Hotel
Transylvania

Hotel Transylvania

a novel of forbidden love

Chelsea Quinn Yarbro

ST. MARTIN'S PRESS
NEW YORK

FOR
CHRISTOPHER LEE

A nous les amours,
et les roses
Act 4, Massenet's *MANON*

Part One

le Comte de Saint-Germain

Excerpt from a letter written by la Comtesse d'Argenlac to her niece
Mlle. Madelaine de Montalia, dated September 13, 1743:

. . . The entertainment provided that night was musical, and Madame la
Duchesse had gathered a truly brilliant assembly for her salon. Even Rameau, though he is sadly aged, attended, but he did not perform. Mlle. la
Trevellon sang Italian ballads, and the King's Own Musicians played several
delightful airs for strings.

Saint-Germain was there—this is not Comte Louis, but another, quite
mysterious gentleman who arrived in Paris only last May—and he played
several pieces of his own composition on the violin and harpsichord. Rameau
congratulated him on his work and commented that he had once met a musical man quite like him in appearance, but that had been long ago, in 1701
or 1702, and the man he had seen was then about fifty, whereas this man is
no more than forty-five. Saint-Germain was truly graceful in his return of
the compliment given him by the great musician. He said that if the man
Rameau remembered had left so clear a picture in his mind, then he (Saint-
Germain) could wish that it were he that Rameau recalled, for certainly no
ordinary man would live so long in Rameau's memory. Rameau mentioned
that the name of the man he had known was il Conte Balletti, and that, like
Saint-Germain, he had been a well-traveled and most remarkable gentleman. . . .

Although we had hoped to see Mme. Cressie there, la Duchesse told us
that she had been ill, and could not attend, so we did not have the pleasure
of hearing her perform on the viola d'amore. We were all saddened to hear
she was unwell, and Saint-Germain was kind enough—there was such an expression in his eyes—to desire his compliments be conveyed to La Cressie
and to say that he had composed three airs for her instrument and was anxious to hear them realized by her skill.

Beauvrai was also there, and noted that all the ladies are fascinated with
Saint-Germain, and predicted that we would be sadly downcast when he
was shown to be a charlatan. Poor Beauvrai, with his scents and jewels and
bandy legs, cannot but be jealous of so elegant and delightful a man as
Saint-Germain is. Beauvrai was part of Saint Sebastien's set, which is a con-

nection no one should boast of. Only his wife's good name and bon ton give him entry to the best of circles, which infuriates Beauvrai. . . .

Your uncle and I look forward with delight to your visit, dear niece. We are pleased that your parents are willing at last to send you to us, for where daughters are concerned, we must be realistic. A woman of your beauty and wit must not be allowed to bloom unnoticed in Provence. Assure your parents that we will take care to bring you to the attention of those hostesses who are most likely to know what is due a woman of your faultless lineage and sensibilities. I trust you will not be shocked by my plain speaking, because I believe that it is best for girls to realize early the practical demands of life.

Until I may kiss your cheeks myself, I commend myself to you and to your esteemed parents, in particular my brother, the Marquis, and beg that they will send you to me before the end of September. I have the pleasure to be

> Your affectionate aunt,
> Claudia de Montalia
> Comtesse d'Argenlac

1

He was known as le Comte de Saint-Germain, although he had had other names, but few in Paris would have recognized even the most illustrious of those names, for the glamorous court of Louis XV cared little for what happened beyond French borders, or before the Sun King had reigned.

There were parts of France, also, which the glittering court did not know, such as the squalid dark street down which Saint-Germain picked his way, his intense dark eyes turned to the task of searching out the piles of filth that filled the night with a smell that was almost palpable. Slums at night, Saint-Germain reflected as his long memories stirred, were the same the world over.

The gentle chuckle of running water was in his ears, and it annoyed him. It was like the sound of an insect, constantly buzzing, reminding him that the Seine was very near.

In the shadows, the red eyes of rats glared out at him, and the gibbering his passing caused made Saint-Germain bare his teeth in what might have been a smile. He had never learned to like rats, though he had often had to live close to them.

At the next crossing he stopped, uncertain of which way to go. No sign marked the alley leading crookedly away from the river. He stared into the dark, then turned down the narrow way. Above him the old buildings almost touched, leaning together, heavy with the weight of centuries. Stepping even more warily now, he trod the rough stones that served as paving.

Up ahead he saw a lantern shine, and he stepped back into the overhang of a doorway to wait for the watchman to pass. He pursed his lips impatiently. There were ways he could slip by the watchman unnoticed, but such doings were often inconvenient, and occasionally led to the kind of discovery he had come to loathe. At least twice before in his long career an impulsive move on his part had exposed him to the full glare of public notoriety. So he waited.

When the watchman was gone, Saint-Germain resumed his walk. In spite of his high-heeled shoes of black brocade, he went silently, his well-knit body moving with fluid grace remarkable in a man his age.

At last he reached the sign he had been told of, the Inn of the Red Wolf. He pulled his long cloak of black velvet more tightly over his finery. He had taken the precaution of leaving his finest jewels at home, save for one flawless ruby sunk in the lace at his throat. Wrapped in the cloak, his dark hair unpowdered, he knew he could go safely among the men who waited in the darkened tavern. With one small, long-fingered hand, he threw the bolt and entered the Inn of the Red Wolf.

The nine men gathered in the squalid taproom looked up guiltily as the door opened, and some of them drew back in fear.

Closing the door behind him, Saint-Germain made a sign. "Good evening, Brothers," he said with a slight bow, his mellifluous voice pitched a little higher, his words slightly more clipped than usual.

"You are Prinz Ragoczy of Transylvania?" asked one of the bolder men after a moment.

Saint-Germain bowed again. "I have that honor." He reflected that the name was as much his as Saint-Germain was. Or Balletti had been. He had used Ragoczy for many years, in Italy, Hungary, Bohemia, Austria, and the German city of Dresden. "You are the Guild, I suppose?" he asked, somewhat disheartened. Sorcerers were always an uncertain lot, and these men were no different. A few had intelligent faces with eyes yearning for the knowledge that had become their deity. But the others. Saint-Germain sighed. The others were what he had come to expect. They were the sly ones, men who operated outside the law, cynically dispensing poisons and abortions to those willing to be blackmailed and to pay. Men of cunning in place of skill, of rapacity instead of passion.

"We were not sure you would come, Highness," said one of the sorcerers. "It grows late."

Saint-Germain walked farther into the room. "I am here at the time appointed. The clocks have not yet struck midnight."

From a nearby church, the six chimes of midnight rang out, solemn warning that the dread hour had come.

"I am, in fact," Saint-Germain said dryly, "early."

"Dead of night," one of the sorcerers murmured, and almost crossed himself. He turned to Saint-Germain, his crafty face twisted into a semblance of goodwill. "We were told you could help us in the matter of jewels."

Saint-Germain sighed. "You French are so obviously greedy."

Two of the men stiffened, and a few of the others smiled ingratiatingly.

The one who had asked about the jewels shrugged and waited for an answer.

"Very well." Saint-Germain strode into the room and took the seat at the head of the meanly laid table. "I will give you the secret of the jewels, upon certain conditions."

"What conditions?" the sorcerer with the greatest interest in jewels asked, too quickly.

"I have certain services which must be performed for me. You will do them, and in as short a time as possible. When these tasks are completed, then I will give you the secret of the jewels. Not before."

The sorcerer scoffed. "And when this service is done, then there will be other services, and others, and eventually you will be gone and we will have nothing to show for our labor but empty pockets." He turned away.

"I have told you you are greedy," Saint-Germain reminded him.

One of the other sorcerers spoke, and this time it was one with the thirst for knowledge in his eyes. "I will accept your conditions. It is true you may betray us, but I am willing to take that chance."

Saint-Germain regarded him evenly in the ruddy light of the taproom. "What is your name?" he inquired, his finely drawn brows lifted.

"I am Beverly Sattin," he said, a trifle nervously, since sorcerers did not in general give their true names.

"English?" Saint-Germain asked in that language.

"Yes. But I have lived in France for many years. May I say that I have looked forward to this occasion for a long time, Your Highness?" He inclined his head with the remnants of the grand manner he must have had as a young man.

"Where were you educated, Sattin?"

"Magdalene College, Oxford," he said, pronouncing it "maudlin." He paused, then went on. "I was sent down in twenty-nine for irreligious practices. It was my second year."

The other sorcerers were getting restless, and the one with the interest in jewels interrupted now. "I can't understand what you're saying," he complained, and signaled the landlord to fill their cups with more wine.

"It was rude of me to exclude you gentlemen," Saint-Germain said gravely in his slightly accented French.

Now the landlord was bustling around the table, his round face glistening with sweat and distress. He glanced furtively at Saint-Germain as he brought another cup and started to fill it.

Saint-Germain raised one small, elegant hand. "I do not drink wine," he said, and nodded a dismissal to the landlord, who bowed as profoundly as his bulk would let him and then hastened away, grateful to be free of those sinister men.

When the landlord was gone, Saint-Germain reached into one of the copious pockets of his black coat, and as the others watched, he drew out a leather pouch with embossed symbols on it. When he was sure he had their undivided attention, he said, "You want bona fides of me, and this is what I offer you." He opened the pouch and in the silence which was accented by the crackling fire, he poured onto the table a dozen large diamonds.

Not one of the sorcerers was unmoved by the sight of the superb gems. The one who had been so eager to have jewels started to reach for them, then drew back his hand, his face frightened.

"Please." Saint-Germain gestured his permission. "Pick them up. Examine them. Assure yourself that they are genuine. Then listen to me while I give you my instructions." He leaned back in the rough-hewn chair and stared vacantly toward the fire as the nine men seized on the diamonds and fell to talking among themselves in hushed voices. When the sorcerers were silent again, he spoke. "I expect that you, Le Grâce, think you have been clever with the substitution you have made," he said without looking around.

The sorcerer who loved jewels jumped visibly. He mumbled that the Prinz was mistaken, and pointed to the English sorcerer. "It must be him, sir. It was not I."

Now Saint-Germain turned to him, his penetrating dark eyes full on Le Grâce's. "Understand me, Le Grâce," he said softly. "I will not tolerate being cheated or lied to. I am not a fool. Sattin did not take the diamond; you did. It is in your inner vest pocket. There are also six fraudulent pieces of glass there. The seventh is my jewel. You have until the count of ten to put it onto the table. One . . ."

Le Grâce could not meet the steady gaze of Saint-Germain's dark eyes. "Prinz Ragoczy . . ." he began, his glance darting to his companions.

"Two."

The English sorcerer Sattin moved restlessly. "Your Highness, reconsider. Le Grâce is not . . ."

"Three."

A rat scuttled near the hearth, chittering in rage, and then was gone.

Two of the sorcerers rose and turned their backs to Le Grâce, one of them saying to the other, "Le Grâce never said his name. The Prinz simply knew it."

"Four."

Involuntarily Le Grâce's hand crept toward the pocket in his vest. His face was rigid with fright. "Prinz, we could talk this over."

"Five."

Sattin moved away from Le Grâce a trifle, and said in English to Saint-Germain, "It is true he is a rogue, Highness, but he is useful."

"Not to me. Six."

"But this is foolishness," Sattin protested. "If you have the secret of jewels, surely this one cannot mean much to you."

"Seven. I dislike being robbed," he said in English. "I dislike being lied to. A man who will cheat me of a jewel will betray me for very little. Eight."

Greasy sweat showed on Le Grâce's face, and he made a swipe with his sleeve to wipe it away. He shifted uneasily in his chair. His mouth was suddenly dry, and he reached for his wine, drinking noisily.

"Nine." Although his voice was no louder, the word sounded like a gunshot in the dingy taproom.

"All right!" Le Grâce blurted, and reached for the pouch in his vest pocket. "All right!" Contemptuously he tossed the pouch onto the table. "Examine them."

A breath passed through the room, and the tension drained from the air. The two sorcerers by the fire came back toward the table.

Saint-Germain took the pouch and opened it. The predicted seven gems fell onto the table next to the other jewels Saint-Germain had spilled there.

"Which is which, then?" Le Grâce asked sarcastically.

Without a word, Saint-Germain reached out his hand to six of the jewels and gathered them into a pile. Then, wrapping a length of napkin from the table around his hand, he struck the jewels with his fist. When he lifted his hand, there was a powder of glass on the table. He looked inquiringly at the others.

"Prinz Ragoczy . . ." Sattin said slowly. "On behalf of our Brotherhood and our Guild, I ask your pardon and forgiveness."

Saint-Germain nodded. "Agreed. Only secure me that man and see that he does not again have access to this guild."

Sattin nodded and turned to the others. "You heard what the Prinz requires." He motioned, and the men accepted his order. "Pesche, and you, Oulen, take Le Grâce upstairs. To the attic room."

The two sorcerers nodded, and went to Le Grâce. "Come," they said, obviously prepared to take him away by force if he resisted.

Le Grâce glared at them. "He's just a trickster. None of those diamonds are real." He looked desperately from one of his Guild Brothers to the next. "They can't be real. They're just glass."

Saint-Germain gave him a cold, bored stare. "Because you are a charlatan, there is no reason to think that the rest of the world is equally dishonest." He reached for the largest of the diamonds and put it on the powdered glass. He tightened the napkin around his hand and brought his fist down full force on the stone. The table sagged under the impact of his blow. When he lifted his hand, the stone, intact, had been driven into the table for half of its length. Saint-Germain opened his hand and pulled away the napkin.

"Your hand . . ." Sattin began.

Saint-Germain put his hand, palm up, on the table. "As you see."

Even Le Grâce did not have the heart to call this deceit. He lowered his head and let his Guild Brothers lead him away.

"You have answered him," Sattin said, a certain satisfaction in his voice, knowing that he had been answered as well.

"Only for the moment," Saint-Germain said with a reluctant shaking of his head. "In a few hours he will have decided that all this was an illusion, and then he will want to discredit me." He touched his dark hair where it was tied at the back of his neck. "Never mind, English. I have more pressing concerns than a discontented false sorcerer."

"You said you had need of a service." Sattin was leaning forward now, and the six remaining men listened, alert.

"In exchange for the secret of the jewels, yes." Saint-Germain looked at the six men. "Which of you is French?"

Four of the men admitted to being French. "And the other?" Saint-Germain asked, waving the English Sattin aside.

"I am Spanish. My name is Ambrosias María Domingo y Roxas. I am from Burgos." He made an odd bow as he added, "I was excommunicated for heresy, and escaped only because my escort to Madrid was careless. They say now that I escaped by sorcery, but it was only my wits that saved me."

Saint-Germain studied the little Spaniard. "I may have use for you later," he said in flawless Spanish. "In the meantime I felicitate you on your escape. You are one of the rare few." He turned his attention to the French sorcerers, and resumed their tongue. "Who among you have dealt with the aristocracy before?"

The sorcerers exchanged glances, and then one, a man somewhat older than the others, said, "I was a majordomo in the Savigny household. That was more than a dozen years ago."

Saint-Germain nodded. "How well can you imitate the manner? Oh, not those of the first consequence, but of the most aspiring of the rich bourgeois?"

The former majordomo shrugged. "I have never tried it, Prinz, but I am certain I know the sort you mean. I can ape the part well enough."

"Then you will be the one to make the bargain for me." He saw the startled expression on the man's face. "There is a gambling establishment in le Faubourg Saint-Germain"—here he smiled to himself—"number nine, Quai Malaquais. The place was built in the time of the thirteenth Louis, and has had an uneven career. It is called Hôtel Transylvania."

"It was called that for another Ragoczy, was it not, Highness?" Sattin ventured when the silence in the room had grown too long.

"I believe it had that name before then," Saint-Germain said, as if he knew little of the matter. "But there was a Ragoczy at that Hôtel thirty years ago."

"Your father?" Sattin's question was echoed in the faces of the other Guild Brothers.

"If you like."

The sorcerers looked at each other, the walls, the light of the fire, anywhere that did not entail looking at the neat figure in the dark clothes who waited patiently for them to give him their attenion once again.

"What is it we are to do about this Hôtel Transylvania?" Domingo y Roxas asked for all the group.

"I desire you will purchase it for me. You may say that I have a sentimental attachment to the name, or the building, if you require a reason for this," he said, anticipating their questions. "I will give you sufficient funds to buy it ten times over. I hope you will not have to spend that much, but whatever it costs, you will purchase Hôtel Transylvania for me. Is that understood?"

"It is, Prinz Ragoczy."

Pesche and Oulen, the sorcerers who had taken Le Grâce from the room, returned, and sat demurely at the far end of the table.

"That little book of l'Abbé Prevost has made an unpleasant name for Hôtel Transylvania," Saint-Germain mused. "It was not so reputed when . . . my father . . . was there. So," he said briskly, looking up from the fire, "you are to buy Hôtel Transylvania without once bringing my name into it. You may say that you are an agent for another, or that you are purchasing the Hôtel for yourself. But at no time are you even to mention my name. If I had wanted it known the Hôtel is mine, I could have used any solicitor and the Police would have knowledge of the transaction within the hour. Your discretion is absolute, I trust?"

"It is, Highness."

"Good." He turned to the sorcerer who had been a majordomo.

"What is your name?"

"Cielbleu," he answered promptly. "Henri-Louis Cielbleu."

"Charming. A name to inspire confidence. You may use that or any other name you would like when you conduct negotiations with the current owners of the Hôtel."

"What will you do with it once you have it?" Pesche asked respectfully, but with curiosity and avarice in his eyes.

"Open it to the world, of course. It has too long been the poor relation to the Hôtel de Ville. That will change."

"Highness . . ." Domingo y Roxas began, "why do you want this place? Is it because you are Transylvanian yourself?"

There was a faraway look in Saint-Germain's compelling eyes as he said, "I suppose it is because Transylvania is my native land, and I have been Prince of the Blood there." His expression cleared. "It is true, gentlemen, that one's native earth has a pull, no matter how long, or at what distances one lives. Say, then, that it is a whim of mine, and let me indulge it. In return, you will have the secret of the jewels. It is not a bad bargain."

Beverly Sattin regarded him evenly. "When must this be done?"

"As soon as possible, my dear Sattin. I wish to own Hôtel Transylvania before October is quite over." He pushed his diamonds into a heap on the table. "You will pay for the Hôtel with these. I think you will find that their value is high enough to meet any price the owner might name. And if the Police learn of my ownership, I will know you for my enemies and will deal with you appropriately." He fingered the diamond he had driven into the table. "You will have to pry this one loose. Make the landlord give you a knife." He rose and gathered his cloak about him, preparing to leave. "I will be here at this hour in ten days' time. You will tell me then what progress you have made."

"Prinz Ragoczy," Sattin said, "what of Le Grâce?"

Saint-Germain drew his elegant brows together. "What an annoyance he is." He fingered the ruby at his throat. "For the time being confine him there. You may take turns guarding him. And be sure that your guard is of flesh and blood, and armed with a heavy cudgel. It would be inconvenient if he should escape." He regarded them once more, thinking that though they were disappointing, he had seen worse.

"In ten days' time, Highness," Sattin said, making a profound bow.

Saint-Germain returned the bow in moderation, then swept out of the Inn of the Red Wolf into the clammy dark of the Paris night.

Excerpt from a letter written by the Marquis de Montalia to the Abbé
Ponteneuf, dated September 21, 1743:

. . . So, my dear cousin, you will understand my concern for my daughter, Madelaine. My wife's arguments have convinced me, but I cannot but
feel grave apprehension should my child fall into certain hands. Madelaine
will arrive in Paris on the fourth or fifth day of October in the company of
her maid, Cassandre Leuf, who has been in service to our family for over
twenty years. I have no fear for her while Cassandre looks after her. But this
is not enough. It is my desire that you watch over her and give her the
benefit of your good counsel, for we both know the temptations rife in the
court of our beloved sovereign.

I am certain you will like Madelaine, for she is a sensible girl of superior
intellect. The Sisters of Ste. Ursule who educated her have praised her
scholarship and were saddened that she felt no vocation for religious life. Indeed, the only complaint that was made of her was that she has little patience with those less intelligent than she, and that she has a certain
disquieting love of the bizarre and fantastic. My wife is convinced that marriage and children will dispel these quirks in a nature otherwise sweet and
responsive. . . .

I have heard through my sister, la Comtesse d'Argenlac, with whom
Madelaine will be staying, that Beauvrai is to be found in good circles again,
on his wife's cachet. I need hardly tell you that any association with
Beauvrai is not to be tolerated. Any of those who were part of Saint Sebastien's set must not be allowed to contaminate my daughter. Let me urge you
to be rigorous in guarding my child from such as those.

. . . Should Madelaine desire to marry, I beg you to be certain that it is
her heart that speaks, and not desire for advancement. All too often marriage
is born of the expectation of others, and not of the strong ties of the heart.
My wife has charged my sister with the task of finding Madelaine a suitable
husband, and to be sure, it would please me to see her happily settled. But I
could not bear to see her life blighted as so many others have been. I rely on
you to know her true heart. . . .

In the name of the God Whom we both revere and worship, and who has
brought you to salvation out of the fires of Hell, I commend myself to you,
and beg that you will remember my sins in your prayers. In this world I
have the honor to be

> Your most humble and obedient cousin,
> Robert Marcel Yves Etienne Pascal,
> Marquis de Montalia

2

"I declare, Comte," Mme. Cressie said, putting one hand to her lovely white throat, "you appear out of nowhere."

Saint-Germain bowed low over the hand she extended to him, his lips not quite brushing her strong, slender fingers. "It is only that when La Cressie is with us once again, all others must pale beside her. If I should spring out of the ground at your side, I would count myself fortunate, for how else would I find my way through all your admirers?"

La Cressie gave a shaky laugh. "Very gallant, sir. But you see, you alone are by me."

"Then it is my greater fortune." Saint-Germain glanced around the crowded room and nodded toward an alcove. "I have been anxious to talk to you, Madame, but I find that this room is a little noisy. Perhaps if we withdraw . . ."

She agreed, and turned with him to the alcove, her wide silken skirts rustling like leaves as she moved. She was dressed in sea green with a petticoat of ivory lace revealed where her skirt was caught up on panniers of very moderate width. Her fair hair was dressed simply, in a style known as the Turtle Dove, and the powder that covered it was scented with lilac.

Beside her, Saint-Germain was greatly contrasted: he wore small clothes and a wide-skirted coat of black silk whose turned-back cuffs revealed a black brocade. In completing the ensemble, he had affected black hose and shoes, so that only his embroidered waistcoat and his impeccably white lace at wrist and throat relieved the severity of his dress. Diamonds sparkled on his buckles, and there was a ruby glowing in the lace at his throat.

As he handed her onto a low seat in the alcove, Saint-Germain mentioned their contrast in dress, and La Cressie sighed. "You are kind, Comte, but I have a mirror. Even my husband has remarked on how I look. I fear my illness has left an effect on me. I see it in the glass." Again she put her hand to her throat, involuntarily touching a neat patch in the shape of a viola d'amore.

"It is true that you are still a little pale," he admitted as he shook out the deep lace ruffles at his wrists, "but such pallor becomes you. With your fair hair and light eyes, you are more ethereal than ever. I see the Marquise de la Sacre Sasseau looking daggers at you with those dark eyes of hers." He studied the long patch on her neck. "A clever conceit, Madame. You will establish a mode, I think."

"Thank you, Comte," she said, uncertainly belying her cool words. "I would like to set a fashion." Her voice was distant, and died away after a moment.

"What is it, Madame?" he asked softly when the silence was long between them.

She looked up suddenly, startled. "It is nothing, Comte, nothing." Her laugh was forced. "I have had some disturbing dreams of late."

"That is not unusual when one is recovering from an illness. Would you like me to give you a potion that would make your sleep easier?"

"You?" she said quickly, guiltily. "No, no, I did not mean that. It was simply that I thought perhaps we should be getting on to supper. I heard the lackey announce it some time ago, and I think now that I am hungry."

Saint-Germain smiled urbanely. He knew that she was not truly interested in supper, and that her appetite was dulled by her weakness, but he offered her his arm, and she laid her hand upon it.

The Hôtel de Ville was enjoying one of its busiest nights. In the grand ballroom, twenty musicians played for many dancers, moving on the inlaid floor like a sea of flowers, so many and varied were the colors of silks, brocades, satins, velvets, and laces they wore. There were card rooms, too, where even the banned hoca was played for dizzyingly high stakes. Here there was little noise, and the expression on the aristocratic faces was grim when there was any expression at all. Other games of chance were being played in rooms apart from the card room, and there the conversation was almost as glittering as the gold louis stacked on the tables in front of the elegant gamesters.

In the supper room, Saint-Germain greeted his many acquaintances with a distinguished inclination of the head and an occasional wave of the hand. He squired Mme. Cressie to one of the more secluded tables, and having seated her, he asked, "What am I to have the pleasure of fetching for you, Madame?"

"Whatever you're having," she answered absently.

"I am not hungry just at present," he said, thinking that it was not quite the truth. "I see that they have hams and chicken for the evening, and what appears to be a dish with deviled lobster." He smiled down at her with the full force of his dark, fascinating eyes. "Perhaps you will be kind enough to let me choose for you?"

She was lost in his eyes, in the depth and promise of them. "Yes," she murmured. "Whatever you think is best." There was a little frown between her brows, and her hand stole again to her throat.

With another careful bow, Saint-Germain threaded his way through the supper crush to the long buffet set out for the midnight repast. As he filled a plate for La Cressie, he paused to talk with le Duc de Vandonne, a youngish man with strange, shifty eyes who was an embarrassment to his family and a shame to himself.

"I hate these functions," de Vandonne said through tight teeth as he pulled at the lace at his neck. "I dread them, and I hate them."

"Then why did you come?" Saint-Germain asked, taking his attention from a venison liver pâté with juniper berries that he had spooned generously onto La Cressie's plate.

"Because if I do not come, then I am castigated by my mother and her two sisters." He spoke in a voice thickened by revulsion. "I cannot escape them: they live with me. So here I am. They expect me to find a wife, to attract some very acceptable virgin to my title and my bed." He sneered. "I have better uses for virgins than that."

"Oh?" Saint-Germain turned back to the buffet. He knew that le Duc had some of the less acceptable perversions, but even then, the remark puzzled him.

De Vandonne giggled, and the sound of it froze Saint-Germain. "Beauvrai said it takes a virgin. I wish we could find one. A real one, I mean. One we could use."

"Use for what?" Saint-Germain raised his brows and molded his features to an expression of faint, polite inquiry, masking the cold dread of certainty he felt.

"Oh, for this and for that," de Vandonne said evasively. "This isn't the place to talk about it." Le Duc's face grew harder. "You aren't one of us, anyway. Though I hear you're a foreigner, and foreigners sometimes go in for this kind of thing." He reached for another glass of wine as a waiter bore a tray by, and swore when his own clumsiness spilled wine on the cascade of lace at his throat. He tossed off half the wine and turned again to Saint-Germain. "Do you like virgins?"

"I'm not in that line, I'm afraid," he said, making a perfunctory bow and returning through the gathering crowd to Mme. Cressie.

"Heavens, I can't eat this much, Comte," she said in pretty confusion as he set the laden plate before her.

Saint-Germain smiled. "Well, do you know, since I am not certain of what you like, I thought perhaps a greater variety would please you. And if there is more than you want, the food itself might add to your hunger, and strengthen your appetite. I cannot help but believe that part of this pallor you complain of comes from lack of food." He seated himself across from her.

"But you do not eat, Saint-Germain," she pointed out.

He waved this away. "I am engaged to dine later. Come, then. The pâté. And after that, some of this excellent aspic or perhaps the eggs à la Florentine."

Mme. Cressie was torn. To have the pleasure of the company of the popular and mysterious Comte was certainly a plume in her social cap, and a pleasant change from the indifference of her husband. But at close range she found Saint-Germain disturbing. His probing eyes, she discovered, were too acute, too capable of finding out the truth, and the disquieting and genuine concern he had shown her threatened to destroy her careful defenses. She nibbled at the pâté and pondered her predicament.

"If you have trouble, Madame, you may tell me," he said to her in a low tone. "I give my word that I will not betray you."

Again she hesitated, struck by his amazing perspicacity. "I am not sure I understand you, Comte."

Saint-Germain leaned forward and said gently, "Clearly, my dear, you are not entirely yourself yet. And even more clearly you are deeply troubled. If you would want to tell me what it is that worries you, perhaps I can suggest something that would be of help to you. I have heard," he said with even more sympathy, "that your husband is not much at home. Now, while I cannot restore lost affection, or inspire it where it does not exist, I may have some remedy for your sorrow."

She sat up, affronted, her face scarlet. "Sir!"

Immediately he saw his mistake. "No, no, Madame misunderstands me." He gave her a wry grin to dispel her lingering doubts. "Although, if that is what you desire, no doubt it would not be difficult for you to find one who would assist you. But consider me excused. It is not that I do not admire you: I find you a delicious woman. But you must realize that I gave up such congress long, long ago."

La Cressie felt her flush fading, and took advantage of the moment to study the strange man across the table from her. He did not have the look of a celibate, but she had to admit there had been no rumors about him, either with women or men. And it was not because no one would have him. Indeed, she remembered suddenly—and the thought brought a ghost of a smile to her mouth—that one or two women had kept Saint-Germain under determined siege for several months, but nothing had come of it. She nodded. "We both seem to have misunderstood."

Saint-Germain opened his hands. "If you misunderstood, what can I be but flattered?" He looked down at her plate. "But you are not eating, Madame. Is the fare unsatisfactory?"

Dutifully she picked up the heavily scrolled silver fork. "I don't wish to give offense, Comte," she said as she took another bite of the venison pâté.

"That would be impossible, Madame," he said, and in this automatically gallant response there was a covert hint of boredom. He adjusted the foaming white lace that spread over his black-and-silver-brocade waistcoat, so that the diamonds pinned in the folds shone like water drops, and the great ruby glowed like the heart of a poet.

La Cressie smiled enviously at the jewels, thinking it unfair that Saint-Germain should have so many magnificent diamonds as well as the huge ruby. Then she banished these thoughts from her mind and turned her attention to the eggs à la Florentine.

Saint-Germain watched her eat, faint amusement lurking in his dark eyes. It was good she was hungry, if only to please him. He touched his hair to be sure that the white powder that was utterly required for a correct formal appearance still clung there. He was sure that his valet, Roger, had done the job with his usual skill, and was pleased when his fingers came away with only the faintest dusting of powder. He nodded slightly to himself, and reflected that each age had had its own absurdities of fashion, and surely powdered hair in France was no worse than perfumed cones of fat in long-vanished Thebes. He dismissed the thought and asked La Cressie, "Is the aspic to your taste, Madame?"

She looked up at him through her thick, fair lashes. "Excellent, as you would expect of this Hôtel. You were right about the food itself making me hungry." She obviously felt self-conscious, for she said softly, "I fear I am very poor company, Comte."

"No, Madame, I assure you. It is a joy to see you at table." That was no less than the truth. "It brings some of the color back to your cheeks."

"That may be the wine I have drunk," she said archly.

"It becomes you." He rose as another supper party came near, as courtesy dictated, and made a bow.

One or two of the new party returned this salutation, and then a small man with bandy legs and the airs of an exquisite stepped forward, staring. He wore a ridiculous wig, with three pigeon's wings over each ear. His coat was of peach satin with gold lacings, and the skirt was stiffly whaleboned. The waistcoat was puce silk embroidered with butterflies, his small clothes the same peach satin as the coat, bringing undue attention to spindly legs, and this was not decreased by mauve silken hose accented with peach clocks. His old-fashioned shoes had high red heels, so that he minced like a woman as he walked. The triple-tiered lace at his throat rose with indignation, and the shine of topazes caught in the light. "Damnation!" he swore in a voice that was raspy from the over-use of snuff, and too loud.

Saint-Germain looked at the man. "Sir?"

"You're the charlatan!" he cried, tugging on the arm of one of his companions. "I've never seen such effrontery. He's here. Next thing, he'll tell you he owns the place!"

A shy smile pulled at Saint-Germain's mouth. "I beg your pardon, but I am certain I do not own this Hôtel."

"Be sarcastic with me, will you?" The man stamped forward, and the skirts of his coat swayed. "I say it to your face, you scoundrel: you're a hoax and a liar."

Mme. Cressie dropped her fork with a clatter and flashed a frightened look at Saint-Germain. He was no longer smiling. His dark, enigmatic eyes rested on the painted, ugly face before him. "Baron Beauvrai," he said pleasantly, "you are determined to force a quarrel on me for no reason. I have done nothing to offend you. You have chosen to single me out to fling baseless insults on me." He paused to see what attention they were attracting, and was annoyed to find that not only had the guests at supper stopped eating to watch, but also that several of the elegant gentlemen stood in the door to the card room, a certain barbaric eagerness in their faces.

"If you swallow that insult, you're a coward as well as a fake!" Beauvrai pulled back smugly and waited.

For a moment Saint-Germain resisted the urge to reach out and throttle the old roué. Pitching his magnificent voice to carry to all parts of the room, he said, "I have always been taught that when in a foreign country a man should behave as a guest, and be willing to respect his host. Certainly it would be both rude and ungrateful to start a brawl here, Baron Beauvrai. I would have thought that a man in your position, with so much scandal behind you, would not want to bring this unpleasant attention to himself. But then, I am not French, as you have pointed out." He felt the hostile reaction to his words, and took advantage of it. "I came here because I had heard fine French taste, culture, and learning praised all over the world. It would be a pity if such as you were to tarnish that splendid reputation."

"Sa-sa!" said one of the men in the doorway, and mimed a fencer's salute.

"I won't be put off!" Beauvrai insisted, but by this time he had lost his momentum. One of his company touched his arm to bring him away, but he shook this off angrily. "If you were a man, you would insist on satisfaction."

"It is not my practice to meet men clearly past their fighting days. It would be most reprehensible of me to kill you. And believe me, Baron, I would kill you." Although he had lowered his voice, his words were heard all over the supper room.

Beauvrai glared at him. "You will regret this," he said icily. He turned back to his party. "I find I have lost my appetite. This room reeks of commoner." He turned on one of his high red heels and stalked from the room.

A young man in rose-colored silk stepped toward Saint-Germain. "I must apologize for my uncle," he said, bowing uncertainly. "There are times he is not quite himself."

Privately, Saint-Germain thought that he had seen more of Beauvrai's true nature in the last few minutes than was usually visible under his occasionally polished veneer. "He is not as young as he used to be," he said to the young man. "Perhaps you might be at pains to be sure he does not stay here too late tonight."

The young man nodded. "It is dreadful. He spent the afternoon with Saint Sebastien." There was an embarrassed pause as many of the diners looked up, startled. "Saint Sebastien has returned to Paris, I am afraid." He made a nervous, resigned gesture. "We asked my uncle not to go, but he and Saint Sebastien spent much of their youth together . . ."

"I see your predicament. And it is difficult for a nephew to restrain an uncle, is it not?"

"Yes." The young man flashed him a grateful smile. "You do realize that, don't you? He is still considered the head of the family, although for a long time his fortune has not been in his hands . . ." Again his voice trailed off. He had spoken out of turn.

Saint-Germain gave the tiresome young Baron a gentle nod. "Such matters are always complicated," he murmured. "Your party is waiting for you," he added with a slight bow, indicating he was satisfied that the subject was closed.

The young man returned the bow with a flourish, saying as he did, "I am grateful that you were willing to excuse my uncle. I will do my best to assure that you will not be troubled again by him."

"Will you?" Saint-Germain said softly as the young man went back to his party, his walk growing more confident as he neared the group. He had never met le Baron de les Radeux before, but had heard him described as having much better manners than sense. Saint-Germain decided he shared that opinion.

"Comte?" Mme. Cressie said, now that the awkwardness had ended. "Will you join me once more?"

Saint-Germain looked down, studying her, a disquieting intensity in his dark eyes. "Please excuse me for the moment," he said musingly. "But be assured that you will see me later. Perhaps you will not be offended if I bring la Comtesse d'Argenlac to share your table?"

La Cressie's face brightened. "Claudia? Is she here, then?"

"I saw her not an hour ago. I understand she has some provincial relative under her wing, but you may be certain that la Comtesse will not allow a countrified relation to bore you."

"Ah, Comte, it is impossible to say when you are serious and when you are joking. Bring la Comtesse immediately, and I am sure I will be delighted with her relative for her sake." She nibbled at some of the food still left on her plate.

Saint-Germain made a leg and went off in search of Claudia, la Comtesse d'Argenlac.

He found her in the ballroom waiting for her niece to finish a set, as she explained when le Comte de Saint-Germain came up and begged her to allow him to lead her in to supper.

"I thought the child would die of fright when we first arrived. There are a great many people here tonight, and she is new to Paris. She said that she was sure no one would notice her in so grand an assembly." She gave a rippling laugh to indicate how ridiculous she thought this.

"If she is dancing, this must not be the case. Obviously someone did notice her." Saint-Germain smiled pleasantly. He liked la Comtesse, and knew that under her frivolous facade was a highly intelligent, acute mind. "Who is this poor girl?"

"Not poor, Comte. She is the only child of my elder brother, Robert. He has lived retired for some years, so you will not have met him. He is le Marquis de Montalia."

Saint-Germain inclined his head, and though he was not a tall man, this graceful gesture gave the impression of height. He was amused when he occasionally caught a tall man trying to duplicate his effect. "Where is this paragon niece of yours?"

"On the dance floor. Dear me, I wish it were not so crowded. I could point her out to you."

"Describe her to me. I'll see if I can find her."

La Comtesse rose on her toes and looked into the moving mass of dancers. "She is in a lavender gown of Venetian silk over an Italian flowered petticoat. Her skirt is caught up with silver ribbons, and she is wearing a necklace of garnets and diamonds. There are diamond drops in her ears. Where *is* that girl?" La Comtesse furled her fan in vexation. She had tried to point out her niece, but it was like trying to point out a figure on a carousel. "There!" she said at last. "Under the third chandelier from the door, with le Vicomte de Bellefont."

"He is the one in blue satin?" Saint-Germain asked, to be certain.

"Yes." La Comtesse let herself smile, and it seemed to Saint-Germain when she spoke that her voice came from far away. "Her name is Madelaine Roxanne Bertrande de Montalia. And while I certainly have an aunt's prejudice, I do think she is lovely."

Under the third chandelier from the door, the niece of la Comtesse d'Argenlac turned in the movement of the dance. Her powdered hair was simply styled, as suited a young woman just entering into society. Her fine brows were the dark color of coffee, emphasizing her laughing violet eyes. Although she was a trifle too slender, her carriage was elegant, and when she raised her chin in response to some comment of de Bellefont, there was a regal look to her.

Saint-Germain let his breath out slowly. "She is the most lovely young woman I have seen in very many years." He watched her sink into a curtsy at the end of the dance. "I predict she will have a great success, Claudia."

La Comtesse demurred, a smile in her eyes. "Come. Let me introduce you. And then you may take us away to supper. I am sure Madelaine is hungry, for just watching the dancing has made me famished." As she spoke, she was threading her way through the dancers who were now leaving the floor. Saint-Germain followed her, exchanging nods of greeting as he went.

"Ah, Madelaine," la Comtesse said briskly as she came up to her niece. She gave de Bellefont a polite curtsy and returned her attention to Madelaine. "Here is someone eager to meet you. I have mentioned him to you in my letters, the man who has us all guessing. Saint-Germain, pray let me present my niece Madelaine de Montalia."

He bowed over her hand, just brushing it with his lips. "Enchanted," he said softly, and smiled at the flush that suffused her face as she floated up from her deep curtsy.

Excerpt from a letter written by Mme. Lucienne Cressie to her sister, l'Abbesse Dominique de la Tristesse de les Anges, dated October 6, 1743:

. . . The dreams of which I have told you continue, and I cannot stop them. Sometimes I fear that I do not want to stop them. I have prayed, but it is in vain. I have even told my husband, but he, of course, thought it funny and advised me to take a lover to banish the thoughts of death from my mind. But it is not death that haunts me, my beloved Dominique. I do not know what this is, but it is not death.

On your suggestion, I went to my confessor, and he said that I was near sin, and should beseech God for guidance, and promised that he, too, would pray for me. He also hinted that if I had children, I would not be so troubled in my mind. I was ashamed to tell him how it is with my husband and me. Achille insists that his tastes are as Greek as his name, and that in Athens his sins were virtues. Yet I am certain that if I had a child by another man, he would denounce me as an adulteress. So I am not to have children, it would seem, and the good Abbé counsels me in vain.

Saint-Germain, of whom I have written before, has sent me three new rondos to play. My viola d'amore is my only consolation. Perhaps I will venture to compose a few airs for myself, since I am doomed to so many empty hours.

I have ordered a violoncello from Mattei. At Saint-Germain's insistence, I tried my hand on one, and was surprised at the instrument. It is shaped like a violin, you know, and is held between the legs like the viola d'amore and da gamba. It does not have the drone strings of the viola d'amore, and at first I found this disconcerting. But the tone was so sweet and its timbre of so fine a cantabile quality, that I could not resist it. Perhaps one day when I visit your convent I will bring my instrument and play it for you. . . .

. . . I trust to the Mercy of God that all is well with you. Let me solicit your prayers for my sleep, and I will not wake with the fear of my soul upon me. Nor will I wake with the memory of unholy rapture in me. It shames me to write this, but it is true. I have had the dream only three times, and when I wake, I am filled with horror at myself. But alone at night, when Achille is with those men who are like him, then I want to dream again, and feel my flesh made fire with pleasure. What am I, that my body betrays me so?

Five years ago, I thought our father a despot to send you to a convent rather than look for a husband for you. But today, I think I would beg him to let us trade places. He arranged marriage for me and not for you because he was certain that no maid with a misshapen foot—as if anyone sees a woman's foot but her husband—would be fit to espouse any but the Church. Forgive me for what I say, but you know it is true.

You have said that your vocation is genuine, but when I recall how we wept together, I am filled with worry. And our father, when he died, confessed he was not easy in his mind about you. Oh, tell me you are happy, my dear, dear sister. Let me believe that one of us is happy. I did not think you were too plain to marry, and your foot did not distress me.

Be patient with me, my Dominique. I am distraught tonight. If you had seen Achille with Beauvrai and those three young men, you would be even as I am. But there. I can do nothing now. So I will await my violoncello and the pieces le Comte de Saint-Germain has promised to compose for me. Perhaps the late hour has made me overwrought, and seeing Achille as he was tonight has hurt my judgment. Our mother told me that I had always fretted over things I could not change, and that it was a foolish waste of time. And certainly Achille is disinclined to change. I have my music, at least, which is more fortunate than Claudia d'Argenlac, who has no children, and whose husband gambles. At least Achille's fortune is intact, and he does not mind what I do with it, as long as it does not affect him.

I will bid you good night, my dear sister. May you know the Peace that is not of this World, and may your soul rest untroubled in the night. With a sister's affection and a penitent's love, I am

Your most devoted
Lucienne Cressie

ᙏᙓ᠖ 3 ᠖ᙓᙏ

La Comtesse d'Argenlac glanced up from her breakfast as Madelaine entered the room. "Ah, good morning, my dear. I hope you slept well?"

Madelaine still wore a smile. "Yes, aunt. I had the most wonderful dream."

"After your triumphs last night, I shouldn't wonder." La Comtesse chuckled, motioning Madelaine to sit down. "What do you want to eat, my dear? There is pastry, of course, and fruit. My cook can prepare an omelet, if you would rather. You must keep a hearty appetite."

"That is what Saint-Germain told me last night. He got me two helpings of the pâté." She seated herself so that the light from the broad windows fell across her, making a pretty pattern on her quilted silk morning dress of blue and white stripes. Her hair, free of powder, shone dark with gold highlights. "If it would not be too much trouble, I would like some of the Chinese tea my father sent with me." She pulled an apple from a porcelain basket in the middle of the table and began to pare it with a small, sharp knife.

"Of course." Without turning la Comtesse issued orders for the tea to a lackey standing in the door. "Have some of this," she said to Madelaine, handing a plate of fruit-filled pastries across the table. "The lemon-curd filling is from my husband's forcing houses. He has said it is his ambition to eat peaches all year around."

"Where is le Comte? I did not see him last night, though he said he would join us."

For a moment a frown clouded Comtesse Claudia's face. "He was with friends. He likes to gamble, my dear. Indeed, it is his one besetting sin, and there are times when I fear I will die of worry." She picked up her napkin. "Ah, it is nothing. I have my inheritance and my holdings, which he cannot touch. If he ruins himself, eh bien, I suppose I will support him. . . ." She sighed and took a sip of the hot chocolate by her elbow.

"Then you are not happy, aunt?" Madelaine looked truly shocked.

"I am happy as I can be, my dear. No sensible woman wishes for more in this world. You need not look far to see how true this is. You remember the woman we dined with last night?"

Madelaine's eyes grew soft as she answered. "Madame Cressie? She looked so drawn and so sad."

"She has been ill," la Comtesse said, as if that were nothing. "One day you will have the misfortune to meet her husband. He is one of those men . . . I do not mean to shock you, but it is something you must be made aware of. There are men in this world who have an antipathy for women. . . ."

Madelaine nodded eagerly. "At home, the good Sisters said that it was often so with the saints, and that those with a real religious vocation fled the world so that they would not have to endure the fires of the flesh—"

Her aunt interrupted her with some asperity. "I am not speaking of priests—although there are those, I think, who would live as Achille Cressie does, given the chance." She clicked her tongue and got back on her subject. "These are fleshly men, Madelaine, and they use one another as women, so they have no need for union with our sex. You will hear of a great many of them. Quite often they are handsome men, of great rank and much respect. Le Duc de la Mer-Herbeux is one such, and I am sure he has no more use for women than Achille Cressie does. But of course," she said with a slight flush and a saddened laugh, "he is kind, very kind. I can think of no one I would sooner trust. And it is most unfair of those people who accuse him of wanting peace with England only because of his English Earl." She shook her head. "You will meet le Duc de la Mer-Herbeux shortly. Aside from private taste, he is no more like Achille Cressie than I am like that dreadful Spanish Baronesa with her sixteen lapdogs and her retinue of priests." Again she paused, saying with insight, "In fact, no matter what may be said, I doubt if le Duc de la Mer-Herbeux and Achille Cressie are very much alike *even* in matters of their private taste."

Madelaine gazed out the window, remarking to the air, "I have often thought, dearest aunt, that even among well-married couples, great diversity exists."

La Comtesse nodded with more emphasis than she knew. "Well, marriage is a special matter, is it not? I know that if Mer-Herbeux were looking for a wife and I were free, I would be delighted to entertain his suit." She encountered a shocked look from her niece and went on, "I assure you, he would make a delightful husband. He is a good friend, most charming, and sincere in his affection. Of how many men may one say that? And if he mislikes women in one sense, well, there are many men who do not keep company with their wives. Is another man so much worse than a score of mistresses?"

"But why marry at all? If Achille Cressie does not want his wife, why does he . . . ?" Madelaine had taken one of the lemon-curd pastries, but had set it aside.

"We all must marry, my dear. Unless there is genuine disgust, and even *then* I have known instances . . . Where monies and estates are involved, marriage is the favored contract. In such circumstances, affection may count for very little." There was a harshness in her voice now, and an expression in her eyes that might have alarmed her niece had it lasted longer. "My dear, marriage is the way of the world. Men may avoid it if they are younger sons, but women can be wives, or nuns, or courtesans, or they become an unwelcome burden. Or," she added with a shaky laugh, "they can become aunts."

Madelaine was staring down at the pared apple lying on her plate. "A bleak picture, aunt."

"Oh, heavens," Claudia d'Argenlac said, mocking her own plight. "Now you will think me a martyr, and I am no such thing. Come, Madelaine," she said in a rallying tone, "there is more to life than one's husband. And to be sure, it would be wearisome having them always fawning after us." She motioned for more chocolate, and acknowledged the service gracefully.

Madelaine realized that the subject had been closed, but she was still curious. "Aunt, why do you tell me about those men?"

La Comtesse lifted her brows. "You were much with Bellefont last night, and I did not want you to set too much store by his attentions."

"Is he one?" she asked in disbelief, and the little knife clattered against the fine china of her plate.

"There are rumors. And the company he keeps is not the best." La Comtesse drank the last of her chocolate and reached for an orange in the fruit bowl. "Also, he might not be an acceptable suitor in your father's eyes, even if he wanted to wed you. He is much too close to Beauvrai and his set."

"Beauvrai?" Madelaine sliced off a bit of apple and nibbled at it thoughtfully. "Is that the ridiculous old man in the dreadful wig? The one with le Baron de les Radeux?"

"You met de les Radeux?" her aunt asked quickly.

"While you were in the card room. De Bellefont introduced us, and I danced with him. He dances very well."

"Did you meet Beauvrai?" La Comtesse realized that this would never do. She had given her brother her word that she would not allow Madelaine to associate with any of Beauvrai's set, and now she had discovered that before Madelaine had been in Paris a week, she had been dancing with Beauvrai's nephew.

Madelaine sensed that her aunt was upset. "De les Radeux pointed him out to me as his uncle. He said that he had not been much in society for the last several years, which explains his odd appearance."

La Comtesse tapped her foot impatiently. "Paulin," she said to her lackey, "I wish you will find out if my niece's tea is ready, and if it is, that you will bring it to her." She nodded to her lackey as he left the room. "I do not want to say this where servants can hear. You must have nothing to do with Beauvrai, my dear. Nothing whatsoever. He is your father's sworn enemy. He may look the fool, but he is Saint Sebastien's crony, and there is no worse company to keep."

Madelaine's eyes were very wide. "I did not mean . . ."

Her aunt continued. "Some years ago, before you were born, there was a dreadful scandal. It was quickly hushed up, for it touched on high places. But at the time, we were all terrified. That was one of the reasons your father left court."

"I *knew* it." Madelaine leaned forward, and the lace fichu on her bosom rose and fell with her excited breath, and where it fanned out in a small ruff to frame her face, it felt suddenly tight. "I knew there was some reason for all this. My father has always said that he grew tired of the sordid venality of the court, but I knew there was something more."

La Comtesse had some difficulty as she went on. "You have heard of the old King's mistress, Montespan? . . . And the accusations of her involvement with certain witches and poisoners? . . . There were several executions. . . . At the time, talk of Black Masses was rife, may God protect us"—she crossed herself—"and in the end, Montespan fell from favor, and in time became most religious, so they say. But there was talk that it was not over, that there were still those who devotedly worshiped Satan at court. Certain accusations were made, twenty years ago, about Beauvrai and Saint Sebastien. Your father, along with a dozen or so other young men, was implicated, but he left the court, and there was no further action taken in his case. . . ." She looked up as the lackey came in.

"The tea, Madame," Paulin said as he set an English crockery pot on the table. "Will Mademoiselle want milk, as the English do?" he asked in a tone that suggested he thought milk in tea was one of the more disgusting perversions.

"Chinese tea is best taken plain," Madelaine said with awful hauteur. "But thank you."

Paulin bowed and drew back to his place by the door.

It took Madelaine a moment to make a recovery, and she masked this well by pouring tea for herself. When she spoke again, her tone was light. "Gossip is always diverting, aunt. But I can understand why you want me to behave so that I do not give rise to any."

"Good girl," her aunt said. Her appreciation of Madelaine's wits deepened. In spite of her youth, Madelaine was neither foolish nor naive. "I knew you would understand."

As she finished her lemon-curd pastry, Madelaine looked up again. "Tell me about Saint-Germain."

Glad to be on safe ground again, la Comtesse laughed. "Has he captivated you as well? I warn you that many another has come to grief over him."

Madelaine drank her tea thoughtfully. "I have heard he has no mistress. Is he as the other men you warned me of?"

"Not to my knowledge. No, that is not what I mean in his case." She ate another section of her orange. "We are all in raptures over him, of course. Such address, such wit. You must hear the enchanting tales he tells at supper. And those eyes. Most of us would sell our souls for such eyes."

"He did not join us at supper last night," Madelaine pointed out as she poured more tea.

"Oh, as to that, he does not eat with the others. I have seen him several times at dinners, but I have yet to see him touch either food or drink. I am sure it is part of the aura of mystery with which he surrounds himself. He has assured me that he sups in private." Quite suddenly she laughed, and the sound was as warm and as free as the laughter of a happy child. "It is always amusing to have a man like that paying court to one. The only mistake is to assume he is serious. Pray do not dwell too much on the pretty things he says."

"Then I should not believe the compliments he gave me?" Madelaine could not quite hide the hurt she felt. Saint-Germain's words had been so delightful, so very much what she had wanted most to hear.

"Well, no," la Comtesse said kindly. "His compliments are genuine. But it would be foolish to read into them more than what they are. After all, no one knows for sure who he is. It is lowering to think that in spite of all, Beauvrai might be right, and the man turn out to be a charlatan."

Madelaine sipped at her tea, her eyes far away. "But he is a Comte. Everyone says so."

"Ah." Her aunt nodded wisely. "But that is because *he* says so, and he has the manner and the jewels to back it up. You must see the carriage he drives—perfection! And his four lackeys wear lacings of gold on their snuff-colored clothes. I have never seen Saint-Germain wear the same waistcoat twice, and most of them have been embroidered silk. Obviously, whoever he is, he is fabulously wealthy. His diamond shoe buckles made me blink the first time I saw them." She finished her orange. "By all means, enjoy his attentions. It does you a great deal of good to be seen with him, for he is very much the rage just now. But do not set too much store by his dancing attendance on you."

Madelaine made a moue of disappointment. "Very well. But it is a shame such a splendid man should be an impostor."

"I did not say that he was—just that he might be. To be sure," she went on after a moment's hesitation, "he claims absolutely no one as kin, which is strange. Everyone must have relatives."

Madelaine frowned. "No one?"

"No one," her aunt announced. "And he is a very rich man, my dear. Rich men *always* have relatives." She pulled at the linen napkin in her lap. "Of course, he is not French, but one would think that someone would have encountered his family somewhere, but no one has, that I know of."

"Where is he from?" Madelaine poured more tea and offered some to la Comtesse.

"No, but thank you, my dear. I cannot abide tea." She brought her mind back to the matter at hand. "That is something else no one seems to know. He has been everywhere, that is certain. His command of languages amazes us all—he has Russian and Arabic as well as all the European tongues. There are some who say he is a sea captain or a merchant." She paused again, obviously still puzzled. "He may be that, of course, but I will wager my eyes and my largest jewels that he did not get that manner on the deck of a ship."

"I heard La Noisse say that she had given him her diamonds and that he had made them grow larger." Madelaine traced a complicated design on the tablecloth with her finger.

"I have heard that, too. And I have seen the diamonds, which most assuredly are larger. He could have taken her smaller gems and given her larger ones, of course, but I cannot see why he would. What does he gain from it?" She shook her head, impatient with these insoluble problems. Pushing back from the table, she said, "I am planning to drive out this afternoon, if you would care to join me. And tonight la Duchesse de Lyon is giving her fête."

Madelaine looked out into the warm sunshine. "If you wish my company. It is a shame I did not bring my mare with me, for I confess I miss riding." The sadness in her face did not seem to spring from the thought of her mare.

"You may hire a horse, if you wish." Claudia d'Argenlac disliked riding, and was startled by her niece's mention of it. "I suppose growing up in the country . . ."

"I rode everywhere, aunt. I felt so free, when Chanèe would race with the wind, and I would use all my strength to hold her." Her face lightened a little at this memory.

"Gracious, I hope you do not plan to ride through the streets of Paris in that manner!" In that instant la Comtesse was very much alarmed; then she considered the matter. "I will ask my groom to inquire about suitable horses for you, and if he finds you a sufficiently proficient rider, then we shall see."

Madelaine turned to her and smiled warmly. "Oh, thank you, aunt. I know I will feel less . . . strange if only I can ride."

"That is settled, then." La Comtesse rose, delighted to see her niece so animated. She felt that Madelaine's adaptation to Paris society was going well, and took advantage of her enthusiasm to ask, "About the fête—what will you wear?"

Madelaine shrugged. "I have not thought much about it."

"Then may I suggest that grand toilette you have, with the cherry-striped satin. It would be wholly suitable, and you have not yet worn it. It is a shame to powder your hair in such a gown, but it must be."

"What jewels should I wear, aunt?" Madelaine asked, entering into the spirit of the occasion.

"Your garnets are sufficient."

"Oh," Madelaine said with an impatient gesture. "This morning Cassandre found that the setting was disturbed. One of the links was almost broken. It scratched my neck." She touched her neck where the lace ruff of the fichu spread out. "I have told her to have it repaired."

La Comtesse shook her head. "A pity. Well, then, the diamonds. You have that collar with the large pearl drop. That should do for the fête."

"Very well." Madelaine rose now, and went with her aunt to the door of the breakfast room, then turned suddenly to embrace the older woman in impulsive affection. "I do not care if my father thinks that it is dangerous for me to come to Paris. I am glad I am here, aunt. And I love you for the kindness you show me."

Pleased and embarrassed by this outburst, la Comtesse freed herself from her niece's arms. "Well," she allowed, "it is no difficulty to be kind to so bright and lovely a girl as you are. Now, let me go, my dear. I must change if I am to be seen abroad in my carriage."

Madelaine stepped aside for her aunt to pass, then followed her out into the wide hallway leading to the front of the house. There was a thoughtful look in her eyes, and she did not speak.

Text of a letter from Beverly Sattin to Prinz Ragoczy, written in English, dated October 8, 1743:

> To His Highness, Franz Josef Ragoczy, Prinz of Transylvania,
> B. Sattin sends his most Rspctfl. Greetings.
> Of the Business which we Discussed some nights since, I have the Pleasure to tell you that the Proceedings of BlueSky have prospered, and that the Desired Outcome is near at hand.
> I beg Your Highness will meet with us in the Accustomed Place on the night of the 9th, where the Documents Your Highness desired will be available.
> At the conclusion of this Transaction, I and my Associates will be most Grateful and Appreciative for the material promised us.
> With the hope that Your Highness's Affairs will prosper, I have the Privilege to remain
>
> > Your most humble, obt. svt.,
> > B. Sattin

❦ 4 ❧

Clotaire de Saint Sebastien leaned back on the squabs of his town coach and sighed. His conversation with de les Radeux had been disappointing, for the boy had no intention of assigning the family coffers to his uncle again, no matter what arguments he used.

The coach lurched over a pothole, and Saint Sebastien cursed. It was bad enough that he would be denied access to Beauvrai's fortune, but he was not certain that he would even have the primary sacrifice he had hoped for. Achille Cressie vouched for his bride, but had been stupid enough to alienate her affections. He did not know if she would be willing to come to the Mass, let alone trusting enough to be the altar and the sacrifice. He tapped his tall cane impatiently. He had to have the woman. This close to his goal, he would not tolerate such a setback.

For a moment his mind dwelt on the Sabbat. He had not officiated at one for almost six years, and he felt his strength declining. He needed that power, born of blood and terror. He thought of the lithe young body of Lucienne Cressie stretched naked beneath him, as the congregation used her or one another until the moment when he would possess her, drawing youth from her like a bee drawing nectar. And later, when All Hallows came, he would possess her again, but this time he would plunge his dagger into her neck and catch the hot blood in the Chalice at the very moment of his ecstasy. . . .

Suddenly the coach swayed and came to an abrupt stop. Angry at this rude interruption of his reverie, Saint Sebastien stuck his head out of the window and looked up toward the coachman's box. "Well?" he demanded.

"I am sorry," the coachman muttered, dreading what was coming.

Saint Sebastien stared at him, his predatory face becoming sharper than usual. "That is not good enough, my man. It is not at all good enough. Give the reins over to the groom beside you. Immediately." He had stepped down onto the road and was most impatiently tapping his high walking stick. "I do not intend to tell you again."

Very, very slowly the coachman climbed down from the box, and even more slowly he bowed before Saint Sebastien. "I thought there was danger, master," he said, not wanting to whine, but needing to delay the punishment as long as possible. "There were three beggars, master. They stumbled in front of the horses."

"You should have driven over them." He was holding the high walking stick lightly now, his hand fondling the cap of polished stone, mounted in lead-weighted silver.

"The horses, master. I did not want to harm your horses."

"That is a lie." Saint Sebastien slammed the stone cap down on the coachman's shoulder, a slight smile curling his mouth at the coachman's shriek. "Put your hands on the road," he ordered implacably.

The coachman started to back away, his head shaking, anger vying with fear for control of him. "No! No!"

This time the jeweled cap struck his knee, and the coachman collapsed beside the carriage, keening in a thin, high voice. He cried out once as Saint Sebastien deliberately took aim and smashed his other knee. Blood spread over his heavy twill breeches and began to soak into the road.

Saint Sebastien licked his lips once as he studied his stricken coachman, his eyes somnambulant with strange pleasure. Then, satisfied, he turned to the horrified groom on the box. "You may drive on," he said as he climbed onto the coach.

"But your coachman—" the groom began.

"What use do I have for a cripple in my household?" Saint Sebastien asked, his voice dangerously sweet. He looked out the window at the few people standing stupefied by the road. His eyes raked over them, and he remarked to the air, "There are those who would do well to be blind at this moment."

Quickly the street was empty. Saint Sebastien said to the groom, "I do not like to repeat my orders. Drive on."

The groom gathered up the reins and gave the horses their office. He was relieved to feel the strong pull on his hands, for it kept them from shaking. He put his mind on the roadway and drove.

The coachman watched the carriage pull away through pain-clouded eyes, and damned the scented, evil man who rode in it. He loathed Saint Sebastien, but at that moment he would have given his life in Saint Sebastien's service to have his legs back again. The pain was intense, and made him nauseated. When he tried to move, there were fires in his body. He realized he might be run over by another coach, and for a moment he wished he would be. He had been shamed, he had been crippled. He struck out with his hand and touched filth.

A shadow fell across him. "Coachman?" said a voice in slightly accented French.

The coachman looked up and saw an angular, elderly man in snuff-colored livery, certain indication that he was a servant from some wealthy household. The coachman groaned. He had had enough of wealthy households.

"I saw what happened." The man had knelt beside him now, oblivious of the dirt in the road. "I would like to help you, sir, if you would allow."

"Leave me alone."

"Were I to do that," the manservant said carefully, "you would be dead within the hour. A coach would crush you, or some of the ruffians who prey on unfortunate travelers would stone you in order to rob you of your clothes." He paused and touched the coachman's shoulder. "What is your name? I am Roger."

He hated to answer, but the manservant would not go away. "I am Hercule."

"Very well, Hercule," Roger said. "I am going to send for the lackeys of my household. We will carry you to our master, and he will surely do all he can for you. You need not fear. He is highly skilled in the use of medicinals."

Hercule scoffed through his pain. "What master would help me? I am a coachman without legs."

There was a wise, old smile in Roger's faded eyes. "My master has often surprised me. I know of one case when he sheltered a runaway bondsman at great risk to himself, and later made sure that the bondsman achieved the revenge he desired."

"He lies." The words came out in shouts.

"Ah, no. I was the bondsman, you see." He rose. "I will be gone for a moment, Hercule. Do not despair."

Hercule was about to throw Roger's kindness in his face, but the aged valet had already walked away. And now that Roger was gone, Hercule felt desolate. It had been easy to reject the old manservant and his master when Roger knelt beside him, but now, lying alone in the road, uncertain when another vehicle might happen along, listening for the approach of thieves and highwaymen, Hercule grew frightened. He was in sight of the gates of Paris, and there were buildings less than a quarter of a mile away. But the travelers who had seen him beaten were gone, and there was no one to help him now that Roger had gone off in a small trap.

As his fright grew, so did his hatred for Saint Sebastien. He felt the acid of it burn in his mind, and he took satisfaction from it. Hatred was stronger and more constant than courage, and it gave him the tenacity to resist the hurt in his legs long enough to pull himself to the side of the road.

The afternoon sun baked down on him, and only the cool autumn breeze brought him respite. He felt the blood drain from him as he lay beside the road, and thought of the smile he had seen in Saint Sebastien's eyes when the first red stain had soaked through his breeches.

Hercule was lying semiconscious a little later when one of the finest coaches he had ever seen came bowling down the road at a smart pace. It was pulled by four matched grays, and even in his agony, Hercule saw that the horses were superb animals. He felt a muzzy bemusement when the coach pulled up where he lay, and the steps were let down.

First out of the coach was Roger, who came directly to him. "Have you been hurt more?" he asked as he neared Hercule.

"No," Hercule answered, finding his tongue unwieldy. "Crawled."

"Crawled?" said the man behind Roger as he came down from the coach. He was of medium height, of stocky but trim build. His elegant, fashionable clothes were black but for fine white lace at his throat and wrists. On his small feet were black shoes with jeweled buckles. His dark hair was unpowdered and confined at the nape of his neck with a neat black bow. Intelligence marked his attractive face, made even more interesting by a strong nose that was slightly askew. He dropped to his knee by Hercule, as if unaware that the dust and filth would ruin his silken garments. "My good man, who did this to you?"

"Saint Sebastien," Hercule whispered, suddenly struck by the gentleman's intense, compelling eyes.

"Saint Sebastien," the gentleman repeated, "Saint Sebastien." Then he turned to his manservant. "Roger, you did well. Bring this man to the Hôtel. I am sure we will find something for him to do. I will attend to him later. See that the wounds are bathed, but apply no bandages. There may be shards of bone in the wounds, and they must, on no account, be pressed."

"Who is he?" Hercule asked Roger as he was lifted gently into the coach.

Roger's master heard the question and answered it. "For the most part, I am le Comte de Saint-Germain, this century."

Excerpt from a letter written by la Comtesse d'Argenlac to her brother, le Marquis de Montalia, dated October 11, 1743:

. . . We attended a salon last night, so that Madelaine would not be overtired from the fête of la Duchesse de Lyon of the night before. At the salon, Madelaine was a great success. Saint-Germain had written some airs for the violoncello and a singer. La Cressie has received her new instrument, and the composer prevailed upon Madelaine to be the vocalist. The works were charming, my dear brother. There was nothing in them even so strict a moralist as you could object to. Madelaine sang very sweetly, and Mme. Cressie said afterward that she had found the duets delightful, and begged Madelaine to sing with her more often. I believe they both requested Saint-Germain to write new airs for them. He said that he felt it would be a shame to deprive the world of their music, and so he supposed he must.

You may imagine, following this lovely evening, what a shock it was to learn that Lucienne Cressie has fallen gravely ill. At least, that is what Achille has given out. I must tell you that I am suspicious of him. He has been even more in Saint Sebastien's company, and in Beauvrai's. There was some gathering at Cressie's late on the 9th. Some are saying that it was only Achille's usual vice being practiced, but I am not so sure, particularly since Lucienne has not been seen since that night. You may call me a fool, brother, but you know what sort of monster Saint Sebastien is, and it is my belief that he is attempting once again to gather together his followers of Satan. Rest assured I will do all that I can to be certain that none of these men so much as talks to Madelaine.

We go tomorrow night to Hôtel Transylvania. Do not fret, for I will not allow Madelaine to gamble. But there is to be a fête, with dancing, and a ballet and a little opera in the Italian style performed, as well as the usual fare. Rumor has it that the Hôtel wishes to rival the Hôtel de Ville. I do not know if this can be done, but it will make for a wonderful entertainment, and all the world goes.

I must congratulate you on your daughter. She is a delight. Her manners are pleasing, she has wit and conversation, and she has an excellent mind. Occasionally she quite astounds me with her erudition. When Saint-Germain was regaling us at supper with his droll stories, she rallied him when he had begun a tale of vampires, saying that to fear them was the greatest folly, since any blood would appease them. All one would have to do was offer them a lamb, or a horse, and the matter was settled. You should have seen the amazement on Saint-Germain's face. He kissed her hand and told her he conceded the match.

Later that night we drank a glass of wine with le Baron and la Baronne de Haute-Misou, and le Baron was recounting some tale he had read by one of the Florentines about the sculptor Michelangelo. Immediately, Madelaine identified the painting in question—the good Sisters who taught her will be pleased to know that the work in question is that in the Sistine Chapel—and told the history of the piece. Le Baron was enchanted. He said that it was rare to find a young woman with erudition to match her face. Madelaine said—and you must not scold her for this, my dear brother, for she was only bantering—that if more women were educated as she had been, le Baron must be enchanted every hour of his life.

I thank you a thousand times for sending my niece to me. I trust you will be satisfied of the good work we make of her time in Paris. Commend me well to your Marquise, and assure her that her daughter is well and that she goes often to Mass. Do not think that because Madelaine's social success is great that I allow her to neglect her religious duties. She is obedient and sincere in her exercises of faith, and her confessor has told me that her soul is chaste. This good man our cousin, is noted for his piety, and has, as I understand it, your approval to minister to her spiritual needs.

I will bid you farewell for the moment, my dear brother. No doubt you will have a letter from me again before too many days pass. May God keep you and your Marquise and give you peace of mind. With all due respect and profound affection, I remain

> Your sister,
> Claudia de Montalia
> Comtesse d'Argenlac

P.S. I have taken the liberty of purchasing a fine Spanish mare for Madelaine to ride. She is a splendid mount, and Madelaine has shown herself to be an excellent equestrienne. Even as I write this, she is with a party, gone to Bois-Vert for the afternoon.

ᵇ̌ᵍ 5 ᵍᵇ̌

Donatien de la Sept-Nuit held the stirrup leather and gallantly assisted Madelaine to mount her new Spanish mare. Around them the other members of the party were climbing back into their saddles for their return to Paris.

Madelaine settled herself onto her saddle, adjusting the bottle-green skirt so that it flowed gracefully down the side of her mare. "Thank you," she said after a moment, with the flicker of a frown in her eyes.

De la Sept-Nuit made a profound bow. "It is always a pleasure. If so little service deserves your thanks, I would willingly perform great deeds, were the rewards commensurate."

She did not answer at once, but had her hands full when her mare sidled under her as the reins were brought up too tightly. "Pray, no more ridiculous compliments, Chevalier. I begin to feel the fool."

Le Chevalier bowed again and made his way back to his big bay gelding. In a moment he had flung himself into the saddle and was moving with a few of his friends. Châteaurose called to him as he came up, "How fares it with La Montalia?"

"More thorns than roses," de la Sept-Nuit admitted as the bay scampered and bucked playfully.

"I've a mind to try for her myself," Châteaurose said as he watched Madelaine bring her mare up beside the snowy-white Andalusian ridden by la Baronne de Haute-Misou.

"It's useless. This time Saint Sebastien is wrong." De la Sept-Nuit lowered his voice to say this, and cocked an eyebrow to the other young men in the party.

Around them, the woods were alive with the golds and russets of autumn. The leaves drifted and crackled on the road, and flitted like butterflies when the wind blew. It was a beautiful, burnished day, full of sunlight that dappled the party with topaz brilliance as they rode under the trees.

"It was a tiresome matter," la Baronne was saying to Madelaine, who listened with a fraudulent air of attention. "The gown was ruined, of course, and there was nothing to do but to give it to the housemaid."

"A difficult matter, certainly." Madelaine schooled her face to gravity and held her mare to a strict trot.

"Well, what can one do? If the cooks will put so much wine into their sauces, we must accept the stains. To be sure, the sauces make the meal, but it is a shame to ruin good satin because beef demands an appropriate dressing."

"Perhaps a special gown to wear at dinner . . ." Madelaine suggested before she had time to consider.

"A gown for eating? For *eating?*" la Baronne almost squealed.

"Why not?" Madelaine asked innocently, developing her theme. "You could have a special dining dress for the occasion of the meal. You could serve a Roman banquet, and everyone could dress in togas and recline on couches. I think that's what the Romans did," she said, frowning a little, then waved to a familiar figure. "Saint-Germain! Did the Romans recline on couches?"

"What is this?" he called. "What about Romans?" He cantered his smoke-colored stallion over to them, and when he was abreast of them, bowed slightly and asked again, "What is this about Romans?"

"Oh, I was suggesting to la Baronne that she might have a Roman banquet with guests in togas and lying on couches. But then I couldn't remember if it was Greeks or Romans who did that."

"Foreign," said la Baronne, and the condemnation in that word was absolute.

"Do not say so," Saint-Germain protested, "when the present King's great-grandfather tried so hard to restore Rome's glory to France."

"Louis the Fourteenth was a glorious monarch," la Baronne announced, looking suspiciously at Saint-Germain.

"Undoubtedly," Saint-Germain agreed, at his most bland. He shot a wicked glance of amusement at Madelaine. "Are you equally admiring of the former King?"

It was la Baronne who answered this question. "Surely there are aspects of the man we must deplore, but it is wise to remember that his second marriage restored much of the tone of the court."

"And the vice and diabolism you despise vanished utterly at the King's command?" Saint-Germain asked gently. "How fortunate for France."

La Baronne said nothing, and it might have been an accident that she dropped behind Madelaine and le Comte, who rode together for a while in companionable silence. Ahead of them, the young men raced their horses in impromptu competition, and behind them came the older members of the party on sedate animals. The sun shone down through the trees in long shafts that brought new shadows and light with every movement.

"I like your horse," Madelaine said after a while. "I don't think I have ever seen one like him."

Saint-Germain patted the graceful neck. "He was given me in Persia. Not many of his kind have been seen in Europe. I believe they are sometimes called barbs." He patted the broad neck again.

Madelaine nodded, then said playfully, "I believe this is the first time I have not seen you in black, Saint-Germain. What is the leather you wear?"

"Elk hide. The tooling shows the story of Saint Hubert and the Stag." He fingered the dark-claret leather that set off the muslin neck cloth he wore. "It is somewhat old-fashioned. The cuffs are sadly narrow by modern standards, but I have had it for some time, and it was made for me in Hungary. I cannot bear to part with it." He raised his brows slightly. "What is troubling you, my dear? You did not call me to your side to discuss Romans or horseflesh. Was la Baronne boring you to tears?"

"Oh, no," she said brightly.

"Then perhaps you were not pleased by de la Sept-Nuit's advances?" He saw her wince as he asked, and knew he had hit home.

"My aunt tells me that I cannot expect much happiness from marriage, and that I would be wise to be practical. I understand that de la Sept-Nuit is rich and on the lookout for a wife. His mother has given my aunt to understand that he thinks I would do him great credit."

"Oh, no." He laughed. "And you do not want to be a credit to de la Sept-Nuit?"

"It may be funny to you, Comte, but I find it demeaning." She gave an angry toss to her head so that he would not see the sudden tears in her eyes. "I feel like a very elegant slave for sale to the highest bidder."

"Madelaine," he said very quietly, and she turned to look at him, pulling her mare back to a slower trot. "Your aunt means kindly by you. It is all she knows to do."

Her throat tight, Madelaine agreed. "She explained what women should expect. But, oh, Saint-Germain, I want more."

He smiled sadly at this outburst. "I know."

She looked at him challengingly. "I have heard that you have been many places, and done things and seen things. . . . I wish I could go many places and do many things."

There was a curious light in his eyes. "Such a life is very lonely, Madelaine."

Now her face was becomingly flushed, and she spoke in a fierce undertone. "Do you think being married to de la Sept-Nuit would not be lonely? Do you think being married to any of them"—she flung one hand toward the roistering young men farther down the road—"would be other than lonely? At least there is *interest* in your life."

After a moment he nodded. "Yes, I suppose my life is, in a way, interesting."

"Well, like last night," she said, changing the subject so that she could restore her calm. "You were talking about using steam to power ships. But you were not like Beauvrai, who wants such things because they bring attention to him, though he does not comprehend one jot about such engines. I could tell when you talked about steam engines that you had thought about them. Saying that as the water pushes a mill wheel, so it could be made to push the water, if the power were in the mill. And using boiling water to move those tubes in circles. I don't see why everyone said it was impossible. I thought it looked very simple."

Saint-Germain grinned, showing neat white teeth. "That is because you have not spent a life learning what cannot be done."

The light left her face. "You are wrong, Comte. And I am learning rapidly."

"Shush, shush, Madelaine." He rode a little closer to her, so that his stirrup leather almost touched the girths of her sidesaddle. "Are you so unhappy, my dear?"

"Yes . . . no . . . I don't know." She did not look at him, afraid that there might be too much compassion in his eyes, and she might betray herself to him. "I know I am expected to marry, and in time I shall grow bored enough and frightened enough that I will." She looked back over her shoulder at the older group of riders. "See where all the women ride, Comte, even the young women? They are old already." She wrenched her eyes away. "In time, I will be like them and think even of you with cynical amusement."

"Madelaine."

"Do not speak to me in that kind way. I cannot abide it. You give me hope and there is no hope." She dug her spur into her mare's flank, and swayed gracefully as her mount bounded ahead.

Saint-Germain rode after her, close enough to catch her if the mare should bolt in earnest, but far enough back so that she could pretend she did not know he was there.

Excerpt from a letter from the physician André Schoenbrun to le Comte de Saint-Germain, dated October 12, 1743:

. . . The physician wishes to assure le Comte that whatever mobility is left in the knees must come from the prompt and expert care that was rendered to the man Hercule. At least movement will be retained in the knees, although it may not be possible for him to walk again. The physician is pleased that le Comte did not order the knees bandaged, as that is what saved the mobility. The manservant accompanying the patient informed the physician that it was le Comte who gave instructions to leave the knees unbandaged, and the physician commends him.

In regard to le Comte's inquiry about work. So long as the man Hercule does not put any weight on his legs, there is no reason he cannot leave his bed as soon as he is fit. His fever has broken, so it should not be long before such gentle exercise as can be done with arms and hands might be undertaken. The physician understands that le Comte is in possession of syrup of poppies, and recommends the administration of such to the man Hercule for pain if that pain is too severe. But the physician warns le Comte not to use it too often, and prays le Comte to remember that the physician has observed that the prolonged use of such medication can result in dependence upon it, which is not desirable.

The physician will take the liberty of calling upon le Comte in ten days' time to examine the man Hercule and see that no infection has arisen, and to satisfy himself that recovery is progressing. If the physician finds it advisable, he will bleed the man Hercule at that time.

If he can be of service to le Comte again, the physician assures him that he would be honored to serve le Comte's household at any time.

Believe me to be yours to command,

André Schoenbrun, physician
le Rue de Ecoulè-Romain

6

Lucienne Cressie regarded the darkening room through glazed, exhausted eyes. Nothing looked familiar, though she had slept in this room almost every night since her marriage to Achille. From the heavy draperies around her bed to the tall, gilt-wood chests against the far wall, it was all as foreign to her as the fittings of the private quarters of a Chinese emperor would be.

Her husband had been with her some time ago. She was not clear in her mind now how much time had passed since he had left, for the wine he had given her must surely have been drugged. She moved weakly, and felt a creeping sickness in her body.

She grasped at the sheets as if she were drowning, wondering what would become of her. Each day she told herself that she could sustain her travesty of a marriage a little while longer, but at night, alone with nothing but dreams to possess her, she felt her courage eroding. At those moments, even prayer did not help her, and that, more than anything else, frightened her.

Now her eyes filled with tears as she thought about the few moments Achille had given to her, his disdain for her suffering, his callous indifference to her pleadings. She had begged him tonight to let her enter a convent. She was even willing to disappear, perhaps to the New World, so that he would not be troubled with her in any way again. He had laughed, saying that if she wished to devote herself to religion, he would take care to give her the opportunity she wanted. He had locked her in the room, as he had the day before.

She had played her new violoncello for a time, but found little consolation in its music, and her mind wandered as the drug took possession of her mind.

Now she lay on the bed, and felt her resistance give way. Achille was planning something for tonight, she knew. The night before, she had listened well into the early hours while Achille and his cronies talked in the library below. There had been sounds like chanting, and, much later, cries and comments that told her the men were enacting what her husband called the Rites of Athens. She closed her eyes and tried to compose her thoughts for prayer.

Dizziness overcame her, and she opened her eyes again in the vain hope that the images would come to rest. Her head ached abominably, and her ears rang.

The room seemed much darker now, and she thought perhaps she had slept, or was still sleeping. When she could not bring the tassels of the canopy that hung at the foot of her bed into focus, she turned her head to the wall. As she stared at the thick folds of the bed hangings, she thought that the cloth moved. She tried to turn away, and found that she could not.

His eyes were warm, very warm and hungry.

It was the dream again, and this time she felt herself move toward the image, shameful joy in her heart. She recognized the guilt of her passion, and surrendered to it, to his warm, insistent mouth, now on her lips, now on her throat. His hands caressed her with a touch as light as gossamer, and full of fire. She could feel his weight beside her, and welcomed it, almost weeping as she drew him toward her.

In some remote part of her mind, she wondered if Achille had sent him to her as a terrible jest, but she could not imagine how even Achille could send a dream.

She felt herself warm and cold at once, and she strained to hold him nearer to her. His touch was gentle, expert, and drew her out of herself. There was a single sharp moment of pain, but it was followed so swiftly by ecstatic languor that it served only to punctuate her rapture. She was drifting, drifting, as insubstantial as music. The warm throb of her violoncello between her legs was nothing compared to this sweet, shining dream that fired her very veins with delight. This splendidly ravished sleep bore her as if on wings, or the wind. She felt her heart open as a flower opens, and slipped away into deep, silent slumber. There was no weight beside her, and the delicious thrumming of her blood subsided to that gentle tide of rest.

It was cold in the room when she woke, and the tumbled bedclothes gave her no protection and little warmth. She was cold, and now that the effect of the drug had dissipated, she felt numb and exhausted.

Guilt assaulted her as well. She knew that such dreams were as deep a sin as the act itself, for she who had committed adultery in her heart was an unfaithful wife in the eyes of Holy Church. Her confessor had told her this was so, and without exception, for adultery was lust, and lust was one of the seven deadly sins. She crossed herself, feeling hypocritical, and pulled the covers about her, shame coloring her face.

The prayers would not come. In vain she tried to fix her thoughts on heavenly things, and each time, she was pulled back to the blissful dream, and the delirious sensuality that it brought, the dream where her body sang a sacrament all its own that the austere example of the saints and martyrs could not dispel.

Her mind was still divided when the door opened and, to her amazement, her husband came in. "Good morning, Madame. I trust I do not disturb you?" His mocking eyes saw her dishevelment as evidence of the drug's efficacy.

"Achille?" she asked, feeling a cold of another kind rise in her. She gathered the bedclothes around her in response to the disgust she saw in his face.

He walked toward her bed. "Come, Madame, come. We have guests belowstairs. It would be remiss of you not to put in an appearance to greet them." He held out his hand to her, and there was an implacability about him. This was not another one of his cruel jokes. This was another matter entirely. "Come, Madame," he repeated.

She frowned. "I am not dressed, Achille. Do you seek to make a mockery of your wife?" She hoped fervently that was all he had planned. "Can you not leave me be?"

"These are your guests, Madame. They are in your home. It would be rude of you not to join us when they have expressly asked for you." He reached for her negligee and tossed it to her. "This is appropriate enough, wife. Put it on and come with me."

Even as she started to obey, some sense in her brought her attention into sharp focus. She knew that there was something terribly wrong, and that Achille was not here for her protection. At the least, humiliation awaited her; at the worst, she dared not guess.

"Do not delay," he ordered her, his face becoming ugly as harsh lines set in it. "The hour is almost past."

"No," she said, backing away from him. She did not know what the hour meant, but she knew now that there was danger and that her husband was leading her into it. "Go away, Achille. I am not well. Please excuse me to your guests."

"They are *our* guests," he said with thinly disguised irritation. "You must come down. Saint Sebastien particularly wants to make your acquaintance." He pointed to the negligee. "Put it on, Madame. I will not wait any longer for you."

She shook her head. "No."

He stared across the room at her, his fists clenching at his sides. Then, with an effort, he walked toward her. "You are my wife. You will do as I say."

Lucienne Cressie had been frightened by Achille before, but she had never felt terror of the sort that raced through her now. She pulled pillows from the bed and threw them as he came nearer, knowing that this was trivial in the face of his rage. There was a heavy glass perfume jar on the stand by her bed, and she threw that, too.

Achille stumbled under the impact of the jar as it glanced off his brow, and swayed for a moment on his feet, his mouth working. Then he lunged at his wife.

Without any hesitation, La Cressie pulled open the window behind her. It was a two-story drop to the garden, and she knew this. Before Achille could grab her, she threw herself out, feeling the night air cold on her body as she fell.

She realized she had been stunned, because she could hear many voices in the house, now that her mind had cleared. She was not dead. She tested her arms, and found that one of her shoulders was dislocated. She had not felt the pain until she tried to move it, and then it struck her with a hammer blow. Inconsequently the thought came to her that she could not play the violoncello with her shoulder thus. She would have to get help, and care.

She heard voices grow nearer, and in the gloom there was a lantern shine. Now she cursed herself for failing in her attempt at death. She knew for her soul's sake she should repent. She was aware that she should thank God for sparing her so that she could make expiation for her sins, for the lust in her flesh, and for her attempted suicide. But the sound of the footsteps was growing louder, and she wished from her heart that she had died.

"We have found her," said a voice she did not recognize, and she looked up to see a tall, thin man of perhaps sixty years, dressed in the height of fashion. His gray eyes were hooded, almost reptilian, and the smile he wore was more frightening than anger would have been.

Behind him came another, older man whose outlandish clothes identified him as Baron Beauvrai, who addressed the man beside him. "Damme, but you get the luck, Clotaire. She's yours for the sacrifice, then."

Clotaire de Saint Sebastien chuckled once, and Lucienne's mouth grew dry at the sound of it. "She can be of use to me, at least, I suppose. We must be sure she is still a virgin. Have Achille and his friend bring her into the library." He knelt beside Lucienne, and ignoring her protests and shock, thrust his hand between her legs.

"No, no, no," she whispered, and tightened her legs.

"Madame," Saint Sebastien said coolly, "do not attempt to impede me. I warn you now that I will not tolerate that."

She started to speak, and struggled against his probing hand. He sighed, and his fingers touched her painfully, intimately. Her head swam, and her legs closed again involuntarily. The pain he gave her this time welled up, cutting through the earlier, duller pain of her fall.

Saint Sebastien stood up. "Good, she is intact. How many of the Circle will take her?" If he saw the horror on Lucienne Cressie's face, he paid no attention to it.

Beauvrai looked hungrily at the woman on the ground. "A nice piece of flesh. It is a shame to have wasted her on one such as Achille."

Saint Sebastien corrected him. "She will not be wasted. For our purposes, we must be glad that Achille prefers men."

"No," Lucienne said, "No. No. No. No. No. No."

Other men had joined them now, among them Achille Cressie. Lucienne saw that there was a red welt on his forehead, and felt some satisfaction in knowing that the perfume jar had hurt him.

". . . in the library. Immediately. We have less than an hour in which to finish the ceremony. It will be three months before we will have the same powerful influences for an Amatory Mass." He was already striding off toward the wide French doors leading into the house.

The men with Achille were delighted to obey. As Achille grabbed her legs, de Vandonne pulled at her arms, ignoring her moan as her shoulder was wrenched again. As they lifted her into the air, she fainted once again.

When she opened her eyes this time, she thought for a moment that her terror had been ill-founded, and that she had been taken to a physician for help. She was lying flat on a table, and there was a crucifix suspended over her head. Cowled figures stood around her. She was about to speak, to offer thanks for her rescue to these good brothers, when she realized that she was still naked, and that the crucifix was inverted. Even as she saw this blasphemy, she looked at the corpus more clearly, seeing the obscenity that had been made of the Body of Christ. The erect phallus was as long as the torso of the figure, and a pentacle was engraved on the forehead. She turned away, crying openly now, knowing that she had not escaped at all.

"Excellent, excellent," Saint Sebastien said, very near at hand. "She is conscious. So much the better." He addressed the hooded men around him. "You may use her as you will until three of the clock, once I have done with her. I will take her maidenhead, and will use her again just as the hour strikes. Keep that in mind. First and last, she is mine. Employ your lusts on her and on each other, but her virginity is mine."

De Vandonne spoke, his voice shaky with excitement. "Will she submit, no matter what we do?"

"She will submit," Saint Sebastien said with such utter certainty that Lucienne despaired. "If she does not, complain to me, and I will remedy that." He nodded to the hooded men. "I think perhaps you had best tie her down. The ropes are fixed in the altar. And put the Devil's Member near at hand. I will need it at three o'clock. Be sure it is hot enough."

"When you are done, who will taste her first?" asked one of the men in a coarse voice Lucienne did not know.

"You must ask our host. It is for her husband to dispose of her. If he does not want her himself." This last was said with an unpleasant laugh.

Achille grinned hugely, and there was genuine amusement in his tone as he said, "Le Grâce is so eager, and we of the aristocracy so rarely have the chance to do something for our lesser citizens . . ."

"*Achille!*" Lucienne cried out with all her soul.

Her husband's words stopped her cry. "Silence her, Le Grâce."

She felt the rough hand cross over her mouth, and the inexpressible horror as her legs were tied, and her arms. She heard the hated voice of Saint Sebastien above her. "Dark Lord, this is for Power."

At the first touch of his intruding flesh, she screamed, writhing in her bonds. Where was her dream now, the gentle hands, the sharp delight of kisses that were as the breath of life? Fierce, hating eyes looked down on her face as Saint Sebastien violated her. She bit her lip to stop the scream in her throat, wanting to keep this satisfaction from her rapist.

Later they tore other sounds from her, and used her in their cruel delights. By the time Saint Sebastien donned the Devil's Member, Lucienne Cressie was only half-conscious, so that this monstrous invasion took only a sigh from her as she passed into unconsciousness again. Some of the Circle watched this moment with gloating faces, but Achille Cressie was not among them. He was deliciously, doubly impaled, and had not the slightest interest in what had happened to his wife.

Text of a letter from the manservant Roger, to his master, le Comte de Saint-Germain, written in Latin, undated:

To my master:

I have continued my observation of Saint Sebastien, as you commanded me to do. It is as you suspected: he is gathering a new Circle around him.

Already they have met, at the home of Achille Cressie, who has given them his wife. She was alive when I left at dawn, but I fear she is distracted from the use to which they put her. Saint Sebastien deflowered her, and after the others were through, raped her in the Satanic manner.

You wished to know who among those attending the circle I recognized. They are as follows:

> de Vandonne
> Châteaurose
> Jueneport
> de la Sept-Nuit
> Le Grâce

If you desire it, my master, I will continue to follow Saint Sebastien. He is vile, master. I pray you will destroy him.

I have taken the liberty of summoning a priest to La Cressie, but the household has refused to admit him. Perhaps you will succeed where I have failed.

This by special messenger, at matins. From my own hand,

Roger

7

Hôtel Transylvania glowed like a box of jewels for some colossal goddess. Every passage was lighted with fine beeswax candles, each chandelier glowed so brightly it seemed to be alive. The Great Hall had been expanded in the latest mode, and a gallery had been added for those who wished to promenade. The only thing that was missing, which would have made the Hôtel a complete success, was the mirror-lined wall in the Great Hall. Since the founding of Versailles, every large building was expected to have mirrors. But in Hôtel Transylvania, the mirrors had been replaced by gigantic paintings of rare beauty. Two were allegorical, showing Zeus at various of his exploits, and one, a somber painting of the death of Socrates, was an authentic Velázquez. Smaller paintings adorned the wall, and all drew exclamations and admiration from the glamorous crowd that flocked there.

The gambling rooms were set aside in the north wing of the gigantic three-story building, and the passage to those rooms was guarded by a new, taciturn majordomo who was seated behind a desk in a discreet alcove. He was a big man, with wide shoulders, a deep chest, and powerful arms. He answered to the name Hercule.

In the rest of Hôtel Transylvania, it was festival time. Several tubs with full-grown orange trees had been arranged down one side of the grand ballroom, and the musicians' bower was filled with flowers. Everyone commented on the extravagance, and secretly envied the wealth displayed in those perishable flowers, for in October, flowers were hard to come by in Paris, and those that were available were terribly dear.

Lackeys and waiters in salmon-colored livery moved through the bustle, performing their services swiftly and unobtrusively. Every man employed by the Hôtel was well-mannered and spoke acceptable French, treating all patrons of the Hôtel with the most becoming deference. The wine was served in the best crystal, the cognac was the finest. The china set out at three luxurious buffets was wonderfully translucent, the silver service a superb example of the most elaborate Italian craft. The food was superb haute cuisine, prepared by a small army of chefs and scullions in the cavernous kitchens at the back of the Hôtel.

La Comtesse d'Argenlac turned to her companion and smiled. "Ah, Marquis, if amid all this splendor you have noticed my niece, she must be complimented in the highest degree. For I protest I have never seen anything to equal this. Everything superior, no expense spared, and all in the best of taste."

Le Marquis Châteaurose bowed slightly. "But this is mere pomp, and tawdry elegance. How can it hope to hold my attention when there is a breathing woman as splendid as Mademoiselle de Montalia to take my eye? All else must pale beside her."

"Of course," Madelaine's aunt said, her eyes narrowing slightly. She had thought this young noble a fine catch for Madelaine, but she found his words too effusive, and it seemed to her this was artistry, and not the sentiments of his heart. She knew that often men of rank sought wives they would be proud of as hostesses, as ornaments to their nobility, for it had been so with her and her husband, and she knew what emptiness was found in such a match. She nodded measuringly. "I will be proud to present you to her," she said automatically, as she led the way through the crush on the dance floor to where her niece stood at the punch bowl talking in a very animated way with le Comte de Saint-Germain.

"My dear," Claudia called to her niece as she drew nearer. "Here is le Marquis Châteaurose come to meet you. He has admired you at a distance, and seeks to know you better."

Le Marquis made a profound bow and rose with a flourish that showed off his gorgeous attire and excellent figure. He cast a withering glance at Saint-Germain, then addressed Madelaine as he kissed her proffered hand. "I have longed for this moment since I saw you first when you rode to Bois-Vert. It has taken me these several days to have courage enough to approach you."

Ordinarily this speech brought a blush and a simper from the women he lavished it on, but Madelaine said, "If you need courage to address me, may heaven help France on the battlefield."

Châteaurose was taken aback. La Comtesse was concerned, as much by Châteaurose's manners as by Madelaine's rudeness. It was Saint-Germain who filled this awkward gap, saying with a smile, "I fear you underestimated the fortifications, Marquis."

But le Marquis Châteaurose had recovered his countenance. "You have no idea," he said to Madelaine, as if he had not heard Saint-Germain, "how refreshing it is to find a girl who says what she thinks. Pray do not curb your tongue for my sake. I find such artless speech charming."

Saint-Germain stepped back and made an almost imperceptible gesture to la Comtesse. "Why did you introduce him?" he asked sotto voce when she stood beside him.

"He asked me to," she answered in the same low tone. "His family is excellent and I have heard nothing to his discredit."

"If you have heard him *speak*, you know something to his discredit. He does not expect Madelaine to believe that drivel he tells her?"

La Comtesse shook her head. "Is there more I should know? You seem alarmed, Saint-Germain. Do you know anything against him?" She was concerned now, for she had realized weeks ago that Saint-Germain knew more of what happened in Paris than any three of her other acquaintances combined.

Saint-Germain did not answer directly, but stood gazing at the far wall in a mildly distracted manner. "I understand you wish her to avoid Beauvrai's set," he said at last.

"At all costs."

He nodded. "Very well. I tell you now that Châteaurose has been seen with Saint Sebastien. Whether he is involved with that set, I do not know for certain, but he makes no effort to avoid them. That much I will tell you. Perhaps you would like me to tell Madelaine something of this? She is so charming a girl, it would be a pity to see her abused."

La Comtesse glanced around the crowded room, and noticed for the first time that de les Radeux and Beauvrai were there. "Please, Comte, please warn her. My brother's fear for her may be unfounded, but I confess that Saint Sebastien alarms me. I cannot forget that La Cressie has received no visitors these last four days, and Achille is often with Saint Sebastien."

"Poor Claudia," Saint-Germain murmured as he kissed her hand sympathetically. He turned to pour her a cup of punch.

She took the cup and sipped at it, then asked with unaccustomed awkwardness, "I do not know if you are willing, but I would appreciate it if you spoke to Madelaine in private. She may have questions, critical questions that could not be answered here"—she gestured to the glittering room—"but in private. . . ."

At the far end of the room the gathering of musicians completed the concertino, and applause rippled through the crowd. The musicians rose, bowed, then prepared to play dance music once again.

"Certainly. I will secure one of the small chambers, if you like. Do you wish to accompany us?" His compelling eyes looked into hers, and it was as if he saw her very soul.

La Comtesse felt divided in her mind. She knew that as her niece's chaperone she was obliged to accompany her, but she also felt that Saint-

Germain was an honorable man, past the age of folly, and discreet. No scandal was spoken of him. No knowing nods and veiled allusions were attached to him. She met his gaze, and her thoughts cleared. It would attract less attention, give rise to less comment if only Madelaine absented herself from the ballroom or the supper room. If she was seen with Saint-Germain, he was only her escort. But if she were seen with her niece and Saint-Germain, particularly as they withdrew, then there would be food for gossip, and might alert Beauvrai, which in turn would endanger Madelaine.

"Very wise of you," Saint-Germain said, and la Comtesse was puzzled, for she did not remember speaking. "I will withdraw with Madelaine in a short while. Perhaps if you were to go into the supper room, her departure will not be noticed, or if it is, all will assume I am bringing her to you."

She nodded, feeling a trifle distracted. She glanced again uneasily in Madelaine's direction, and saw her still in deep conversation with Châteaurose. "Oh, dear," she said to herself as she watched her niece and the gorgeous Marquis.

"Do not be troubled," Saint-Germain told her, and went on gently. "You are as good as a mother to her, and it is not surprising that you worry for her safety. But I promise you she stands in no danger now from Saint Sebastien, and I will do my utmost, I promise you, to be sure she never will."

La Comtesse turned to him impulsively. "You are so kind, Comte. I cannot help but wonder why you do this."

At these words, Saint-Germain laughed. "You need not think it is because I have designs on Madelaine's honor. Let us simply say that I have as little use for Saint Sebastien and his set as you do."

La Comtesse knew she would have to be content with that answer, unsatisfactory as it was, and she was secretly pleased that Saint-Germain had told her that he disliked Saint Sebastien. The niggle of doubt that had risen in her mind was quieted, and it was with a much calmer conscience that she made her excuses and turned toward the supper room.

A few moments later, Saint-Germain offered his arm to Madelaine. "A thousand pardons, Châteaurose, but la Comtesse has charged me with the pleasant task of escorting her niece in to join her at supper."

Châteaurose was not the least discomposed. "If you would appoint me your deputy, Saint-Germain, you would not be bothered, and I would have the pleasure of being in Mademoiselle's radiant presence still longer."

"It is no more bother for me than it is for you," Saint-Germain pointed out, and held his arm ready for Madelaine. "You have danced with her, and been at her side for half an hour, Châteaurose. You have the advantage of me there, in that I do not dance. Do not begrudge me the few minutes it will take me to lead her from here to the supper room."

"It will be as night to me until she returns," Châteaurose said sternly, as if accusing Saint-Germain of perfidious dealings.

Saint-Germain had paid him no attention. "Come, child. Your aunt is waiting." He smiled rather mischievously at Châteaurose. "You will have to find a better ploy in my absence. This one was most unsuccessful."

The little orchestra grew louder as the members swung into a set of variations on two popular arias by Handel. Saint-Germain did not hear the remark made by Madelaine. The gabble of voices and the suddenly loud music drowned her words, and he held up a hand for her silence until they were out of the room.

When they had swept through the double doors and into the long hallway, Madelaine repeated her comment. "I'm grateful for your timely rescue."

Saint-Germain's eyes very nearly twinkled. "Was he boring you?"

"Worse," she said, not objecting or even questioning when Saint-Germain led her down a side hall away from the supper room. "It is all very well to be told one is attractive, but I know that I am not the loveliest woman in the room. Madame de Chardonnay and la Duchesse Quainord are much prettier than I am. And," she went on, warming to the subject, "to be spoken to as if I were just out of the schoolroom—"

"Which you are," Saint-Germain interjected in some amusement as he opened the door to a small withdrawing room.

Madelaine paid no attention to this. "And could only understand one word in five!" Then she realized where she was and looked around in surprise.

The room was not large, but it was furnished in the first style of elegance. Two sofas flanked the hearth, where a low fire smoldered under a carved marble mantel. On the far wall, another Velázquez hung over a table of inlaid rosewood and gilt, which held a number of morocco-bound books, a telescope, and an astrolabe. On the wall opposite the fireplace, fine silken draperies of Chinese brocade covered the entrance to an alcove, with a narrow, monastically hard bed hidden behind the opulence.

Saint-Germain handed Madelaine to the nearer of the two neat sofas, which were upholstered in Persian damask. "Pray sit down," he said softly, and walked across the room to the table where the telescope and astrolabe lay. "I have something to discuss with you."

At last Madelaine had taken stock of her surroundings, and all her training overrode her instinctive trust of him. "Where are we?" she asked, trying to show no outward concern.

"We are in one of the private rooms." He was toying with the telescope, not looking at her.

"And my aunt . . . ?"

". . . is at supper, as I told you. We will join her later."

There was steel in her voice when she said, testing him, "And if I should want to join her now?"

"Then, of course, I will escort you." He picked up the telescope and fingered its fine brass casing. "A wonderful instrument, the telescope. And yet, Galileo was forced to deny its evidence. A pity."

Madelaine glanced at the door, and saw that it was not locked. The key hung there, and one of the door handles pointed down. Her curiosity was piqued, and she settled more comfortably onto the sofa. She knew that if she were discovered with him, alone, that she would be terribly compromised, but an inner surety told her that she was safe. "A man discussing Galileo is not very loverlike."

"No." Saint-Germain put the telescope back on the table. "What I have to say to you is not very loverlike. It is for your protection to listen to me."

She arranged her extravagant taffeta skirts around her with considerable skill. "Very well, Comte. I will listen." She smiled in spite of herself as she saw the quick flash of approval in his dark eyes.

There was a moment of silence while Saint-Germain leaned against the table, his hands thrust deep into the side pockets of his wide-skirted coat. "What do you know of Satan?" he asked her in a matter-of-fact way.

"Satan is the Enemy of God and Mankind, the Fallen Angel, who aspired to the Divinity of God. . . ." She hesitated, then went on. "He was set upon earth to torment us with temptations and deceptions. . . ."

He shook his head wearily. "Not the answers of the Sisters, please. What do you know of the Power called Satan?"

She looked confused. "I told you."

"Then you must learn anew," he said with a sigh. He flung his head back, then lowered it again, as if searching for the right place to begin. "There is a Power, which is only that. It is like the rivers, which nurture us and can destroy us. Whether we are prosperous or drowned in floodwaters, the rivers are still the same. So with this Power. And when it lifts us up and opens our eyes to goodness and wonders, so that we are ennobled and inspired to kindness and excellence, we call it God. But when it is used for pain and suffering and degradation, we call it Satan. The Power is both. It is our use alone which makes it one or the other."

"That is heresy," she began without conviction.

"It is the truth." He watched her, and saw the years of the Sisters' training war with her own good sense. At last he was sure she would reserve judgment. "Grant me that, then, for the sake of argument. There are those who use the Power as Satan, and for that they create much sorrow."

"And they will spend eternity in Hell," Madelaine said promptly with some satisfaction.

"You know nothing of eternity," he said sharply, but the compassion in his dark eyes took the sting from his words. "There are those in Paris," he went on in another tone, "who gather to invoke the Power as Satan. They are preparing for two of the festivals they keep: one at All Hallows' Eve, and one at the winter solstice. At the first there is a simple sacrifice, and they have already selected their victim. But at the second their Rule requires that they sacrifice a virgin, both in her body and her blood."

Madelaine would have given much to find a bantering word to turn his warning aside, but all she could do was watch him with widened eyes, her heart racing.

"Your aunt has told me that your father was once involved with Saint Sebastien's set. It is Saint Sebastien who seeks to make this sacrifice, with the help of Beauvrai and others. He has already made one minor sacrifice —at least, he felt it was minor—and he has grown stronger. I do not mean to frighten you, Madelaine, but you must not have anything to do with any of Saint Sebastien's Circle. And that includes young Châteaurose."

"Châteaurose? He is nothing but a foolish dandy." She tossed her head as punctuation.

"That is your newly found sophistication speaking, not your soul. And your soul will always prevail over the other."

She stared at him, bemused.

"Your soul is like a sword, bright, shining, and will always pierce through deception to the truth. Do not doubt what it tells you, ever, Madelaine."

"I know what it tells me now," she whispered, but he did not seem to hear.

"Tell me," he said, as he looked, unseeing, at the hearth, "when Châteaurose speaks to you, how do you feel?"

She shuddered, surprised at her depth of revulsion. "I feel as a flower must when a great worm crawls over it."

"Yes," he breathed.

"But," she objected, shocked by her own words, "he is nothing. He has done nothing . . ."

"Do not underestimate any of them, child. That way is your downfall."

She studied her hands. "And you? Why should you care what becomes of me? Why do you warn me?"

He turned away from her, and dared not look at her radiant face, and the dawning of understanding in her eyes. "It is not important."

"If you will not tell me, then perhaps I should find out for myself."

Suddenly his eyes, now filled with emotion, found hers, and he took one hasty step toward her. "Your life is so sweet, and so dreadfully short, I do not think I could bear to lose one hour of it to them."

She had risen, and her cheeks were pale. "Saint-Germain!"

He laughed gently, and resumed leaning against the table, self-mockery twisting his mouth into a painful smile. "No, you need not fear me; you will take no harm from me. I find no joy in assault and its fear. I have not forced myself on a woman for more than five hundred years. And certainly not in the sense you mean."

It was very still in the little withdrawing room. Three branches of seven candles each glowed, filling the room with soft amber light.

"Five hundred years?" She tried to scoff, but the sound caught in her throat. "How old are you?"

"I do not remember," he said, turning away from her once again. "I was old when Caesar ruled in Rome. I heard Aristotle teach. Akhenaten praised the likeness of the bust I commissioned of his beloved Nefertiti in Amarna. No one has found its ruins yet, but I walked there when the city was new."

"You have never died?" She felt her hands grow cold as she asked.

"I think that perhaps I did die once, long ago. I don't remember. Certainly I have seen enough of death to know how fragile and how precious life is."

She felt tears in her eyes, for there was such loneliness in his words that her heart ached for him.

"Oh, do not pity me. I have had more than my share of death. I think I have been mad at times, and then I bathed in blood. I sought out wars and cruelty. I remember the circus in Rome, and I disgust myself. And more recently, when I returned to my homeland, I used patriotism as an excuse to take lives and revel in it." He looked toward her again. "So you see, the reverence I have now for you and your brief life is dearly bought."

"Saint-Germain, are you so unhappy?" she whispered.

But he was still speaking. "I drink the Elixir of Life, and I do not die. I cannot die." He put his hand to the lace at his throat and fingered the ruby nestled there.

"With all those centuries, you still have concern for me?" There was wonder in her voice as she felt her fear evaporate.

"Of course." At his soft words, she looked at him, seeing something in his beautiful, unlined face that she had sometimes seen in fine paper, a kind of translucence that told her more of his age than wrinkles could have. "When I was young," he said as he watched her closely, "I was considered a tall man. Now, I am less than average. Four, five hundred years from now, and I will be thought a dwarf." He came toward her, and when at arm's length, reached out and gently touched her face with his small hands.

"Saint-Germain," she said softly, and reached to confine his hands.

"Do not tempt me, Madelaine. You do not know what I desire . . ." He broke off, mastering himself. "Come, I will take you to your aunt." His manner was brisk now, and he dropped his hands and stepped back, shutting her away. "Remember what I have said of Saint Sebastien, and be careful. I will guard you, but your wits are your best protection. Use them. And do not be too proud to ask for help."

She took his hand again. "This Elixir of Life," she said, her eyes fixed on his. "How do you obtain it?"

He kept his distance, admiring her courage, knowing that it would take so little to possess her. He thought of the eventual consequences, and sought to stifle her longing. "I drink it," he said harshly. "Ask Lucienne Cressie."

Madelaine nodded. "I thought so. Was it you who made her ill?"

"*No.*" His voice was low, but filled with feeling. He pulled his hand free. "She took me because there was no one else. If there had been another, I would not have approached her."

"Does she know it is you?"

He laughed once. "She has dreams, my dear. Lovely, sweet dreams, and for a little time she blossoms. Then morning comes, and all is the same." He stopped again.

"The Sisters told us of horrors in the night, unholy and undead things that drink the blood of Christians, stealing their souls in foul embraces. But you say that La Cressie is happy?"

He damned himself for the tenderness he felt for Madelaine. "Apparently," he said dryly.

A shy, knowing smile crossed her face. "Saint-Germain, my garnets have broken their chain again," she said, touching her necklace. "There is a cut on my neck. I am bleeding."

Involuntarily his eyes flew to her throat, and grew dark as he saw the blood there. "You do not offer me a sheep or a horse?" The words, which he had wanted to be flippant, were almost a plea.

"Only if you need more than I have."

Once again Saint-Germain laughed, and this time with true enjoyment.

"I need no more than what can be put into a wineglass." He stopped, seeing her face. "But it is not without risks," he added quickly.

"What risks?" Her violet eyes were alive, and she was smiling.

"If I drink too deeply . . ." He came toward her and touched her shoulders. When he spoke again, his voice was very low. "If I drink too deeply, or too often, you will become as I am when you die. And you will be thought unclean and unhallowed, and you will be hounded by misguided ones, and despised by the world."

"You are not despised," she pointed out.

"I have been. But I have learned."

"But surely you can drink once, without harm," she insisted, her face alight with eagerness and her words made light by happiness. "Saint-Germain, oh, please . . ."

"I can still take you to your aunt."

"No, Comte." She left his side, moving swiftly to stand in front of the door. "I did not understand how a woman could hold her honor without consequence when compared to love. But I have seen the way of the world. I have studied those around me. If I must live as my aunt lives, as all the world lives, then I will know, at least once, what it is to be loved."

This time the smile that brightened his face was new to her, and she felt her pulse race as he walked slowly toward her. His hand came up and undid the clasp on her garnet necklace, which fell, unheeded, to the floor. "Well? Are you certain?"

His hands were on her now, warming her with easy, delightful caresses. Surely, gently, he sought the sweet weight of her breasts, lifting them reverently from the restrictions of her corset, cradling them as he felt them swell in his hands. He moved that last step closer and folded her into his arms, kissing her eyelids, her mouth, and then, almost dizzy with the ecstasy of it, set his lips against her neck.

She gave a soft shout of triumph as she tightened her arms around him, feeding her rapture on the sharp passion of his kisses.

Excerpt from a letter from la Comtesse d'Argenlac to her husband, le Comte d'Argenlac, dated October 14, 1743:

> . . . So, my dear husband, I trust that you will assist me in this arrangement I have mentioned. November will be dreary, and all the world will welcome a fête such as the one I have planned.
>
> I am aware how dear your forcing houses are to you, but I would count it very much a token of your affection for me if you would be willing to pro-

vide fresh fruit for all the guests. Your apricots, in particular, are always much praised and much admired.

I have hired the Queen's dancers for entertainment, and Saint-Germain has promised to compose new airs for Madelaine to sing. As La Cressie is still abed, he said he will consider accompanying her on the clavier or the guitar. Madelaine is delighted, of course, and I know that this will assure a great deal of interest in the evening.

Your sudden departure for the country very much surprised me, and I was seriously alarmed for your safety until your message reached me. I was saddened that you had come to such straits as these. If you had told me sooner, this predicament might have been avoided. I have authorized a partial payment of your debt to Jueneport, which will ease your situation somewhat, at least for the present. Let me urge you once again to abandon your gaming, which has proven to be so disastrous to your good name and your interests. Your man of business has told me that you can no longer secure mortgages on your estates. Until our conversation of yesterday, I was unaware of those mortgages. Pray disclose the whole of your debts to me, and I will arrange with my brother and my man of business to discharge the most pressing of them. Otherwise, I am very much afraid that you stand in danger of prosecution and default.

I look forward to your return, my dear husband, and until I have the felicity to see you again, I am always your obedient and affectionate wife,

Claudia de Montalia
Comtesse d'Argenlac

8

"You damned idiot," Saint Sebastien said softly as he ran a contemptuous glance over Jacques Eugène Châteaurose. "You knew she did not like frivolity and hollow compliments."

"But how should I have guessed it? She is not yet twenty; she was raised in the country and taught by nuns. My manner should have overwhelmed her. You know that it has been successful in the past." Châteaurose picked up one of the books that lay open on the desk and started to thumb through it.

"Put that down," Saint Sebastien ordered, and waited until Châteaurose had obeyed him. "I do not want to hear your excuses, Châteaurose. I am not prepared to accept failure on your part, particularly in this instance. You do understand that we must have that girl at the winter solstice, don't you?"

Châteaurose was noticeably paler. "You have told me that, and I believe you, Saint Sebastien, but it was more difficult than I thought. She is not what I expected. . . ."

"I have asked you not to make excuses for yourself. If you continue in this vein, you will annoy me." He rose, his crimson lounging robe brushing the floor as he strode across the library. He stood for a moment contemplating a shelf of the works of Greek philosophers and Roman poets.

"I will try again, if you like. I will approach her differently," Châteaurose said eagerly, starting toward Saint Sebastien.

"I did not say you were to come near me," Saint Sebastien reminded him gently. "You must learn that one of the Rules we obey in this Circle is the Rule of Order. If you cannot learn that, then you will be expelled in the manner described in the contract you signed when you joined us."

In spite of himself, Châteaurose turned scarlet. He stammered, "I . . . I do not know . . . what you mean . . ."

"That is a clumsy lie, Jacques Eugène," Saint Sebastien informed him. "Nevertheless, I will remind you. If you break our Rule of Order, you will be cursed by the Circle, and banished from our ranks. So that you may not speak ill against us, your tongue will be cut out. So that you cannot give testimony to our detriment, your hands will be struck off; so that you will not be able to identify us, your eyes will be burned out, and you will be at the mercy of the Circle for one night, after which you will be left nude on the highway to live or die as it chances." During this recitation, Saint Sebastien had stood quietly, the tips of his fingers touching, and held just below his chin, as if in prayer. At the conclusion he turned to Châteaurose. "I trust you recall your obligations?"

Châteaurose tried to achieve an ingratiating smile. "I did not mean anything, Saint Sebastien. It is only my frustration speaking. I did not want to fail with the girl." Inspiration struck. "It was so awkward because Saint-Germain was there."

"That poseur!" Saint Sebastien snapped, turning abruptly. "Surrounding himself with mystery, claiming on occasion to be immortal!" He stared down into the fire that blazed in the hearth, filling the library with a ruddy glow. "He interferes with me to his ruin!"

Suddenly Châteaurose was very much afraid of the lean, evil man who confronted him with cold, condemning eyes. "What shall I do with him? Do you want me to get rid of him for you?"

There was a flash of something immensely threatening in Saint Sebastien's eyes, which was gone almost before Châteaurose was sure he had seen it. "Yes," he said, drawing the word out. "Yes, you may rid me of him. I want him gone. But I do not want the Circle implicated in any way. Do you understand? You may find an excuse to challenge him, or you may hire bravos to assassinate him, or you may find a way to discredit him, but at no time, *at no time*, is there to be even the merest whisper of the Circle's involvement."

Châteaurose swallowed nervously. "Very well."

Saint Sebastien took a turn about the room, very much lost in thought. His hands were locked behind his back, and his crimson lounging robe rustling on the floor accented the restlessness of his reflections. At last he paused by the tall windows that overlooked the wide expanse of a topiary garden. This ordinarily impressive view was marred by the first real rain of October, and the sullen low clouds cast a leaden pall over the whole of Paris.

If this marring of his prospect disturbed Saint Sebastien, he did not show it in his face or his manner. A slight, satisfied smile pulled at his mouth, and he turned away from the window to face Châteaurose. "Le Comte d'Argenlac gambles, as I understand it?"

"Yes," Châteaurose answered, puzzled.

"He is very much in debt, is he not?"

"Yes. And his estates are mortgaged. He does not admit it, but he is entirely dependent on his wife."

Saint Sebastien let out a pleased sigh. "Good. Excellent. To whom does he owe money?"

"Everyone," Châteaurose said in disgust. "He is worse than a drunkard when dealing with cards or rouge et noir. I myself have seen him lose twenty thousand livres in an hour."

"A considerable sum. No wonder he is in so much trouble. Do you know what his feelings are about this? Does he want to be dependent on his wife?"

"No, he hates it. Sometimes I think," Châteaurose went on with rare insight, "that he ruins himself only to ruin her."

"Then perhaps he would be willing to trade some of his difficulties for the chance to have revenge on his wife through her protégée." He was musing now, and his smile was more sinister.

"Do you mean turn La Montalia over to us to annoy his wife?" Châteaurose was incredulous at first, but even as he spoke the words, he saw merit in the plan. If there should be repercussions, they would fall to d'Argenlac. He nodded as he thought this idea through. "I think he might do it, if approached properly."

Saint Sebastien sank into a low Turkish chair. "To which of us does he owe the most?"

Châteaurose would have liked to sit, but he did not dare. He compromised by resting his arm on the mantel, crossing one booted leg over the other. He was dressed for riding, and his coat skirts, front and back, were pulled back and buttoned over the hip, which not only made riding easier, but showed off the lining of gold-and-black twill against the ocher English wool of the coat and neat riding breeches. His muslin neck cloth was edged in Belgian lace, and except for the worried expression he wore, he was the epitome of the compleat aristocrat.

Saint Sebastien's fingers tapped ominously on the arm of his chair. "Do you know, or will you have to find out? If it is the latter, you have until nightfall to deliver the information."

"No, no, it's not that," Châteaurose said hastily. "You startled me, that's all. I think d'Argenlac owes the most to Jueneport. His wife has settled some of the debt, but not all, I think. The amount is greater than d'Argenlac admitted to." He considered this a little longer. "I believe there is a question of the estate in Anjou. I am not sure, but I think that Jueneport holds a private note on it, and so far, there is no sign that d'Argenlac will be able to redeem it."

"Would he want to?" Saint Sebastien had crossed one leg over the other, and the satisfaction was back in his face.

"Oh, yes, I am certain of that." He avoided the cold ferocity of Saint Sebastien's eyes. "The Anjou estate is where he has his forcing houses. I think it would kill him to have to give them up."

"Good," Saint Sebastien said dreamily.

"And there is the matter of what he owes de Vandonne, which is trivial beside the debt to Jueneport, but still considerable. As I recall, jewels were involved. I do not know how the matter stands at the moment. I cannot tell when de Vandonne is boasting and when he is telling me the heart of the issue."

Saint Sebastien shrugged. "It is of no consequence. We will deal through Jueneport first, and if there is no satisfaction there, then I will talk with de Vandonne."

There was a knock at the door, and on Saint Sebastien's command, it opened and Saint Sebastien's manservant Tite came in.

"What is it, Tite?"

"Le Grâce is here, mon Baron. He wishes to speak with you. He says it is urgent."

Saint Sebastien regarded the taciturn servant appraisingly. "I am not accustomed to receiving calls from such as Le Grâce. I trust you denied me?"

"No, I did not. I was certain you will want to talk to him." Tite came farther into the room and waited.

"Now, why?" Saint Sebastien said, waving Châteaurose aside.

Tite came stalking up to Saint Sebastien and held out his hand. When he opened it, he revealed an uncut diamond of slightly bluish cast rather larger than a hen's egg.

Saint Sebastien sat up abruptly, and Châteaurose swore.

"He says that the Sorcerers' Guild was given the secret of jewels by a strange man claiming to be Prinz Ragoczy of Translyvania."

"Is it genuine?" Châteaurose asked, awed by the huge stone.

"Le Grâce claims that these stones are made in the alchemist's oven, the athanor. Apparently, whoever the man is, he has a formidable secret, even if the stone is not real." Tite regarded his master evenly, and waited while Saint Sebastien stared into the fire, apparently seeing nothing.

Eventually he said, "Show him into the blue salon, Tite, and tell him I will join him directly. I want to know more of these stones."

Tite bowed and withdrew, a cynical grimace settling on his features as he closed the door.

"Well?" Châteaurose demanded impulsively as soon as they were once again alone.

"Prinz Ragoczy, Prinz Ragoczy. Where have I heard that name?" Saint Sebastien directed his gaze toward the rain-spangled windows. "I should know that name—"

"What about the jewels?" Châteaurose interrupted him. "Will Le Grâce give us the secret?"

"Certainly." The calm in Saint Sebastien's tone made the word frightening. "One way or another, we will learn the secret." He rose from his chair and paced down the library. "I will want you to proceed on this matter with Jueneport and d'Argenlac. That girl is mine. She has been promised to me since before her birth, and I will not let her go. I charge you with the matter, and I remind you that I will not tolerate your failure. Remove Saint-Germain from our path and distract the aunt. She will be given us on a platter by her uncle."

Châteaurose bowed deeply. "As you wish."

Saint Sebastien was almost at the door when he turned and said softly, "If you fail, Châteaurose, you will regret it more than you can imagine." Then he was out the door, leaving Châteaurose alone, feeling very cold, though he stood in front of the fire.

Text of a document written in Latin on parchment, sealed in a chest in Saint Sebastien's library, dated August 19, 1722:

By the names of Asmodeus, Belial, and Astoreth, by the Vow of the Circle and the Oath of the Blood, by the Rule and the Sign:

I, Robert Marcel Yves Etienne Pascal, Marquis de Montalia, promise the Circle and its leader, Baron Clotaire de Saint Sebastien, that upon the birth of my first legitimate child, I will mark that child for service to the Circle in whatever way the circle sees fit.

I affirm that I am at present unmarried, but am betrothed to Margaret Denise Angelique Ragnac, and that any child born of this union will be recognized by me as legitimate, and be my heir if male.

Should I default in any way on this agreement, may the advantage which has been secured for me be forever revoked, and neither the sea, nor the land, nor the sky be sufficient to hide me from the wrath and vengeance of the Circle and the Powers of Satan, which shall endure for all eternity. Signed and witnessed this day, and to be without limit in my life, or until such time as my firstborn child shall pass the age of twenty-one years without being taken in service to the Circle.

Sworn to in the mortification of the flesh and the Rites of Blood:

Robert Marcel Yves Etienne Pascal
Marquis de Montalia

Part Two

Madelaine Roxanne
Bertrande de Montalia

Excerpt from a letter from l'Abbé Ponteneuf to his cousin, le Marquis de Montalia. Dated October 16, 1743:

. . . I have had the felicity of hearing your daughter perform some airs, with Saint-Germain accompanying her on the guitar. They were practicing for your sister's fête, and Madelaine was kind enough to invite me to listen. I confess I am not overly fond of the guitar—it lacks the subtle tones of the lute and does not have the celestial sound of the harp. Yet I will allow that Saint-Germain plays it prettily, and that the music he has composed shows Madelaine's voice to advantage. I was pleased to read the text of the airs, for the sentiments expressed are wholly acceptable to me, and I am certain would be to you. It is to Saint-Germain's credit that he does not follow the modern taste for dissonant chords and jarring melodies. His music, on the contrary, harks back often to the old forms, even to the modal harmonies of several centuries ago.

Occasionally Madelaine must confront Beauvrai or Saint Sebastien socially, which is lamentable, but cannot be avoided without giving a serious affront, which would lead to scandal and gossip, which would significantly reduce Madelaine's chances of making an acceptable match. I have taken the liberty of giving her a little warning about Beauvrai and Saint Sebastien, telling her that their reputations are such that her name must be sullied if she is seen with them. This is no prevarication on my part, for it is perfectly true that it would harm her immeasurably to be seen with them. I did not think it wise to reveal the truth of the matter to her, for such knowledge could not but stain that sweet innocence which makes her so truly admired.

. . . Your inquiry of the 8th, regarding Madelaine's religious devotions: I am honoured to tell you that you have no reason to fear for her soul in any way. She is good, chaste and kind. She attends Mass on the Lord's Day and on Friday, and makes her confession on Wednesday or Saturday. Her devotions are genuine and her faith sincere, even as you told me.

Your concern over Saint-Germain would also appear to be groundless. When questioned about him, Madelaine said that she found his attentions flattering, and certainly an asset to her socially, but that an alliance with a man of his age and background was out of the question. To be doubly sure, I talked to Saint-Germain himself. He was generous in praise of Madelaine, complimenting her on her singing and her excellent mind. But there was nothing of the lover about him. Indeed, I have not seen him show her any particular attention greater than what he shows to other ladies, except in the matter of music, which is easily understood. He was equally attentive to Mme. Cressie until she fell ill a short while ago. Be certain, my dear cousin, that your daughter is not on her way to losing her head to Saint-Germain, nor he his over her. Your daughter has superior good sense, and you need not fear she will give her heart against the wishes of her family. In our conversations, when I have sought to school her in the ways of the world, she has made it plain that she perceives her duty and does not shrink from it. Of course you would want her to respect the man who will be her husband, and to regard him with affection. Madelaine has the presence of mind to be aware of these necessities, and has assured me that she will bestow her hand circumspectly.

Let me, mon cher Robert, again plead with you to make peace with God and the Church, for the days of men are few, and your life is short and full of sorrow. Your errors are long past, and your repentance is profound. Do not despair of the Infinite Mercy of God and Holy Mother Church. Dearer to God is he who has sinned and repented, who has lost the way and come again to it with a full heart, than those who are without error the whole of their lives. Confess, my cousin, and make your Act of Contrition, so that you may again take Communion and be among those who taste the Body and Blood of Christ. Pray to the Virgin for intercession. You have said that your sin is great, for you denied the Lord. But Peter did even as you have done, and he knows glory in heaven. What God will forgive in Peter who was His friend, he will forgive in you. Give me your promise that you will go at last and make confession. . . .

You may be certain that I am always watching over your daughter, and that I will be swift to chastise her for error if she surrenders to temptation. She has always the lives of saints and martyrs to guide her, and my exhortations.

In the Name of the Lord, in Whose eyes all men are His children and each other's brothers, I send you my blessings and the assurance that you are ever in my prayers. For the Redeemer came for us all, mon cousin, and in His name I have the honor to be

Your most devoted cousin
l'Abbé Alfonse Reynard Ponteneuf, S.J.

1

When the pen sputtered for the third time, Madelaine flung it down in disgust.

"What is it, my dear?" her aunt asked her from her seat at the window. They were in largest of the withdrawing rooms, a good-sized salon of slightly old-fashioned design, where six high windows gave the north and western prospect that in most instances was pleasant, but today was marred by a thin, persistent trickle of rain that lacked the gentle grandeur of a good downpour and at the same time gave all its disadvantages.

La Comtesse had had her embroidery frame moved nearer to the windows so that she would make full use of what little light there was. She looked up now, tugging absentmindedly on a strand of wool. "What is the trouble, my dear?"

"This pen!" Madelaine shook her head vehemently. "I will never get all the directions written, never." She glared at a stack of sealed notes of fine cream-laid paper. "That's only fifty-seven. There are over three hundred of them."

"Well," Claudia said reasonably as she set another petit point stitch, "you may summon Milane and give the task over to him. You," she pointed out, "were the one who said you wanted to help with the fête."

"I must have been mad." She pushed away from the little table where she worked. "Oh, aunt, never mind. I have a headache. That visit from le general this morning has put me in a bad temper. As if anyone *cared* about the Austrian Succession. What does it matter if the Elector of Bavaria or Fredrick is on the throne?"

"Well," her aunt explained as she worked her tapestry, "you see, Madelaine, while Fleury was alive, we had years and years of peace, which the generals hated." She was busy for a moment with her yarns, then went on. "Now Fleury is dead, and the King's mistress is in favor of war—very foolish of her, I think. It will cost her His Majesty's affections one day, you mark my words. We all have learned to despise Maria Theresa of

Austria, and now that the English support her, it is obvious that there must be war."

"It's stupid. It's stupid and wasteful!" Madelaine had gone to the windows and stood looking out. She was very pretty in that wan light, her dark hair showing the fine warm color of her flawless skin to perfection. She was simply dressed in flowered taffeta over a simple petticoat of eyelet linen. Her panniers were very moderate, even for morning at-home wear. A wide sash of rose satin circled her narrow waist, and because it was cold in this great house, she had draped a Spanish fringed shawl around her shoulders and tied it below her bosom. A ribbon of the same rose satin as her sash was threaded through her hair, catching up the long curls in an artless cluster.

"The King wishes the world to know that he will govern for himself, as did his great-grandfather. Oh, it is foolish, for there are able men around him who thrive on such work, and he, poor man, does not truly enjoy the tedium of government. Dear me," she added, breaking off. "I did not mean to sound disrespectful of his Majesty, who, naturally, is a glorious monarch." She turned her attention to her needlework for several minutes, and then said, in quite another voice, "Do not worry, Madelaine. The fête will be a success. You will be overwhelmed with compliments and attention, and will very likely spend the next day abed, recovering from all your gaiety."

"Oh, aunt, I did not mean it. I am out of sorts. I think it must be the weather. I was promised to ride this morning, but this rain . . ." She turned abruptly from the windows and walked back toward the table.

"It *is* hard to stay indoors when it would be delightful to be outside," Claudia allowed as she carefully selected another length of yarn, holding it against her canvas. "How vexatious," she said in a different voice. "They may say what they will, but these hanks came from two different dye lots. Well, I suppose I must work on the background until I have the time to consult with the dyer." She sighed and pulled a long twist of light-blue yarn from her needlework box.

Madelaine, who was busy trimming a new pen, did not hear most of this. She looked critically at the ink in the standish, and tipped a little water into it. "It might have been this," she said to the air. "The ink is getting dreadfully thick."

There were six more addressed invitations in the stack when the door opened and le Comte d'Argenlac strolled into the room, his fashionable dress revealing that he had arrived some little time before, and had put off his traveling clothes. He was a good-looking man in his thirty-ninth year, but in his wife's company he had the manners of a sulky boy.

"Gervaise," his wife said, rising cordially.

He kissed her hand with more form than interest. "Good day, Claudia. I see you are well." He turned to Madelaine. "I see you are both busy. I hope you are still enjoying Paris, Mademoiselle." His tone said he would like nothing better than for her to go away.

"I find Paris delightful. But the rain does not please me." She had given him the curtsy that good manners required, and was mildly affronted when he did not return her so much as a nod of the head.

"Gervaise, dear husband, you must not behave so. Here is my niece, very correctly acknowledging you, and you act as if she were made of air." She smiled as she said it, but Madelaine saw le Comte set his jaw.

"I beg your pardon for my lamentable behavior," he said, with a bow that would have been more appropriate for a Duchesse.

"Comte," said his Comtesse with disastrous candor, "it is not Madelaine who annoys you, but me. I would prefer that we talk in private. And if you want to vent your spleen, do so at me when we are alone, my dear. Involving my niece in our petty quarrels only serves to make matters worse."

Madelaine was already at the door. "Excuse me, aunt. I see that you and your husband have much to talk about, and I will leave you alone. You may send to the library for me when you want me."

Her aunt gave her a harassed smile and said, "Yes. Very well. It is unfortunate, but you are right, my dear. I must talk to my husband alone for some little while. I know you enjoy reading, so will not apologize for isolating you in this way." She had her hand on the door, and as soon as Madelaine's skirt had rustled through it, she closed the door firmly and turned with a sinking heart to face her husband.

"My compliments, Madame," le Comte said, his almost handsome face flushed. "You cannot even greet me without disgracing me."

Claudia reluctantly crossed the room toward him. "It was not I who insulted Madelaine. But let that go. It is not what is bothering you." In spite of herself, she extended her hands to him. "Ah, Gervaise, why did you not trust me? Why did you not tell me long ago how it is with you?"

"So that you would pity me, and gloat? No, thank you, Claudia. Give me credit for more pride than that." He chose one of the old-fashioned chairs by the fire and sank down onto it.

"Certainly you have pride," his wife said in a slightly exasperated tone. "And it must be painful indeed for you, who have never had the least need to study economy, to be forced to do so now. But you must understand that you are in very serious trouble."

"No more." He held up his hand. "How I handle my affairs is no concern of yours."

She approached him again and dropped to her knees beside him, looking up at him with sad hazel eyes. "But it is my concern, Gervaise. If you cannot settle your debts, and your fortune is exhausted, the King will require that my fortune be used to that purpose."

Le Comte nodded savagely. "Now we have it. *Now* we have it. Your precious fortune would be used. It doesn't mean anything to you unless your fortune is involved." He pushed her hand away.

"That is not so," she said in a low voice, and felt herself precariously near tears. "Gervaise, please. You cannot want to bring ruin on us. Only consider what that means. It is not just your estates and this house we would lose . . ."

"You would like it if we lost the estates, would you not?" He pulled his hand from her. "You have always wanted me to come to ruin. That way, you will make me stop at home, and be at your beck and call, like some despicable lapdog." He pushed out of the chair. "No more tears, Madame, if you please."

"Very well," Claudia said as she got slowly to her feet. "Here you have been home less than an hour—it is less than an hour, is it not—and already we are quarreling, and over such senseless matters." She pressed her hands together and forced herself to stop trembling. "Do you know what it would mean to be poor, Gervaise?" she said in a moment. "Do you have any idea how we would have to live? In what circumstances we would find ourselves? No?"

"You are being melodramatic, Claudia," he snapped, but without conviction.

"I saw Lorraine Brèssin last spring," she said rather remotely. "I saw where she lived. It was not bad enough that Brèssin bankrupted them. When he killed himself, he made certain that his family would have nothing to do with Lorraine. She and I are the same age, and she looks fifty. Her hair is grizzled, she dresses in worse gowns than my chambermaid. Her two daughters—do you remember them? They had no skills but their looks and pretty speech, and they were taken by brothel keepers. The daughters of le Vicomte de Brèssin are common whores, Gervaise," she said with a stifled sob.

"Well, you need not worry yourself about that, Madame. We have no daughters, or sons for that matter, to be sold to brothels. So if we lose my fortune and yours, we will hurt none but ourselves." He strode to the door. "Control your tears, Claudia. It is bad enough having you rescue me. To have you weep is more insult than I can bear." He pulled the door open and stood for a moment, watching his Comtesse. "I suppose you must be thanked for paying my debts. But I will be grateful if, in future, you let me handle my own affairs!"

She nodded, standing very straight. "As you wish, Gervaise," she said in a strangled voice.

"I am going out. Do not expect me to dine with you." He had the satisfaction of seeing her composure break. Claudia covered her face with her hands and wept. "Good day, Madame."

Once outside of the withdrawing room, Gervaise strode down the long hall toward the stable room. He had taken great satisfaction from his conversation with his wife, but now he felt certain doubts. He did not, in fact, know how he was going to rescue the pitiful remains of his fortune. He had had some very disturbing letters from his man of business, but he refused to admit that perhaps Claudia had been right to pay what she could of his debts for him. He swore, and paused as he heard a lackey call to him.

"What is it, Scirraino?" he demanded impatiently as the servant came up to him.

Scirraino bowed and said, "There is a person to see you, master."

Gervaise started, thinking that perhaps it was about his debts. His man of business had warned him about that possibility. "Did he give his name?" He said the words more loudly than he had intended, revealing his nervousness. He glanced over Scirraino's shoulder. "Where is he?" Again the words were too loud, and he grimaced, glancing at the door to the library, which he suddenly realized was ajar. He opened the door, stepping quietly into the room.

Madelaine was sitting at the desk by the fireplace, a branch of candles giving light to the old leather-bound book she was reading. She leaned on her elbow, her hand against her neck, rubbing idly at the skin. There was a secret smile in her violet eyes.

"Mademoiselle," Gervaise said rather sharply.

Madelaine looked up sharply, somewhat confused, and rose to bob a curtsy to her host. "What is it, sir?" she asked, seeing the desperate light in his eyes.

"Nothing. Nothing." He looked around the library as if he had never seen the room before. Then he turned back. "What are you reading?"

Madelaine glanced down at the book. "Latin poetry. Here, let me read this to you." She picked up the book and twisted so that her own shadow did not fall across the page. " 'Jucundum, mea vita, mihi proponis amorem/ Hunc nostrum inter nos perpetuumque fore./ Di magni facite ut vere promittere possit/ Atque id sincere dicta et ex animo/ Ut liceat nobis tota perducere vita/ Aeternum hoc sanctus foedus amicitiae.' Isn't that beautiful? To promise love for eternity, and friendship."

This was a turn of events Gervaise had no idea of how to handle. His own scholarship was shaky, and anything in Latin roused him to panic. Now, to stand in his own library and have his wife's niece quote poetry to him, and that in Latin, was beyond his tolerance. "Very pretty," he said as he turned to the doorway, prepared to make his excuses and bolt.

But his lackey Scirraino was back, and leading another lackey, this one outfitted in deep blue with red lacings on his livery. "I have a message for you, sir. For your ears alone."

"Yes, yes, of course," Gervaise agreed quickly, glad to escape from Madelaine. He sketched a bow in her direction, saying, "Do not let me interrupt your reading, Mademoiselle. The library is yours for your stay, if you like." As he got to the door, he turned his attention to the lackey.

"My master sends you greetings," said the lackey, and Madelaine, only half-listening, thought she heard Jueneport's name mentioned, but she was not sure, and soon turned her attention to Catullus, thinking that the good Sisters of Sainte Ursule who had educated her would be shocked if they knew to what worldly use she had put her Latin. Softly she read the words. "*'Da mi basia mille, deinde centum, dein mille altera, dein secunda centum, deinde usque altera mile, deinde centum . . .'*" To have a thousand kisses, and a hundred, until they were without reckoning. She closed her eyes and remembered Saint-Germain's touch, and his kisses.

Several minutes later she was shocked out of her reverie by the sound of Gervaise d'Argenlac calling for his coach, and the burst of activity his order provoked. She realized the library was cold, and, rather guiltily, that she had stayed away from her aunt much longer than she had planned.

With a sigh she closed the volume of Catullus and left the room.

Text of a letter from the sorcerer Beverly Sattin to Prinz Ragoczy, written in English, dated October 17, 1743:

> To His Highness, Franz Josef Ragoczy, Prinz of Transylvania,
> B. Sattin sends his most Urgent Greetings.
> The Egg and Nest of the Black Phoenix are missing. BlueSky has been Beaten, and is near to Perishing. Oulen is missing, with the Treasure mentioned. We have searched, but there is no sign of it.
> I Pray that Your Highness will lend your Assistance to the Guild in this Calamity. If it is Possible, come to us at the Place where we met before, at Your Highness's Earliest Convenience.
>
> Yours, etc., in haste,
> B. Sattin

2

"Well?" Saint-Germain said without ceremony as he came into the tap-room of the Inn of the Red Wolf. Feeble rays of the setting sun gave a ruddy glow through the years of grime that caked the windows and made the room appear darker and bleaker than it had first seemed to be. The floor was littered with scraps of food and stains of sour-smelling wine.

Beverly Sattin was the sole occupant of the taproom, and he rose promptly as Saint-Germain came in. "Your Highness"—he made a deep bow—"Your Highness must excuse me for so unseemly a summons . . ." he began, speaking in English.

Saint-Germain also spoke in that language. "Have done with fripperies, then." He pulled off his black cloak, to reveal his usual black-silk attire beneath it. "I do not have long, and there are a great many questions you must answer. I came as soon as I had your message, Sattin. You will do me the favor of being equally punctilious."

Sattin fidgeted for a moment, looking as uncomfortable as a student asked to recite a piece he did not know. "Le Grâce is gone," he said.

"I know. I told you to keep him under locks with a guard." There was steel in Saint-Germain's voice. "Why was this order not obeyed?" Over the years he had learned that severity would often serve where reason would not. He sensed the dithering in Sattin, and drove his lesson home. "I am not a patient man."

Now Sattin was even more uncomfortable, but he gathered his wits and spoke. "He *was* under guard. In the attic room on the third floor. We did not secure the window. It is a killing drop to the street. We did not think he would try to escape that way."

"You were wrong, it seems."

Sattin opened his hands helplessly. "We were wrong. I know that is not an excuse, Highness. But we were certain he was secure. Domingo y Roxas kept guard the first night, and the next day the duty fell to Ciel-bleu. We traded off the watch equally, making sure that Le Grâce got his meals and some little exercise. The room is very small, Highness. And when he asked for more blankets, we gave them to him. It is cold in that room, and the weather has turned. He tore the blankets and made a rope and let himself out of the window to the street. We did not know until Oulen took his breakfast to him the following morning that Le Grâce had fled. . . ."

"And you did not see fit to notify me." Saint-Germain tapped his small hands on the back of one of the rough chairs.

"I thought it best. He must have left Paris. There was no point in searching for him. He could be on his way to America by now."

"He did not leave Paris. Continue." His eyes bored into Sattin's, and the English sorcerer grew frightened.

"We . . . we notified some of the others in the city that Le Grâce had run away, and that he was not acceptable as a sorcerer, and possibly in danger of being taken by the law. All one must do is mention the law, and we all treat the afflicted Brother as if he were an adder."

Saint-Germain nodded. "And after you alerted the other sorcerers and magicians, what then?"

"Nothing. So far as we know, Le Grâce has vanished." He faltered. "But you say he is still in Paris?"

"He is. One of my servants has seen him." He looked across the tap-room. "Is this where you study alchemy?"

Sattin shook his head quickly. "No. Our facilities are in the adjoining building. At the moment, Domingo y Roxas and his sorer are working on the Green Lion there."

So these were alchemists of the modern school, Saint-Germain realized. They had women to perform those procedures that were thought to be female, and men for those considered male. And for the hermaphroditic processes, both artifex and sorer would work together. "When may we interrupt?" he asked, smiling wryly.

"After sunset. Once the sun is gone, it is useless to continue." He said it automatically, but thought it strange that so great a man as Prinz Ragoczy did not know this.

"You see," Saint-Germain said, by way of explanation, "I have studied with other schools. In the Persian and Muhammadan schools, women are not permitted. In China, only castrates are allowed to perform certain of the works. You must not wonder at my question, Sattin."

The expression on Sattin's face was that of a Dominican confronted with heresy. "It is not possible to do the Great Work in any other fashion."

"Of course," Saint-Germain agreed, bored. "Tell me how you came to lose the athanor and the crucible?"

"I do not know." Sattin turned away and stared into the black maw of the hearth. "Cielbleu has been delirious and cannot tell us. Oulen has disappeared as if into the air. No one has seen him. No one." He turned impulsively to Saint-Germain. "You must believe me, Highness. We did not know this could happen. The athanor was heated when it was taken. The process was working."

"Quite a feat." He considered the alternatives for a moment. "Well, Sattin, either one of your own Guild Brothers is working with the thieves, or someone has learned your secret. Either way, your Guild is in grave danger of exposure. If I were you, I would not remain long in this neighborhood. If the law does not find you, whoever took the athanor will." He glanced at the windows, which were now quite dark. The taproom was lost in murky light, with only two branches of tallow candles to ward off the gloom. "Let us go to the laboratory. It is dark enough that Domingo y Roxas will not be hunting the Green Lion any more today."

Reluctantly Sattin rose. "Follow me," he said, feeling a desolation of spirit that left him fatigued.

Saint-Germain pulled on his cloak, and as he secured the fastening, he touched the ruby in the lace at his throat. "I wonder," he said to Sattin, "if Le Grâce is part of this theft."

"It would be impossible."

"Impossible?" Saint-Germain's brows rose. "Do not say impossible, Sattin. That way leads to blindness." He stood in the door waiting for Sattin, and saw a strange expression come into the English sorcerer's eyes. "What is it?" he asked.

Sattin hesitated, then plunged recklessly ahead. "I was recalling something I had read. There was a man who visited Helvetius, almost a century ago."

"Yes?" Saint Germain said pleasantly.

"He gave him a piece of the Philosopher's Stone."

"How fortunate for Helvetius."

"In his book, he describes the man. He said he was of medium height, with dark eyes and dark hair, small hands and feet. This stranger spoke excellent Dutch, but with a slight accent that might have been northern. He rarely raised his voice, but he had a great presence to him, and authority."

Saint-Germain nodded, his face enigmatic. "Why are you telling me this, Sattin?"

"I did not realize until this moment," Sattin said almost dreamily, "the resemblance between you and that man."

"How old was Helvetius' visitor? Did the good man bother to mention that?"

"He said he was possibly forty-two." Sattin was puzzled now, and he lingered by the table in the center of the taproom.

"And how old would you say I am?"

"No more than forty-five."

Saint-Germain held the door open insistently. "You have your answer, Sattin. Let us not waste any more time."

But Sattin stared at Saint-Germain with covert worry as he led him down the darkened street toward a house near the Inn of the Red Wolf. Around them the night was full of the last sounds left over from the day. Here and there were sounds behind closed doors, some of them boisterous, some of them more sinister. Over the stench of the slum hung the odor of cheap food cooking in grease. Lean cats lurked in the shadows, drawing back as Sattin and Saint-Germain went by them.

"Here, Highness," Sattin said deferentially as he pulled open a side door to the house that was quite the most ancient of the buildings on the street. "We do not have much, but we follow our calling as best we can."

Saint-Germain had seen alchemist's laboratories from the land of Khem, which gave the science its name and was now called Egypt, through their development in many countries, in many ages. He knew that this one would be hot and smelly, and he was not disappointed.

"Prinz Ragoczy," said Domingo y Roxas, turning to the opening door. "I hardly dared to hope you would come. We are disgraced by Le Grâce." He smiled at this feeble jest.

"It is of no matter. I know where Le Grâce is, and will do my poor best to discover if he knows aught of the athanor's present whereabouts." He turned to bow to the older woman with stern, dedicated features. "Madame?" he ventured.

She gave Saint-Germain a no-nonsense nod as she wiped her hands on the stained apron that covered her plain woolen dress. "Good evening, Your Highness," she said in a wonderfully low voice.

Domingo y Roxas shot her a quick look, then bowed. "Madame is Iphigenie Ancelot Lairrez," he said. "She is my sorer, and vastly skilled in the Discipline. She came to us from the Guild in Marseilles."

"Enchanted," Saint-Germain said, liking the piercing eyes of the woman, and her calm assurance and realizing with a pang that she reminded him of Olivia, who had died the true death more than a century ago. "You and Domingo y Roxas chased the Green Lion today. What fortune in the hunt?"

"We achieved the Lion, but he did not devour the Sun," she said, begrudging him each word.

"My congratulations." He walked farther into the room, glancing around him at retorts, basins, vials, jars, bellows, crucibles, and all the other equipment of the alchemists' art. At the far end of the room stood a brick construction that resembled nothing so much as a permanent beehive. "I see you still have an athanor for your other experiments," he remarked.

"We have had this one for some time," Sattin explained hastily. "We found that we had to build changes into our newer one. The platinum gears you required could not be fitted into the old athanor."

"Of course." He studied the small, specialized oven. It might have been worse: the design was only a hundred years out of date. He had seen many of far older vintage in use in many places. "Whoever took the athanor, then, knew what it was they wanted, and where to find it."

"We fear so, Prinz," Sattin admitted, then added hastily, "It must not have been Le Grâce, for he did not know what we had done."

"Are you sure of that?" Saint-Germain asked, and watched as the three alchemists fell silent. "You did not tell him, but there are others in the Guild who might have. Where is Oulen? You say that Cielbleu cannot tell you who beat him. What if it was one of your Brotherhood? And are you so certain that it wasn't?"

Domingo y Roxas looked sharply at Saint-Germain. "Prinz Ragoczy, what you suggest is unthinkable. If it is as you say, then we are all betrayed."

Saint-Germain's eyes rested on the little Spaniard. "You say this, who escaped from the Inquisition? They did not take you because you were protected, Ambrosias."

Mme. Lairrez nodded suddenly, saying, "It may be unthinkable, but you are right, Prinz. It has happened, and either way, we are discovered." She had taken off her apron as she spoke. "We will have to move, of course."

"That is the wisest course, Madame," Saint-Germain agreed.

"But we cannot!" Beverly Sattin interrupted in English. "There is no place for us to go. Not with Le Grâce gone and our Guild exposed to its enemies."

Domingo y Roxas did not understand Sattin's words, but he was in agreement with him. He said, "We have no one to turn to, Prinz. We are at the mercy of the authorities unless there is a safe place we can seek out. We were prepared against this day, but all our preparations are wasted now."

"Unless a safe place is found, we must leave Paris very soon," Mme. Lairrez said with great determination. Saint-Germain's respect for her increased. She was obviously the most practical member of the Guild, and possessed a stern common sense that was lamentably uncommon among sorcerers. She looked at Saint-Germain with steady gray eyes, and said with candid dismay, "We are in a great deal of danger, Highness. We are without any friends."

"If Le Grâce is still in Paris . . . as you say he is . . ." Sattin faltered, then bit his lower lip. "We have Cielbleu upstairs. We dare not move him far."

Saint-Germain inwardly cursed himself for a fool, but he said, "You are overlooking one obvious possibility."

The three alchemists turned to him, suspicion and hope in their faces.

"There is a place where you may go, safely." He hated to expose himself in this way. He had survived as long as he had through knowledge and caution. But he could not let the Guild be taken by the law, for that would ultimately expose him. And he could not allow Saint Sebastien to reach them through Le Grâce, for there was far more danger from the Circle than from the ponderous forces of the Paris police.

"What place?" Sattin demanded, finding the Prinz's sudden hesitation disquieting. He studied Saint-Germain, desperation twisting his features into a travesty of a grin.

With a wry smile Saint-Germain said, "You can go to the cellars of Hôtel Transylvania."

Text of a letter from Mlle. Madelaine de Montalia to her father, le Marquis de Montalia, dated October 19, 1743:

To my very noble and dear father, Marquis de Montalia:

It hardly seems I have been gone from home so long, and yet, my cherished father, you are always in my thoughts and my prayers. There is nothing in Paris, grand a city as it is, to compare with the beauty of our home. I have often waked at dawn and longed for the sight of our park which spreads out like a vast skirt of green with that lovely frill of woods where the preserves are. Even in the Bois-Vert there is nothing to compare with it, for I am always aware that the great city is no more than an hour's ride.

As my aunt must certainly have informed you by now, we are to have a fête on the third of November, and we are all in a bustle already with preparations. Nothing could exceed your sister's kindness to me, and her warm heart and generous interest make me love her for herself as much as I love her by obligation of blood. And I am not the only one to so value her. Every day I see proofs of her worth, and the affections in which she is held by all. You told me that you had some slight reservations in sending me to her, but there can be no sufficient reason for this. It is true that she lives the Grand Life, and is much in society, but this has not impaired her virtue nor her tone of mind. She is an excellent woman, and you should be grateful to her for her desire to assist me in the world, for I have seen quite a few who would take shameful advantage of this trust.

L'Abbé Ponteneuf did me the honor of attending a practice hour I had with Saint-Germain last week. He is a worthy man, full of good counsel, and wholly aware of the pitfalls of the world. It is true that on occasion he desires overmuch to protect me from the dangers of society, and try as I might, I cannot convince him that whatever causes him worry, he should tell me, that I may be more on guard against those dangers.

Aside from our practice session, I have seen little of Saint-Germain. He has given me a few books to read, some of Roman philosophers and in an improving tone. He has also given me a few of the *Lives of the Saints,* that I might be more familiar with the sacrifices demanded of us in this life. His knowledge is vast, and of an elevated nature, and I am certain that you would find his company a refreshing change from the dreary chatter that so often passes as conversation in good society.

Tomorrow night we go to Hôtel Transylvania for a concert and a cold supper. There will be gambling, of course, but that is in a separate part of the Hôtel, and one can easily ignore it.

I think so often, dear father, of the strictures you have laid on me concerning the hollowness of court life, and being here only reinforces your wisdom. Most of the people here are shallow, unaware of the world beyond them, unwilling or unable to rise above their surroundings and see the variety of their people. De la Sept-Nuit, who my aunt says might offer for me, is not an evil man, I think, but thoughtless and consequently cruel. He has no concern for any other than himself, because he was never taught to regard the feelings of those other than himself. And it appears that the life in Paris only makes this worse. He has fortune, education of a sort, is pleasing of face, and of the first style, but he would ride past a starving child without ever hearing its pitiful cry, or seeing its emaciated state. No wonder you shun these people as you do.

But consider this: you are an example to them, as well, and if you hide forever in Provence, what can they learn of you, but that you are a recluse with your head in the clouds? I am sending you an invitation to the fête in November, and I pray that you will come. It would delight me to have you at my side, so that you should see how I go on in this vast ocean of society.

In the time I have been here I have come to see many things which I did not understand before. Reflection on the teaching of the Sisters has brought me to a new sense of faith, at a depth which I had not known until this time. We are not in a world of life and death only, my father. There is a compassion that transcends the brevity of life, and makes bearable our pitiful mortality.

If my mother has returned from her brother's estates, I hope you will tender her my duty for me, and commend me to her. For yourself, you have my filial respect and devotion, and my willing obedience to your orders and affections. With this continuing assurance, I am always

Your devoted daughter,
Madelaine Roxanne Bertrande de Montalia

❧ 3 ❧

The lackey in deep-blue livery with red lacing bowed as he opened the door to the little salon, announcing as he did, "Le Comte d'Argenlac, Baron Saint Sebastien."

Saint Sebastien looked up from his reading and nodded curtly as Gervaise d'Argenlac came uncertainly into the room. "Baron Saint Sebastien?" he said uncertainly. "You wanted to see me?"

"Yes, d'Argenlac, I did." He rose from his deep chair and regarded his guest with hooded eyes. "I am, as you may perhaps know, a friend of Jueneport."

Gervaise had almost cringed at the mention of Jueneport, and Saint Sebastien felt a surge of inward satisfaction. Evidently the interview of two days before had badly frightened d'Argenlac.

"You need not worry, Comte," Saint Sebastien said smoothly, setting his book aside on a small rosewood table. The salon had three such tables, and its high ceilings were decorated with murals showing a disturbingly realistic *Rape of the Sabines*. At the far end of the room a low fire burned, for though the rains had stopped, there was a crisp bite to the air, which chilled the bright sunlight pouring through the high windows.

"I am not worried, Baron," Gervaise lied. He still held his tricorne and cane, and seemed uncertain of what to do with them. "I confess," he said, turning from Saint Sebastien's contemptuous gaze, "I cannot think why you would want to speak with me."

"You may call it a whim, Comte. Perhaps you would like to sit down." He motioned to a chair, and waited while Gervaise sat, his tricorne clutched over his knees.

Saint Sebastien strolled to the windows and let Gervaise wait.

"I . . . I found it curious, Baron," Gervaise said at last, his voice unnaturally high, "that one of your lackeys should have brought me a message from Jueneport."

"You did?" He turned slowly and was glad to see that le Comte d'Argenlac was squirming like a schoolboy. "I meant for you to wonder."

"But why? What interest do you have in me?" He wished now that he had had the foresight to wear his full formal scarlet satin coat with the rose-and-gold embroidery on the cuffs instead of the simple light-blue traveling suit of English superfine wool. He felt like a peasant beside the luxurious lounging robe Saint Sebastien wore. An unpleasant thought crossed his mind. "I don't owe you money, do I?"

His host let out his breath in a long, satisfied sigh. "If you mean did you lose money to me, no, d'Argenlac, you did not. But it may surprise you to learn that you do, in fact, stand in my debt. De Vandonne has had need of ready cash and was willing to sell me a few of your notes of hand." He went to one of the small tables and opened the shallow drawer, taking a sheaf of paper from it. He made a show of thumbing through these, saying at last, "My dear Comte, do you always bet for such tremendous sums? I would think, in your position, you would not want to be so profligate."

Gervaise felt color rising in his face. "You mistake, Baron. I do not play to lose."

"Do you not?" Saint Sebastien's voice was tinged with polite disbelief. "I would not have thought it." He put the notes down again.

"Well?" Gervaise said after a few moments of silence.

"Oh, I was simply wondering when you would find it convenient to redeem them."

This time the silence was noticeably longer, and when Gervaise spoke, it was with considerable difficulty. "I have not . . . a great amount of . . . ready money by me . . . just at present. . . ." He fingered his neat neck cloth, which was suddenly much too tight. "My man of business . . . will have to arrange . . . matters. It might take a few days."

"I would not think you could arrange it at all," Saint Sebastien said pleasantly. "I was under the impression that all your real property is heavily mortgaged. Perhaps I am wrong, but that was what Jueneport led me to believe." He toyed with his elegant snuffbox as he spoke, but did not open it or offer any to his miserable guest.

"There are mortgages," Gervaise admitted at last. "But I fancy I can find sufficient funds to redeem those." He pointed to the notes on the table.

"You mean that you can force your wife to pay them," Saint Sebastien said with obvious distaste.

The expression of chagrin and disgust on Gervaise's face told Saint Sebastien more than he realized. "Yes, that is what I mean. And she will pay them. You need not fear."

Saint Sebastien took a leisurely turn about the room, his face inscrutable. "I see you dislike using your wife's fortune," he said as he stopped by the hearth.

Gervaise shrugged.

"If it were possible," Saint Sebastien went on, looking into the fire, "if there were a way for you to pay off your debts without your wife's help, would you be willing to take it?"

"There is no such way." The desolation of these words brought a smile to Saint Sebastien's eyes, but Gervaise did not see it.

"Tell me," Saint Sebastien mused, "your wife's niece, the de Montalia girl . . ."

"She's a pert-tempered child!" Gervaise snapped.

"Very possibly. The de Montalia line is at all times unpredictable. But I understand your wife is giving a fête in her honor?"

"Yes, on the third of November." He was faintly curious. "Do you want to come?"

"I? Certainly not." He turned to face Gervaise now, his eyes almost expressionless. "I have only thought that you might do me a favor as regards her—"

"Madelaine?" Gervaise interrupted, very puzzled now.

"Yes, Madelaine. Robert's first and only born child."

"What do you want with her?" Alarm pricked at Gervaise's neck, but he steadfastly ignored it. He felt no particular partiality for Madelaine; in fact, he thought her far too bright and self-possessed for her own good.

"I want to discharge an obligation of her father's. I trust she will be able to do this."

"To do what?" He did not quite like the way Saint Sebastien's face looked, the reptilian cast to the eyes and the unpleasant sneer in his smile. He sat a little more forward on his chair. "Le Marquis de Montalia has been invited to the fête. You may discharge your obligation to him."

"Indeed?" Saint Sebastien clicked his tongue, and strode to the windows. "Robert is coming to Paris, after all these years. Who would have thought it."

"I do not understand you," Gervaise complained.

"This does not concern you." He moved back to the fire, a restless light in his face now. "It is an old, old matter, Comte, of personal interest only." He tapped his hands on the mantel and then murmured, "There is much less time, then. We must handle this otherwise." He turned to Gervaise, speaking briskly. "Your debts: would you like to discharge them?"

Gervaise made a gesture of despair, and confessed. "It is impossible, Baron. I have not the resources to do it."

Saint Sebastien seized on this. "Suppose it were possible. Suppose I could make it possible? Would you do one small service in return for me?"

Suddenly Gervaise felt the full force of his alarm, and his hands grew clammy. He found he could not meet the ferocity of Saint Sebastien's cold eyes. "What service?"

"A minor one, Comte. Very minor," he soothed. "You have a small estate not far from Paris. It is called Sans Désespoir, appropriately enough. If you are willing to do this little thing for me, Comte, you should be truly without despair for as long as you are wise in games of chance." He regarded d'Argenlac cynically, knowing that for Gervaise gambling was like an illness, a possession, and that it would not be long before he once again depleted his fortune and was forced to turn, resentfully, to his wife.

"What am I to do? What do you offer me?" He wished his need were less acute, as he sensed that he might be able to realize far more from Saint Sebastien, had he time to bargain.

"Sans Désespoir is surrounded by a large park, I believe, and shares hunting preserves with two other nearby estates?" He let the plan come together in his mind. He thought it would work, and would put Madelaine de Montalia into his hands before her father arrived in Paris.

"Yes. Le Duc de Ruisseau-Royal is to the north, and on the east le Baron du Chaisseurdor. Our families have hunted there together for six hundred years." He put his hands out in front of him and was startled to see they were trembling. He thrust them back into his pockets. "I do not hunt much, myself. I have no taste for the sport."

"But La Montalia does. I have heard that she is a daring horsewoman who has been heard to complain that she misses the long gallops she had at home. And with the rigors of the fête before her, she might very well find a few days in the country a treat. You will make up a party, Comte. Very select, and most attractive. You may allow your Comtesse to make up the list, so long as de la Sept-Nuit is included. He has expressed great admiration for the girl, and I want to give him an opportunity to know her better."

"I see," Gervaise said eagerly, needing desperately to know that he would not be doing anything where he might be held at fault.

"Of course, there will be hunting. Not the most vigorous of chases, for we don't want to see the girl exhausted before her triumph. A few runs in the afternoon, and pleasant evenings away from the demands and bustle of the city—it is just what she will find most enjoyable. And your Comtesse will agree. Be sure of that."

Gervaise thought this over, and saw that it would indeed put him in good odor with Claudia. But a nagging doubt clung to him. "How will this benefit you, Baron? And why should you pay me for extending my hospitality to the young lady?"

"Ah, that is my concern. Only see that de la Sept-Nuit is there, and that they hunt together. It will more than satisfy me."

One ugly thought came to his mind. "I do not want the girl compromised under my roof. If de la Sept-Nuit wants to seduce her, let him do it here, in Paris."

Saint Sebastien achieved a sly laugh. "No, that is not what de la Sept-Nuit wants. I can safely promise you that he will not seduce her." There was nothing reassuring in the bland smile he gave Gervaise. "Only let her hunt with him in the country, Comte, and you will be amply rewarded."

"Why?" He knew he had to ask the question, and he rose as he said the word.

"I have made that clear. De la Sept-Nuit wishes to know her better, and I have promised that I will help him to make the match if he can." Saint Sebastien rummaged in his pocket and at last retrieved what he searched for. "Here, Comte, a token of my good faith."

"What is it?" Gervaise stepped back and looked suspiciously at Saint Sebastien's closed, extended hand.

"Partial payment. Come, Comte, take it. You will find it of use, believe me."

Gervaise took a few reluctant steps forward and held out his hand, half-expecting to have something loathsome dropped into it.

"There. You will find that Guillem of Le Hollandais will be able to cut it for you." He dropped the uncut diamond into Gervaise's hand, and smiled a little at the joy in his face, which was quickly followed by fright. "It is genuine, Comte. I would guess that it will bring a sizable sum."

Gervaise's hand closed convulsively around the gem. "I do not understand," he muttered.

"There will be four more of at least that size to puzzle you after the sojourn at Sans Désespoir. It will also be my pleasure to give your notes of hand to you then, for burning." Saint Sebastien had strolled toward the door, and now he rang for a lackey. "I will wish you a pleasant stay in the country, Comte. And a happy conclusion to our association."

"Certainly, certainly," Gervaise said, close to babbling as he picked up his cloak and his cane and tricorne. Relief made him giddy, but dread was a spur to his departure. He nodded to the lackey with satisfaction, and bowed his way out of the room.

When he was gone, Saint Sebastien once again rang for a lackey, and this time asked for the pleasure of Le Grâce's company.

It was some little time before the sorcerer came up from the cellars, and he made his apologies for the stained apron he wore as he came into the little salon.

"Never mind," Saint Sebastien snapped. "Tell me, how many of those jewels can you make in the next ten days?"

Le Grâce rubbed at his chin. "I don't quite know. I am getting one to two a day at present. As long as the carbon is kept molten and the gears resist the gases of azoth, there should be jewels for several weeks more. Beyond that, I cannot say, not without finding Ragoczy again. He's the one with the secret."

"Ragoczy, always Ragoczy!" Saint Sebastien crossed the room in rapid strides, his lounging robe of quilted silk spreading out behind him like a wake. "I must find this Ragoczy. If he knew the secret of the jewels, he might know others as well. I want that knowledge, Le Grâce. I want you to find this man for me."

Le Grâce paled. "Baron, I cannot. I have been cast out of the Guild, and I take my life in my hands if I—"

"You take your life in your hands if you displease me, Le Grâce. Remember that. Remember, also, that I can reward you far more richly than can any of the Guild." He turned on the sorcerer. "You are of use to me only so long as you can produce the jewels. After that, unless you have more to offer me . . ." He shrugged and walked toward the fire.

"But I dare not search them out," Le Grâce pleaded.

"You dare not defy me," Saint Sebastien corrected him. He picked up the elegant gold-plated poker by the hearth and stirred at the logs that burned there, giving a cruel laugh as the sparks spattered onto the high polish of the floor. "You remember La Cressie, Le Grâce? You took her first, when I was done. Do you remember how she looked? Do you remember how she writhed? And that was only rape, Le Grâce. That was not torture, or the Mass of Blood. Think about that when you seek to defy me."

Le Grâce's throat was dry, but he managed to croak out a few words. "I'll try, Baron."

Saint Sebastien did not look at him. "Good."

"I'll go tonight."

Le Grâce was almost out of the door when Saint Sebastien's words stopped him. "Do not think to escape me, Le Grâce. If you try to run, I will find you and bring you back. And I will have no mercy, Le Grâce."

"I had not considered it, Baron." Le Grâce bowed, though Saint Sebastien did not turn to acknowledge it.

"Do not lie to me, either, Le Grâce. Find me this Prinz Ragoczy, and you will be rewarded. Fail me, and be punished." He jabbed viciously at the logs.

Le Grâce opened his mouth in a desperate grimace. He wanted to scream. How much he longed to be back in the attic room at the Inn of the Red Wolf with Oulen, alive, outside. He should not have killed Oulen, he realized now. He had ruined his chances of coming back to the Guild. But he had stabbed Oulen after forcing him to help carry the athanor to the special carriage that had brought it to Saint Sebastien's hôtel. And he had beaten Cielbleu, which only made matters worse. He mastered himself enough to say, "I will find Ragoczy," to Saint Sebastien before letting himself out of the little salon.

Saint Sebastien chuckled as he heard the door close and Le Grâce's terrified flight down the hall. He stood by the mantel, smiling down at the shapes he saw in the fire.

Excerpt from a letter from le Marquis de Montalia to his sister, Claudia, Comtesse d'Argenlac, dated October 24, 1743:

. . . I was amazed at the speed at which the post brought Madelaine's letter to me. Only five days, my dear sister. Say what you will about the disastrous foreign sense of Louis, his domestic policy is sound. I am delighted to have heard so quickly from my daughter, and with so warm greetings as fill my heart with gratitude to you and to her confessor, l'Abbé Ponteneuf, who has also written to me of late. She tells me that she has come to value the virtues that survive, rather than the pleasures of the moment, and this has given me a new lease of strength, as if an insufferable burden had been lifted from me. I have always known that she is an honorable child, and her confidences in her last letter confirm this.

She has written to ask if I will come to her fête, adding her entreaties to yours. If the dearest women of my life rank themselves against me in this way, what can I do but consent? You tell me it would do me good to see Paris again, and to renew my friendships of my youth. Some of those, of course, are best forgotten, but others, I do confess, tug at my heart and prompt me to be with you for the fête. Though it is unwise, I cannot deny the urgings of my heart. I will leave the day after tomorrow and will arrive in Paris on the first or second of November. I trust I may stay with you and your Comte for several days. I am also writing to l'Abbé Ponteneuf to be sure he and I may spend a few hours together, for I yearn to have the benefits of his learning and his sincere fervor. He almost persuades me that there is hope and that I may yet find the peace which has so far been denied me in this world.

My wife continues her stay at her brother's estates, and will not be joining me. I had her message this morning, and have dispatched one of my grooms with a note to her, outlining my intentions and telling her where a letter will find me. Her brother, as you may have heard, has married again, and his wife is at her first lying-in. Margaret, out of devotion to him, has gone to attend to his children of his first marriage. She is much loved by her nieces and nephews, and I do not want to pull her away from the pleasant duty of seeing another Ragnac into the world. She and I, as you know, live very much apart, and I do not see that I have the right to impose on her at this time. Being her husband, I have the right of command, but she is also devoted to her brother, and it is a bond I do not wish her to sever, for should anything happen to me, it is to him she must go for her home and protection.

Your concern for Lucienne Cressie alarms me. Surely her husband cannot be as much in the wrong as you suggest. I realize that if he has indeed succumbed to the fleshly vice you describe that it would be most difficult for her to submit to his wishes with a good grace. But it is not for her, or for you, my dear sister, to challenge a husband's right to the schooling of his wife. It is true she may have much to bear, but as a wife, it is her duty, and certainly, her privilege to minister to the wants of her husband. Religion and law both enforce this view, and everywhere we see the wisdom of this. The examples of the saints teach us the virtue of obedience and the blessings of marriage are such that any woman must acknowledge that the firm rule of her husband is the strong protection from idleness and folly. If Lucienne Cressie is without the fruits of union and the joys of motherhood, she is certainly in a better way to finding grace, free from the pollutions of the body. Let not her disquiet and the worldly disappointment she professes lead you into interfering with her life. Instead, counsel her to accept meekly the role that Heaven has decreed for her, and to submit to the pleasure of her husband. Her tractability and her gentle example may well turn him from his ways and bring him again into the acceptable behavior of a husband.

. . . It has occurred to me that the proper dress for evening must have changed since my days at court. I hope that your Comte or some other will tell me what I must do and how I must dress so as not to disgrace my daughter or you. I doubt there is time enough to order full clothes for me, but I am sending a sheet with this which includes the measurements taken this last summer by my seamster, and it should afford a gentleman's clothier the information necessary to make, at least, small clothes and a coat for me. I am more than willing to meet the price he demands for this rapid service. But I request you, my dear sister, that though the current mode is for bright colors, not to indulge your fancy for them at my expense. I am a somber man, and a coat of russet silk and brown velvet cuffs would be grand enough for me. None of your lilacs and peaches, please, as it would be against my nature. If russet silk is not available, I leave the matter to your discretion. Err on the side of sobriety, I pray you. I believe I have suitable shirts in cream silk, and matching lace. I thank you in advance for this help you give me. The thought of the fête fills your days, but I trust that you or your Comte will take my measurements to the clothier for me.

Until I greet you myself, I thank you again from my heart for your warm hospitality to my daughter and the consideration you have shown her, as well as your affection that comes to me with your invitation. I look forward to seeing you both once again, and to enjoying the brightness of Paris. In all things I have the honor to be

> Your devoted brother,
> Robert Marcel Yves Etienne Pascal
> Marquis de Montalia

4

"Saint-Germain, you are not attending," Jueneport said as he looked up briefly from his cards. "Are you betting on this hand or not?"

"What?" he said, mildly distracted. "Oh, the game. No, I think I will not play the set out." He tossed the cards onto the table face-up, showing what was plainly the winning hand.

The other five men stared for a moment, and Jueneport remarked, "Your wits must surely be wandering if you will leave the game with such a hand and five thousand livres on the table."

Saint-Germain gave him a sweet, insincere smile. "That is why I go. Where is the challenge if I hold such cards as these?" He had pushed away from the table, and now rose slowly. "Continue your amusements, gentlemen. I am going to find solace in the supper room."

Jueneport hooted at this. "But you never eat, Saint-Germain." He looked at the others for confirmation, and was met with knowing snickers.

"True enough, Jueneport, I do not eat in public. But there is conversation to be had, and some wit. Perhaps I can console myself with the company of one or two of polite society who are not addicted to drink or games of chance." He said this with flippancy, and it brought a fresh gush of laughter from the others, and none of them saw the dreadful fatigue at the back of his eyes. He made a bow, flourished his scented lace handkerchief, reminded Jueneport that his luck was quite out, and with one last quip sauntered away toward the Great Hall of Hôtel Transylvania.

"Good evening, Hercule," he said to the majordomo as he passed through the door to the north wing.

"Good evening, Comte," Hercule answered with a perfectly straight face.

"Who is here tonight, Hercule?" He paused, decidedly elegant in his chaste black velvet. The silver embroidery of his brocaded cuffs and waistcoat set off his fine silver lace and gave a warm, winy cast to the ruby at his neck.

"All the world, Comte." By not so much as a flicker of respect did he betray his employer. "You may find la Comtesse d'Argenlac in the ballroom, I think, unless she has gone in to supper."

"I see." Saint-Germain's eyes were fixed on the magnificent Velázquez that hung across the Great Hall from him. He said in a louder voice, "Do you think the owner of the Hôtel might be persuaded to part with that picture?"

"I doubt it, Comte," Hercule replied with perfect civility.

"I would pay a good deal for that work," Saint-Germain continued, reminding himself that he had. "Well, I bid you tell your master, whoever he is, that I have an especial love of Velázquez."

De la Sept-Nuit, chancing to walk by at that moment, grinned. "Offering for that painting again, Comte?"

Saint-Germain, affecting surprise, looked up. "Oh, I did not see you, Donatien. Yes, I am trying once again, and still to no avail."

"If you keep up your determined interest, we will all be betting on your chances." He turned to his companion for confirmation, but Baron Beauvrai paid no notice to this conversation.

Beauvrai was startlingly dressed tonight, even by his own extravagant standards. He wore his most elaborate wig, which was tinted with delicate blue powder. This was secured at the back of his neck with a large satin bow spangled with golden stars. His coat and small clothes were of jonquil watered silk, whose broad claret-colored revers and cuffs could not be said to set it off to advantage. A straw-colored waistcoat of peau de soie was embroidered with turquoise floss, which was undoubtedly meant to complement his turquoise silk hose and gold shoes. He had completed the ensemble with pale-blue lace at throat and wrists, and had drenched himself with violet scent.

Saint-Germain contemplated Beauvrai in silence, and punctuated this with a short sigh. "As always, Beauvrai, you leave me speechless."

Beauvrai shot a swift glance at him, regarding Saint-Germain's somber dress. "I'd rather look a man than a priest," he said with what was obviously intended to be withering contempt. "From what I hear of you, you have no more claim to manhood than you do to the title."

With a disarming smile, Saint-Germain inclined his head. "Mon Baron, if to be a man is to emulate you, I fear I must always be a disappointment." He was about to turn and leave Beauvrai sputtering with rage, but a chance remark from de la Sept-Nuit caught his attention, and he paused.

"When you're at Chaisseurdor's, will you spend an evening with our party at Sans Désespoir?" de la Sept-Nuit was asking Beauvrai in an effort to turn his attention from Saint-Germain.

"What? Chaisseurdor? Oh, oh, yes. I suppose I might. I'll be spending a week there. Chaisseurdor won't miss me for one night." He pointedly ignored Saint-Germain.

"Bring him along," de la Sept-Nuit suggested, prepared to steer Beauvrai into the gaming rooms.

"The thing is, he doesn't like d'Argenlac. They quarreled about the preserves ten years ago, and the thing hasn't been patched up yet. Damned silly, the both of them, if you ask me. Don't worry, Donatien, I'll take the time to visit Sans Désespoir. I want to see how you do the pretty with La Montalia."

"I will do well enough, do not you worry." He clapped Beauvrai on the shoulder, and exchanging knowing winks, they went into the north wing of the Hôtel.

Saint-Germain stood in the Great Hall for fully two minutes, a vacant expression in his dark eyes, which belied the thoughts racing in his mind. He wandered across the fine expanse to the Velázquez, pausing once to nod to a party of late arrivals. Looking up at the splendid antique faces, Saint-Germain felt a pang of loneliness, remembering how he had gazed eagerly at this very work when the paint was still oilily wet, when the artist himself had asked him if the figure of Socrates had the full weight of doom on it. Then, and now, Saint-Germain thought that ragged, unworldly, argumentative old Socrates would never have recognized himself in that austere figure of Velázquez's imagination, but he had refrained from saying so to the great painter.

Walking rather slowly, Saint-Germain made his way toward the supper room. The alarm he had felt at Beauvrai's words with de la Sept-Nuit did not lessen as he considered them. He recalled the invitation la Comtesse d'Argenlac had sent him to join her party at Sans Désespoir, an invitation which he had refused, not wanting to tempt himself with the sweet, impossible nearness of Madelaine.

Her image rose in his mind, and he tried to push it away. He could not afford to desire her, to care for her, for that way led to exposure, not only of him, but of her. For one blind instant he pictured the cruel stake pounded into Madelaine's exquisite body, and the thought was hurtful to him.

"Comte," said a voice near him, and he looked up quite suddenly to see Claudia d'Argenlac walking toward him on the arm of le Duc de la Mer-Herbeux. She was decked out in a grand toilette of the palest green satin embroidered with morning glories over a petticoat of ruched Austrian silk with bows of matching Belgian lace the color of English roses.

Saint-Germain recovered himself and made la Comtesse a profound bow. "I am delighted to see you," he said, knowing it was almost the truth. "I will not ask if I find you well, as the look of you tells me that. With all your plans, I would not be surprised to discover you alone in a corner recruiting your strength for the fête of the third."

La Comtesse laughed merrily, the smile in her eyes almost as bright as the shine from her heavy emerald necklace. "Ah, no, my dear Comte. My husband has arranged for us to go to the country tomorrow, and make a little stay there while the hôtel is being made ready for the fête. If you had been to see us more often these past few days, you would know that."

"I had your invitation," he reminded her, and turned his attention to le Duc. "I am very pleased to see you in Paris again, sir. I trust that your venture in London met with success?"

"A modicum of it, Comte," de la Mer-Herbeux admitted. "The English pride themselves on being reasonable, but in the question of Austria, they seem singularly irrational."

Saint-Germain smiled. "You must forgive them, de la Mer-Herbeux, if occasionally their desires run counter to those of France."

La Comtesse put up her hands. "Gentlemen, gentlemen, please, do not talk politics. It is all I have heard this last hour, and I cannot bear one more moment of it." She smiled at Saint-Germain. "Comte, I know you will support me. Do you take me in to supper and tell me tales of anything that has not to do with politics."

Saint-Germain raised his brows at le Duc. "May I have the honor?"

De la Mer-Herbeux relinquished la Comtesse's hand on his arm. "By all means, Saint-Germain. If I must not speak of politics, I fear I will not be able to entertain her at all." He bowed to Saint-Germain and kissed la Comtesse's hand, then turned to stroll away in search of more like-minded company.

"I thought I would spend the whole evening listening to him," la Comtesse whispered to Saint-Germain in obvious relief. "I know he has done a great service for France, and I know that the King is tremendously impressed with his diplomatic skill, and I know he is a most gifted statesman, *but* I swear I am perishing of boredom."

"I will do my poor best to remedy that," Saint-Germain said as he led her toward the supper room.

"Comte," she said lightly, "I have wanted to tell you my excellent news for the last several days, but you have not been to call on us."

Saint-Germain kept his voice neutral. "I have been lamentably busy, my dear. It is not that I wanted to stay away, believe me."

La Comtesse laughed again. "Madelaine has said that she feared you had grown tired of us, and had forsaken our company, but I thought perhaps you were otherwise engaged."

Inwardly, Saint-Germain felt quick sympathy for Madelaine, so vulnerable to him, and he wished she were not so vital, so much to be cherished. "If there is to be music for your fête, as you have asked, Claudia, I must at some time write it," he said easily. "When the new works are finished, you may be sure you will see me, probably unto surfeit."

She turned as he escorted her through the doors of the supper room. "Never that, Comte. In fact, I was myself disappointed that you are not able to join us at Sans Désespoir."

"Well, that cannot be helped." He led her through the closely packed tables to one some way apart from the others, and held her chair while she skillfully maneuvered her wide panniers into it. "Tell me what I may bring to you, and when I return, I want to hear your good news."

"Select what you will, my dear Comte, so long as it is not rice à l'Espagne. I have dined out twice this week, and at each place we have had rice à l'Espagne. Madelaine has said that if we have it one more time she will take to playing castanets."

"Very well, no rice à l'Espagne." He had turned to go to the buffet, when he found he could not resist asking, "Will Madelaine be joining us? If she is coming, I must secure another chair."

"She may be in later. When last I left her, she was dancing with le Marquis de la Colonne-Pur. He is certainly captivated with her, Comte."

"I am not surprised," Saint-Germain murmured, and he turned to visit the buffet.

He took somewhat longer than usual, finding his thoughts in a turmoil he was anxious to conceal from Claudia's disastrously acute mind. When at last he returned to the secluded table, he brought her roasted duck in orange sauce, a salad of spinach and wedges of Italian marrow, a little curried shrimp, and a glass of moderately sweet white wine. He set this before her and settled himself in the chair opposite.

"Now," he said as he waved away la Comtesse's thanks, "what is this wonderful news you speak of? You are so radiant, and your happiness shines like a branch of candles in a dark room. You are almost another woman, my dear."

La Comtesse d'Argenlac took some of the wine and gave Saint-Germain a roguish smile. "Ah, Comte, you will be so very happy for me." But it was hard for her to begin. She set down the glass and studied her plate for some several moments before saying, "As you have probably guessed, the relation between my husband and myself has on occasion been strained. . . ."

"Yes, I was aware of that," he said gently, his voice very low.

She sighed, shaking her head. "I was very much afraid that he had come close to ruin, for his man of business was greatly alarmed, and he urged some very drastic and unpleasant measures. I . . . I had the opportunity to alleviate the more pressing demands made on him, which, I promise you, made our way much easier for a time."

Saint-Germain said nothing, wondering how much of her personal wealth had been spent on her foolish husband.

"Just when I was sure that we were in desperate straits, Gervaise astounded me. He had a private legacy from his father, one he had made no mention of before, because he had no idea of its worth."

"A private legacy?" Saint-Germain's mild disbelief was echoed in the rising tone of his voice. "What, pray, was this private legacy?"

Now la Comtesse turned her happy face to him fully. "It is truly an answer to my prayers. His father, it seemed, had come into the possession of a very, very large uncut diamond, which Gervaise has had cut, and the stone now is said to be worth more than sixty thousand louis." She placed her hands together and delight laughed in her eyes.

"An uncut diamond?" Saint-Germain said slowly.

"Yes. He brought it to me a few days ago. It is amazing that gems can look so commonplace, is it not?" She turned her attention to her supper, starting with the salad.

"His father left him an uncut diamond which he has at last decided to sell?" He did not expect an answer. His eyes were turned toward the window, and one hand toyed with the ruby at his throat.

Claudia, glancing at the window, gave a little gasp. "Why, Comte, how strange. See? From where I sit, you have no reflection."

Saint-Germain glanced up sharply, his eyes darting to the night-darkened windows, which reflected back the glittering images of the guests at supper. He realized that he had been careless, so preoccupied was he with his concern for Madelaine. He moved his chair slightly. "It is the angle. If you were where I am, then you would disappear, my dear."

"You gave me quite a start," she admitted, her laugh now sounding forced.

Saint-Germain rose and loosened the tassel which held back the sculptured velvet draperies. The heavy fabric glided across the windows, blotting out the night and the figures in the glass. "There. We need not be distracted searching for each other in the reflections." Once again he sat. "You must tell me more about this lucky chance that has befallen your husband. I gather you knew nothing of this before now?"

"Not so much as a whisper. That is why I feel so relieved. Gervaise told me that until his man of business reminded him of it, it had not crossed his mind these ten years."

"Why, how fortuitous," Saint-Germain mused. "I am very pleased for you, Comtesse. It is a timely rescue indeed."

"Yes," she agreed. "Now I can be easy. It is as if a weight had been lifted from my shoulders. I am quite in charity with my husband once again."

"That is obvious, Claudia. You must accept my felicitations." There was nothing particularly happy in either his face or his tone, but she did not appear to notice this.

"Yes," she said. "Thank you, Saint-Germain. You have been very kind, listening to me, giving me the solace of your presence and your wit. I must confess," she added artlessly, "that when Gervaise first suggested this stay in the country, I was terribly afraid it meant that he was wholly rolled up, and was escaping from his debtors, but it was no such thing. To be sure," she went on, more sternly now that she had given the matter some thought, "I am not pleased that de la Sept-Nuit is to be part of the company, but with seven others, there can be little danger. It is not what I would want, but I do not desire to put myself at opposition to my husband's wishes, particularly now, when things are better between us at last."

Saint-Germain nodded, studying the flicker of uncertainty that crossed her face. "Claudia, if you are not easy in your mind, you may count me your friend and rely on my confidence."

She turned swiftly to him. "Oh," she said, realizing he had caught her concern. "It is nothing, Comte. Truly, it is nothing. But you are generous. I have always said you were generous, even when you first arrived in Paris, and so many were suspicious of you. . . ." She put her hand to her face. "Dear me, I did not mean that as it sounded. . . ."

"I know what was said of me, Claudia. I still know." He smiled, genuine amusement in his eyes. "You all wonder who I may be, or what I may be. I know the answer, and I find a pleasant entertainment in watching you all guess." He picked up her hand from where it lay on the table and carried it to his lips. "Never mind, Claudia," he said, seeing the shine of tears in her eyes, knowing she was far closer to hysteria than he had thought at first.

"It is only that . . ." She stopped for a moment, trying to collect herself. "It is dreadful for me to say it, Comte, but I feared at first that he had lied to me, and that this was something else. Until he showed me the stone, I didn't believe him." She was plainly abashed by this confession.

"It is understandable," he remarked dryly.

But she rushed on, "Even now, I cannot help it. I find myself afraid that this is all a dream, and that I will wake to discover bailiffs at the door and our hôtel sold out from under us." She dashed her hand over her eyes. "What will you think of me?"

"Nothing to your discredit, Madame." His compelling eyes sought hers, and when she was fully aware of this penetrating gaze, he said, "You are not to be frightened again, my dear. You have been through a terrible time, but now you will recover. If there is other danger, you will face it well, for you are quite courageous. Remember that."

Her hand touched her cheek, and her eyes faltered. "I do . . . not know what . . . to say. I am overtired, I think. Every little thing oversets me." She looked down at her plate. "I must finish supper."

Saint-Germain frowned slightly, realizing that Madelaine's safety hung in the precarious balance of her aunt's sensibilities.

She had taken her fork up eagerly, and rattled on about the food as she ate, saying that the duck was superb, that she had never had so fine an orange sauce. Between bites she commented fulsomely on the excellent meals always served at Hôtel Transylvania. She could not bear to speak of her worry again.

Saint-Germain put an end to this with another question. "I have heard that you have called at hôtel Cressie, to inquire after Madame. What do you hear of her?"

Claudia's inconsequent flow of words stopped abruptly. She put down her fork and said, "The poor woman. I could not see her. Achille has forbidden her to receive her friends."

"So I am aware," Saint-Germain said with a certain asperity. "I have called there myself, once or twice, but could not gain admittance." He thought of his two attempts to see her alone in her room, coming as her dream again. But there was always a servant with her, and Lucienne Cressie had no chance to sleep alone.

"I fear for her. I have written to my brother, asking him what he feels I should do. I know that in general it is wrong to interfere between man and wife, but it cannot be so in this instance." There was a flush to her cheeks now, and a ghost of the spirited girl she had been at twenty showed in her determination.

"If it were possible to show she had been mistreated, then her relatives might wish to arrange for a separation for her." Saint-Germain waited for la Comtesse's thoughts.

"I don't know," she said slowly. "Her parents are dead and her only sister is an Abbesse. She has three aunts, but I am not certain that their husbands would be willing to take her in unless there was reason to believe that she was in serious danger. . . ." She looked away from Saint-Germain, a pall of desolation over her attractive features. "Oh, dear. I feel so *helpless.*" The cry was as much for herself as for Lucienne Cressie.

"Hush, my dear," Saint-Germain said, putting a steadying hand on her arm.

"Ah, pay no attention!" She had lifted her arm as if to ward off a blow. Then, quite suddenly, her expression lightened and the protecting gesture became a wave. "Madelaine!" she called, beckoning to her niece, who was seen coming into the supper room on the arm of le Baron de la Tourbèdigue.

Across the room, Madelaine looked up as she heard her name called, and she said something to her escort.

That elegant young man in mauve satin bowed to her wishes and led her through the tables with the air of one clearing a path for one of the better Roman emperors.

"Aunt," Madelaine said as soon as she was near enough to make herself heard over the general babble of voices, "I was hoping I would find you. I am simply famished after all this dancing. De la Tourbèdigue here is determined to wear the shoes off my feet."

Saint-Germain had risen at her approach, and now held the chair he had vacated for her. "Good evening, Mademoiselle," he said, not allowing his eyes to linger on her face too long.

She gave Saint-Germain a brittle smile. "Good evening, Comte. I suppose I must thank you for the chair. I have seen so little of you that I think I must stand on ceremony with you, out of strangeness."

Saint-Germain let this pass. "Will you allow me to bring you some supper, Mademoiselle? Undoubtedly you want to speak with your aunt—"

Here de la Tourbèdigue interrupted, very eager to please. "No, pardon me, Comte, but it would be my honor to serve Mademoiselle. You have already had the pleasure of serving the aunt; you must allow me the privilege of serving the niece." He flourished a bow and went off before Saint-Germain could object.

"Who is that puppy?" he asked, as soon as de la Tourbèdigue was away from the table.

Madelaine turned to Saint-Germain, and her words were sharp. "He is my admirer. My devoted admirer."

"Ah, Madelaine," her aunt said, shaking her head at this.

"No," Saint-Germain said with a rueful smile, "I deserve your severity, Mademoiselle. But I fear your mockery of a man of my age when you are sought by so many much younger and more acceptable gentlemen." He gave Madelaine a swift, speaking look and saw the answering fire in her eyes.

"You may not be as young as most of Madelaine's suitors," Claudia d'Argenlac observed, "but you have twenty times their address."

"At least that," Saint-Germain agreed with a wicked chuckle. He looked once more at Madelaine. "I am desolate that my affairs will not allow me to join you at Sans Désespoir, but I find that I must be away from Paris for a few days." He stepped back and had almost made his bow to the two women when Madelaine stopped him.

"Oh, Saint-Germain, I wish you were going to be there. I have missed our musical afternoons."

"Rest assured that I am busy with some new works for your fête." He looked across the room. "See, here is your devoted young Baron returning, Mademoiselle. I must leave you, but he will certainly entertain you."

Madelaine turned her pleading violet eyes. "But I was hoping to see you."

He gave her an enigmatic smile, and relented a little. "Perhaps you will," he said softly.

Text of two letters from le Comte de Saint-Germain to his manservant, Roger, and his majordomo, Hercule, respectively, written simultaneously with the left and right hands, dated October 25, 1743:

My dear Roger/Hercule:

I find that I must be away from Paris for three or possibly four days. This is a matter of some delicacy, and I must attend to it in all privacy. To that end, I will travel alone, going on horseback, and without companion or escort.

Should my absence be commented on, you may say that there is good reason for it, but that you are not at liberty to divulge it for fear there be embarrassing repercussions in high places.

If I do not return to Paris within five days and you have had no word from me, or if word comes without my signet on it, I authorize you to begin a search in the manner known to Roger. You may use Sattin and Domingo y Roxas to assist you, but on no account will you ask help of anyone else. Police and clergy alike are to be avoided.

My Will and instructions for my interment are in their usual place. You may open such if my absence is longer than twenty-one days.

I charge you to carry out my orders as you hope for salvation.

                                        Saint-Germain
                                        (his seal, the eclipse)

5

Even the overcast sky could not detract from the joy of the afternoon hunt. The park and preserves adjoining Sans Désespoir were full of the richness of autumn. Leaves covered the ground, crackling under the horses' hooves as Gervaise led his guests in pursuit of a young stag, though almost none cared if they did not run it to earth.

Madelaine took the third jump ahead of everyone, her riding habit of burgundy velvet flying and her eyes alive with joy. She was mounted on a big, rawboned English hunter that ate up the distance with unflagging speed. She steadied him for the long gallop to the next fence, and felt her heart lightened. It relieved her of the nagging loneliness she had felt since she had left Paris three days before. She told herself that it was the city she missed, and not Saint-Germain.

Behind her, the rest of the party had cleared the jump, save for Gervaise's cousin, le Chevalier Sommenault, whose horse had balked at the fence and had sent his rider hurtling through the air over his head, to land, winded but unharmed, in a drift of beech leaves.

"Ahi!" shouted de la Sept-Nuit as he spurred his big Hanoverian bay up beside Madelaine's mount, matching its stride with her hunter's. "You take the shine out of us all. Such style! Such courage!"

She held her horse firmly, her gloved hands sure on the reins. "Pray do not crowd me, Chevalier. The path is very narrow."

"Crowd you? I'd have to catch you to do that." He showed her a smile as free from malice as he could make it. "You're a splendid horsewoman."

"You should offer your compliments to my father: he taught me." She did not like de la Sept-Nuit, and found his nearness grating. She wanted to be rid of him, but knew that unless he was tossed on a jump, there was no way for her to escape.

De la Sept-Nuit's smile broadened. "You need not be modest, Mademoiselle. You are most praiseworthy." He held his horse back a little as the trees grew denser, letting her move ahead of him.

Madelaine ground her teeth. She had found in the three days she had been in de la Sept-Nuit's company that she wanted nothing to do with him, with his elaborate courtesy and his greedy face. The very thought of the flattering offer he had made to her aunt for her hand made her ill.

Gervaise thundered by them, perilously close to their horses, his big chestnut stallion tossing his head at the bruising pace his rider set. Le Comte d'Argenlac was a reckless rider, and only his great skill kept him from killing himself in the saddle. He yelled something incoherent to de la Sept-Nuit, waved hugely, and spurred past them.

Far ahead, beyond the trees, the young stag leaped a fence and bounded over the stream beyond, onto the holdings of le Duc de Ruisseau-Royal, headed for the dense forest that stretched away into the north.

"That will teach us a lesson." De la Sept-Nuit laughed, raising his voice enough to carry to Madelaine. "Is your mount up to it? Take care, or you'll come to grief."

"I trust he is sound," Madelaine said through clenched teeth, not so loudly that her unwanted companion could hear her. She was glad now that she had not insisted on riding her Spanish mare, for this grueling pace would have sapped her strength dangerously.

They were out of the trees now, crossing the open meadow to the fence that marked the limits of Gervaise's land. Already the owner himself was across it, and was wisely fording the stream beyond, holding his sweating horse on a direct point to the opposite bank.

Now Madelaine felt her English hunter gather under her, and she tightened her leg on the horn of her sidesaddle. The horse surged upward, and Madelaine leaned forward against the neck of her hunter; then, as he crested his jump, she stretched backward in her saddle, her head almost brushing the horse's rump. Immediately the horse had touched all four feet to the ground, she came up straight, shortened her rein, and urged her mount toward the stream.

De la Sept-Nuit's Hanoverian was right behind her, and le Chevalier shouted to Madelaine, his enthusiasm getting enough ahead of his judgment that his horse almost stumbled, and de la Sept-Nuit had to collect his mount to keep him from going down on his knees.

Gervaise was quite out of sight in the wood now, and the rest of the hunt had fallen behind. A crisp breeze had come up, rustling the leaves around them and sending the heavy clouds scudding across the sky.

Madelaine glanced around swiftly, and felt a twinge of fear, worried that she might be caught alone with de la Sept-Nuit. Her horse was into the stream now, and she held him on course to the far bank. She found herself wanting to spur the hunter hard into the forest, to get a great deal of distance between her and the young nobleman who was still less than two arm lengths away. There was a resounding crash from the fence, and two more riders parted company with their horses. Madelaine felt her fright congeal in a solid lump at the base of her throat.

Over the stream at last, she pushed on toward the forest, but knew that Donatien de la Sept-Nuit was enjoying the chase now, playing with her as a cat plays with a mouse. For a moment she considered challenging him, demanding to know what he wanted of her, but then dismissed the thought almost as quickly as she had formed it. She had no desire to put herself at such a great disadvantage, for it would be a simple thing for de la Sept-Nuit to compromise her, and then there would be no choice but to marry him.

The trees were quite near, and she sank her spurred heel into her hunter's flank, and felt satisfaction as he drew away from de la Sept-Nuit's Hanoverian. Once in the woods, she would have a chance to put more distance between them. She ducked her head in anticipation of the many low limbs that waited in the waning light.

It was cold under the trees, and she was forced to rein in to a canter. The ground here grew rougher, more uneven, and her hunter was beginning to labor under the furious pace. Madelaine set her hands on the reins, grimly determined to ride the hunt out. She knew that Gervaise was ahead of her, and she told herself that her aunt's husband would not refuse her the protection she so ardently sought.

A swift glance back over her shoulder told her that she was indeed pulling ahead of de la Sept-Nuit. She could hear the steady pound of his horse's hooves, but he was far enough behind her that she began to hope that the track would offer her a chance to be free of him. She looked about her, ready to take full advantage of any opportunity the woods presented.

The track wound deeper into the forest, and began to lose its clear markings. Huge pines and ancient oaks commanded the view, dominating the dusk they themselves created. Here the track became more tortuous, winding among the formidable old trees.

Ahead, the track forked, one branch leading up a slope and away from the marked pathway. The other branch kept to the lower way, a little broader than the other, clearly marked, and free from rocks. The disturbance on the second path showed that several horsemen had come that way no very long time before.

Madelaine did not hesitate. She dragged heavily on the rein, tugging the hunter toward the upward path. The big English horse faltered, then raced up the narrow way, flecks of sweat foaming on his neck as he bounded over the tumbled rocks.

At the top of the rise, with a screen of trees between her and the main track, Madelaine reined in, holding her restless, panting mount still while she listened for de la Sept-Nuit to pass. She had almost convinced herself that she wanted to follow him when she recalled the many hoofprints on the track below.

In vain she told herself that it was another hunting party, that she was letting her apprehension overwhelm her, that her aunt's husband would be waiting for her, solicitous of her well-being.

Tired, worried, far from Sans Désespoir, Madelaine took stock of herself. She knew she could return to the main track and follow it to where Gervaise and de la Sept-Nuit were, but something told her she must not do that. After a moment, she slipped out of the saddle, twitched the reins over her horse's head, and began to lead him along the lesser track, wondering where it might lead. She knew that she would have to walk the hunter a way, for the big horse was too hot; his mottled gray coat was dark with sweat, and his breath came in great heaving gusts. She tugged on the rein, and began to walk.

It was awkward going, for the long train of her habit was forever catching on things, and the hunter was restive. She began to wonder if she would find her way to safety that night, or if she was fated to spend the time wandering the forest. The wind, too, was stronger, and the trees moaned to one another, lashing the limbs like flagellants doing penance. Where the sky was visible through the branches, there were threatening clouds, growing darker now that the afternoon was so far advanced.

She had gone perhaps a quarter of a mile when she heard the sound of hoofbeats not far behind her. She paused, and put her hand to the hunter's nostrils to keep him from whinnying. It seemed a ridiculous precaution for her, since the moment before, she had been anxious to be found, but now there was a grue down her spine, and her heart beat more quickly.

Listening carefully, Madelaine was sure she heard four or five horses. With the three casualties, that was the number of riders who had set out on the hunt. It could not be those horsemen who came after her.

On impulse, she tugged her hunter off the trail and into a thicket some way back from the track. She stood there in the dim light, not daring to move. She was grateful for the fallen leaves now, because the hunter had left no telltale prints leading to her hiding place.

The sounds of the chase grew louder, and then six horsemen burst into sight, their faces hard and their horses steaming. Madelaine felt herself grow cold, for the rider at the lead of the group was le Baron Clotaire de Saint Sebastien, and beside de la Sept-Nuit was Baron Beauvrai.

Madelaine's eyes grew wide, and her face paled. She put a hand to her throat and wished that she was not trembling. Saint Sebastien! Dread weakened her knees, and she felt herself slump against the shoulder of her hunter. She knew she must get away. She must not be caught by those desperate men.

They were gone now, and only the sound of their plunging horses kept her aware of the great danger that confronted her. She told herself to think clearly, to put her fright aside so that her wits would save her. She heard the hoofbeats growing fainter, and as they receded, she felt her courage return.

She secured the reins to a tree branch so that her horse could not wander, and then she raised her voluminous velvet skirt and began to untie her four petticoats. One by one she dragged them to her ankles and stepped out of them until there was a large heap of crumpled linen at her feet. She was colder now, but her movements were freer. Bending down once more, she pulled the little knife strapped to the top of her boot from its sheath. Her father had given her that knife so that she could cut herself free from the stirrup should she ever fall. Now she put it to another use, cutting long strips from her petticoats and spreading them around her like diapers.

It was hard work, and she felt herself grow tired long before the task was done. But at last there were enough of the linen rags for her to wrap each of her hunter's feet in muffling cloth, and she set to work on that task. She was certain that Saint Sebastien would still be searching for her, and she did not want chance noise to bring him to her side.

It was almost dark when she finished swathing and tying the horse's hooves, and she was much colder now. It was going to be a hard night. And she would have to ride through it if she were to escape her enemies.

She was about to pull herself up into the saddle once again when it struck her that the men hunting for her would be looking for a figure riding sidesaddle. She nodded to herself and unbuckled the girths of the saddle and pulled it from her hunter's back. She put it down with some little regret. It was a fine saddle, and had been made for her. If there was rain that night—and a covert look toward the tiny patch of sky overhead confirmed there would be—the saddle would be ruined. She thrust it under the thickest branches of a low-growing pine and told herself that it might not be too badly damaged.

With hardly more than a sigh, she cut the heavy velvet skirt up the front and up the back, then bent over one last time to secure the flapping hem around each ankle, making herself surprisingly serviceable breeches.

At last she was ready. She unfastened the reins from the branch, and taking a handful of mane in her left hand, vaulted clumsily onto the hunter's back. It took her a few moments to accustom herself to riding astride and bareback, but she had been excellently trained, and it did not take her long to get her balance and adjust her seat for the ride ahead.

The hunter was fairly rested, and did not object to moving off into the deep woods. She tried to glance back toward the track, but the dusk was thick, and the track was lost in the gloom.

It was more than twenty minutes later that she heard the sounds of pursuit once more. She pulled in the hunter and listened carefully, trying to discover where the hoofbeats were coming from. She thought for a moment that she had been mistaken and that it was only the sound of branches knocking together, but it was not so. The next gust of wind brought the sound to her, louder. She realized, as she listened, that the hunters had fanned out and were moving through the forest in a wide swath. She threw her head back to stifle a sob, and felt despair grow in her like some exotic disease. Her escape seemed so useless, so meaningless. But the memory of the cruel smile on Saint Sebastien's face forced her to action. Cautiously she urged the big horse forward, hardly daring to go faster than a walk.

Night had settled in in earnest, and the dark slowed her progress even more. The third time she found herself almost swept from her mount's back, she was ready to weep with vexation. Only the continuing sound of the search near her kept her silent.

There were scratches on her face and arms now, and her hair was disheveled now that her hat was gone. Even one of her pigskin gloves was torn, and she felt her hand growing cold as the wind touched her skin and lashed out at the trees, bending them before its invisible might.

Suddenly Madelaine saw a glimmer of movement off to her left, and her horse shied, snorting.

There was a soft moaning in the forest as the trees braced themselves against the onslaught of the gale.

Madelaine reached for her boot to grip the knife there, thinking that if she were to be ravished by Saint Sebastien's men, she would at least fight them until she was overpowered. She might even be able to kill one or two of them before they could rape her.

A shape in the brush moved nearer, and her horse almost bolted.

She sat up straighter, holding the sliding, frightened hunter firmly in check. She looked through the woods, and in the dark saw a low, gray shape crouching in the underbrush. Her eyes narrowed as she stared; then, trembling violently, she saw it plainly and knew it was a wolf.

Involuntarily she looked about swiftly for more of the sinister gray forms, but she could see no others. Her pulse was as loud as the wind in her ears, but she held her fear as firmly as she held her horse.

The hoofbeats behind her were nearer, and she could hear an occasional shout as Saint Sebastien and his men called to one another in the darkness. Carried on the wind, their words had the eerie sound of madness in them, as if the air itself was touched with their malevolence.

Now the wolf circled in front of her, keeping well back from the terrified horse. It whined, then yelped, starting away into the dark, then once again circling back toward Madelaine, never coming close enough to panic her mount into bolting.

Madelaine hesitated, studying the strange behavior of the wolf. She had almost satisfied herself that it was alone, that no pack ran with it, when it began to bark. It was a strange sound, not like the friendly tumult of dogs. This was lorn, ageless, as desolate as the mountain crags, as primeval as the close-crowded trees around her. Something about that wild, lonely cry tugged at her heart, and she longed for one insane moment to be able to run on four paws away from the horror behind her.

The hunting party grew nearer, and Madelaine fought down her rising panic. She forced herself to watch the wolf, looking for that one moment when the strange gray animal would be far enough away that she could push past it without terrifying her horse still further. Thinking of the monstrous men who chased her, and comparing them to the gaping mouth of the wolf, Madelaine knew that she would much prefer to take her chances with the wolf. That, at least, would be a clean death. Or she might be able to kill it. As her horse reared, she wondered if she could force him close enough to the wolf to trample it into the ground with flashing hooves.

With a kind of desperate bravado, she reached up with one hand and tugged the comb out of her hair, so that her dark tresses streamed out behind her on the wind. She held on to her plunging horse with her knees, waiting.

Now the wolf had circled back again and was whining more loudly, starting off into the darkness of the forest, then moving back where she could see it once again.

Quite suddenly Madelaine remembered something that Saint-Germain had said to her in that elegant little room at Hôtel Transylvania. The words sounded in her mind as clearly as if he had spoken them in her ear. *"Your soul is like a sword, bright, shining, and will always pierce through deception to the truth. Do not doubt what it tells you, ever, Madelaine."*

She shot one swift look over her shoulder, then kicked at her horse's sides, moving away from the hunters into the dark, following the liquid gray shape of the wolf.

It seemed to her that she had been following the wolf for half the night, even farther into the forest, when she saw ahead of her the looming shape of a building. She slowed her horse and carefully approached the structure, saying nothing, making no noise that might alert the inhabitants that she was near.

The first few drops of rain had fallen, and Madelaine was achingly exhausted. She circled the building once and was startled to realize that it was an ancient church, abandoned, yet intact, its heavy arches and squat pillars indicating its great age.

Gratefully she slid off the horse, and after looking over her shoulder nervously, pushed on the thick oaken door of the church.

Old metal screamed as the doors were opened, but the ancient hinges grudgingly admitted her. She stared into the darkness of the narthex, denser than the dark of the rainy night. On impulse she turned and tugged at the bridle, pulling the English hunter into the church. His muffled hooves made little sound on the stone floor, and he whickered once, before coming to stand in the little space of the narthex.

Madelaine secured one rein to the door bolt, then turned into the church itself, noticing that in spite of its obvious disuse, the altar was still in place, and there was a slight smell of incense on the musty air. She walked up the aisle, and genuflected automatically before the crucifix, murmuring a brief, incoherent prayer of thanks.

When she turned again, she saw him.

"Madelaine," he said in his deepest tone, and held out his small hands to her. He was dressed in a military-like uniform, with somewhat loose breeches and a heavily frogged tunic of bottle green on black. He wore high cavalry boots and a fur hat, and the smile in his dark eyes filled her heart.

"Saint-Germain," she cried, and ran into his arms, pressing her face into the curve of his neck.

"Hush, hush," he whispered, holding her tightly against him. "You must not be afraid, Madelaine, my heart. You are safe here. Saint Sebastien will not come onto consecrated ground."

The words caught her, and she said rather wildly, "If you are here, this cannot be consecrated ground. The Sisters have said—"

Saint-Germain gave a bitter laugh. "The Sisters do not know everything. All of my kind can walk on consecrated ground. Most of us are buried in it." He felt her stiffen in his embrace. "There. I have said it, and you are horrified." He freed himself from her arms and went toward the altar. "It is not safe to have much light in here, for though the windows are small and high, it is possible we may be discovered." He pulled flint from his sleeve, and steel. "There are a few oil lamps in the choir," he said by explanation as he struck the spark.

In a moment a faint, soft glow suffused the choir, and Madelaine could see him more clearly. She noticed he was rather leaner in the face than she had seen him last, and he moved as one who had run a long way.

Behind the altar there were now revealed several huge murals, done in an antique style, showing a forbidding Christ with His hands spread to show the marks of the nails, surrounded by clusters of tiny saints and martyrs dressed in courtly garb of the eleventh century. To one side was a representation of what was probably Saint Jerome, for an old stylus pen was clasped in one hand, and a leather-covered book was opened with the other.

"I did not know," Madelaine whispered, moving toward the mural. "It is very beautiful, isn't it?"

Saint-Germain was looking steadily at her. "Very."

She turned to him. "How do you come to be here?"

"I said I would protect you." He came toward her and gently touched the scratches on her face and arms. "You are so much in need of protection."

She flushed at this. "I did well enough in the wood. I escaped and came here." She looked at him again. "The wolf . . . ?"

He shook his head ruefully. "I could not leave you to Saint Sebastien. I know you are brave, I know you are resourceful, but I feared for your safety."

She took his hands in hers and held them fast. "I am grateful, Saint-Germain. I do not like to think what would have happened . . ."

"And you feel safer with me, knowing what I am?" He looked into her face, and he felt his resolution weakening. He broke away from her.

She gave a little cry of entreaty. "Saint-Germain. Saint-Germain, don't do this. No. No. Listen to me. Please." The sound of her voice brought his reluctant eyes to hers. "What did you save me for, if you abandon me?"

His words were lightly ironic as he answered. "You know that what I want to do will not save you."

She reached out for him again. "But it is not so, Saint-Germain. You walk on consecrated ground. You are not damned if you do this."

"Not in the usual way, certainly," he agreed in a neutral voice.

She studied his face in the dim light, seeing the shadow of agony there. Gently she came up to him again, and gently she reached to touch him, her fingers tracing the line of his jaw and the wry curl of his lips. "Communion is partaking of the Body and Blood of Christ, is it not?"

"You know that better than I," he said, trying to pull away from the temptation of her warm flesh.

"If blood is a sacrament, then what we have done is a sacrament." She was near him, and her eyes yearned for him.

"Oh, God," he said softly, in his private torment. "You are willing, but you do not know what may happen to you. Can't you see that my very desire makes me dangerous to you?" He had taken her by the arms and was shaking her tenderly. "Madelaine, I burn for you, but I cannot. I cannot."

"It is cold here, Saint-Germain. If you are not by me, I will die, and it will be a death that lasts until the Last Trumpet. You would not do that to me."

"No," he said, taking her into his arms again.

"Can you hold me and not love me?"

He was silent for some time, and there was only the soft sound of the rain, which had begun to fall heavily. "You are precious to me. I think I have longed for you always."

She turned slightly in the circle of his arms. "Then don't deny me," she whispered hungrily. "Touch me, oh, touch me."

His hands were already on her, and then he lifted her, carrying her to the rear of the sanctuary, laying her on the old choir stall. As the saints and martyrs watched, with lips and hands he worshiped her.

Excerpt from a letter written by l'Abbé Ponteneuf to Madelaine de Montalia at her aunt's husband's estate, Sans Désespoir, dated October 28, 1743:

. . . I was most pleased to learn of your esteemed father's visit, and I look forward to several happy hours in his company. You, I know, will welcome his loving care and attention, for certainly it is a wise daughter who cherishes the wisdom and condescension which must mark every father's love.

Your little sojourn in the country is surely a delight to you. No doubt you have spent much time in pleasant walks and delightful rides through the countryside. Although I am not familiar with Sans Désespoir, I know that the scenery there is much admired. You must certainly be grateful to le Marquis d'Argenlac for this opportunity to recruit your strength for your fête. Not every young woman is so fortunate as to have relatives who are willing to cater to her in this way.

. . . Your father has charged me with the happy task of explaining to you the duties of a wife, since it is hoped that that joyous change in estate is not far off. Let me urge you to reflect on the words in Scripture, and the virtues attributed to Our Lord's Mother, the Immaculate Virgin, Who is ever willing to aid us in salvation for the sake of Her Son. Think of this holy Mother's chastity, of her devotion, of her selflessness, of her humility, of her generosity, of her charity, of her meekness in submission to the will of the Holy Spirit. These are qualities which must be the goal of every wife, though none can hope to attain such perfection. It will be your honor to serve your husband in all things, gladly to accept his word as your law, and to submit to his demands, that you might be fruitful and blessed with children. School yourself to think only of his good, of his needs, and that way you will find true happiness.

You have been enough about the world to know that there are wives who set themselves in opposition to their husbands, who defy their marriage vows and wallow in sensuality and the lusts of the flesh. What a dreadful fate is theirs! They are despised by their families, scorned by their children, and when at last they die—alone, friendless, without the adoring presence of their children—then they see their sins and know that they have just begun to taste the bitter draft prepared for them.

While your father is in Paris, I hope we may discuss this more, so that you will be fully sensible to the joys of a woman in her married duties. It is not seemly for a man, let alone a priest, to say more, but your father, and certainly your aunt, will be willing to describe the rites of marriage and the privileges of the marriage bed. More I am not able to say to you, except to assure you that the man who finds favor in the eyes of your family will be best able to instruct you in what he finds most becoming.

You will return soon, as I understand it, and begin the final preparations for the fête. It is said that you will have an opera sung on that occasion, by le Comte de Saint-Germain. A great honor for you, my daughter, and one of which I am certain you are sensible. For a man of his experience to be pléased to make you such a present must certainly put you much in his debt. You will I know, acknowledge this with the humility and grace that so distinguish you.

I charge you to remember me to your aunt and her husband, and assure them that they are always in my prayers, as you are, my daughter.

With the love that Christ bade us have for one another, and with the blessings of my hand and your father's hand, I am always

Your reverent cousin,
l'Abbé A. R. Ponteneuf, S.J.

6

Ambrosias María Domingo y Roxas held the contraptions aloft so that Hercule could see them better in the dim light of the cellar. "There. It is to Prinz Ragoczy's specific design: horn and wood on the braces, and a joint of steel and formed bronze. The straps are of leather, and they buckle so." He demonstrated this, fitting one of the braces along his arm.

The part of Hôtel Transylvania where the sorcerers had set up their alchemical laboratory was at the lowest section of the cellars, almost directly under the north wing, where the gambling rooms were. A storeroom directly overhead blocked any noise or smells, preventing the Guild's activities from disturbing the elegant throng.

Hercule glanced uneasily around. He did not like these strange men and the somber middle-aged woman who worked with them. And the strange device that Domingo y Roxas was showing him looked more like an instrument of torture than anything else. "What are they?"

Beverly Sattin answered the question from his place by the athanor. "They are braces. They are for your legs." He indicated the crutches that Hercule used. "His Highness gave us the design because he wanted you to walk again."

Hercule moved forward awkwardly, hating himself for being crippled. He realized in a rush that he was near weeping. He put one hand to his eyes, and almost fell as he overbalanced.

The stern expression on the woman's face relaxed somewhat. "You hate your infirmity, do you not?" Iphigenie Lairrez asked in a deep, melodic voice.

For a moment his bitterness overwhelmed him, and he said nothing. At last he became aware of the sorcerers' eyes on him, and he muttered, "Yes."

"Eh bien, then why not try these braces? The Prinz has said it is his desire that you have the use of your legs, and he has assured us that these will be most successful."

Hercule knew nothing of this Prinz they spoke of so reverently, but he did know that his master, le Comte de Saint-Germain, thought highly of the strange people working in this cellar. He hesitated, then said, "But I cannot walk. A surgeon was sent for. He has come twice. He has said it is impossible. See?" He steadied himself and swung one leg. "It bends. Which is something. But if I put my weight on it, I fall." In an eruption of self-disgust that startled him as much as the sorcerers, Hercule threw one of his crutches across the room, and leaned heavily on the large oaken table beside him.

Mme. Lairrez put her hands on her hips. "That was foolish. If you are helpless, then you would be wise to make use of whatever is offered. Including these braces." She bent to pick up the crutch, but did not return it to him.

Sattin turned again to the athanor, murmuring a few words about ingrates in English.

"Very well," Hercule said defiantly as he looked around the darkened cellar. Even with four branches of candles, the gloom of the place was oppressive, made more so by the stink coming from the strange oven they called an athanor.

The woman came closer to him, her compassionate eyes belying the severity of her face. "I have your crutch, if that is what you want. If it is not, then let me help you to put on one of these braces. We are under a certain obligation to Prinz Ragoczy. You may help us discharge a part of that obligation." As she spoke, she motioned to Domingo y Roxas. "A chair, Ambrosias. The poor man is about to fall."

At that moment Hercule hated her for her acuity. He glared at her and the others as he settled cautiously into the old backless chair that was set for him. When he had made himself as comfortable as possible, he waited tensely for what the sorcerers might do.

Domingo y Roxas nodded, then took one of the braces and knelt at Hercule's feet. "I must remove your boot, señor. I will do it carefully, so that you are not hurt." He took the heel of Hercule's boot in his hand. "Perhaps you had best hold onto the arms of your chair. I do not know if I will do this well."

The broad coachman's boot was drawn off, and Hercule admitted to himself that the little Spanish sorcerer had done it well, and kindly.

"Now, you see," he went on, setting the boot aside, "I must untie the lacing of your breeches. So. And now, I lift your foot." He raised Hercule's leg. "Now, you see, here is where this fits against the foot. It is not unlike a sole of a shoe, is it?"

Hercule grudgingly admitted that the piece of the mechanism against his foot was indeed something like a sole.

"And this, do you see?" He set the two side bars in position, bars which were made of horn and wood. "This is what makes the brace strong. Here, on each side, you see, is the joint. His Highness tells us that it works like knees do. The steel above and the bronze below. You see the tongue of the laminate here and here?" He pointed to small projections that came down at the front of each knee joint on the brace. "That will keep you from having the joint bend too far backward. It will only bend forward, just as your own legs do."

Tentatively Hercule reached down and fingered the small projections. "But is it strong enough?"

Domingo y Roxas frowned. "I would not have thought so, but see." He picked up the other brace, straightened the joint, and then tried to force the thing to bend the wrong way. When he put the brace down again, he was panting a little with his exertion. "I am surprised myself."

Hercule had watched this demonstration in dawning amazement. He had tried to convince himself that he would grow resigned to being crippled, and had known this was not so. Now he sensed a chance, a promise he had never thought to have. He swallowed hard and felt his throat tighten.

"This strap goes, so." Domingo y Roxas fitted it around the majordomo's thigh and tightened the buckles. "The leather is braided, so that it will move with you, and of double thickness for extra strength." He stood up. "There. You may try it."

As Hercule looked up, he saw that the other sorcerers were watching him intently, and he licked his lips. "I do not know . . ."

Mme. Lairrez came toward him, holding out a hand to him. "Steady yourself, my good man."

Reluctantly Hercule took the proffered hand. "Thank you, Madame," he said stiffly as he pulled himself to his feet, using the one crutch to keep himself upright. He swayed for a moment, then stood, his weight on the crutch and his hand in Mme. Lairrez' firm grip.

"Go on," she said to him, her very sternness an encouragement.

Hercule nodded brusquely, then hesitated while he prepared himself. Gingerly he began to shift his weight, expecting at every moment to tumble to the floor. But the brace held. He stood almost erect, and though his leg trembled, it did not bend. Seconds turned into minutes, and slowly, slowly, Hercule let out his breath, saying in awe, "God and the Devil!"

It was like a signal to the others. Sattin gave a curious little whoop and clapped his hands. Domingo y Roxas crossed himself as he felt tears come to his eyes. Mme. Lairrez let go of Hercule's hand and stood back smiling.

"The Prinz was right," Sattin said to himself.

"We must learn this secret," Domingo y Roxas said softly. "It is a great secret."

But Mme. Lairrez was more cautious. "Time to learn this when the man walks," she said measuringly as she watched Hercule.

At those words Hercule's face fell in a manner that would have been comic if he had not had his very soul in his anguished eyes. "But I stand," he said.

"That is not the same thing." She gave him his other crutch. "You will have to try."

Revulsion filled him. He tried to push the crutch away.

"Do not be foolish," Mme. Lairrez snapped. "You have not walked since you were assaulted. Even if the braces do work and you will be able to walk, you have not used your legs with your weight on them for many days. You are weak. And you are unfamiliar with the workings of the brace. It will do you no good to fall."

This time when she held out the crutch, he took it, fitting it under his arm resignedly.

"Now," Mme. Lairrez said. "Come toward me."

Hercule gripped the crutches and made his first uncertain step, letting the brace take his weight for an instant before he allowed his crutch to support him. His next step was as it had been since Saint Sebastien had broken his knees, a dragging shuffle that embarrassed him more than hurt him. He tried again, rather more confidently. The brace still held. He stopped. "Give me the other one," he commanded them.

"Certainly," Mme. Lairrez said, and moved the chair for him to sit once more.

This time the fitting went faster, and as Mme. Lairrez adjusted the brace, Sattin said to Domingo y Roxas, "Perhaps Prinz Ragoczy knows of a remedy for Cielbleu."

Domingo y Roxas thought of their Guild Brother lying in an attic room, his face vacant. "No," he said sadly after this consideration. "Horn and wood and steel and bronze cannot restore a mind, my friend."

Sattin nodded after a moment. "It was a hope only. I did not think it was possible." He raised his voice somewhat. "Majordomo, are you ready?"

Hercule was watching the adjustments that Mme. Lairrez made, concentration in every aspect of his body. "I will be so very shortly."

He had made three halting turns around the cellar, his confidence increasing as he familiarized himself with the braces, when the stout wooden door was thrown open.

Everyone stopped, looking fearfully toward the spill of light from the storeroom above. There was a figure in the door, made shapeless by the long traveling cloak that fell in thick velvet folds from the intruder's shoulders.

"Good afternoon," Saint-Germain said as he stepped into the cellar, pulling the door to behind him.

Sattin was the first to speak. "Highness, we were not expecting—"

"Neither was I." Saint-Germain cut him short.

Hercule made his way toward his master. "Comte," he said, smiling at last. "The Prinz of these sorcerers has done this for me." He was aware that it was a breach of social rules for him to address his master in this way, and felt a certain chagrin, anticipating the sharp rebuke reminding him of their separate stations in life.

It did not come. "I am pleased to see you so, Hercule. In a little time I expect to install you as my coachman." Although he spoke with sincerity, there was a certain preoccupation in his wry smile.

"We have made the braces to your specifications, Highness," Sattin said in English. "Horn and wood bonded together in opposition; a most innovative concept."

Saint-Germain shrugged. "Hardly innovative. The Scythians were using bows made in this way a thousand years ago. Adapting the technique to Hercule's needs was a simple matter." He took off his point-edged tricorne and pulled his cloak from his shoulders, revealing traveling dress of dark-wool-drab coat with fur edging at cuff and collar, in the Hungarian manner, over a cambric shirt and cravat of spotless white. His boots were high, with a wide-turned cuff just below the knee. His dark hair was unpowdered and confined at the nape of the neck with a simple black bow of very modest size. Save for his ruby stickpin, he wore no jewels. He tugged the black Florentine gloves from his small hands, frowning intently.

In a moment he seemed to recover himself. "I have been gone three days, Sattin," he said in English. "I am most pleasantly surprised to see what you have accomplished. It does you great credit, all of you. You may be sure that my gratitude will manifest itself in a manner useful to you."

"Thank you, Highness." Sattin bowed, then hesitated. "I wonder, Highness, if you have not decided on the expression of your appreciation, if I might make so bold as to request one of you."

Saint-Germain raised his fine brows in question. "Go on."

"It is the athanor, Highness. To make the jewels, we must have a newer one, one that is more sound and can take greater heat. To be sure," he added quickly, "this is a fine one, but it is not adequate to the task."

"I know," Saint-Germain said shortly. "Very well, Sattin. I will consider it." He turned away from the lean English sorcerer to Domingo y

Roxas and addressed him in Spanish. "This is most excellently done, and shows precision of thought. How much of the work did you do, my friend?"

Obviously flustered by this familiarity, the little Spaniard stumbled over his words. "I . . . We . . . My sorer and I . . . We carried out your orders, Highness. We prayed at each step of the way, and calculated the influence of the heavens so that the work would prosper."

"Admirable." Saint-Germain's tone was sardonic. "You and Madame Lairrez and Sattin. Who else."

Domingo y Roxas bowed very low. "We are entirely at your service, Prinz Ragoczy."

"I see. And Cielbleu?" Saint-Germain asked him very gently.

"He does not improve. The surgeon has seen him, and says that there is nothing he can do." He made a gesture compounded of frustration and despair. "What can a surgeon know? He has knives to cut the body, and when the patient dies, then he has a multitude of reasons why it was not he who brought the death."

"It is a pity." Saint-Germain now spoke in French with his slight Piedmontese accent. "I am willing to have other physicians treat him, if that is your wish. I doubt that they will be able to help him much, however."

Mme. Lairrez nodded. "So I think. It is not his body that suffers, but his mind." She stared down at her hands. "As you say, Highness, it is a pity."

Saint-Germain had a certain grim amusement in his voice. "I see we understand one another tolerably well, Madame."

Hercule, who had kept to the side, puzzlement on his rough features, interrupted now. "You are the Prinz Ragoczy they keep talking about!"

By not so much as a hair did Saint-Germain appear shocked at this accusation. "Among other things, yes. I come of a very old line."

"I . . . I did not mean . . ." Hercule stammered, horrified at his own temerity.

"It is not a title I generally use." Saint-Germain was at his most urbane. "But in certain circles I have a reputation associated with it."

Thoroughly flustered now, Hercule looked away from the keen, mocking eyes of his master. "Of course. I do not question—"

"Of course you do. And you deserve my answer. I am one of an ancient Carpathian house. Through the years, those of my blood have had many titles, and have allied themselves with the first families for centuries." He smiled a little sadly as memories stirred. "I believe one of the Orsini popes was in our number. And there were a few of the Caesars in my line. But that was a long time ago." He had a fleeting, anguished memory of Medicean Florence but could not speak of it.

Two of the sorcerers were obviously impressed with Saint-Germain's recitation of his noble credentials, but Mme. Lairrez was not. "An illustrious line is something to be proud of," she allowed grudgingly. "But you must earn the respect bestowed on its members, or you are naught."

"Very true," he admitted. "Have you complaints of me?"

She shook her head, ignoring the whispered corrections of her companions. "No, Highness. I do not." She turned suddenly from the penetrating dark eyes that he had leveled on her.

Satisfied, he nodded. "Bon. I would not like to think that you found me wanting." He motioned to Hercule. "Come. Follow me. I have instructions for you. As for you"—he indicated the sorcerers—"your new athanor will be in your hands by the end of this week. You have my word. I hope it is sufficient bond, Madame Lairrez?" With an ironic bow, he went to the door, Hercule trailing in his wake.

The sorcerers said nothing until the door closed behind him.

"Now, Hercule," Saint-Germain said as they climbed the stairs to the storeroom, "I have work for you. While you get the use of your legs again, you will continue as majordomo of this establishment."

Hercule, moving as fast as he could, panted a little as he answered. "Yes, master. What am I to do?"

"I want you to watch all who come here, particularly any you see with Saint Sebastien or Beauvrai. If you suspect anything, let me know as soon as may be. Take care not to be noticed."

"Saint Sebastien?" Hercule demanded, stopping his ascent and glaring up at Saint-Germain, two stairs above him.

"Yes." He waited as he watched wrath mount in Hercule's face. "You will not know him, Hercule. You will be my majordomo, and what has my majordomo to do with Saint Sebastien?"

"He crippled me!" Hercule cried out.

"With those braces, you will not be crippled much longer." He went a little farther up the stairs, then stopped. "Hercule," he said softly, "I rely on you in this. Keep silent about all you know of me, and you will yet be revenged on Saint Sebastien." He had reached the top of the flight now, and turned again toward the hallway stretching beyond.

"For vengeance on Saint Sebastien, I would protect the Devil himself."

Saint-Germain laughed softly. "Would you?" He shook his head, then said in quite another voice, "Tell Roger to have my coach ready tonight at midnight. Tell him that it concerns a violoncellist he knows of who is in great travail. I have promised to help this musician, for the danger grows greater."

Hercule pulled himself up even with his master. "I will."

Saint-Germain looked down at the cloak he still carried over his shoulder. "I must get into more appropriate dress. Tell Roger to meet me in my quarters. And, Hercule."

"Yes, master."

"As you value your life and soul, keep your silence."

Hercule stood dumbfounded as Saint-Germain favored him with a terse, mirthless smile. "If you do not hold your soul in such esteem, then keep silent for the debt you owe to me, for my life and soul are also forfeit." He turned away at those words and strode down the hall.

Text of a letter from the physician André Schoenbrun to le Comte de Saint-Germain, dated October 30, 1743:

> André Schoenbrun, physician in la rue d'Ecoulè-Romain, presents his compliments to le Comte de Saint-Germain, and his regrets that the man, Cielbleu, did not recover from the beating he had suffered. He asks that le Comte understand that it was not lack of skill on the part of this physician, but that the beating was too severe to allow for recovery.
>
> On the other matter which le Comte was kind enough to discuss with him last night: the physician Schoenbrun wishes now to assure le Comte that he is willing to assist le Comte in the venture he outlined, and begs him to believe that the physician will meet him at two of the clock at the gates of the hôtel Cressie.
>
> As per his discussion with le Comte, physician Schoenbrun agrees to take the coach provided by le Comte and escort the woman le Comte will bring to him to le couvent de la Miséricorde et la Justice de le Rédempteur in Brittany, where she is to be put into the care of her sister, l'Abbesse Dominique de la Tristesse de les Anges.
>
> Le Comte has given the physician to understand that a certain peril attends this venture, and for that reason the physician willingly accepts le Comte's offer of an armed guard. Obedient to le Comte's instructions, the physician will seek no lodging, but rather drive through the night. The physician also promises to undertake to provide himself with sword and pistol, and expresses his appreciation to le Comte for the timely warning.
>
> Because le Comte has suggested that the woman to be escorted might well be somewhat deranged, the physician will take this opportunity to supply those composers which he feels will be of benefit to the woman.
>
> Until the second hour of tomorrow, the thirty-first of October, at the gates of hôtel Cressie, I have the honor to remain
>
> > Yours to command,
> > André Schoenbrun, physician

7

It was rather closer to four than three in the morning when le Comte de Saint-Germain at last strolled into the fine gambling rooms in the north wing of Hôtel Transylvania. He was dressed in a wide-skirted coat of black silk, and his usual black small clothes and hose. But instead of a black waistcoat, this time he wore one of the most pristine white satin embroidered with white floss. Against it his scattering of diamonds shone with additional brightness, and the ruby in the thick fall of Mechlin lace at his neck seemed to have darkened.

Le Duc de Valloncaché looked up bleary-eyed from the rubber of picquet he was playing with le Baron Beauvrai. "So late, Comte? I quite despaired of seeing you."

Saint-Germain bowed to him and smiled a little. "I fear the business I had earlier this evening detained me a trifle. But I hope you will not hold that against me. I am entirely at your service now."

De Valloncaché chuckled. "I fear I must protest this cavalier treatment of our engagement. I cannot have it spread about that there is one better than I at rouge et noir."

"If there were," Beauvrai said nastily, "it would not be that impostor. The game, de Valloncaché." He waved his elegant cream-colored lace back from his hands and smoothed the front of his glass-green brocaded coat, unbuttoning two more of the tiny ruby buttons that hid in the rust embroidery that replaced the revers on this coat. Under it he wore pantaloons of rose silk and a waistcoat of lemon and orange stripes. His hose were of a soft fawn color tonight, and his shoes were Turkish blue.

Shrugging, de Valloncaché said, "What am I to do, Comte? Beauvrai has the right, and I fear our game must wait."

Saint-Germain smiled easily. "I am willing to postpone our match, or to stay and wait your pleasure this evening."

Le Marquis Chenu-Tourelle, who had overheard this, turned to his companion, le Duc de la Mer-Herbeux, and gave him a knowing wink. "And what was it, Saint-Germain, that kept you away so long?"

If Saint-Germain caught the innuendo in the words, he gave no sign of it. "I was visiting a musician, who is leaving soon for a long visit away from Paris. I wanted to pay my respects, and, as such things will, it took more time than I had thought it would."

"Musicians!" Beauvrai scoffed. "When do those of our station visit strummers and plunkers?"

"He is a composer, Beauvrai," de Valloncaché said, at his most conciliating.

Beauvrai was not put off. "Paying respects to a musician!" he scoffed. "I tell you, that man is a charlatan." He picked up his hand once more and refused to look again at Saint-Germain.

"Beauvrai's in an ugly mood tonight," de Valloncaché said by way of apology to Saint-Germain. "I'm winning, you see. He cannot bear to have me win."

Unruffled by Beauvrai's rudeness, Saint-Germain bowed slightly and said, "If it falls in well with your plans, de Valloncaché, I will play hoca until you are ready to pit your skill against mine." He turned away, prepared to walk toward the far corner where the banned hoca was played, but he was stopped by a word from le Marquis Chenu-Tourelle, delivered in a low tone, but malicious, and loud enough to carry.

"I call it damned convenient that le Comte should come so tardily that he need not risk so much as the diamonds on his vest in play."

Although he did not turn toward that mocking voice, Saint-Germain addressed him in words that carried by their very softness. "If there are those here who seek to play with me, I am more than willing to accept the challenge of a game. Let them but name their pleasure." He stood, a neat figure in black and white at the center of that gorgeous room, one hand still holding an unfashionably short cane, the other just fingering the hilt of his dress sword. He seemed in that moment to have gained several inches on his moderate height, filling the room with his presence.

Le Marquis Chenu-Tourelle hesitated, and when he spoke again, he had lost much of his cocksureity. "We play picquet here, at ten louis the point."

Saint-Germain smiled. "Why not twenty, to make it worth your while?" At last he gave up his position at the center of the room, coming across the thick Belgian carpet to the table where Chenu-Tourelle sat with his friends le Duc de la Mer-Herbeux and Baltasard Aubert, Baron d'Islerouge. At the next table, le Duc de Vandonne turned from his card game with le Chevalier de la Sept-Nuit, and one of them nodded to d'Islerouge.

"Which of you," Saint-Germain said as he took his seat, lifting the skirts of his coat to keep them from being crushed, "is going to give himself the pleasure of fleecing me?"

"It was my challenge, I believe," Chenu-Tourelle said quickly, with a sharp glance at de Vandonne.

"I will be delighted." Saint-Germain smiled tightly.

Somewhat belatedly, d'Islerouge blurted out, "No. Chenu-Tourelle. I have a claim to the next game. Let me play the first rubber."

"Well?" Saint-Germain raised his brows, waiting. "Which is it to be?"

D'Islerouge turned startled eyes on Chenu-Tourelle. "You have been playing all evening," he reminded le Marquis. "I have not done much tonight. Nom du nom, but I am bored. Let me play the first rubber. If I lose, you take up the gauntlet."

Chenu-Tourelle moved aside with the faintest of nods to le Marquis d'Islerouge, a sly smile in his dissipated young face that contrasted oddly with the almost virginal look of his attire: pale-blue-satin coat, waistcoat of silver brocade; small-clothes hose, and lace of impeccable if rather wilted white. He slid a stack of gold louis across the table and nodded to de Vandonne. "I propose to back d'Islerouge, at whatever odds you like. Who will take my wager?"

There was a rustle of excitement in the room, and a few of the late-staying gamblers drifted toward the table, among them a long-headed, lean and skittish young English Earl who resembled his own high-bred horses to an uncomfortable degree. These men had a hunger in them, the hunger of risk, that could not be sated until they were ruined.

D'Islerouge dealt, and bent his attention to his cards, considering his discards and hoping to sum up the strength, if any, of Saint-Germain's hand.

Compared to his opponent, Saint-Germain was almost negligent in his play, discarding almost with indifference, a slight frown of impatience showing between his fine brows when d'Islerouge paused to consider his hand.

"But this is a jest," de Vandonne said softly. "Look at Saint-Germain. He's not even paying attention. Two hundred louis on d'Islerouge to win this hand and the rubber."

"Taken," de Valloncaché said promptly, having stopped his game to watch this match.

Three more men had come to the table now, sensing rare sport in the picquet game.

"I'll back Saint-Germain," said one voice too loudly.

Le Comte did not turn, but said, "Go home, Gervaise. Your Comtesse would be glad of your company."

Gervaise, already somewhat flushed with wine, turned a darker red and said in a sulky voice, "I only wanted to lend you my support."

"Did you?" Saint-Germain made another one of his casual discards and leaned back in his chair while d'Islerouge pondered what next to play.

"There! You will not have the ace if you discarded the king!" he said in triumph.

"I am devastated to disappoint you," Saint-Germain said as he revealed his traitorous ace. He looked at the men around the table, and knew that their attention was caught. "I trust one of you will keep count?"

The laugh that this remark evoked was not a pleasant one. D'Islerouge shifted uneasily as Saint-Germain shuffled the cards and dealt them.

This time the game went more slowly, though Saint-Germain still played in his offhand way. D'Islerouge knew now that he would not win nearly as easily as de Vandonne had said he would. The older man in black and white might seem disinterested, but d'Islerouge realized that it was because nothing he had done had yet tested Saint-Germain's wits.

"I wager a thousand louis that Saint-Germain will rise the winner by more than a hundred points," Gervaise d'Argenlac cried out, and Saint-Germain's brows twitched together in a moment of irritation.

"I'll match that, d'Argenlac," Chenu-Tourelle said lazily from his chair at d'Islerouge's elbow. "And go double that my man rises the winner by a hundred points."

The English Earl laid a stack of guineas on the table, saying in dreadful French, "I think that d'Islerouge will lose, and stake these in proof."

"My three, Comte," d'Islerouge said through tightened teeth.

"But my pacquet, Baron."

Most of the candles had guttered when the third rubber ended. Saint-Germain moved his chair back and regarded the money and scraps of paper on the table. "It is almost dawn, d'Islerouge."

The glow had long since gone out of d'Islerouge's face. Now he was haggard, and the nervous way he touched his cards showed most eloquently the straits he now found himself in. "I did not realize . . . What do I owe you, Comte?"

Saint-Germain raised an eyebrow and looked sardonically at Gervaise d'Argenlac. "What is the amount? I am certain you know. Pray tell the Baron."

Gervaise licked his lips, then laughed, saying, "You owe Saint-Germain eighteen thousand, two hundred forty-eight louis."

D'Islerouge blanched at this figure. "I . . . I will need time, Comte. I did not realize . . ."

Saint-Germain waved this away. "Certainly, Baron. Take all the time you need. I will await your convenience." He rose now, still neat, even his powdered hair flawlessly in place. "Come, de Valloncaché, do me the honor of your arm to your carriage."

"Of course," de Vandonne said nastily in a voice loud enough to cut across other conversations, "we understand why Saint-Germain is anxious to leave."

There was a mutter at this, for many of the men had lost a great deal of money in those three hours of play.

De Valloncaché, counting his winnings, looked across the table. "Be a good loser, de Vandonne." He turned to Saint-Germain. "I will be with you in a moment, Comte. But you have added to my riches tonight. I want to settle with Chenu-Tourelle and Broadwater."

The English Earl was already handing over two tall roleaus of guineas to de Valloncaché, saying, "Well, my luck was in tonight, but I was too cautious. You were right to risk all, Duc. It's a lesson to me."

"It's a lesson to *me*," d'Islerouge murmured darkly, and turned to hear what de Vandonne whispered to him.

"Forty-two thousand louis!" Gervaise crowed, giddy with success as he pushed up to Saint-Germain. "Forty-two thousand louis! Now Claudia will see that I do not always lose."

Saint-Germain was unmoved. "No, you do not always lose," he said softly. "Do not be foolish with your winnings, Gervaise."

Le Comte d'Argenlac dismissed this warning with a wave of his hand. "I know my luck is with me, Comte. If I am doing well tonight, think of the All Hallows' fête at Maison Libellule. If my luck holds, I will be a millionaire again." He smiled dreamily at this prospect.

Worried by this, Saint-Germain put one small, beautiful hand on Gervaise's arm and turned the full force of his compelling eyes on him. "D'Argenlac," he said, his voice musical and low, "do not gamble. Do not think that you will win at Maison Libellule. Do not sacrifice what you have gained."

Gervaise laughed lightly. "Oh, I know you will not be at the fête. Claudia told me that you will have your musicians at our hôtel to rehearse that little opera of yours. But there will be other games, Comte. You need not concern yourself with me." He sauntered off, more drunk with his winnings than with wine.

Saint-Germain was still staring after him when he heard de Vandonne speaking once more. "You saw how he played. He hardly looked at his cards. Yet he won."

There was a sharpness in de Valloncaché's tone now. "Leave it alone, de Vandonne! D'Islerouge lost in fair play, and that's the end to it."

"Fair play?" d'Islerouge demanded, color mounting in his drawn cheeks.

The room had suddenly become very quiet. No one spoke as all eyes turned to Saint-Germain.

For a few moments le Comte did nothing. Then, quite slowly, he rounded on d'Islerouge and said easily, "Pray be direct with me, Baron. I gather you think that I have cheated you."

D'Islerouge swallowed hard. "Yes."

"I see," Saint-Germain said, his eyes narrowing.

"Don't be any more foolish than God made you, Baltasard," de Vallon-caché snapped.

Behind him, Baron Beauvrai barked out one derisive laugh. "He's a damned coward. Wouldn't meet me when I tried to call him out." He flicked his lace handkerchief over the brocade of his coat. "Common!"

Now that he had actually accused Saint-Germain, d'Islerouge felt a cold, sinking fear that the elegant foreigner might be as successful a swordsman as he was a card player. "Well, Comte," he said with false bravado, "do you take my challenge?"

Saint-Germain's dark eyes studied him, revealing nothing of his thoughts. "It is not my habit to accept the challenge of a man young enough to be my son," he said slowly.

"Coward. Craven," de Vandonne taunted him.

"It is not you I will meet." Saint-Germain cut him short. "D'Islerouge has bought himself the right to say such things of me, but not you, mon Duc." He turned back to d'Islerouge, nodding once. "Very well. I accept your challenge, Baron."

Cold to the soles of his feet now, d'Islerouge bowed stiffly. "Appoint your seconds, and they may wait upon mine."

Saint-Germain held up his hand. "No, no, d'Islerouge. I have the right to choose the time and place. I choose this room, and now."

The hush which had hovered in the air deepened, and de Vandonne looked up in surprise.

"Certainly," Saint-Germain went on at his most urbane, "you have friends here who will act for you. I trust that I may have the support of de Valloncaché"—le Duc nodded as his name was mentioned—"and if you insist on form, I believe one of the other gentlemen here would be so obliging as to assist us."

"One will do," d'Islerouge said numbly. He looked about him rather wildly, passing over de Vandonne and saying, "De la Sept-Nuit, will you be my second?"

De la Sept-Nuit rose slowly. "Very well, Baltasard. I will accept the honor." He made no attempt to hide his scorn.

D'Islerouge, already regretting his challenge, writhed in mental agony at the smooth condemnation patent in every motion, every look of de lä Sept-Nuit. "Weapons?" he said in a voice he did not recognize as his own.

"Swords." Saint-Germain was already pulling off his black coat and tucking up the ruffled lace at his wrists. "If you ask the majordomo, I know he will provide you with dueling foils." He unbuckled his dress sword. "This is worse than useless," he said as he put it aside.

With a quick nod, de la Sept-Nuit went from the room, le Duc de Valloncaché in his wake.

Belatedly, d'Islerouge took off his coat, and then tugged at his fine lace jabot, pulling it from around his neck and tossing it aside, his eyes, on de Vandonne, filled with a curious combination of rage and puzzlement.

"Gentlemen," Saint-Germain was saying in a calm way, "if one or two of you would push these tables aside, so there is room enough . . . ?"

Even Beauvrai was happy to assist in this work, shoving the elegant cloth-topped table where he had been sitting all the way back to the wall. He dragged his chair after him and sank into it, smug satisfaction spread cat-like over his face.

Saint-Germain was about to remove his shoes when a glance at the window showed him the tarnished silver color of dawn. He stopped, and rebuckled the shoes.

D'Islerouge saw this and scoffed to de Vandonne, "He is asking for a fall, is he not? I wonder if he realizes that I will not be satisfied with less than his life."

De Vandonne grinned unevenly. "You will best him, mon Baltasard, and we will reward you." He took d'Islerouge's hand, holding slightly longer than was seemly.

"Are you ready?" de la Sept-Nuit asked as he came back into the room with de Valloncaché close behind him.

Saint-Germain straightened up. "May I suggest that you close and lock the door? It is not a time to be interrupted, I think." He glanced once around the room, then said to his second, "De Valloncaché, it might be wise if those candles were put out. They're almost guttered anyway. And if one of you would build up the fire . . ." He did not appear to think it odd that a French noble should be put to lackey's work.

"I will see to it," Chenu-Tourelle said quickly, moving to the grate where three logs smoldered. He pulled another log from a neat stack by the hearth, and with judicious care shoved it onto the dying fire. A spurt of flame took hold of the bark, crackling eagerly.

"What are your terms, d'Islerouge?" de Valloncaché asked in the suddenly silent room.

"To the death."

De Valloncaché bowed, and walked across the carpet to Saint-Germain. "The terms are—"

"I heard." Saint-Germain turned, testing his dueling sword in his hand. "I accept, on one condition."

"What condition?" d'Islerouge flung at him.

"That if I should best and spare you, you will reveal who put you up to this." He met d'Islerouge's startled gaze with his steady, intent one. "Have I your word?"

D'Islerouge looked about him again, this time rather wildly. "Yes, yes. Very well. You have my word." He turned his back on Saint-Germain.

"Have you any instructions for me?" de Valloncaché asked Saint-Germain, preparing to meet de la Sept-Nuit at the center of the room.

"My man Roger knows what to do, if anything must be done. Speak to him." He knelt and made the sign of the cross. "For any transgressions in my life, may I be absolved."

On the other side of the room, d'Islerouge burst out with derisive laughter.

But already de Valloncaché had met de la Sept-Nuit, and they were exchanging a few words. De la Sept-Nuit nodded and said, "Gentlemen, to your positions. Saint-Germain, if you will, to the east. D'Islerouge, in the west." His dress sword pointed out the areas. "Very well, gentlemen. Do you draw back?"

"No," snapped d'Islerouge.

"Saint-Germain?"

"No."

"Eh bien." De Valloncaché held his dress sword crossed with de la Sept-Nuit's while the duelists saluted each other, and then, bringing their blades sharply upward, they sprang back, barely moving fast enough to escape d'Islerouge's ferocious attack.

As d'Islerouge rushed forward, Saint-Germain moved his sword from his right to his left hand, turning to protect himself, and forcing d'Islerouge to expose his right side as he closed with him. Seeing his danger, d'Islerouge brought his blade down viciously, the point set to rake Saint-Germain's thigh.

There was a movement of Saint-Germain's wrist and d'Islerouge's blade glanced harmlessly away. Saint-Germain turned with the same controlled grace that was sometimes seen in Spanish bullrings. His hands were steady, and there was a set, sad smile on his mouth.

When d'Islerouge moved in on him again, he was more circumspect, handling his blade warily, unused to a left-handed opponent. He feinted in tierce, and was parried and very nearly pinked by the fast response from Saint-Germain. He stepped back, breathing a little faster, and set himself in form for a long fight.

Saint-Germain did not seem to press him, but d'Islerouge knew that he was losing ground. He did not have the eye or the skill of the older man, nor the strength of wrist. Saint-Germain fenced in the Italian manner, with subtlety and grace that might have awed d'Islerouge under other circumstances. Try as he would, he could not break through Saint-Germain's defenses. It was only a matter of time until Saint-Germain wore him down, exhausted him, and finished him.

Desperate now, he looked for a chance, and saw it. He made a clumsy feint, pretending to stumble, and saw Saint-Germain fall back, his point dropping while d'Islerouge recovered himself. In that instant he reached for a chair and threw it across the room.

It caught Saint-Germain at the shins, and brought out a cry of protest from the men who watched them.

"No!" Saint-Germain ordered, and his voice had absolute authority. His point flew up and he moved closer to d'Islerouge, his white waistcoat ghostly in the pale light.

D'Islerouge had struggled to his feet and he steadied himself to meet the attack. Steel scraped on steel and he was again driven back. He was sweating freely now, and he knew he stank of fear. Saint-Germain was still meticulous, and there was not even a slight moisture on his upper lip to betray his exertion.

They closed again, and this time Saint-Germain met d'Islerouge's attack with a stunning display of the art of fence, all but forcing him into the fireplace before deliberately stepping back to allow d'Islerouge a moment to regain his breath.

When the young man had somewhat recovered himself, Saint-Germain said, "I am willing to consider the matter settled between us, Baron."

"No . . . no . . . To the death." He brought up his blade and saw that the point wavered.

Saint-Germain sighed. "As you wish. En garde." Apparently he had lost the zest of the game, for now he drove a ruthless, forceful attack on d'Islerouge, determined to end it.

That end came suddenly. Saint-Germain's blade slipped inside d'Islerouge's defenses, but instead of pinking him in the shoulder or driving the point home through his chest, Saint-Germain passed under d'Islerouge's arm.

Startled, exhausted, d'Islerouge tried to follow this movement, and succeeded only in cutting a gash in Saint-Germain's white waistcoat before stumbling, to fall heavily on his back.

As he looked up, he saw Saint-Germain standing over him, his sword point only a few inches from his neck.

"I am satisfied, d'Islerouge. Are you?"

Anger gagged his words as d'Islerouge glared up at his adversary. He spat.

"I do not want to kill you," Saint-Germain said in an even tone. He held the foil steady, waiting.

"Very well." The words were so quiet that even Saint-Germain was not sure he heard them. D'Islerouge slid away from the point of the sword. "I am satisfied," he declared, his face ravaged by the agony of defeat.

Saint-Germain stood back and offered his hand to d'Islerouge, who ignored it. In a moment he turned away and looked at the seconds. "I leave you gentlemen to see that my condition is met. One or the other of you may deliver the information to me before sundown."

There was a rush of talk now, as all the pent-up tension released itself in an eruption of words.

Saint-Germain walked slowly across the room, feeling very tired. "I'm too old for this sort of thing," he said quietly as he came up to de Valloncaché.

"It certainly looked like it," de Valloncaché agreed with laughter. "That was the most beautiful match I have ever seen. Tell me, do you always fence left-handed?"

"Not always." Saint-Germain sank heavily into a chair and cast an involuntary glance at the windows. The sky was now a pale lilac, touched with long gold fingers. "Not a moment too soon."

De Valloncaché had walked away, and returned holding Saint-Germain's coat. He held it out, then muttered a word to himself.

"What?" Saint-Germain roused himself from his thoughts.

"Your waistcoat is ruined, Comte. That slash runs right down your ribs. It got the shirt, too. You're very lucky. He might have had you."

Only now did Saint-Germain finger the huge rent in his waistcoat. "Impressive," he said dryly.

This seemed to remind de Valloncaché of an earlier thought. "Whatever possessed you to wear a white waistcoat, Saint-Germain? You're always rigged out in black."

Saint-Germain smiled slowly as he rose and pulled his coat over his shoulder like a cape. "It was to express my purity of purpose, Duc." He put the dueling foil down and began to walk toward the door, where seven men still waited to congratulate him.

Excerpt of a letter from la Comtesse d'Argenlac to Mme. Lucienne Cressie, dated October 31, 1743; returned unopened to la Comtesse on January 11, 1744:

. . . My dear Lucienne, you do not know how much you and your superb music are missed by everyone. Last night Madelaine told me that she had been longing to hear you play at her fête, which is only four days away. This brings her entreaties as well as mine.

. . . We do not know how ill you have been. I am sorry to tell you that Achille tells us nothing, and try as I will, I can get no more from him than a certain confirmation that you are not well. If you will but allow it, I would willingly send my own physician to wait upon you. Custom may require that one consults a physician only with one's husband's consent, but I think we may agree that in your case this is a matter that is well beyond Achille's responsibility. . . .

It is quite true that Baltasard Aubert Baron d'Islerouge is betrothed to Olympe de les Radeux. Her brother is furious, but Beauvrai, who wanted the match from the first, is, of course, delighted. I remember you said these six months past that it would be so. You are always so acute an observer of us all, I wonder how you can bear not to receive visitors during your convalescence. I promise you the latest gossip would soon bring you out of yourself, and help you to good health once more.

Saint-Germain has told us that he will not compose for the violoncello again until you are sufficiently recovered to play. Now, you must take pity on us. To be robbed of your presence and Saint-Germain's music is beyond anything. He has written a little opera for our fête which I know would delight you. Tonight he brings his musicians to rehearse it, and I am quite filled with anticipation. Do recover quickly, so you may hear this work. I know it would please you.

. . . When I think of you locked away in that house, I feel almost dizzy. That dreadful man—forgive me for saying it of your husband, but we both know that he has no more use for you than a mouse has for a terrier—will not allow us to speak of you, and when we ask of you, says nothing but common-place things.

You must write to your uncle, or your sister. You cannot stay under that roof any longer, my dear. It wrings my heart to think of you in such travail. If there is anything I may do for you, any friend I may approach on your behalf, say you will let me know. Someone must be willing to help you to free yourself from that hateful Achille.

Come to me, my dear, and if you wish it so, you will never again return to hôtel Cressie. I offer you my hospitality for as long as you may need it. If you do not want to abide in Paris, or fear reprisal for your actions, I will plead with my brother. He has told me not to interfere, but he will change his mind when he hears of your circumstances. He must see that your plight is beyond that of marriage. Together we will convince him, if you will but give me the office to approach him.

I am sending this by messenger, and he has my instructions to see that it is indeed taken into the house. He will wait for an hour for your answer. If you can contrive to give him a message or a billet, he will bring either to me as quickly as may be.

Until I may see you for myself, my dear, believe me always

> Your most sincere and devoted friend,
> Claudia de Montalia
> Comtesse d'Argenlac

Part Three

le Baron Clotaire Odon
Jules Valince Pieux
de Saint Sebastien

Excerpt from a letter from le Baron Clotaire de Saint Sebastien to le Chevalier Donatien de la Sept-Nuit. One of a series dated November 1, 1743:

. . . For whose benefit did de Vandonne stage that little travesty yesterday morning at Hôtel Transylvania? You have sufficient wit to know that this kind of thing will not serve our purposes. And the murder of d'Islerouge was clumsily handled. No one will believe that poseur Saint-Germain killed d'Islerouge, not after that duel with some of the finest of our nobility as witnesses, and Saint-Germain wholly triumphant. It is far more likely to be thought that he was murdered to keep him from delivering the information he was in honor bound to reveal. That this is indeed the fact of the matter in no way lessens the stupidity every one of you has displayed in this business.

. . . Fast on the heels of that imbecilic duel came news that Lucienne Cressie has disappeared. Achille can offer no reasonable explanation for her disappearance, even after Tite and I asked him personal and forceful questions in private. If you should happen to call on Achille, you will find him abed, and his bruises may give you pause. Consider them carefully before you embark on any more foolishness.

The sacrifice of La Cressie's maidservant in her mistress's place was at best a stopgap measure. You have consistently failed to fulfill your obligations to the Circle, my dear Donatien. If you would stay with us, you must do better in future. Those parts that make you a man are almost as acceptable a sacrifice as the blood and virginity of young women. I beg you to remember this. For if you, through your actions, fail to deliver Madelaine de Montalia to the Circle for sacrifice at the winter solstice, then you will take her place as that sacrifice. I promise you this: you will be emasculated, de la Sept-Nuit, and your body used as the Circle sees fit. No doubt you will recall what was done to Lucienne Cressie? Much the same may, in other ways, be done to you. And when the Circle has finished with you, I will myself flay you. Think of your skin hanging in tatters from your hands and feet, Chevalier, and do not bungle again.

I suppose it is too much to hope that we will still have Gervaise d'Argenlac to command. I hear that he won a great deal last night, and even with his ability to create his own ruin, it will take a while for him to be in desperation again. He was useful to us when ruin faced him, but now he is a danger. He may be on his guard against us, which means we will have to tread carefully. If Chenu-Tourelle is to join the Circle, he must rectify our position with d'Argenlac. We risk discovery if one of us moves too much in d'Argenlac's affairs. He must be forced back to danger again, before his wife can secure herself with him. He must be made to believe that his wife is working to his destruction and complete subjugation. In that alone may we hope to have his help in taking Madelaine.

Be reminded then that I am depending on you to deliver Madelaine de Montalia to me not later than the tenth day of this month. She is mine, promised to me before she was born, and I will not be thwarted in my claim to her. I will require forty days to make her ready for the sacrifice, so that her will is amenable to ours. I must have that time with her or her death will be wasted. I will not tolerate any more interference. She must come to our altar to give up her virginity and her life to our Power. Each of us must use her after our own fashion, so that her blood may release us. Mere degradation is abhorrent to me. She must be annihilated, extinguished in body and soul utterly.

You, and Jueneport and Châteaurose, are charged with delivering this woman to me within ten days. I will accept no excuses if you fail. No reason will be sufficient. There will be no place in France far enough from me for you to hide, and no horse fast enough to carry you beyond my vengeance.

There is one more task for the Circle which must be settled soon. I have ordered a few of the Circle to search out this mysterious Prinz Ragoczy, who Le Grâce says is still in Paris. He may be difficult to find, for it is obvious that he is a man of great power and may be reluctant to share his learning with us. If we have him in our hands by the time we perform the ritual at the winter solstice, we will be in a position of even greater strength. It will be possible to force the secret of the jewels from him, and any other secrets he may possess—even, perhaps, the secret of the Philosopher's Stone, if he has it. His death, done properly to release his power to us, is much to be desired. To sacrifice Ragoczy and La Montalia together, one in the flesh and the other in the mind, will benefit every one of us greatly.

Be warned, then, Donatien. You have much to gain from the Circle: wealth, power, the ready fulfillment of your desires. But you have much more to lose. And your life is the very least of the risk. I beg you ever to be aware of that, so that you will be inspired to discharge your duties successfully.

In this and all things I have the honor to be

> Eternally at your service,
> le Baron Clotaire de Saint Sebastien

Ahead on the bridle trail le Comte and la Comtesse d'Argenlac rode side by side. Gervaise was talking eagerly, explaining to his wife for the fifth time how he had won so much money the day before. "And on the duel," he added with renewed enthusiasm, "I put ten thousand louis on Saint-Germain to win that, at three-to-one odds. This very morning I sent a draft to Jueneport discharging my most pressing debts to him. And I still have twenty thousand left, and that will double in the next week, I am sure."

La Comtesse did not appear to be listening. She looked very young and vulnerable in her light-blue riding habit with the military cockade in her fashionable hat. "Be satisfied with these winnings, Gervaise," she said pleadingly. "We might leave Paris, and live on your Anjou estate, if you like. You have always said you are happiest there."

"But you love Paris, Claudia," he objected, with a tinge of malice.

"Of course," she agreed. "But I do not like worrying and doubting, and being half-mad, fearing that our hôtel will be taken away or that my estate will be forfeit to your gaming debts. I would far rather live out of the world without worry than endure more years of this."

"But I have just told you," Gervaise explained with exaggerated patience, "that my luck has changed. It will all be different now, you will see."

"Oh, Gervaise." She sighed, feeling resigned, helpless.

"There you go," he accused her. "You doubt me, you have no faith. No wonder I cannot win. You condemn me and revile me. I can do nothing worthwhile in your eyes."

"It's not that," she said, knowing that he would not listen. She looked back over her shoulder to the two riders behind them, calling out, "Madelaine, if you want your gallop, this stretch is very nice. It is clear for a considerable distance. Saint-Germain, will you ride with her?"

Madelaine turned bright eyes on her companion. "Will you? Say you will." Without waiting, she called, "You had best pull to the side of the path, dear aunt. I can be quite a reckless rider." She gave one taunting glance to Saint-Germain, then spurred her Andalusian mare to a bounding gallop.

Saint-Germain gave her the lead of less than a minute, then urged his smoke-colored stallion after her, waving once to la Comtesse as he raced by her.

On one side of the wide path rose formal woods, the trees almost bare now, making weird shadows with their empty branches. On the other side, between neat, ordered banks, ran a shallow river, moving swiftly to join the Seine, scolding itself as it ran. This parkland was well-kept, manicured for the nobility who used it, so that rude nature would not intrude too roughly on well-bred sensibilities.

It was a chill autumn day of the sort that promises winter in every shadow and in its very stillness, as if the season were holding its breath in anticipation. Thin streams of clouds clung to the very top of the sky, tingeing it light gray, like a stone vault impossibly distant. Several leagues away, a fine, thin line of smoke rose straight up the emptiness between earth and heaven. The keen air smelled faintly of that smoke, and of mushrooms.

The bridle path was well-tended, groomed expertly so that no rider need fear for the safety of his mount or watch for a treacherous gopher hole or root lying in his path. It was a path made for this kind of day, and for one last mad race before winter took the joy out of riding.

Laughing, her fawn-colored habit flying around her, and her face glowing in the wind her headlong gallop created, Madelaine rode in fierce exhilaration. She had not been on horseback since that dreadful day on the hunt at Sans Désespoir, and she had feared that the memory of that terrifying chase would cast a pall on her pleasure. But it was not so. She could wish this run would last forever.

Saint-Germain's barb was closing with her. The sound of his mount's hooves was very near, gaining on her. She did not look back, but heard him shout to her, "Keep to my offside!"

Obediently she eased her mare to the right, making room for him beside her. They rode that way for several minutes, sharing the speed and the bite of the cold instead of words as the horses stretched out to full speed.

When they had covered some distance, they saw not far ahead a bridge over the shallow river. Saint-Germain called to her, "Pull up at the bridge! We'll wait for the others!"

Madelaine was about to object, hating to give up this wild intimacy, but she could feel her mount begin to strain at the pace. With mild regret she pulled her mare in, dropping from gallop to canter, to trot, and finally to a slow walk, letting her hands slacken their hold on the reins. They were much nearer the bridge now.

Saint-Germain swung out of the saddle, leading the barb along the path while the horse cooled. They seemed quite alone in the afternoon.

"Shall I dismount, too?" Madelaine asked when they had gone on a little farther.

"Only if you want to," Saint-Germain replied, looking up at her.

"I would like to be with you."

There was a strange smile in his eyes. "You are with me, my dear, more than you know." He shook off his abstraction. "I'll give you a leg up if you need it later."

"What did you mean?" She had bent in the saddle to hear him, and was a little frightened to find him now so remote.

He turned to her. "That you are with me? I have tasted your blood. You were right to compare it with Communion. It is that, when there is love."

She felt questions suddenly jumble together, and impulsively asked the first one that came to mind, "Saint-Germain, are you a Catholic?"

"Upon occasion."

Madelaine scowled down at him. "Upon occasion?" she echoed, bemused. She shifted in her sidesaddle for better balance.

"Well, I have not in the general sense been baptized, though in the past I have supported the Church and made endowments when such a course was wise. Of course, I do not take Communion," he went on in a different voice, a slight smile lingering about his wry mouth, "or, not in the usual way."

She slapped at him playfully with the end of her rein. "I didn't mean that." Her delight faded, and was replaced by a quiet withdrawn expression. "In the church, Saint-Germain . . ."

He shrugged. "It is not what you think, Madelaine. Do not mistake what I am with Saint Sebastien's Circle." He looked away from her, across the softly running river, his face enigmatic. "It is the fault of your prelates, who have confused the heretical and blasphemous worship of your Christian Devil with the doings of those of us beyond death. Most of what is said of us is superstitious nonsense. I do not deny the miraculous nature of the life of Jesus. From what I have read, he, too, rose from the dead."

Madelaine tried to look shocked, and failed. "Saint-Germain."

"It is common belief that one born at the winter solstice will be a vampire." He saw her flinch at the word, but went on. "If that is so, it certainly puts a new light on the resurrection. And in memory of Him, blood is drunk, is it not?" The words were flippant, but his tone was not. "Oh, I know, my kind should fear the cross and cringe at the mention of God, if you believe the folk tales. But just as many of us lie in consecrated ground, so we lie under crosses, and in churches, before altars. Yet we walk. It is not the sacred signs that stop us, Madelaine. I can hold a crucifix in my hand and suffer no torment for it. You would find it otherwise with those who worship the Devil, the Power used for evil and destruction. It is they, not I, who cannot endure the cross. It is they, not I, who are not able to touch the symbols of the Power as God."

Madelaine had let her mare wander toward the bridge, and as the Andalusian set her hooves on the old paving stones, Madelaine checked her. "I forgot about water," she said, turning to Saint-Germain.

He, too, had stepped onto the bridge. "You need not worry. I am protected." He looked up at her, and the wan light made auburn glints in his neat, dark hair, for he had removed his tricorne and was carrying it tucked under his arm. "Yes, that belief is quite true. In general, I cannot cross running water. But you see," he added as he stopped to lift one leg and touch his boot heel, "I learned long, long ago to fill my soles and heels with my native earth. As long as I am shod, I need not fear sunlight or running water."

She laughed aloud. "And I thought your shoes were thicker because you were vain! I was certain that you wanted to be taller!" Alarmed by her outburst, the mare tossed her head and almost broke into a trot. Madelaine controlled herself and gave her mount's neck a reassuring pat to quiet her.

He laughed, too, and much of his somber mood fell away. "Madelaine, my heart, you are a minx."

"If I am truly your heart, then it matters not to me what else I am." Her sudden intensity forced him to look up at her, and to see the passion in her eyes. "When will you come to me again? When, Saint-Germain?" She waited for an answer, and when one did not come, she went on in a low voice. "You must come to me, Saint-Germain. I couldn't bear it if you did not come to me. Say you will. Say it."

Saint-Germain studied the rein in his hand as if he had never seen it before. "Madelaine, I have warned you what might happen. It is not just the blood, though that is part of it, but the closeness. If I taste of you again so soon . . ." The words stopped.

"Then let me drink yours. Please, Saint-Germain, as you love me."

He had closed his eyes as if in pain, and at last said, "No," very softly.

"Why not?" Impatiently she pulled her legs free of her saddle and slid to the ground beside him, turning to him with her demand. "What you give me is ecstasy. Do not forbid me to share that with you?"

His words were louder, and harsher. "Yes. I forbid it."

"Why?" She stood at the crest of the bridge, blocking his way. "Why?"

"Very well," he capitulated. "If you were to taste my blood, Madelaine, you would most certainly become a vampire. You would be as I am." He turned to look over the river, feeling a certain vertigo that he always experienced when crossing water.

"Is that so terrible a thing to be?" She came closer to him and looked into his face. "Can you tell me that it is terrible?"

"It is very lonely." He found it hard to return her gaze, knowing what he would see in her eyes. If she were not so willing, he would not be vulnerable to her. Not since Demetrice, more than two hundred years before, had a woman caused such tumult in his life. Often in the past, he had been either their dreams, as he had for Lucienne Cressie, or a hated thing, to be avoided. Yet Madelaine knew him, knew what he was, and did not shrink from him. She sought his embrace wide-awake, and met his desire with her own. He dreaded the loss of her, and at the same time wished to protect her from the consequences of his passion.

The river ran under the bridge, clattering against the ancient stones like an impatient officer knocking for admittance. In the chill waters the gray sky was muted by the ripples spreading over the surface like gooseflesh. The two horses were reflected with the bridge and a dark-haired young woman. But of Saint-Germain there was no sign on those rushing waters.

"Is that all? Just loneliness?" She put her hand on his arm and smiled inwardly when he did not pull away. She stepped closer still.

Still he did not turn. "It is very dangerous. We are hated as much for our immortality as for our . . . feeding."

"And is it any more dangerous for you than it is for me to live now as I do? Was I in less danger at Sans Désespoir than I am with you? Does my mortality guard me against Saint Sebastien? Saint-Germain?" Gently she turned him toward her. "Can not you believe in my love for you? Does it mean so little to you that you will shut me away from you?"

He hesitated only a moment, then pulled her into his arms, holding her against him. He made a last desperate attempt to turn her from him. "You are not the first, Madelaine. Or the last. No matter what happens between us."

Her eyes yearned up at him. "I know."

Gently he touched her mouth with his, the kiss almost chaste. He felt her body quiver with emotion, and he relented. "No, I do not mean that. What I feel is only for you. You do not have my love exclusively, Madelaine, but uniquely."

She rested her forehead against the firm line of his jaw. "I am glad," she said, and could not help giving a satisfied chuckle.

Looking back along the bridle path, he said with regret, "Your aunt and her husband will be along shortly." He tightened his arms around her.

"Isn't there time?"

"No." With one hand he touched her face. "I will come to you, Madelaine, since you will have me. After your fête, I will come to you."

She caught his hand in one of hers. "Promise!"

There was mild surprise in his face as he raised his brows. "I have said it, my heart. My word is sufficient."

She seemed about to insist on the promise, but something in his manner gave her pause. Lifting his hand to her lips, she kissed it once on each small finger. Then quickly she stepped back from him, pulling her horse around to remount.

He stood beside her. "Here. Give me your foot." He waited until she had readied herself, then tossed her up onto the saddle.

"Thank you," she said, her formality returning again.

"Ah. Look there," he said, pointing toward two riders who had appeared around the gentle bend in the bridle path. "La Comtesse and her Comte. Not a moment too soon." He vaulted into the saddle without recourse to the stirrups.

"They have seen us," Madelaine said, waving. She let her mare walk off the bridge, turning to say to Saint-Germain, "I am glad we have had this time alone. It would have been dreadful to have remained uncertain."

"You were uncertain?" He pulled his stallion alongside her mare. "Mademoiselle, I will fear you are trifling with me if you say such things."

She spoke the next words softly, but he heard them. "I was never uncertain of myself. I only feared that perhaps you would not want me, or would tire of me after the first time. I know I am very young . . . particularly to you. It would have broken my heart if you had been seeking sensation. I could have borne outright rejection better than that."

He let his intense gaze rest on her for a moment. "You need not fear: the last time I sought sensation that way, Heliogabalus was Caesar. I lost my taste for such sport more than a thousand years ago." He turned his horse's head toward the approaching riders, and went on, in quite another voice, "The opera for your fête is to be a surprise, my dear, and I will not tell you more than that."

"Madelaine! Saint-Germain!" La Comtesse d'Argenlac had raised her riding crop to wave.

They returned her salutation, Saint-Germain remarking to Madelaine as le Comte and la Comtesse came abreast of them, "I am looking forward to meeting your father, Mademoiselle. I understand that he is to arrive to-night."

Grateful for this deft turn to their talk, Madelaine said, "Yes, that is when we expect him. He has not been in Paris since before I was born. It will be delightful to watch him discover the city all over again. I hope I may prevail upon you to take him to those places where it would not be appropriate for me to go."

"Oh, I can do that," Gervaise offered with a swift, challenging glance at his wife. "I suppose you will allow that, Claudia."

La Comtesse turned away, speaking in a somewhat muffled tone. "You must do as you think best, Gervaise. If you wish to be helpful to me in entertaining my brother, what can I be but grateful to you for your interest?" She took an unsteady breath and turned to Saint-Germain. "I must thank you for escorting Madelaine, Comte. I am sure our conversation would have bored her. So much contention for so little a matter! One would think that we had nothing better to do than displease each other to no purpose."

"So little a matter," Gervaise said with a certain malice in his smooth voice. "But now we are in perfect accord. Are we not, my love?"

"Certainly," la Comtesse agreed, too promptly. She gave the horizon a furtive glance, then said at her brightest, "Why, I did not realize how far advanced the day is. If we are to be at our hôtel when my brother arrives, I fear we must turn back now. I hope you do not mind, my dear niece. I do not want to take you from your pleasure."

Madelaine encountered a quelling look from Saint-Germain, and said tactfully, "Why, to see my father must be the greatest pleasure I may have. If it is acceptable to you, let me set the pace back to your hôtel. Saint-Germain," she said over her shoulder, "I would be happy for your company, but I know I must not keep you. I will look for you at the fête. And I promise I will not spy on your rehearsal of the opera."

Saint-Germain bowed low in his saddle, his tricorne over his heart. "Thank you, Madelaine. It has been an enchanting afternoon. Comte, Comtesse, your most obedient." He wheeled his stallion and set it for the bridge. "Until tomorrow, then."

But he waited on the far side of the bridge for some little time, watching Madelaine as long as he could see her, a brave figure leading her troubled aunt and her husband back toward their hôtel at a smart trot.

Only when she was completely gone did he cross the bridge again, and follow after them.

Excerpt from a letter from l'Abbesse Dominique de la Tristesse de les Anges to her sister's unknown benefactor, dated November 2, 1743:

. . . The physician who was good enough to accompany my poor Lucienne to this convent has told me that with good nursing and the help of God she may well be restored to her reason and some portion of her health.

I cannot thank you enough for your kindness on her behalf. That you sent her violoncello with her, so that she might have the solace and consolation of her art in this retreat, reveals the goodness of your soul. If you have aught to fear of God at the Last Judgment, you may be sure that your efforts on my sister's behalf will mitigate in your favor. No one, learning of her suffering, could have done more for her, or with greater care for her protection and good name. That you have rescued her without scandal shows how great is your concern for her.

Schoenbrun told me that you do not desire to be known, as much for Lucienne's benefit as for your humility. It is no doubt true that if it were known by anyone near her husband, efforts would be made to compel you to speak, thereby exposing her to punishment by the law and to forced obedience to her husband. I know that it is the duty of a wife to accept the judgments of her husband, and to submit meekly to his bidding. Yet, from what I have heard from Lucienne, her husband has been an adulterer in unnatural ways, and has eschewed the company of women, including his wife. No doubt this is not a marriage in the Eye of God, and even the Holy Virgin does not ask that those not in her service deny the flesh, but rather admonishes women to pray for the blessings of children, and bring fruits of their marriage to God in testament of their mutual respects and affections.

Be assured that I and the good nuns here will guard my sister and keep her safe until she is ready to go again into the world. If she should prefer not to return to Paris, we will be at pains to be sure she lives in a manner suited to her rank and station. Already I have written to our cousin, who is Cardinal Glaivefleur. He lives in Rome, and is a man of the most excellent repute. I am certain he would willingly be guardian to Lucienne and give her the sanctuary of his house as well as the setting for her to realize her talents in a most congenial atmosphere. Perhaps you will agree that it will be best if she does not see Achille Cressie again.

The Good Virgin, who is our help and font of intercession before the Majesty of God, will think on you kindly, and will hold you in her mercy for the delivering of my sister from the mouth of hell. You will always be in my prayers, for though I do not know your name, the God of us all reads our hearts and sees you as beloved among His children.

I must not be long at this letter, for I wish to send it with the physician Schoenbrun, who returns to Paris within the hour. I have had that good man's promise that should I wish to reach you, a letter to him will find you.

I will take the liberty of informing you of Lucienne's progress from time to
time, so that you may be certain of her recovery and salvation.

From the bottom of my heart and with the blessing and gratitude of my
soul, in this world and the next, in pious gratitude

> Believe me your most devoted in spirit,
> Dominique de la Tristesse de les Anges
> Abbesse, la convent de la Miséricorde et
> la Justice de le Rédempteur

❧ 2 ❧

Rain had been falling steadily for more than two hours when the coach pulled up at last before the side entrance of hôtel d'Argenlac. The horses were steaming, and the wheels and crested side panels of the coach were heavily spattered with mud.

A shout from the coachman brought lackeys running from the hôtel, and in a few moments lanterns were brought to illume the wet, blustery night.

The door of the coach opened, and the steps were let down for a staid, middle-aged servant in green livery. He held a long cane in one hand, prepared to give it to the other man about to descend.

"Thank you, Eustache," said the owner of the coach as he stepped out of the cumbersome vehicle. In the light he was revealed as a man of slightly more than middle age. His hair, unpowdered, was the color of steel, though it had once been of a rich, dark brown. Of slightly more than middle height, he was amazingly slender, with the lined, haunted face of one driven to fast often in expiation of his sins. He was dressed in well-made but drab and slightly old-fashioned clothes. Simple muslin sufficed for his neck cloth, and there was no lace at his cuff. His shoes were of a practical design, with very little heel on them. He turned appraising eyes toward the door, and it was seen that these were of a pale blue almost the color of ice. He addressed one of the lackeys. "Be good enough to tell la Comtesse that her brother has arrived."

The senior lackey bowed and went ahead into the house, giving orders for le Marquis de Montalia's baggage to be brought to his room, and setting the door open in welcome.

Apparently the arrival of the coach had been noticed before the lackey's announcement, for Madelaine came running down the hall, her walking dress of pale rose billowing around her as she came. "Father! Father, welcome!" She threw herself into his arms as he crossed the threshold, laughing for joy. "Oh, how I have *missed* you."

Le Marquis de Montalia returned his daughter's embrace, then held her off from him. "Madelaine, I have missed you. But look at you, my child. Such fashion. Such finery. I would not have known you, I think."

"Don't say that," Madelaine said quickly, putting her hand through his arm. "You would always know me, father, would you not?"

He gave her a sad smile. "Of course I would. I did not mean to distress you, my dear. I meant only to tell you how well you are looking. I sent a child away, I protest, and am met by a woman. It is the fate of every parent, I suppose."

She walked with him down the hall, smiling at him, holding onto his arm confidently. "We were just at supper, and I know you will want to join us. My aunt's chef is superb, father. He has a way with veal that will amaze you: the sauce is made with mushrooms and herbs and wine, and the veal is stuffed with pâté of chicken livers and bacon. I know you will love it."

"But I must not dine yet, my child," he said with a slight ripple of laughter in his voice. "I have been traveling all day, and I know I must reek of the road."

"I am sure no one would mind," Madelaine said, a melting persuasion in her voice.

"I would mind, my child. You must allow my eccentricities. I cannot sit down to eat in this dirt. I would ruin the meal for everyone else." He kissed her on both cheeks, then said, "It will be less than an hour before I join you. Eustache has my things, and as soon as he has been shown to my room, the appropriate clothes will be laid out. I may not have been in Paris for the last twenty years, but I know what is due my hostess."

Madelaine raised her chin, a stubborn set to her face. "I would rather have you join us now, my father."

It was perhaps fortunate that at that moment the senior lackey appeared, bowing to Madelaine's father. "I have taken the liberty of showing le Marquis's servant to his rooms. If it is convenient, I will do myself the honor of directing you there now."

Le Marquis de Montalia nodded to the lackey. "In a moment. I thank you for your attention," he said, handing the lackey a livre doucement.

"How long will you be? Do not take too long, father."

"I will take not one moment longer than is necessary. Tell my sister and her esteemed husband that I will join you as soon as may be. And pray do not wait for me at table. I am rarely hungry after a long journey. Some vegetables, an omelet, and a few slices of meat will suffice me."

"I will see that my aunt sends the order to her chef." She gave her father an impulsive hug.

"That is not wholly becoming in young ladies, my child," he said in mild reproof. "As a Father, I am overjoyed that you still show me this unaffected attention, but you must remember that in the world, such actions do not add to your credit. Be willing to be formal with me now, Madelaine." He took her hand and kissed it gallantly. "I will be with you within the hour."

The lackey, who had been watching this as if he were a wooden statue, came to life and said to le Marquis de Montalia, "Follow me, sir, if you will be so good."

"Thank you," le Marquis said. He turned down the hall and up the stair.

Madelaine watched him go, doubt surging through her like a strange dark tide. She was delighted to see her father, this was true, and she felt her love for him well up as it always did. But the remoteness she had long sensed in him, the isolation between them, was stronger now, and if she did not know better, she would have been willing to take her oath that he had been upset at the sight of her. Certainly there was no word to betray him, yet the reserve she had always known in him felt stronger now, and deeper.

She walked slowly along the hall back toward the dining room. The veal in sauce did not tempt her to hurry now. There was the hint of a frown in the angle of her brows, and she moved as if she were locked inside herself. Pausing by one of the windows, she stared out into the streaming night, one finger following the silver progress of a drop on the other side of the glass as it slid downward. How much she wished that Saint-Germain were with her now. It was less than an hour since he had left with his musicians, promising to see her for a moment the next day. She wanted him now, so that she could pour out her confusion to him, and feel safe in the warmth of his eyes.

Realizing that she would be missed, she abandoned her vigil at the window and walked toward the dining room with a purposeful stride.

This room was on the north side of the hôtel, facing onto a little terrace so that in pleasant weather the french doors could be kept open allowing a cool breeze to pass over the diners. On nights like this it was made cozy with several trees of candles, a large fire, and thick velvet draperies over the windows to keep out annoying drafts.

The dining table was made of fine cherry wood, and could seat twenty-four. Three crystal chandeliers hung above it, making ghostly patterns on the green-and-white-striped walls, for the candles were not lighted. At one end of the table Claudia sat, and at the other, Gervaise. Two large epergnes made conversation between them impossible without shouting, and so the room was silent when Madelaine opened the door and took her place at her aunt's right hand.

"That was Robert?" La Comtesse smiled a little wearily.

"Yes. He has gone to his room to change clothes. He asked that we do not wait for him." She studied the food on her plate as if it were a wholly unfamiliar and possibly hostile life form.

"What is it, my dear?" her aunt asked when the silence was oppressive once more.

Madelaine shook her head. "Nothing. Or probably nothing. He seemed so . . . strange. . . ."

"Well"—Claudia picked up her third silver fork and helped herself to some winter pears poached in brandy—"I should not refine on it overmuch, Madelaine. He is undoubtedly tired from his long journey, and returning to Paris after so many years might distress him. He did leave because of scandal, remember. He could find this return visit somewhat distressing." She rang a bell beside her plate and in a moment two lackeys came into the room. "You may remove this course, and serve the meat at once."

"Very good, ma Comtesse," one of the lackeys said, and set to work clearing the third course.

From his end of the table, Gervaise beckoned to the other lackey and issued an order in a low voice. Then, recalling his duty as host, he said, "Is there anything your father might like, Madelaine?"

To her own consternation, Madelaine flushed. "Oh, yes. I had forgot. He would like some vegetables, an omelet, and a few slices of meat. He will not want it for a little time, so they need not rush in the kitchen." She looked at her aunt, a mild shock in her eyes. "I do not mean to give orders in your house."

La Comtesse patted her hand. "Do not talk nonsense, my dear. You may do as you wish. And when you make requests for your father, I must be pleased for his sake."

Madelaine felt the color in her face subside. "Thank you, aunt Claudia. I do not know why I feel this way so suddenly."

La Comtesse gave a knowing smile. "With your fête the day after tomorrow, you do not know?" She gave an indulgent chuckle. "To be sure, I cannot imagine what there is to claim your attention. Merely your own fête, with three hundred guests coming—"

"Three hundred?" Madelaine was deeply shocked.

"That is what my replies have been so far. I daresay there will be more, for there are always those who come at the last minute, and I don't know why, but they inevitably bring half their friends. We may anticipate a great crowd Sunday night. Thank goodness almost all the preparations have been made." She looked up as the lackeys returned with the meat course, and she saw that Gervaise had been brought a third bottle of claret. She felt her heart sink, knowing that heavy drinking led inexorably to another bout of gambling, but she rallied her spirits and said, "Gervaise, see? Collops of suckling pork in a wine sauce with crab. Say you will have some."

Gervaise cast one eye at the new platter and three side dishes and snorted with disgust. "No, thank you." He reached unsteadily for the new bottle and poured a generous quantity into his glass.

"The meat is not red, Gervaise," his wife pleaded with him. "You need have no scruple to eat it on Friday." She pressed her hands together, and realized that the delicacy set before her would taste like sawdust now that she knew Gervaise was bent once again on his own destruction.

"Do not trouble yourself over me, Madame, I pray you." Already his speech was slurred, and there was an ugly sound to this command.

"I am sorry." The words were very soft, wrung from her heart. She put one fine hand to her eyes, then said to Madelaine, "There, my dear. I will be fine in a moment. You must not let me alarm you. I . . . I must be more tired than I knew, so that every little thing may set me off. Do not worry."

The effect of these reassurances was to make Madelaine more apprehensive than ever. "Dear aunt, why do you say that?"

"I am being foolish." She gestured rather wildly. "It is nothing. Here. Have some of this excellent pork. We will break Onfredo's heart if we do not eat this dish." She motioned blindly to the platter. "Onfredo is always so considerate. It is wrong to turn back his splendid fare, Gervaise. Why do we pay him such an outrageous salary if we do not want him to cook for us?" She did not expect an answer to this, and did not get one.

In the hopes of helping her aunt to master herself, Madelaine said, "I have heard that Onfredo is the envy of all your friends. Why is that?" She accepted a helping of the pork and put a few of the peas in a sauce of cheese and cream on the plate, nodding to the lackey to dismiss him.

Grateful for this, Claudia flashed her niece a quick smile of appreciation. "You have eaten here for more than a month, and you need to ask? Onfredo comes from one of the greatest schools in the world. His uncle and his father have been chefs to royalty. Onfredo accepted employment here because he wants to experiment without the criticism he might have in a greater establishment. I am more than delighted to have him attempt any dish he wants, for not only does this give my table a reputation no other has, but it is wonderful to think of a few great masterpieces bearing the title *à la Claudia*. There are three such already." She looked toward the head of the table and for an instant there was despair in her face as she watched Gervaise fill his glass yet again. She turned back to Madelaine, determined to be cheerful. "He's frightfully temperamental, of course, as befits a genius of his sort. But the food he prepares is worth it."

"I heard," Madelaine said, falling in with her aunt's frame of mind, "that he once threatened to commit suicide if he could not get fresh fennel and a particular variety of fish for a new recipe he had in mind."

Claudia made an airy tinkle of laughter as she tasted more of the pork. "He is *always* threatening to commit suicide over something. He was in utter desperation about all Friday dinners until l'Abbé assured him that it was only red meat that could not be served, so that suckling pigs, of this sort, or veal, could be part of the meal. Onfredo delights in these tantrums." She looked once again at her husband, and saw him toss off the last of his wine as he took the neck of the bottle.

Gervaise rose unsteadily and looked down the table, something very close to contempt in his face. "Madame," he said, his voice thickened and his tongue unruly. "I will leave you to your meal. Greet your sanctimonious brother for me, and give him all the complaints you like. I have had a billet from Jacques Châteaurose. We are going for the play at the Hôtel de Ville tonight. I am devastated to be deprived of your company." He wavered through a bow, then wove out of the room, wine dribbling from the bottle he carried, marking his progress.

The dining room was very still for some little time after le Comte had gone. At last Claudia put her hands to her face and let out the harsh, racking sobs she had held back most of the evening.

Madelaine waited for a moment, then rose and secured the door so that they would not be interrupted by servants. She then took one of the huge linen napkins from the chest by the fireplace and dropped it into the vase of fresh-cut flowers that stood on the chest.

When she was sure the napkin was thoroughly soaked, she pulled it from the vase, wrung it out, and went back to her aunt. "Aunt Claudia," she said firmly, but with considerable sympathy, "you are too distraught. Come away from the table for a moment or two and compose yourself. I have a damp cloth here. Let me put it over your eyes, so that they will not be red and swollen when my father joins us."

Between her sobs, la Comtesse agreed, allowing Madelaine to help her rise and guide her to one of the straight chairs by the fire. She held onto Madelaine's hand, her whole body shaken with her tears.

"There, aunt, do not weep so. I know that you have much to bear with, but you must not do this to yourself." Madelaine bent to wipe the older woman's face with the napkin. "See how cruel you are to your beauty. You must not weep." To Madelaine's surprise, Claudia took a few shaky breaths, quelling her outburst.

Finally, when the tormented moment was over, she looked up at Madelaine, taking the napkin into her hands and wiping her face with care. She did not paint her face overmuch, but tears were ruinous to her splendid eyes, and she knew it. "Ah, my dear, I did not mean to behave so." She forced herself to breathe as deeply as her stays would allow. "It is only that sometimes I let myself become overwhelmed by matters I cannot control. It is kind of you to help me so. I am sure I need not tell you that I would not want Robert to hear of this."

"You may depend on me, aunt. My father is a good and upright man, but he is not always wise, I think." She stood back from the Comtesse, a vacant look on her face.

"What is it?" Claudia asked of her.

"Oh, nothing. I was wishing that Saint-Germain were here, for he is so expert in awkward moments." She took the napkin and set it in one of the unused glasses on the table. "But we will have to do our best." She paused, her head tilted. "I think that my father is coming. There is someone in the hall. Please do you sit down, my dear aunt, and we will go on with our meal. There is no need, as you say, to distress my father with what has occurred."

Claudia had already risen and was standing by her chair at the foot of the table. "Indeed," she said, with a greater sense of purpose than before, "you are very right, my love. Open the door for Robert. I know we will do well."

Madelaine had already pulled back the latch, and opened the door with a smile as she saw her father come nearer.

He was woefully out of fashion, his coat skirts ridiculously narrow, the pockets too high, and no one had buttoned the top three buttons of a coat for more than a decade. But the cut of the garments he wore was masterful, and the dark-dove color of ribbed faille was unobjectionable. He held out his hands. "Well, my child, you are come to meet me?"

She took his hands in hers. "My aunt and I are all eagerness to see you." She stood aside for him to enter the dining room.

Brother and sister looked at each other across a distance that was measured in years as well as paces. Claudia smiled uncertainly, giving le Marquis a slightly more formal curtsy than was the custom in families. Robert made a bow, but without flourish.

"Ah, Robert," Claudia said at last, and came across the room to take him in a friendly embrace. "It has been too long."

Her brother held her, then stood back to study her. "It has," he agreed. "But the years have been kind to you, Claudia. I would not believe that you are thirty-seven years of age. You do not appear to be more than thirty."

Claudia took the compliment gracefully, and guided Robert to the seat on her left. "I beg you sit down and join us. You will have just what you want, but this suckling pig is delicious."

As Robert sat down, he looked a little uncomfortable. "But where is your husband, Claudia? I had hoped to renew our acquaintance this evening."

Claudia had sufficient presence of mind to dismiss this airily. "Ah, Robert, Gervaise is all that is vexing. He made an engagement for tonight without consulting me, and felt that he could not break it without giving offense. I trust, since you will be with us for some time, that you will forgive him for tonight."

Robert inclined his head, accepting this without question. He had not seen his sister for many years and so did not know that the brittle laughter and too easy manner were danger signals, saying more than words of her precarious state of mind. "Well, perhaps later, then. I had forgot the demands of the world. You need not fear I will be harsh with him." He smiled at the two women, and was flattered when he saw them exchange quick glances, thinking that they grew out of concern for him.

Excerpt from a letter from le Marquis Chenu-Tourelle to le Marquis de Montalia, dated November 2, 1743:

. . . I was first captivated by your wonderful daughter when I saw her at a fête at Hôtel Transylvania. I had the pleasure of being her partner for several dances, and learned then that her demeanor and sweetness are more of an inward quality than mere beauty of countenance. Her wit inspires my respect, and her goodness fills me with admiration.

As I have not heard of other offers for her, I am making so bold as to address you directly, in the English manner, and say secret and myself out of France forever, and you may continue that I would find it an ultimate victory of my life if you would be willing to accept me as your son-in-law. My fortune and rank are the equal of hers, and besides the attributes of my position in life, I offer her my devotion and the security that affection must bring.

Yet, I do not seek only your approbation. Before this matter is settled, I wish to see her alone, to find, if I can, if she will take me to her heart. My sentiments for her are such that if she will not have me for my own sake, I would rather relinquish any claim to her freely, so that she may bestow her heart as well as her hand. For that reason, I propose to call at hôtel d'Argenlac on the fourth of this month for a private interview with Madelaine. If you will allow it, Marquis, I will take her for a turn in my carriage, chaperoned as you wish. It would be my hope that, free from the constraints of those gala occasions that would seem to rule our lives, she will open her heart to me, even if only to say that I must not hope to win her.

. . . I will do myself the honor of making myself known to you at the fête tomorrow night that will be held at hôtel d'Argenlac. There may be questions you wish to ask me, or it may be that you will refuse my suit. I know that whatever you tell me, it will be motivated by your concern for your daughter, and not by worldly considerations. Such worth must always be respected and be held as an example in this world, where only too often we see sons and daughters bartered in marriage like so many head of sheep.

It is my fervent wish that you will look with indulgence upon my requests. Certainly your daughter's welfare will be of the utmost importance to you, even as it is to me. I beg that you will find it in your heart to let me hope, at least until she has had the chance to speak her mind to me and reveal what lies in her heart.

With the most respectful greetings and most cordial regards, I have the distinguished honor to be

> Your most devoted and hopeful
> Samson Guilbert Égide Nicole Herriot Yves
> Marquis Chenu-Tourelle

❦ 3 ❧

The doors of hôtel d'Argenlac stood open, flanked by lackeys waiting to receive the cloaks, hats, and other accouterments of the glittering train of guests who had begun to arrive for the fête at the stroke of nine. All the rooms on the ground floor were ablaze with lights, every chandelier shimmering with long white beeswax candles. At each corner of every room, tall trees of candles added to the brightness, and all the wall sconces twinkled merrily.

Madelaine stood beside her aunt in the receiving line, her beautiful face pink with excitement. She wore a grand toilette of platinum lustring whose shine challenged the myriad candles. The hem was heavily embroidered, with a great many jewels worked into the embroidery, which showed the waves of the sea where tritons and nymphs disported. The corsage of the dress was cut somewhat low, and was also embroidered heavily, accenting the jewels of her choker necklace, which were tourmalines and sapphires. From her sleeves, which reached to her elbows, there fell three tiers of light-blue lace, and her petticoat was of ruched satin sewn with seed pearls. Her powdered hair was simply dressed and framed her lovely face with two small ringlets.

Beside her, her aunt stood in a magnificent sack-back dress of lavender. Three lace bows marked the center of the corsage and framed the neckline, harking back to fashions of over two hundred years ago. Her petticoat was of matching lace, and she had a lace ribbon in her powdered hair, which was dressed on stiff-woven horsehair pads to create an enchanting confection. Her only jewels were bracelets of flawless diamonds set in gold.

Le Marquis de Montalia was dressed in the fine russet velvet he had stipulated, and his revers and broad cuffs were of brown satin. Next to his sister and daughter he was almost staid, but the delight in his face more than made up for his conservative dress.

Guests had been flowing through the door almost as torrentially as the rain had been falling. By ten o'clock the splendid rooms were packed to bursting, and Claudia was feeling very pleased with herself indeed. Madelaine had just turned to address a quiet word to her, when she stopped and smiled at the elegant figure in the door.

"Saint-Germain!" she cried impulsively, curtsying to him with mischievous formality.

He made her his most profound leg, kissing her hand in perfect form before allowing her to rise. "Well, my dear, you quite take my breath away."

She beamed at him. "You are very fine yourself tonight. The black frogging all the way up the coat is *very* taking."

He smiled at her audacity. "It is my humble wish to please you," he murmured.

"Double-strand garters, too. It will be the rage, I think," she said, surveying him critically. From his waved and powdered hair to his black brocade shoes, he was flawless. The black Chinese brocaded silk of which his coat was made showed phoenixes rising from their own black ashes. His waistcoat was almost as long as the coat, and was also black, but with embroidery of the darkest red, depicting an allegorical unicorn hunt. Against his black hose the silver double-strand garters stood out with startling effect, and the ruby clasp that held them firmly below the left knee glowed as if alive. Deep cuffs were turned back to his elbow, and were of black velvet edged at the false buttonholes in silver. He had a great profusion of the finest Belgian lace in pure white, setting off the familiar ruby at his throat. His dark eyes rested on Madelaine for just a second, so that only she could read the passion there.

Turning to le Marquis de Montalia, he bowed with respectful style and said, "I am Saint-Germain. No doubt I have the honor to address Robert de Montalia?"

"I am he, sir," Madelaine's father said, liking the severity of Saint-Germain's dress, but wondering at his manners.

"It is a pleasure to meet you at last. I have heard so much of you from la Comtesse and your daughter. It is a privilege to meet a man held in such high esteem by his own family."

Le Marquis looked somewhat puzzled and said, "You are certainly gracious, sir, but I cannot fathom your meaning."

Saint-Germain sighed inwardly. Robert de Montalia was not precisely a fool, but he did not have the swift and penetrating wit of his daughter, and even his acceptance of compliments was tinged with gentle melancholy. "Perhaps you have observed how it is that a man might be praised by the world in general but held in abhorrence by those who must live with him. It is when those closest to us, who know our most intimate faults and love us still, praise us to the world that we know something of real merit."

Robert de Montalia bowed slightly, and decided that there was no harm in Saint-Germain. Obviously le Comte was of middle age, foreign, with a decided cosmopolitan air, and given to indulging Madelaine for his harmless amusement. "Even they can be mistaken, upon occasion. But I agree that those who are closest to us in general must be our severest critics and our staunchest supporters."

"This is dangerously near to a philosophical discussion, and I will not tolerate this at my fête," Madelaine said brightly. "I must stay at the door for another half-hour, but then we will dance. I suppose I must ask Gervaise to lead me out for the first one." She turned to Saint-Germain. "And what time is my little opera?"

Her father was about to admonish her gently for this sudden imperiousness, but Saint-Germain answered her question meekly. "We will perform at the stroke of midnight, Mademoiselle, so that we will not sully the Sabbath with mere theatrics."

Madelaine's eyes glowed. "I do not know if I can wait, my friend. Will you tell me nothing of the work?"

"I doubt if Saint-Germain enjoys your pertness, Madelaine," her father said. Turning to le Comte, he went on, "Even the Sisters of Ste. Ursule who were her teachers had little to complain of besides this occasional mild arrogance, and her delight in the grotesque."

"Had I ever been a father," Saint-Germain said with a gentle smile that equaled Robert de Montalia's in beneficence, "I would wish that my child had the same high courage and inquiring mind that Madelaine possesses."

Robert de Montalia was relieved. He realized that Saint-Germain's kindness to his daughter sprang from his own childlessness. "To be sure," he said, and turned to address a remark to his sister, when yet another figure appeared in the doorway.

The grayish, reptilian eyes met le Marquis de Montalia's for one derisive moment as he strolled into the entry hall. "I beg you will excuse this late arrival, but your husband's invitation did not reach me until my evening meal." He bowed over Claudia's hand. "Enchanted, Madame, I promise you." Every line of his bearing revealed his contempt. His cloth-of-gold coat, by its very finery, mocked them. He flourished a handkerchief of Venetian lace as he bowed to Madelaine's father. "I trust that even as old an acquaintance as I may take this opportunity to renew a neglected friendship."

Claudia shot an anguished look toward her brother, who had turned as pale as linen. "Mon Baron," she faltered, trying to imagine what could have inspired Gervaise to invite her brother's greatest enemy to the fête. "You need not introduce me," he said easily. "I have seen Mademoiselle on other occasions, though I cannot remember being formally presented to her. But my old association with her father has long made me perceive a certain link with her." He took Madelaine's hand. "I feel sure we will know each other better before the year is quite out."

"Alas, that there are so many people in Paris, Baron. I wonder if I can spare the time."

For once his daughter's alarming speech brought no rebuke from her father, who stood as if turned to marble, disaster in his ice-blue eyes.

"And, Saint-Germain . . ." Saint Sebastien went on, turning to le Comte, "I heard of your little contretemps at Hôtel Transylvania. Certainly an odd setting for a duel, but foreigners like you are always odd."

Madelaine's face paled, for she had not heard much about the encounter Saint-Germain had had with d'Islerouge.

"And now," Saint Sebastien went on musingly, "the young man is dead. Curious how these things happen. I cannot dream how you might benefit from his demise, yet you must forgive me for speculating about it." He feigned embarrassment. "A thousand pardons, Comtesse. This is not the style of talk suitable for so festive an occasion. My apprehensions have got ahead of my manners." He bowed his deepest, then paused to regard Saint-Germain once more. "You must excuse me, Comte, but I confess I was surprised when Beauvrai described the duel to me. I had, until then, been of the opinion that you were unwilling or perhaps unable to defend your honor."

Saint-Germain inclined his head graciously, murmuring, "It is strange how one may be deceived by appearances, mon Baron."

"Yes," Saint Sebastien agreed, drawing out the word. He held his handkerchief to his nose as if shutting out a noxious odor, but his eyes were narrowed in unpleasant speculation as they rested on Saint-Germain. Then, when the entryway was quite still, Saint Sebastien turned and sauntered off toward the ballroom.

The entry hall was quiet for some few moments longer, becoming almost unbearable before Robert de Montalia turned his horrified pale face to his sister. "What is the meaning of this? Claudia? How dare you have Saint Sebastien here? You knew I forbad it!"

La Comtesse spoke in a stifled scream. "I did not know, Robert, believe me. Gervaise invited him. I had no idea—"

"He is evil! Unutterably evil. The thought of his hand touching my daughter sullies her in my mind, Claudia. He defiles us all. He might do . . . anything." As fast as his anger had risen, it fell. His shoulders drooped, and there was all at once a noticeable tremor in his hands. "Merciful Mother, what have I done?"

"It is not that bad, father, indeed it is not." Madelaine had rushed to le Marquis de Montalia's side, her throat strangely tight with tears. "You must not allow that terrible man to ruin my fête." She turned her desperate eyes on Saint-Germain. "Will you help me, Comte? It distresses me to see my father so much upset."

Saint-Germain's magnificent eyes rested on her face, and there was an unreadable expression in them. "Very well, Madelaine, if you wish." He said to le Marquis, "Would you care to come with me, sir, while I see to the setting of the stage and the placing of my musicians? You might want to hear one or two of the airs that will be sung."

"I thank you, but no," le Marquis said with formal stiffness.

Instead of accepting this obvious and straightforward cut, Saint-Germain smiled affably. "But come, de Montalia. When will you be able to hear the great Ombrasalice practice again? There are few castrati who can compare with him."

Robert de Montalia stood uncertainly, as if poised for flight. He took Madelaine by the arms, saying violently, "You do not know what I have done. I should not have let you come. Why did I allow it? I knew the danger. Do you understand that, child? I knew. I *knew* even when I pretended that it did not exist. And Saint Sebastien knew, or why did he come back to Paris? Why is he here, if not for you?"

There was fright and more than a little anger in Madelaine's face. She pulled back out of her father's grasp. "This is not the time or the place!" she said sharply. "If I do stand in some danger, I beg you will not advertise it to the world."

Before de Montalia could say more, Saint-Germain touched him gently on the shoulder. "Marquis, your daughter is quite right. Surely what you have to say to her can wait until you are able to be private with her. In the meantime, may I suggest that we see to the musicians? Perhaps if you tell me of what you fear, together we may work out a solution."

He let himself be pulled away from the door, but said to Saint-Germain, "You are a dilettante. You know nothing of what may become of my daughter."

"Then I hope you will enlighten me." He had taken le Marquis away from the entry hall, and now led him down a hall toward the library, where the musicians were waiting. "Turn your thoughts away from your worries for the evening, I beg you. If not for your sake, for your daughter's." He held open the door to the library and was greeted by a rush of sound that came to a ragged halt as he closed the door behind him and Robert de Montalia.

A tall, soft-featured man in splendid dress stood by the fireplace, an expression of intelligent concentration on his smooth face. "Saint-Germain," he said in a voice of great sweetness, as high as a boy's.

"Good evening, Aurelio." He turned to his reluctant companion. "May I have the honor to present Aurelio Ombrasalice to you, my dear Marquis? This is le Marquis de Montalia, the father of the woman our little entertainment honors."

There was a general murmur among the musicians, and a woman whose ugliness made her stunningly attractive came forward and curtsied respectfully to Robert de Montalia.

"This is Madame Inez Montoya, who will sing the Persephone tonight. I trust the theme of Persephone and the God of the Underworld will not strike you as improper fare for your daughter."

Le Marquis, who was looking at the musicians, made an abstract gesture. "It is not too dreadful a topic. But there is an abduction, isn't there?" He scowled.

Saint-Germain met this reservation with a charming smile and the full power of his eyes. "I will ask Ombrasalice to sing that for you now, and if you find anything in it to offend you, he will not sing it." He turned quickly and said, "Aurelio, will you do that for me? I know you are engaged only to sing a performance, but I would count it as a favor."

The tall singer graciously nodded. "I will sing that one aria. But softly."

"Thank you, my friend. I appreciate this greatly." Saint-Germain motioned de Montalia to a seat and waited while the ten musicians tuned their instruments, an inscrutable expression on his face. He did not think that Robert de Montalia would hear the message in the aria that was meant for Madelaine alone. When the instruments were tuned and the players had given an expectant look to Saint-Germain, he explained, "The aria, mon Marquis, is in two parts, a largo, and then a passage for the violins, followed by an andante espressivo. Gentlemen, any time you are ready."

The brief introduction in D minor went through the strings in descending triads, ending in two chords played pizzicato. Aurelio Ombrasalice stood away from the fire and sang in his strong, high voice:

In my realm of shadows
Unravished by the sunlight I raged
And I knew not why.

Your laughter in the meadows
Demented me as it flew and surged
Assaulting the sky.
Oh, Persephone, I am undone by love
And what my love must have!

The strings began to modulate into the major, and picked up tempo.
Saint-Germain watched Madelaine's father, and realized his message was
undiscovered. He nodded once to himself as Ombrasalice began the more
difficult second half:

In darkness burning for your light
That, burning, casts away my night.
The fire that burns for you, my own
Gives light no one will ever ever see
The wind that blows through time, my own
Will never blow to me, will never blow to me.

The strings capped off the aria with a lingering restatement of the second theme, then slipped into the minor again to end the piece. Aurelio
Ombrasalice looked rather critically at le Marquis de Montalia, and when
the musicians had stopped playing, said, "I would not like to give up the
aria, Marquis. It is very good for me."

"It is somewhat unorthodox," Robert de Montalia said at last. "I am not
familiar with the meter or the harmonies."

"They are based on Greek poetry and song," Saint-Germain said, thinking of the ancient times when flute girls performed in Athens. "The story
being Greek, I felt such a conceit was appropriate. But if you find the
piece too disturbing . . ." He left the rest unsaid and did his best to ignore the anger in Ombrasalice's face.

"No, no, I cannot see that it would disturb Madelaine. It is perfectly
within the bounds of propriety, and I must say," Robert de Montalia
added handsomely, "that your entertainment is a most flattering gift. I am
sure that Madelaine is deeply flattered." He rose, and was about to leave,
when Saint-Germain said, "Stay awhile, Marquis, and I will bear you
company."

He did not wait for a reply, but issued a few final instructions to the
musicians, then went to the door, closing it firmly.

"Now, mon Marquis, I had best tell you that I know you are in some
trouble relating to Saint Sebastien." He put up his hand to stop de Montalia's protests. "Whatever that may be, I want you to believe that I am
yours to command at any time."

Le Marquis de Montalia had become somewhat stiff again. "I thank you for your concern, Comte, but I cannot imagine that there is any trouble in my family that requires attention other than mine to remedy."

"Of course." Saint-Germain had almost reached the ballroom, but paused to try once again to gain de Montalia's confidence. "If it should happen to be otherwise, you may call on me at any time. I would be deeply complimented if you would."

Robert de Montalia felt a twinge of alarm; then an idea came to him as he remembered his own hatred of Saint Sebastien. "Is it that you, too, have a matter to settle with le Baron?"

Saint-Germain opened the door to the ballroom. "Yes. I have a debt I would like to pay."

"I see." Robert de Montalia nodded. "I will keep your offer in mind, Comte." He bowed once and turned away into the gorgeous assembly, and it was not until the fête had ended that he spoke to Saint-Germain again.

"A great success, Comtesse," le Comte was saying to his hostess as he bowed over her hand. In spite of the late hour, he was still absolutely precise in dress, and his powdered hair was neatly in place.

Claudia smiled warmly at him. "If it was, you must certainly take much of the credit, Saint-Germain. The *Persephone* was a triumph."

"Thank you, Comtesse, but I fear it is a rather trivial work." He obviously did not expect her to disclaim, for he had said this with such complete candor that there was no way to contradict him.

"It was very much enjoyed. Madelaine was in raptures."

"Was she?" Saint-Germain smiled secretly. "Then I am amply rewarded."

Le Marquis de Montalia overheard this as he came into the entry hall, and he added, "I fear she will grow too much in her own estimation, Comte. But it was a pleasant work, and you have afforded us all a unique pleasure."

"I will tell the musicians, Marquis. It was their skill that made the music live." He had signaled for his cloak, and waited while a lackey fetched it, reminding him, "It is black velvet, with red frogs at the throat."

"I remember, Comte," the lackey had said, and was returning now with that garment over his arm, prepared to help Saint-Germain on with it.

"No, thank you. I will carry it. The rain has stopped for the moment." He took the cloak, then said to Robert de Montalia, "Tell me, has Saint Sebastien left? I thought I did not find him among the guests after the *Persephone.*"

"I do not know." Le Marquis de Montalia glanced about uneasily.

But Claudia answered him. "Saint Sebastien had the ill grace," she said with acid sweetness, "to leave after the overture to your work. He excused himself on account of boredom."

To the surprise of the others, Saint-Germain laughed. "Well, he is at least an honest critic." He was still smiling as he said to la Comtesse, "Pray tell Madelaine that I will see her at the appointed time. I noticed she is still with the intrepid ones in the ballroom." He directed his next words to le Marquis. "De Montalia, of that matter we spoke on earlier— believe me, I have never been more sincere in my life."

He did not wait to hear what Madelaine's father might answer, but strode swiftly to the door and out into the night.

It was less than an hour later that Madelaine opened her window on the third floor of hôtel d'Argenlac in response to a gentle tapping and the faint scrap of a melody she had heard earlier that night.

"Saint-Germain?" she whispered as she saw the man who clung to the sill of the window. "How did you . . . ? It is a sheer drop . . ." She dismissed these questions, standing back to give him room. "However it was, come inside now."

There was a sibilant rustling, and Saint-Germain stepped into the room. He was no longer dressed for the fête, having put away his finery in exchange for a simple sleeved waistcoat of the darkest brown, burgundy small clothes and hose, and a shirt of natural muslin. The powder had been brushed from his hair, and it was simply confined with a burgundy ribbon. He pulled fine Austrian-made gloves from his small hands. "It is cold out," he remarked as he set these aside.

"Then sit here by the fire." She motioned to a chair, waiting until he had seated himself before sinking to the floor beside him. Her night-rail was of Indian silk, and the material clung to her body. She did not lean against him, but pulled her knees up and dropped her chin on them.

They sat together this way until Saint-Germain touched her shoulder gently. "What troubles you, my heart?"

She did not answer him at once. "You were in a duel. You could have been killed."

"Killed?" Saint-Germain stifled a laugh. "To kill me, Madelaine, my spine must be severed completely. A sword, a stake, perhaps one of those unpleasant new bullets, anything that breaks the spine will kill me. One of my blood was killed by a collapsing building in Rome. And fire. I can burn, like all living things. But a duel? I was not in the least danger from that impulsive, unfortunate young man." He stared out the window. "I wish I knew who killed him."

"Why?" she asked, sensing his unease.

"Because then, my heart, I would know who wanted me dead." He stopped abruptly. "Of course, I do have a fairly good idea who is behind it," he added dryly after a moment.

"Is that why you're not wearing black?" She met his glance, challenging. "I noticed. Do not think I have not eyes."

His laughter was soft, low. "I know you have eyes. And so have others. As it is well-known that le Comte de Saint-Germain wears only black and white, a man in dark brown and burgundy cannot be he. I am not anxious to have rumors about our attachment reach unfriendly ears."

She turned her head to one side. "If this is not Saint-Germain, who visits me, then?" Under her bantering tone there was worry.

"Oh, Graf Tsarogy, if you like. I have used that name at Schwalbach. Or Lord Weldon. I think I used that in Leipzig and Milan. Or Comte Soltikoff, who I was in Genova and Livorno. There are other names, of course. You may choose the one you find most attractive."

She shook her head, a dislike in her face. "Stop it, Saint-Germain. I do not like it when you do this. I begin to fear that you will change as you change your name, and that when you are no longer Saint-Germain, you will forget me." She had turned from him, so that he saw her profile only.

There was a saddened amusement in his voice. "Do you really think that, Madelaine?" He reached out and caressed her shining dark hair, made ruddy where the light of the fire touched it. "Do you think that I will ever forget you?"

"You have lived a long time," she said in a small voice. "You will live much longer. It would be easy to dismiss me . . ."

He dropped to one knee beside her, like a knight to his liege. "You have my word that I will not forget you. We are bonded, you and I. I promise you that I am not toying with your life." His words were harsh, and there was more sternness than ardor in his manner.

She could not meet his eyes as she felt the blood rise in her face. She remembered reading in the Old Testament of a love as terrible as an army with banners. At the time, she had not understood. Aloud she said, "This is not sweet languor, is it, Saint-Germain? All my life I have been told that passion is the right of men, and surrender the right of women."

"And instead you want to conquer?" He moved nearer.

She nodded uncertainly. "And then I become frightened, and I say hateful things." Her hands clenched at her side. "I see the beautiful women around me, I hear them talk about you, I see the way they look at you, and I think how long you have lived, and I want to drive them away so that you will not leave me. I could not bear to have you leave me." She struck out at him with her fists. "I know it does not make sense!"

He did not stop her blows. "Are you jealous: you need not be."

"Yes! Not really. I am sometimes, when I think you will forget me, or grow tired of me. You will go away to be a Russian czar or an Arab mathematician. You could do that, couldn't you?"

He was tempted to laugh, but he did not. He contained her hands in his. "I will certainly go away from time to time. I must go to England soon. I have given my word to Mer-Herbeux. But I will always come back to you. In your life, and later in mine, I will never desert you. Love is not for the weak, my heart. You must have courage." His dark eyes were glowing now. "You are blood of my blood, Madelaine. It would be as impossible for me to leave you as it would be for me to cross the Seine barefoot. Even if blood did not bind us, I swear to you that love would."

Madelaine smiled, warmth filling her though she shook her head. "But for you, blood is part of the love, isn't it?"

He paused. "It is all I have, my dear. When I became a vampire, I lost certain living abilities. Most of the time I do not find this an inconvenience. Yet for you I could wish to be a man and love you with all the pleasures of the body."

She rose to her knees beside him, pressing against him, letting the force of his passion draw her nearer. "It does not matter." She forestalled his objection. "No, do not remind me that I have never lain with a man. If I had had a dozen lovers, I would feel no different."

"Perhaps," he murmured, but held her more tightly as he kissed her shining hair.

Her senses ran together, so that it seemed she could taste the pressure of his arms around her, that she could feel the light of his eyes, that she could hear the passion of his seeking hands. She breathed in sharply, as if tasting air for the first time, and felt him wait, checking his need for her until she could share it.

"I will shatter for joy," she said, breathless. "I wish, deeply, deeply, that you could feel what I do." She looked full into his face. "You will not let me taste your blood?"

When he spoke, his voice was a caress. "Do not concern yourself. If delight could make one mad . . ." He had taken off his sleeved waistcoat, and she pulled at the buttons of his muslin shirt. He stroked her neck and shoulders, then held her face in his hands. "It is late, Madelaine. I ache for you."

"Yes, oh please, yes." She turned and let him ease her back against the thick white carpet before the fire. Her veins were afire now as his lips sought hers.

Earlier that night he had plucked melody from a harpsichord for her, and now he made music of her body. There was great tenderness in his eyes as he unfastened her night-rail and slid it reverently back from the soft curve of her shoulders, her breasts, her waist, her hips, her thighs. Where he had parted this night garment he clothed her with the warmth of his touch and his kisses. Each touch, every motion, wakened her inmost harmony.

Madelaine trembled violently as her body rose to fill his hands, to press still closer to his mouth and the delicious rapture he gave her. Her intense need, until that moment unrecognized and unknown, surged through her. She gave a cry as his small hands pressed her intimately, learning the whole of her.

Now he had stretched beside her and was drawing her ever nearer to him—his presence, his compelling nearness, shutting out the lesser fire in the grate, the room, the world. Then, at last, his mouth was against the curve of her neck. She threw back her head and her eyes closed in triumph and elation as his passion overcame her.

Text of a letter from the sorcerer Le Grâce to le Baron Clotaire de Saint Sebastien, dated November 4, 1743:

From Le Grâce to Saint Sebastien, most profound greetings.

Obedient to your commands, and anxious to discharge your orders, I have sought diligently, mon cher Baron, in the hope of finding where the remaining members of the Sorcerers' Guild have gone. I can learn little of them, but that they have not left Paris, for old Valenaire in la rue de les Cinq Chats saw the English Sattin but two days ago. Others have spoken to Domingo y Roxas, but there is no information on their location. Valenaire thinks that they have put themselves under the protection of a powerful noble, but you would have known of that.

But there is another matter that puzzles me, mon Baron. You have told me to find Prinz Ragoczy, so that you may have the secret of the jewels from him. Yet, it seems strange that you should ask that of me when you yourself have spoken to the man. Just last night, when I spoke to you before you entered the hôtel d'Argenlac, you ordered me to depart immediately, and I did not know why until I saw that you were deep in conversation with Ragoczy. To be sure, he was dressed in all his finery, but it was certainly the same man. It was not just the black clothes that made me think it was he. No one else moves like that, or has such eyes.

I do not wish to be impertinent, mon Baron. No doubt you have reason for keeping me occupied on a fruitless chase. If you were testing me, I cannot understand what you thought to gain from this. But if this is a clever ruse to save the secret of the jewels for yourself and your noble Circle, then

I warn you that I will tell the others of the deception. Unless you offer sufficient inducement for me to keep to myself what I know.

I will call at your hôtel tonight, mon Baron, and we may discuss this further. A handful of diamonds guarantees my silence. Two handfuls, and I give you my word that I will take your secret and myself out of France forever, and you may continue to deceive those foolish young men as long as you like. It is up to you.

Le Grâce

❦ 4 ❦

Le Marquis Chenu-Tourelle extended his hand to Madelaine and stood aside as she stepped up into his finest town coach. Next, he bowed respectfully and stood aside as Madelaine's maid Cassandre followed her mistress, smiling ingratiatingly at le Marquis for the distinction he had shown her.

He smirked to himself as he turned to give his instructions to his coachman. "As I told you earlier. You need not be in haste, Henri. We are not expected for more than an hour. It would be well to be gentle with the horses." He saw the nod from his servant on the box before he climbed into his magnificent vehicle with a polished expression of sincere attention. "If you are ready, Mademoiselle, we will depart."

Madelaine shrugged slightly. She did not like this exquisite gentleman with his chaste pastel clothes so much at odds with his dissolute face. "When you will, Marquis."

"At your pleasure, Mademoiselle." He rapped on the ceiling with his cane of clouded amber, which was chosen to complement his superb day wear of pale coral and ecru. There was a response from the coachman as his whip snaked over the heads of the team and the coach moved ahead, away from hôtel d'Argenlac.

It was a splendid carriage, with long swans' necks holding the complex leather springs that made the carriage sway heavily over rough ground but eliminated all but the most disastrous of jostles and bumps usually provided to travelers over the worn Parisian streets. It was painted a pale olive green with accents in chocolate brown and gold. The crest of le Marquis was blazoned on the door panels, a red tower topped with snow, edged in black on a field of ermine. The patent-of-arms was an old one, going back to the reign of Philippe Auguste.

The inside of the coach was of the finest sea-green velvet, the squabs thick and wonderfully soft. The rest of the interior was finished out in heavy satin the color of straw and edged at the door frames in petit point. The coach was pulled by four matched horses of a pale dun whose manes and tails had been bleached white. They were all of excellent confirmation and action, and the off-wheeler was ridden by a postilion in the traditional green-and-tan livery of the Chenu-Tourelle household.

"Very fine, Marquis," Madelaine said when they had been riding in silence for some little time. She actually thought that the Marquis was too fawning, that his coach was overly modish, and that dun horses with bleached manes and tails were an affectation, no matter how excellently they pulled the carriage.

"It is, isn't it?" he agreed affably. "I am ultimately complimented if it pleasures you."

"I have never seen such a stylish rig," she said truthfully, at her most neutral.

Chenu-Tourelle favored her with a wide smile. "It is that, certainly. I wanted it all of the best. I dare to hope that my desires have been realized." He filled these last words with painfully obvious double meaning, leaning forward to touch Madelaine's hand as punctuation.

Madelaine withdrew her hand and gazed determinedly out the window. Her jaw had a decided set to it, and there was a forbidding aspect to the way she sat, making Chenu-Tourelle reluctant to venture another conversational gambit. It was Madelaine who spoke next, when the coach had rumbled on a little farther, and she appeared to address her remarks to the air. "How perplexing it is, to have so little time, and only a small portion of it begrudged to one. Desires, learning, hope—all of them pale in the face of time. And yet, we are so profligate with what is most precious, that we spend vast amounts of it amusing others at our own expense."

Le Marquis Chenu-Tourelle interrupted her thoughts. "It is very true, Mademoiselle. I have often observed that boredom is the fate of the superior man."

Startled from her thoughts, Madelaine looked at le Marquis, and there was unquestionably real annoyance in her face. "I beg your pardon?"

Taking this as an invitation to expound further, le Marquis continued silkily, "It is the way of the world, Mademoiselle. Enjoyment, entertainment, are hard-won. How many times have I been forced to accept invitations to please my friends, when I would far rather seek more private pleasures." He smiled tentatively, hoping that he had not said something too shocking to her.

Certainly Madelaine looked alarmed, but not as Chenu-Tourelle had feared. "Oh, you are all alike! Boredom! Boredom!" She brought her fists together in her lap. "It is not pleasure that is short, Marquis, it is *life*. I am nineteen years old, and all but a little of my life has been wasted. In ten years, what then?"

Although this was rhetorical, Chenu-Tourelle put in, "I hope I will have some say in that, Mademoiselle."

"In ten years," Madelaine went on ruthlessly, "I will be a wife, with children and empty, empty days. . . ."

"Not, I fancy, if your children are like other children." Chenu-Tourelle gave an indulgent chuckle as he reached for her hand again. "Children, the devotion of your husband, the comforts of religion—is that so very bad?"

"Yes!" Madelaine ignored the warning look in Cassandre's eyes. "There is learning, and travel, and discovery. If I had a true vocation, I would be with the Sisters of Sainte Ursule, so that I could learn. Perhaps I could travel, see other places. But I have no vocation, and my father is not a diplomat." She considered a moment. "There was a girl, her name was Ranegonde Chamlysse, who was at school with me. Her father is le Comte de Etenduní. She has lived so many places—Turkey, Rome, Stockholm. She was even once in Russia, which she said was quite strange. When she left, it was to go to India with her father. The Sisters said that it was wicked to take her so far from her country and the safety of her family, but, oh, I would have gone in a moment, and I would have killed anyone who tried to stop me." She dared Chenu-Tourelle with her eyes to contradict her.

Misreading the danger signals in Madelaine's flushed face, Chenu-Tourelle said, "The Sisters were quite right, of course. De Etenduní has always been a trifle strange, taking his family on those missions of his. And you, hearing his daughter talk, imagined all the romance such a venture would bring. You see yourself surrounded by luxuries and admired by exciting men. But if all I have heard is true, it is not so very comfortable in those strange lands."

"You are a great fool," Madelaine said measuringly. "What do I care about comfort when there is so much to *know*."

At his most stiff, le Marquis said, "I think you would find, Mademoiselle, that the pleasures of knowledge are few in less civilized lands. But of course, you know best. Do not let me impose on you."

His formality seemed to amuse her, breaking the spell. She laughed, leaning back against the squabs. "I have let you impose on me already. And truly, I meant to be good, and do as my father wishes. He said that you wish to marry me, but that is not so, Marquis. It cannot be so."

"It is my fondest hope," Chenu-Tourelle said through his teeth.

Madelaine shook her head. "No. You would find me boring in very short order, and would be back to your gaming and mistresses, and I would find myself alone and the subject of pity or ridicule, as so many wives are. And why should it be otherwise? It is, as you say, the way of the world."

This masterful summing up of the situation did not mollify le Marquis. "Very well, Mademoiselle, since you will not have me, there are those who want you, and with less honorable intent." He saw the incredulity in her eyes and took grim satisfaction in it. "Yes, you never thought of that, did you? I may be a hateful bargain to you, but there are fates infinitely worse. You say that you will not accept me. So be it, Mademoiselle." He rapped on the ceiling of the coach with his cane.

"What are you doing?" Madelaine demanded.

"I am changing my orders." He called to the coachman. "I have changed my mind. I wish to go to the other destination."

"What other destination? Where are you taking me?"

Chenu-Tourelle smiled unpleasantly. "I am taking you to those who have use for you."

"Who?" Madelaine's knuckles were white, and a sickening fear closed around her heart, and she seemed to hear the sound of the chase near Sans Désespoir.

"Le Baron Clotaire de Saint Sebastien and his particular friends have promised me certain . . . rewards if I bring you to them. I said I would do it if you refused me. You have chosen your own fate, Mademoiselle." Relaxed for the first time, he crossed his shapely legs at the ankle and began to finger the knob of his cane.

Madelaine felt her courage fading, and she forced herself to say, "I did not think you were so vile, Marquis. But we are in the streets of Paris. If I call out, surely I will be rescued. Take me and my maid back to the home of my aunt and I give you my word I will not say anything to your discredit, now or later." She knew she lied, for she thought, even as she said the words, of Saint-Germain.

"You may call out if you will, Mademoiselle. That is up to you." He made a quick motion with his hand, and pulled the thin blade from his cane. "But I think you will not."

Madelaine bit her lip as the sword point wavered in front of her face. She felt Cassandre tense beside her and said, "Do nothing. I think he would use it at the least excuse." She felt pride that her voice was as firm as ever. Crossing her arms deliberately, she studied Chenu-Tourelle. "May I know why you are doing this? What reward have you been offered?"

Chenu-Tourelle waved the sword a few inches from her face, enjoying her discomfort. "I do not know if I should tell you."

Desperately she tried another line. "Do you know why Saint Sebastien would want me? He does not know me. He has hardly spoken to me. If it is the enmity of my father . . ."

"Enmity, Mademoiselle. It is his right to have you." He reached with his free hand into his capacious pocket, withdrawing a flask, which he held out to Madelaine. "Do me the courtesy of drinking this."

"No," Madelaine refused.

"If you do not drink, I will kill your maid. Right now." He shortened his arm for the stroke, delighted to see the fear in the older woman's face. "Drink the wine, Madelaine."

"You need not," Cassandre said faintly.

But Madelaine had already taken the flask and set it to her lips. Her eyes crackled with hatred as she finished the wine and held the flask out to Chenu-Tourelle. "An inferior vintage, Marquis."

"It is sufficient for my purpose. It will not be long before the drug takes effect, ma belle."

Madelaine's chin tilted up. "It cannot be too soon for me, as I will then not have to endure your company. I *knew* I should have nothing to do with you. But you convinced my father, did you not? And I hated to disappoint him." She turned a little toward Cassandre. "It will not do to make a scene. Do not be alarmed when I faint. Chenu-Tourelle has this all planned out. Are we not fortunate?"

The bitter sarcasm stung le Marquis, who gripped his sword more tightly. "If you think to weaken my resolve . . ."

"What? Mere scruples keep you from your delightful reward?" she marveled in spite of her thickening speech. "I cannot think it."

Desperation filled Chenu-Tourelle as he glared at Madelaine. He had wanted her to be contrite, to beg him for mercy, so that he could relent gallantly, saving her from Saint Sebastien in spite of le Baron's claim. He decided to remind her of her position. "It is Saint Sebastien's right to have you. Ask your father. I am not doing wrong by bringing you to him."

Cassandre, distressed to see Madelaine becoming sleepy, tried to rouse her, chafing her wrists and pressing a clean cloth to her forehead, ignoring the vague motion that meant to turn her away. "Do not be frightened, my little one," the maid whispered in her terror.

"He has no right to me," Madelaine said slowly, overly precise in her pronunciation as she fought the drug.

Delighted to have this opportunity to shock her, wound her, Chenu-Tourelle drew the moment out as long as he dared. "But that is not so, Mademoiselle. There is a document—I have seen it. Your father signed it with his own blood." He touched the corsage of her dress lightly with the point of his sword, snicking a bit of the soft material, exposing a little of

the rounded flesh above her corset, but not marring the beauty. He saw
her try to pull away and felt much better. "That document, ma belle, gave
you to Saint Sebastien before you were born. From the womb you belong
to him."

The muzziness of the drug was darkening her mind, but Madelaine understood enough to feel acrid disgust fill her. "Gave . . . me . . . ?" Then
there was a rushing in her ears, and she did not feel Cassandre's trembling
hand on her face, or see the slack-mouthed, evil smile that possessed
Chenu-Tourelle as he watched her slip into unconsciousness.

Text of a note from the sorcerer Beverly Sattin to Prinz Franz Josef
Ragoczy, left in his quarters at Hôtel Transylvania, written in English,
dated November 4, 1743:

> To His Highness, Prinz Franz Josef Ragoczy of Transylvania,
> Beverly Sattin sends his Most Respectful Greetings.
> I Regret to say, Your Highness, that we may have been Discover'd, and
> by Le Grâce. I have taken the Liberty of seeking you out, but finding you
> away from your Quarters, I am Taking Advantage of the moment to Inform
> you of the Circumstances of this Unfortunate Development.
> Earlier today, Domingo y Roxas took himself to la rue de les Cinq Chats,
> where there are Those who supply us with our Needs for the Great Work.
> In general we are all Most Cautious when venturing abroad, but the Morn-
> ing being not far advanc'd, Domingo y Roxas did not think it Necessary to
> be as Circumspect as is our wont, a Folly for which he is most heartily
> repentant. He (that is Domingo y Roxas) went to the shop of Valenaire,
> who has often had our Custom, and Desir'd Valenaire to provide certain
> Salts and other Compounds we requir'd. It Happened that while Valenaire
> was Occupi'd with this Request, another Person came into the shop. So
> Strange was this Person's appearance (Domingo y Roxas has describ'd the
> Fantastical Manner in which he was Drest) that he (that is, Domingo y
> Roxas) Remark'd on it to the Person, for he Fear'd the Stranger was some
> Lunatic recently Escap'd.
> This Solicitation was answered in French, and with such Mockery that
> Domingo y Roxas' Suspicions were Rous'd. He found excuses to Linger in
> the shop until the Stranger had Purchas'd some several Compounds for his
> own use, and when he (that is, the Stranger) left the shop, Domingo y
> Roxas followed after him. Anxious to Discover whither the Stranger was
> bound. You may Imagine his (that is, Domingo y Roxas') Confusion when
> the Stranger went strai't to the Inn of the Red Wolf. There, inside the tap-
> room, he Cast off his Garments, and Domingo y Roxas saw that it was Le
> Grâce!

Le Grâce stay'd at the Inn some time, drinking wine and Swearing that he had found the means at last to Riches and a Safe Life. Domingo y Roxas, who Continu'd to observe him through a small, dirty window by the Chimney, thought he heard Le Grâce boast that a Great Lord was to give him money and jewels to buy his Silence in a Particular Matter.

Seeing that Le Grâce was Quite Drunken, Domingo y Roxas Hastn'd away to tell us of this Dreadful Occurence.

Le Grâce is not Dead, as we Hop'd. It is Certain that he will do us Some Mischief if he can. That he Recogniz'd Domingo y Roxas is Sure, for he (that is, Domingo y Roxas) was quite without Concealment. The very Tone of his (that is, Le Grâce's) Speech with Domingo y Roxas shows that he Knows more of us than is Safe. We Dare Not Ignore the Threat Le Grâce Represents.

Your Highness, let me Urge you to be On Your Guard. You, We, are Everywhere in Peril. I pray that you, at your Earliest Opportunity, do us the Honor of granting Private Speech with us. I have Ask'd your Manservant to Alert you should he see you before you Read this.

At twelve of the Clock, I am always

> Your most humble, Obednt. Svt. to Command,
> Beverly Sattin

5

Saint Sebastien rounded on Le Grâce, the glitter in his hooded eyes singularly unpleasant. He spoke languidly, but the ferocity in his face was not disguised. "Perhaps," he said to Le Grâce, who sprawled inelegantly on the brocaded sofa by the largest bookshelf, "you will be good enough to tell me, Le Grâce, what it was you sought to accomplish with this?" He held up the grubby sheet of paper with Le Grâce's clumsily written blackmail threat on it.

Le Grâce shook his head, possibly to deny the message was his, or perhaps to clear his head of the wine he had drunk so liberally a few hours before. He wiped his stubbled chin and slurred out a few words. "It . . . wasn't that . . . way, Baron. You mis . . . understand me."

"I doubt that, Le Grâce," Saint Sebastien said sweetly as he tapped the letter against his hand. "You threatened me with exposure. No," he said sharply as he saw Le Grâce prepare to interrupt, "do not deny it. You fed me this nonsense about the man in black and white! You chose your subject unwisely. Do not think that I will tolerate deception. Or threats."

"But I'm *not* lying," Le Grâce protested in vain.

"You would do better to admit your error, Le Grâce." Saint Sebastien came over to the sofa and leaned one arm on its back. The velvet of his lounging robe brushed Le Grâce's cheek, and for an instant Le Grâce thought he would scream. "If you think to distract me with your stupidity, I warn you you will fail."

"I tell you, he is the man!" Le Grâce twisted away from Saint Sebastien, only to find that the fine, long hand on the back of the sofa had grasped his collar and was twisting cruelly.

"What must I do to convince you, Le Grâce? I cannot allow you to continue this way." The pressure on the sorcerer's neck increased as Saint Sebastien turned his hand delicately. "I am not a patient man, Le Grâce. I warn you that you are only increasing my anger with this foolish persistence."

Le Grace's face had turned an unhealthy mottled color, and he tugged frantically at his neck cloth. "But it's *him!*" he insisted, gasping.

Saint Sebastien sighed resignedly. "Very well, Le Grâce. Since you are unwilling to tell me . . ." He stood back, releasing his hold on Le Grâce's neck cloth.

Pleasantly surprised by this turn of events, Le Grâce was about to rise when he heard that smooth, hated voice behind him. "Do not move, Le Grâce," Saint Sebastien said icily. "I have not given you permission to move."

"But surely—"

"Nor have I given you permission to speak." He spoke with silken charm as he walked around the corner of the sofa into Le Grâce's range of vision. "I am not finished, Le Grâce. I must beg you to stay with me yet a while." He fingered the long, thin whip he carried lovingly, and the whip twitched in his fingers as if it were alive.

Le Grâce felt himself grow cold. "Ah, Baron . . ." He shifted on the sofa, trying to block the blow he feared. "I tell you, I didn't lie."

"But I don't believe you." He had moved closer now, relishing the fear in the sorcerer's eyes and the sudden stink of his sweat.

"I know you don't. It's not my fault you don't know about Ragoczy." He cowered away from the tall, lean figure hovering ever nearer, his hands caressing the whip.

"Poor Le Grâce," Saint Sebastien purred. "You are a bungling liar and a fool, but you have your uses." He stepped back to give his arm play. The motion was so quick that Le Grâce had not realized what it meant when the sjambok fell against his jaw, opening his flesh to the bone.

With a cry made up of pain, betrayal, and desperation, Le Grâce clapped his hand to his bleeding face as he lunged at his tormentor.

"I had this whip from a man who had been a slaver," Saint Sebastien informed Le Grâce as he stood back, waiting for his next opportunity. "It is made from the rhinoceros, from the pizzle, to be precise. It is oiled and stretched, oiled and stretched, until it cuts more deeply than steel. But you have found that out, have you not?" He played with the heavy whip, letting it writhe on the floor as he held it easily. Somewhat dreamily he went on, "When he gave it to me, he demonstrated it." The whip coiled on the floor. "He had a reluctant slave of his own, and he amused himself for an afternoon with this. At times I think the slave's blood still stains the lash." On the last word, he brought the whip into play again, this time letting it fall full force across Le Grâce's shoulders.

Le Grâce bellowed and tried to roll away from the whip, but it fell again, this time tearing open the flesh of his back and bringing bile into his mouth. "No! No!" He tried to push away from Saint Sebastien and the next assault, and succeeded in turning the sofa onto its back.

The loud crash of furniture brought swift results, for the door to the library flew open, and Tite, Saint Sebastien's personal servant, came into the room. "Master?" he asked anxiously.

Saint Sebastien shrugged. "No, Tite, it is not I who is hurt. It is poor Le Grâce, there. You must take him away for a while, and be sure that his wounds are looked to. I have not finished with him yet. He has not given me the answers I want." Le Baron was flushed and speaking in a jerky, excited way. He still held the whip, but now the long, ominous strand of leather was quiet, sated.

Tite grunted as he went to Le Grâce, who had staggered into a corner of the room, where he crouched, one arm up to deflect more blows. His face and back were spattered with blood now, and from the deep cut on his jaw more blood welled. The sorcerer whimpered, all the while trying to press closer to the wall as Tite approached him. His progress left a swath of red on the fine wall covering.

"Take him to the stables. You know the room." Saint Sebastien had regained a little of his grand manner. He wiped his face with a heavy silk handkerchief and dropped the handle of his whip to the floor. "I will want to talk to him within the hour. Remember that."

Tite had grabbed for Le Grâce, his big arms holding the terrified sorcerer in an easy grasp. "The stables. As you wish, master." He started toward the door, his face impassive, apparently unaware of the groans of pain Le Grâce made every time he moved at all.

"Yes. I think I want to use him myself. The Circle may have others, but I think this one is for me." He neatened his lace jabot and fixed a beatific smile on Le Grâce. "You may lie to me. You may cheat me. It does not matter. You may also die for me, Le Grâce." He reached out and flicked the edge of the wound on Le Grâce's face. "It is said that the face gives the greatest hurt, after the loss of manhood. I wonder."

Le Grâce was too cold now to say much, and he could not bring himself to open his mouth.

"Go out by the terrace," Saint Sebastien ordered Tite. "I don't think it would be wise to have the other servants see him."

Tite nodded as he went to the wide french doors that filled one wall of the library. Beyond them a gray veil of rain had dropped over the world, leaching the color out of it. When Tite pulled the door open, a cold breeze chilled the room. "The room in the stables," he repeated as he stepped out into the rain.

"It was such a promising morning," Saint Sebastien lamented as he went to close the door behind Tite. He stared meditatively out at the drowned afternoon, his mind on nothing in particular. There was a faint, predatory smile on his mouth.

He was pulled from this contemplation by the sudden rattle of wheels on the flagged sweep of drive that curved around the hôtel Saint Sebastien. He looked up, and the smile broadened, for in the mist he could just make out the outline of Chenu-Tourelle's ridiculous new coach. Filled with energy now, as if the sight of the coach had revived him, Saint Sebastien turned back into the library, shut the french door behind him, and pulled on the bell rope to summon a lackey.

Almost immediately the library door opened and a young lackey in Saint Sebastien's red-laced deep-blue livery came in and bowed respectfully. He did not lift his head as he waited for orders.

"I gather we have company, Maurice," Saint Sebastien said pleasantly. "I believe I saw le Marquis Chenu-Tourelle arrive just now. I trust, I do trust that he has been welcomed?"

"He has, master, and his guests."

"He *does* have guests? How charming." Saint Sebastien nodded, then waved his hand negligently. "I will want a note to be delivered. Not immediately. It must arrive at hôtel d'Argenlac no earlier than nine tonight. I will give it to you now. I might be busy later."

"The message will be delivered as you say, master."

"Of course it will. Life is much easier when you obey me implicitly, is it not, Maurice?" He bent to pick up the sjambok, and let the lash curl lazily through his fingers. "No, not today, Maurice. Today I have other things on my mind. But it would be unwise of you to forget this." He fingered the end of the whip and watched Maurice turn pale. With a sigh he abandoned this sport, and strode to the secretaire near the wall. "I will not take long, Maurice. Then you may take me to my guests. Where have you put them?"

Maurice stammered his answer. "One of them . . . one was . . . in a swoon. . . . But le Marquis . . . he . . . he . . . said to take her to your private study." The last words came out in a panicky rush.

Saint Sebastien interrupted himself in trimming his writing quill. "My private study. How thoughtful. Is anyone else with them?"

"No. No. Le Marquis, the young lady, and her companion, who is distraught."

"Indeed?" Saint Sebastien said solicitously. "How unfortunate. We must remedy this situation. In a moment I will attend to it. But this note, first, I think. Yes." He had finished trimming the quill, and now pulled out the standish and two sheets of hot-pressed paper. Saint Sebastien smiled at the bold embossed crest at the head of each sheet. It was an old,

old patent-of-arms, granted to his many-times-great uncle in the days when the Inquisition destroyed the Knights Templar. In memory of that occasion, the arms showed a cinc-foil, each branch of which contained allegorical figures: topmost was a goat seated on a throne, then a skull inverted to make a cup, next a candle burning upside down, followed by a mandrake root, and last the tall, fearful hat of the Inquisition.

Saint Sebastien's gaze lingered on this device lovingly, and he wondered if that Inquisitor ancestor of his would be surprised to discover that the heretical, blasphemous practices he had so rigorously stamped out were being used by his own blood. Recalling some of that worthy priest's painstaking records describing the Question of suspected heretics, Saint Sebastien thought he saw in the meticulous details of torture a dim echo of the delight he himself found in giving suffering.

His mind strayed again to Madelaine. He knew exactly the use he would make of her, and it pleased him to think of the agony her death would bring not only to her but also to Robert de Montalia. Saint Sebastien nodded. He found the idea attractive. He had not intended to tell de Montalia much more than that he had Madelaine, but he reflected on the matter, and realized that if he detailed his intentions, Madelaine's father would be driven to frenzy.

He caressed his wooden-faced lackey with hot eyes, assuring himself that his servant was thoroughly frightened before drawing the paper forward. His smile broadening, he began to write.

Text of a letter from le Baron Clotaire de Saint Sebastien to le Marquis de Montalia, delivered by hand shortly after nine on the night of November 4, 1743:

My very dear and long-absent friend, Robert, Marquis de Montalia, I send you greetings and my most cordial wishes for your welfare along with my compliments.

How sad I was not to have known earlier that you would once again return to Paris. When I think of the many hours we spent together, twenty years ago, I am desolated to think that you would forget to tell me of your visit, so that I could arrange some appropriate entertainment for you.

But fortune has favored me, dearest Robert. At last I have found a way to tender my respects in a manner befitting our long years of friendship, the protestations of which have endured through our separation. The obligations of our association are not easily forgotten, Robert.

By now I would imagine that you are cherishing fond hope for your daughter's future as la Marquise Chenu-Tourelle. No doubt you think that she dines tonight with the family of le Marquis.

I regret my lamentable duty to inform you that I have reclaimed my property, which you have been so tardy in making available to me. Surely you did not think to escape that obligation. Particularly when Madelaine is so much admired and her manners so charming. As much as the young men, I find her to be utterly entrancing. It could hardly be otherwise, she is so lovely. I will admit that I will find it difficult to wait the necessary number of days before we offer her in sacrifice. But in that time, of course, she will have a service to perform for us all, and a way to prepare herself for the winter solstice. I am certain I will find ways to amuse her, my dear Robert. Tite, for example. You do remember my manservant, do you not? He still is best pleased when he is feared, and I know he can be very terrible. I will take her virginity, of course, but Tite should be next, don't you think? It will be so much easier for the others when he is through with her. I have never known anyone to resist Tite for long.

Think of it: your daughter, my property, on the altar, bound, naked. She will lie there every night for forty days, Robert, and every night she will be used. When I have had her, Tite will enjoy himself for one night, and he will use his own methods to bend her to our will. When this is done, the rest of the Circle will be given access to her, for their pleasure as it suits them. There are quite a few of us, and some of that number have longed for this opportunity.

No doubt you remember Beauvrai's tastes still. What will Madelaine think, I wonder, when she is used by three at once? It is a pity that Beauvrai is so rough, for I am certain he will not be able to contain his passions when he is given his time with Madelaine. He will probably ask de la Sept-Nuit to join him, for Donatien also enjoys roughness. Do you remember that ingenious device that Beauvrai was working on, that allows him to penetrate front with his flesh, and back with the heated Devil's Member? He has done quite a lot of work with it these last few years. I gather by the reactions of other offerings that the process is quite painful.

By the time we pull her living heart from her, she will be happy to die, Robert. We will have defiled her in every way we know. However our fancy inspires us, that will we do, short of killing her. We will violate her, assault her, disfigure her, torture her, so that her death will be pleasing in the Eye of Satan.

If you had given her to us at the beginning, this need not have happened. She would then be one of us, and would participate with us rather than be our offering. For her degradation and death you have none to blame but yourself. Think of that while you search for her in vain.

This I promise you: I have found a new place for the Circle to make its sacrifice. No one will suspect us. You may torment yourself with that thought, and with the thought that every moment your child suffers adds to my power.

I do not forgive you for betraying your oath. I do not forgive you for taking my property out of my reach. I do not forgive you for raising her in the manner of the Sisters. In short, I hold you to blame, and I warn you now that with the new year, you will be marked by the Circle, and your life will be of no value.

Let me warn you that if you attempt to find us and we snare you, that will not save Madelaine. It will only mean that your death will happen all the sooner. Two sacrifices will be better than one. I beg you to consider this before attempting any fruitless rescue or futile petitioning of the King. His Glorious Majesty Louis XV could not issue orders in time to save your daughter. At the first hint that you have attempted such a ploy, Madelaine will die, my friend.

Should you find someone foolhardy enough to aid you in your search for your daughter, do not place too much dependence on any victory. There are enough of us to take care of twenty more like you. And anyone assisting you would, of course, be subject to the same penalty as you are. Isn't it enough to lose your daughter? Let your friends live, Robert.

Until our reunion, late or early, it is my pleasure to be

Saint Sebastien

6

Even as he woke on his monastically comfortless bed, Saint-Germain felt himself possessed of deep foreboding. His eyes searched his sleeping alcove, as if trying to read the cause of his alarm in the gathering dusk. He put his hands to his eyes, and a frown clouded his brow. The frown deepened, and then he nodded as if giving himself a signal. With a quick movement he had slipped to the floor, his loose robe of dark Egyptian cotton brushing the floor as he pushed aside the curtain masking his alcove, and walked into his sitting room.

This was the same room he had brought Madelaine to not so many days ago. For a few moments he thought he could see her garnets shining on the floor, and Madelaine blocking the door, her face filled with yearning. He smiled at the memory but it faded to be replaced with worried malaise.

One candle burned on the mantel, and Saint-Germain used this to light the others in the tall branches. The room glowed, but its warmth did not communicate itself to its occupant. Saint-Germain tugged at the bell rope, his mind still probing restlessly to discover the source of his alarm. He touched the astrolabe, as if seeking answers from it.

"Master?" Roger said with a curt nod for form's sake as he came into the room.

"Um?" Saint-Germain turned, saying, "Close the door, Roger. What I have to say is private."

Roger did as he was told, waiting patiently for his instructions. He carried a towel over one arm and held a basin in the other hand. These he set down as he watched Saint-Germain move quickly about the room.

"I think it had better be a bath," he said slowly as he paused by the fireplace. "A bath, and then simple clothes. I think the linen breeches, or wool. And that shirt I was given in Persia, the one with the signs worked in Russian embroidery. And the wide-cuffed boots. Make sure that the heels and soles are well-filled. I sense I will have need of that protection tonight."

"As you wish," Roger said.

"Prepare my elk-leather riding coat, too. I will be leaving as soon as I have the bath." He stopped as he saw the note from Beverly Sattin propped against the mantel. He pulled the two crossed sheets open, reading swiftly, his face growing grim. "Le Grâce has seen Domingo y Roxas," Saint-Germain said as a brusque explanation as he burned the letter, holding the paper until he was sure the message would leave no trace in the ashes.

"When?"

"This morning. Sattin does not think he knows the Guild's present location, but that is scant comfort. If Le Grâce knows that the Guild is still in Paris, he will find a way to follow them, and then there will be a great deal of trouble." He untied his cotton robe. "That is all for the moment," he said, then changed his mind. "On second thought, Roger, send Hercule to me. I have some instructions to give him before I bathe."

He knelt to build up the fire in the grate, and found himself staring into the flames, held by the thought that they were vast, all-consuming. He felt as if he would find Madelaine in the flames, and in spite of the heat, he leaned farther forward, almost scorching the cotton of his open robe.

The door opened again, and Hercule came into the room. He stood just inside the door, still somewhat awkward with the braces he wore, but no longer using crutches. "Master?" he said when Saint-Germain did not turn.

"Hercule," le Comte said dreamily, still looking into the fire, "I have need of you, either tonight or tomorrow."

"Yes? What am I to do?" He hesitated, then closed the door.

With a quick, almost finicky motion, Saint-Germain brushed the ashes from his hands and rose swiftly. "I will need my barb for tonight, but by tomorrow I should have need of my coach. As you love me, will you drive for me?"

Hercule grinned hugely. "I would drive to hell, master, only to hold reins again."

Saint-Germain did not smile. "You may well do just that. I ask you to consider this before you accept: there is great danger, I fear, in what we will do. If you fail me, I am dead. And you may not live, either."

"Tell me," Hercule said after a thoughtful pause, "does this danger come from le Baron Saint Sebastien?"

"Yes."

"I see." Hercule looked steadily at le Comte, and when he spoke, there was steely resolve in his words. "If your danger is from Saint Sebastien, and I may do anything to bring him to ruin, though it cost me my life and soul, I would do it. And think myself cheated if you denied me my vengeance."

Saint-Germain nodded, his opinion confirmed. "I will need my traveling coach, Hercule. I entrust you to have it ready. You will have the heavy team harnessed, for we will have to go far and go quickly if we are to escape."

"But where?"

"We will be bound for England. My friend Mer-Herbeux has a number of messages he would want me to deliver for him in London, clandestinely, of course. No one will wonder at my sudden departure. And it will allow us to do two things at once."

"Who will go with you?" Hercule asked, thinking of the road to Calais. "I will have to arrange for a change of horses along the way, and I do not know how many will travel with you. Or do you travel alone?"

"I think not alone," Saint-Germain said slowly. "Roger will come after me in the second coach, but that does not concern me or you. I may take up one or two of the sorcerers working under us, in the cellar. It may not be wise for them to remain here."

Hercule nodded, remembering the cold-blooded ferocity of Saint Sebastien. Anyone left behind would be in grave danger from him. "I will carry them," he said.

"Good. Roger will tell you where the coach is to meet us, and at what hour. You will follow Roger's instructions exactly. He speaks for me, and with my authority." He hesitated, then continued. "I charge you most particularly to be sure that there is a fresh layer of earth under the floorboards of the coach. You will find the appropriate earth in a special crate in the stables. Roger will show you. Be sure that the earth is laid under the floorboards before you start out. It is most important."

Confused by this unorthodox request, but committed to helping Saint-Germain, Hercule repeated, "It is important. I will see that it is done as you wish."

"You must not fail me in this, for it is my strength—the good earth that has nurtured me all my life. And I will need its strength after dealing with Saint Sebastien."

Hercule bowed. "As you order, master. I will obey you." He was prepared to withdraw, and wondered if he should wait, since he had not been dismissed, though Saint-Germain appeared to have forgotten him.

"Hercule," he said distantly, "I think you had best warn Sattin and the others. They must be prepared to leave on short notice. There is a concealed tunnel that runs toward the river. It is part of the old monastery vaults on which the foundation of this building is laid. The monks used it for escape when their monastery was under attack. It is below the third cellar, and a trapdoor will take them there. It is set in the northwest corner of the cellar, and takes them into a very old burial chapel. The tunnel is in the vault next to the chapel, on the north side. If they cannot leave here unnoticed, they must use that tunnel, or we will all be very much in danger of discovery."

"Then we are to leave soon?"

"I am not certain, Hercule. I would think that by nightfall tomorrow I will know what we must do, and where. If you have no word from me by sunset tomorrow, hold yourself in readiness here, no matter what happens, and no matter who gives you instructions to the contrary. Have the coach ready, the horses harnessed, and three or four heavy rugs in the coach, as it will be cold."

"Do we want postilions or outriders?"

"One outrider is all. I leave it to you to find someone who is trustworthy. Perhaps you know of someone already.

"If I have not come to you before the dawn day after tomorrow, you must assume that Saint Sebastien has won. In that case, find Cardinal Fouet at Chambord. Tell him what you know of Saint Sebastien. Tell him also that Saint Sebastien, along with Beauvrai and others, celebrated an Amatory Mass on the body of Lucienne Cressie, who is in retreat in Brittany, at la couvent de la Miséricorde et la Justice de le Rédempteur. She will supply any proof that is needed. And, Hercule," he added very carefully, "do not let yourself be caught with this knowledge. Should you fall into Saint Sebastien's hands, be sure that you are a dead man. Too many lives ride on your silence." He looked up as the door opened and Roger stepped into the room. "What is it?"

"The bath is ready," Roger said. "I have secured a vial of holy water, and I have put the Host into your pyx. If you need them."

Saint-Germain nodded. "Thank you, Roger," he said. "I will be with you directly." He turned once more to Hercule. "Remember what I said. If you have faith, be shriven tonight."

Hercule was rather white around the mouth at these uncompromising words, but he said, "I will see the priest within the hour. St. Sulpice is not far from here, or Saint-Germain-des-Près."

"Bon. But do not tell the priest more than he needs to know. You cannot confess for Saint Sebastien. Do not reveal more than you must."

"My sins alone will be absolved," Hercule promised, then limped awkwardly from the room.

Roger said nothing while Saint-Germain looked into the fire, one small hand fingering the embroidery on the standing collar of his robe. "You do not think me wise to trust Hercule."

"No."

"I trusted you, once, Roger, before I knew you."

"With good reason."

Saint-Germain raised his brows. "And you doubt Hercule? Now, why?"

"He is a servant, master. He has always served Saint Sebastien. Obeying is a habit with him. Saint Sebastien has hurt him, it is true, but habits are not easily broken. He might, faced with his former master, find that he cannot deny him."

"Perhaps," Saint-Germain said softly. "And yet, do you know, I think he will not betray me. I think that hatred is raw enough in him that all the years that have gone before have been burned from him, as much as last year's logs on the hearth."

Roger nodded diffidently, but it was clear he had not put his doubts aside.

"Come," Saint-Germain said crisply, breaking away from the contemplative mood that had held him to the hypnotic dance of the flames. "My bath, and then the pyx."

Roger stood aside as Saint-Germain swept out of the room.

Text of a letter from l'Abbé Ponteneuf to le Marquis de Montalia, dated November 4, 1743, returned to l'Abbé by la Comtesse d'Argenlac on December 17, 1743:

Mon cher cousin, I greet you in the name of God and the Virgin.

I had hoped to receive your daughter this afternoon, so that she and I might have that little chat you have so much desired. Undoubtedly her maiden confusion has overcome her and she is reluctant to discuss so intimate a subject with me, though I am her confessor. Your note, which I had the felicity to read this morning, informing me of the request of le Marquis Chenu-Tourelle, explains much, and I certainly hope that Madelaine is aware of the honor done her by that distinguished young gentleman.

It is my intention to hear her confession on Wednesday or Thursday, and at that time I will once again attempt to turn her mind to the delights of marriage and the sweet duties of a wife. She has read my letter that touches on these things, and has said she found it most instructive.

You had mentioned her scholarship before, and I am pleased to tell you that she continues to occupy her mind with worthy matters. Her readings in history are commendable, though she does read of matters not truly fit for an unmarried woman's eyes. To be sure, it is sad to reflect that so much of history is not suitable reading for those gently born and gently reared. She has said that until now she did not understand much of the sorrow and misfortune of others around her, but that the reading of history has given her a new perspective of humanity, and where she was confused before, she now perceives humanity in truer colors.

Your concern for your daughter is most commendable, Robert. I know that your affection has done much to make your daughter the excellent young woman she is. But it is not only her soul which concerns me, but your own. How often I have exhorted you to make your confession and be received again into the bosom of Holy Mother Church. As you think on Madelaine and her future, you must think as well of your own. It is not wise of you to delay that moment when your soul is once again in Holy Communion with the Mercy Seat. Think, Robert, of the great emptiness that will fall on you if you cannot attend the marriage of your daughter. It would shame her if you had to refuse to take Communion with her at that joyous time. Think of your grandchildren, who are so far off. You will want them to enjoy the protection of the Church, and take part in all the ceremonies and celebrations that give meaning to our discourse with God through His saints.

I most earnestly pray you will come to confess, my cousin. It is important not only to me, and your cherished daughter, but it is of vital importance to you. It is your soul that stands in danger of eternal damnation. You cannot deny that when one is older, time grows increasingly precious, and it behooves you to think on your mortality and to reform your ways before the coming of the Dark Angel.

Believe me, I pray for you daily, and beg Our Lord and the Virgin to touch your heart and bring you truly repentant to us once again. It is not for worldly glory that I do this, but for the salvation of your soul. In less enlightened times, you would have been treated more severely, and even today, in Spain, you would find that your rejection of the tender love of the Church Triumphant would place you in a most unpleasant position. To be sure, the misled days of Torquemada are gone, but the Inquisition still keeps to its sacred obligation. It is sobering to think of the suffering of the body in this life, but it is much less frightful than the suffering of the soul in Hell. Do not think that you will escape that. Accept your contrition now and spare yourself an eternity of pain.

But I have said sufficient on this head. For now, you have my assurance that I will avail myself of the opportunity to talk to your daughter and abjure her to make her husband's wishes her own, his will her will, and to love his law and his chastisement even as those of us in religious life love that flail that purges our errors.

In the most prayful and faithful respects, I am in this world

> Your cousin of blood and your brother as
> we are children of God,
> l'Abbé Ponteneuf, S.J.

7

In the elegant dining room of hôtel d'Argenlac, all pretense at conversation had come to a halt. At his end of the table Gervaise started his second bottle of Bordeaux, and ignored the turbot of beef stuffed with mushrooms and fresh lobster that had been broiled in butter. Neither that succulent dish nor the two varieties of vegetables, one done in the Genoese manner, tempted his palate from the lure of his wine. He cast a jaundiced eye at the next course waiting on the sideboard and sighed audibly.

"What was that, Gervaise?" Claudia asked too quickly, her eyes turned toward her brother, who sat at her right hand.

"Nothing, nothing." He picked his glass up by the stem and held it up so that the light shone through the wine. "I was thinking that I should depart soon. It has struck nine, and I am engaged to meet Lambeaugârenne at ten. I doubt I will have time to finish more of this supper of yours. You will be pleased to have time alone with Robert, I am sure. You may gossip about the family and complain of me to him until the candles gutter, for all I care." He was about to swing himself unsteadily to his feet when one of the lackeys opened the dining-room door, very much flustered. "Well?" Gervaise demanded.

The lackey began uneasily. "There . . . there is a message, master. It is brought by a messenger. . . ."

"I will read it in the yellow salon," he said peevishly recalling the bet for six thousand louis he had lost that day. His face filled with petulance as he remembered that encounter. "The goose should have won," he muttered, as he reconsidered the race between a goose and a hare. "The goose has wings."

"My dear . . . ?" Claudia said anxiously.

"I beg your pardon," the lackey dared to interrupt, "but the letter is not for you, master, it is for le Marquis de Montalia."

Robert turned, startled and strangely afraid. "For me?" He had a fleeting thought that perhaps Madelaine required his support at hôtel Chenu-Tourelle, but he put this from his mind. "I thank you for bringing it to me." He held out his hand for the message and waited as the lackey placed the sealed sheets in his fingers. He started to put it down beside his plate, for it was terribly rude to read such messages while at table.

"No, Robert, pray read it." Claudia looked toward the lackey. "Who brought the message?"

"A servant in dark blue and red," the lackey said. "I am not familiar with the livery."

But Robert de Montalia obviously was. His face had gone the color of chalk, and quite suddenly his hands were unsteady. Even Gervaise shook his head truculently, knowing that his capricious invitation to Madelaine's fête the night before had brought much abuse on his head. "Sounds like Saint Sebastien's man," he said, to forestall any accusations against him.

"Yes," Robert said quietly. "Do you mind?" he asked his sister as he reached for the sealed sheets. One look at the cinc-foil signet on the seal confirmed what Gervaise had said. It was Saint Sebastien. He broke the seal and spread out the two crossed sheets, reading slowly, as if translating a difficult foreign language.

"Ah, Holy Mother," Claudia said to herself as she watched the expression on her brother's face become a mask of anguish. "Is it Madelaine?"

"Yes." Robert crumpled the two sheets and flung them across the room with a sudden oath. He rose from his chair, his sudden movement upsetting his wineglass, spilling the burgundy over the pale damask tablecloth.

"Saint Sebastien?" Gervaise said, puzzled. "She went out with Chenu-Tourelle. What has Saint Sebastien to say to her?"

Robert had ground his teeth. "He is my enemy," he said. "He has kidnapped Madelaine. He says . . . I dare not repeat what he says."

"There is a mistake," Gervaise said, for the first time wondering if there was. He took a hasty mouthful of wine, wiped his hand over his lips and said, "Look here, de Montalia, I know Saint Sebastien. He has said that he wants to renew your friendship of twenty years ago. He's probably asked Chenu-Tourelle to bring that girl of yours to his house, and wants you to join him. He is a trifle forbidding, but you must not be put off by that."

"A trifle forbidding?" Robert's voice had risen, and he held his fists at his side like wooden mallets. "He is dangerous, he is evil! He tells me in that . . . that pernicious letter that he is going to make a sacrifice of my child!" He stopped abruptly, seeing his horror reflected in his sister's eyes.

"Sacrifice? What sort of nonsense is that?"

"It is not nonsense," Robert said heavily. "Saint Sebastien intends to offer Madelaine in body and blood to Satan." He covered his eyes with his hands. "I must stop him."

Gervaise tried to scoff, and almost succeeded. "Offering to Satan? The last of that happened when Montespan was the Sun King's mistress. The police put an end to it, you may be sure."

"Gervaise, don't," Claudia begged him.

"No, it did not end then," Robert said, as if the words were dragged from him. "It became invisible, it became secret, but it did not end. And Saint Sebastien leads the Circle now. I know. I know," he said more loudly, stopping Gervaise before he could speak. "I know, because I was once part of that Circle. I know that he will do what he has promised to do to Madelaine, because I gave him that right before she was born." His voice broke, and tears coursed down the seams of his face. "God forgive me, I did not know."

Claudia had risen and taken her brother into her arms. She regarded her embarrassed servants with distress, but mastered herself enough to issue a few terse orders. "Paulin, I will want some brandy for le Marquis. Fetch it at once. Soussère, send word to the stable to harness the racing carriage. Aiguille, remove the dishes and take them back to the kitchen. Tell my chef that we have had tragic news and cannot do his artistry justice." She smoothed Robert's hair back from his face and looked at him. "We will find her," she said with a conviction she did not feel. "We will find her and bring her to safety. You may leave shortly. Gervaise will go with you—"

"But Lambeaugârenne . . ." Gervaise objected.

"I am sure Everaud Lambeaugârenne can wait one night to fleece you, my dear," she said with asperity. "Send him your regrets."

"But this is all a mistake!" Gervaise insisted.

"Then the sooner you take Robert to Saint Sebastien, the sooner it will be resolved and you may keep your appointment with Lambeaugârenne." She looked up at Robert. "You will find her, dearest brother. You will."

"Oh, Holy Blood of Christ," he said, his shock deepening.

"Send for help, Robert, write a petition to His Majesty immediately. I'll see that it's delivered at once. I'll explain to him. When he understands, King Louis will authorize Saint Sebastien's arrest," Claudia advised, trying to turn his thoughts from the malefic visions the letter had conjured in him.

He glanced down, murmuring, "I have ruined your beautiful table-cloth. I did not mean to."

"It is nothing," she said gently. "Come, Robert, you must get your coat, if you are going out on such a night as this. Gervaise will go with you. All will be well, I am certain of it." She disengaged herself from Robert's arm as she said this, and then said to her husband, "You will need a coat, as well, Gervaise. There is a storm coming."

"Oh, very well," Gervaise grumbled. "I'll be at your disposal within a quarter of an hour. I must write a note to Lambeaugârenne. Servant," he said tersely as he made the most perfunctory of bows.

When he was gone from the room, Claudia gave her full attention to Robert. "Where is she?"

"At hôtel Saint Sebastien, I would guess. The letter came from there." He paused. "I was told that I would be killed if I tried to come after her, and that anyone who helped me would also be killed. I would not object, if Gervaise does not wish to accompany me."

"And let you go alone among those dreadful people?" Claudia was incredulous. "Gervaise knows several of those men. They will not harm him, Robert. They know he is a gambler and often drinks too much. He represents no threat to them. You might, but you are not known in Paris, and few would miss you if you were to disappear. With Gervaise it is otherwise. If he were not to spend five days out of seven at Hôtel Transylvania or Hôtel de Ville, half of Paris would hear of it." She said the words in a flat bitterness that told Robert, more than ranting would, of the state of her life with Gervaise d'Argenlac.

"Are you very unhappy?" he asked ruefully.

"No, of course not. Perhaps a little," she amended, then added, "I daresay if we had children it would be otherwise. A man without heirs does not feel he has a great investment in his own future." She turned her thoughts from this unproductive route. "He will be good company for you, Robert. He can deal with Saint Sebastien. It may require money—"

"I doubt it," Robert interpolated.

"Or other payment, but it will be made." She crossed the room to the marble-fronted fireplace, realizing as she did so that she had become very cold. "I have some advice to give you, my dear, and I hope you won't despise it."

"What is it?"

"Send a lackey to Saint-Germain." She saw the distaste in her brother's face and hurried on. "Hear me out before you say no. Saint-Germain is not French, and he is almost wholly immune to scandal. He may not seem so, but I understand that he is formidable in a fight. He fought a duel last week that surprised half of the beau monde. He is fond of Madelaine, and I know would be willing to assist you."

Robert strove for composure, and said to his sister in a forcibly contained voice, "It is demeaning enough to ask your husband to involve himself in this sordid affair. I will not ask someone outside of our family, let alone a foreigner, no matter how fond he is of Madelaine, to become involved in something that would surely disgust him." He licked his lips, as if cleaning a bad taste from them. "I am afraid I must leave you now if I am to reach Saint Sebastien in time. Pray that I do, Claudia."

"With all my heart, Robert." She resisted the urge to run to him and weep. With an effort, she kept herself by the fireplace, her face showing concern unmarred by doubt. "I will pray. Do bring Madelaine as swiftly as may be."

"I will," Robert promised, then went to the door and was gone.

Now that she was alone, Claudia let herself shed the tears she had held back. It was a ragged, tearing grief that was like a physical pain. She knew that her face was mottled red and white, and that her evening coiffure was quite ruined, but that did not matter. So lost was she in her despair that she did not hear the carriage pull away from hôtel d'Argenlac, nor, twenty minutes later, did she hear a single horse arrive.

Her first awareness came when a well-known voice spoke from the doorway. "My dear Comtesse."

Claudia raised her sorrow-filled face to the familiar stranger in the door. "Saint-Germain."

"I must ask your forgiveness. I would not let the lackey announce me. I was afraid you would refuse me." He came across the room to her. She saw that he was dressed for riding, and wearing even more severely simple clothes than usual.

"I . . . we . . . there was bad news earlier."

"Madelaine," he said, and it was not a question.

"Yes. She has been . . . detained. . . . And Robert has gone to fetch her—he and Gervaise. . . . They will be sorry to have missed you."

"I doubt it." He dragged a chair near to her. "If Madelaine were merely detained, it would not take both her father and your husband to bring her home. And you, my dear," he added in a kinder tone, "would not be weeping. Tell me what it is."

"Robert does not want—"

"If your tiresome brother does not want help, then he is a greater fool than I thought." Saint-Germain took one of Claudia's hands in his. "My dear, believe me, I would not interfere if it were possible for le Marquis to save your niece alone. But it is not possible. They are determined to kill Madelaine, are they not? Saint Sebastien and his Circle?"

She made a helpless gesture. "I don't know. Robert had a letter . . ."

"A letter? Did he take it with him?"

"I don't . . ." She looked up, some of her despondency dropping from her. "No. He threw it away. It should be . . ." She looked about the floor. "There. By the second tree of candles."

Saint-Germain rose and retrieved the letter, flattening the crumpled sheets so that he could read their message. His face became more and more grim as he read. When he was finished, he handed the letter to Claudia. "Burn this," he said shortly. "Do not read it, just burn it." He took a turn about the room, his eyes smoldering, their darkness becoming more intense.

Claudia obediently held the letter to the flame of one of the candles on the mantel. "Is it that serious, Saint-Germain?"

"I am afraid it is." He stopped his pacing and studied her. "Saint Sebastien is planning to kill her. And that is the least of it."

Claudia put her hand to her mouth. "But surely . . ."

"And if you would help her, there are some things you must do."

She nodded, finding this sudden authority in Saint-Germain disturbing. He had always been compelling, but she had told herself it was merely a trick of the eyes. But now she saw his force without the courtly facade, and she realized that he was much more formidable than ever she had thought. "Tell me, Comte. I will do anything I can for my niece."

"Good. First you are to send a messenger to la rue de Ecoulè-Romain to a physician named André Schoenbrun. He is as accomplished as any in the medical arts, and he is very, very discreet. You may have his services as you require, and not worry about unpleasant rumors spreading."

"Do you think Madelaine will need a physician?"

"Very likely. She will also need a priest. Who is her confessor?"

"L'Abbé Ponteneuf. He is a cousin of ours."

Saint-Germain frowned. "I have heard her speak of him. She does not like him, and is afraid that he tells things he should not. We will require another. I leave it to you to find a priest, preferably a young one, with courage and excellent silence. There must be such a one in Paris."

Claudia nodded numbly. "A priest," she echoed.

He paused as he fastened his cloak again. "I cannot stay. Every minute I delay, there is greater danger. If you are correct, I will find your brother and husband alone with Madelaine at hôtel Saint Sebastien, and we will all return to you before midnight. But if it is otherwise, you will not see us until after dawn, perhaps. If none of us have returned by nine of the clock, send word to my servant Roger. He has instructions from me."

"I will," she said, her tone firmer than it had been when he arrived. "Godspeed, Saint-Germain."

Saint-Germain lifted his brows. "Godspeed? Why not?" And then the door closed, and Claudia heard the firm, quick tread as he left hôtel d'Argenlac.

Text of a letter from the physician André Schoenbrun in answer to one from la Comtesse d'Argenlac, dated November 5, 1743:

The physician André Schoenbrun of la rue de Ecoulè-Romain sends his respectful compliments to la Comtesse d'Argenlac and wishes to inform her that he has received her note of the earlier evening requesting his present at her hôtel as soon as is possible.

The physician is pleased to agree to la Comtesse's kind request and will present himself to her in the hour before dawn. At that time, the physician would appreciate it if la Comtesse will provide him with more information on the nature and characteristics of the ill or ills he is to treat. Medical art being what it is, the physician is reluctant to proceed blindly.

In the event that la Comtesse's fears prove ill-founded, the physician will recommend a nurse of experience and pious disposition to watch over the victim she mentions. Oftentimes it is the soul that suffers more than the body, no matter how deeply abused the physical being may be. The physician has, on more than one occasion, seen how a man may die of fear or of despair that cannot be traced to a physical ill. Indeed, it is the opinion of the physician that the mind and soul alone bring about apoplexy and all its ills, for the physician has noted that such events most often occur when the victim is at his most choleric. It is otherwise with women. Women of the most submissive, meek, and mild temperaments alone are prey to apoplexy. Where overt hostility in the male brings on the apoplectic stroke, women succumb to the ill in the opposite case.

But it is not the intent of the undersigned to dwell on matters that must be of no interest to la Comtesse. He craves her indulgence of his unseemly enthusiasm, and begs that la Comtesse will believe him to be

Hers to command,
André Schoenbrun, physician

8

As her senses returned, each added its own unpleasant burden to Madelaine's fear. Her hands and feet tingled, and when she tried to flex them, she felt ropes binding her wrists and ankles, and realized that she was tied down on a cold stone surface. Her mouth grew drier as her muddled memory threw off the last of the drug. What had she done under the drug's influence, she wondered, that she had to be confined in this immodest and hideously uncomfortable manner? She opened her eyes, and a kind of dizziness seized her, so that she closed them once again to shut out what she had seen.

"So you are awake," said the cultured, hated voice. "I am relieved."

She felt his fingertips and nails as he drew them lightly over her abdomen. She said quite distinctly, "If you do that again, I will be sick."

Saint Sebastien chuckled nastily. "You must not promise me such treats. You will make me too anxious." He touched her flesh again, this time tracing the arch of her ribs. "You are wonderfully firm. That means strength and health." He ran the end of his tongue over his lips. "No," he said rather breathlessly to himself. "No, not too soon. Now there is only anger, and there must be terror and capitulation before more is done. She must welcome her ravishers and her humiliation."

Madelaine knew that she was meant to overhear this, and that Saint Sebastien intended that it should frighten her. She steeled herself against the words, swallowing down the bile that rose in her throat. Slowly she tested the bonds again, and found that they were only too secure.

"My dear," Saint Sebastien murmured, "when you arch your lovely body and twist in that painful way, I can hardly resist succumbing to your charms." He paused long enough to draw his nails over her body from her neck to the soft cleft between her legs. "It is not time for that yet. There are other things I must do before that." Quite suddenly he pinched her skin at the hip, under her breasts, and on the upper arm.

Madelaine's eyes stung with tears and outrage, but she bit back the sound that surged in her. When she was sure she could speak without screaming, she said, "May God damn you."

Saint Sebastien spread his mouth in a soundless laugh and let himself respond at his most urbane. "You are a little late, my dear. As your father should have told you."

"No." Madelaine blinked as against a threatened blow.

"So you know something of his oath," Saint Sebastien said speculatively. "Who could have told you?"

"What oath?" It was a clumsy distraction, and she knew it. Her heart seemed to solidify as she watched Saint Sebastien, hating herself for letting herself be so visibly eager for a denial of what Chenu-Tourelle had said.

"The one he gave many years ago. Before you were born, my dear." He put his hand between her legs and played negligently with the delicate tissues. "He gave you to me, Madelaine, to be mine utterly." On the last word he brutally thrust three fingers deep inside her, smiling slowly as she shrieked and pulled futilely in her bonds, her thighs working to close against his casual, vile intrusion. "Not yet, not yet, my dear. Resign yourself to my will." He moved his hand and pain shuddered through her. "Not tonight, but tomorrow night, I will take your virginity. I will not be the only one to use you. And as the nights pass, our uses will grow with our imagination. You think that this hurts you?" He chuckled as her movement confirmed it. "This is the merest taste, Madelaine. Remember that." He moved back from her, leaving her panting, the sheen of sweat on her body though she shivered with fear and cold.

"Tonight," he went on with a grand gesture, "you remain here with me some little while." He glanced around his study as if the room itself were a pleasant discovery. "At the dark of night, which comes in the third hour after midnight, we will join the others."

"The others?" The words were hushed with dismay.

"There are quite a few of them. You will find many familiar faces, Madelaine." He strode around the room, taking satisfaction that her eyes followed him wherever he moved. "Those who have desired you will be gratified. Those who despise you will find the means to vindicate themselves. In the next forty days we will take away your humanity, my dear. And when you are nothing, you will die for the forces of Satan, for whom destruction is pleasing." He tugged at a bell rope, and almost instantly the door was opened by a tall, large man of saturnine face and greedy eyes. He was wearing the dark-blue-and-red livery of Saint Sebastien's household. "This is Tite, my manservant. He is your guard, my dear. Do not think that your beauty or your anguish will rouse pity in him: he takes pleasure in hatred."

Tite nodded, his eyes flicking over Madelaine's nakedness. "Five have arrived," he informed his master without taking his attention from her. "When will I have her?"

"Tomorrow night, Tite. After I do. She will be yours for the rest of the night." He said this as if giving a child a sweet. "Bring the others in. And her maid."

With a bow compounded of groveling and insolence, Tite withdrew.

Saint Sebastien stood by the door for a moment, then went to a large closed case that stood against the far wall. He opened the case and selected a few items from its interior, closing it once more as he turned back to Madelaine. His sjambok was coiled around one arm, and he held a short device in his hand that looked like a bamboo whisk broom. He held up the latter, considering it critically. "I think this will be best," he said to her. "It does not generally break the skin."

Madelaine felt a cringing fear begin, which she fought down. She would not give him the satisfaction of seeing her courage crumble. The marble table top felt even colder now.

"Good," Saint Sebastien approved. "It would be a pity if you were broken too soon. It is your resistance that makes the final degradation so potent." He tapped the stubby bamboo whip against his hand.

Once again the door opened, and five men came into the room. Madelaine gasped as she recognized them. There was de la Sept-Nuit, with an expression of lewd anticipation in his face; beside him Châteaurose, who appeared nervously excited; with him was Achille Cressie, who showed Madelaine one contemptuous sneer before resuming his conversation with de les Radeux, who had come with his uncle, le Baron Beauvrai.

Châteaurose ambled across the study to the heavy table where Madelaine was tied. "Well met, Mademoiselle," he said at his most respectful. "You have no idea how delighted I am to see you this way."

"We're all delighted to see you this way," de la Sept-Nuit agreed. "And you cannot imagine how much I am looking forward to knowing you better." He, too, came to the table and looked down at her. "Charming, I protest," he said with insolent grace.

Madelaine said nothing, but an angry flush mounted in her face and neck.

A shocked cry from the door made her turn to see Cassandre, her maid, dragged into the room by Tite. "Oh, Merciful God and all the saints," she wailed.

"Tite," Saint Sebastien rapped out, "silence her."

"That I will," Tite said, and brought his huge hand down on Cassandre's neck. The blow was a heavy one, and Cassandre, middle-aged and exhausted with the appalling events of the day, slipped to the floor in a heap without resistance or protest.

The men had all gathered around the table where Madelaine lay now, and were silent, preparing for the task ahead of them.

They had not long to wait, for shortly Saint Sebastien said with languor, "I think we must turn her over. This"—he showed them the bamboo whip—"works best on the buttocks and thighs. You, Donatien, take her arms, and you, mon cher Baron"—he gave Beauvrai a formal bow—"her feet. The rest may untie her bonds and retie them when we have her in place. Be careful when you turn her, as she is very likely going to fight."

Achille had looked curiously at the bamboo whip, his interest piqued. "Is that a comb, Saint Sebastien?"

"I am loathe to disappoint you, Achille, but we will not use the combs for a few days yet. And those must be used only on the soles of the feet. No, this is quite different. Shall I show you what it does?"

Though she had twisted, pulled, squirmed, and tried to bite, Madelaine had been ruthlessly turned prone and retied. Her head dangled over the end of the table, and her legs, still forced wide apart, were beginning to ache. She gritted her teeth as Saint Sebastien once again fondled her, promising the others that they would be allowed the same privilege after he had demonstrated the bamboo whip.

"It is used thus—the strokes very fast and light, hardly more than taps. The rhythm should be even," he said as he used the bamboo on her buttocks. "You say that this is dull. But wait. In a few minutes you will see the excellence of this little Chinese whip. I have always found that the Chinese are a most ingenious people."

Already Madelaine was feeling the effects of the bamboo. Blood rushed to her buttocks, and the skin started to swell, making each blow more agonizing to her as the sensitivity increased.

"Do you see?" Saint Sebastien asked. "Ten more minutes of this, and the skin would enlarge to twice its normal size, and she would experience the keenest agony if so much as a drop of water touched the skin, or a feather."

"Will you do that?" Beauvrai asked hungrily.

"Not yet, I think. But certainly we must do so before we are done. Think of possessing her when her body cannot endure to be touched. That must be for later." He was about to continue, when there was a sudden breaking of glass and splintering of wood as one of the french doors at the end of the study burst open and Robert de Montalia stumbled into the room, followed by Gervaise d'Argenlac. The shattered remnants of the french doors spread around their feet.

"*Stop!*" Robert de Montalia shouted as he brought his musket to his shoulder, aiming it unwaveringly at Saint Sebastien.

Most of the men around the table had the grace to be shocked, and Châteaurose looked embarrassed. Only Saint Sebastien was unperturbed, and even, judging by the smile that pulled at the corners of his mouth, amused. "Good evening," he said when he was certain that Robert would not pull the trigger at once. "I see you have decided to join us."

"Stand away from her."

"No." He nodded mockingly. "Your daughter is in my hands, Robert. As you gave me your word she would be."

"You can't do that!" Robert's desperation bordered on insanity now, and his voice rose to a scream.

"Why? Because you wish to reserve that honor for yourself?" He gestured to his companions. "I am sure these gentlemen will wait, if that is your pleasure. You have a right to her, after mine." He tweaked Madelaine's swollen buttocks, and the cry that escaped her brought new torment to her father's ravaged face.

"Let her go, Clotaire," Robert said hoarsely. "Let her go and I will stay. No matter what you do, or how long it takes you to do it. I will stay."

"Of course you will," Saint Sebastien agreed affably. Then, with feigned amazement: "Surely you did not think I would allow you to leave, did you? You read my note, I assume. You, of all people, should know that I meant what I said."

Gervaise, who had drunk most of a bottle of wine in the carriage ride to hôtel Saint Sebastien, gathered his fuddled wits and moved uncertainly toward the table. "Lord God of the Fishes," he slurred. "What are you doing to Madelaine?"

"We are making a sacrifice." Saint Sebastien motioned Gervaise away with a disdainful flick of his hand.

But Gervaise was not to be put off. He had a drunkard's tenacity, and had reached a pugnacious stage in his inebriation. "You can't make a sacrifice of a noble. It isn't done. What are you sacrificing her for, anyway? Tell me that."

"For power," Saint Sebastien snapped, as he brought up his hand again. "Robert, you choose your allies most unwisely."

"Damn you for a pernicious whoreson," Gervaise roared as he reeled toward the table. "You don't strip a lady of quality and beat her for the amusement of your friends, Saint Sebastien." He peered at the others. "There's something damn wrong about this," he said slowly.

Ignoring Gervaise, Saint Sebastien said, "I am not a patient man, Robert. The more you prolong this little melodrama, the less charitable I will be with you."

"Stand away from my daughter," Robert said icily.

"I think not." Saint Sebastien did not turn as he issued his orders. "Tite, if I am shot by this foolish man, I give you leave to kill him in any way you like, with the help of our friends here." He motioned his servant to move aside, out of Robert's line of fire.

"Killing," Gervaise announced, though no one appeared to listen, "is a matter for the courts. We need a magistrate." He pushed away from the table and set out across the broken glass for the gaping hole where the french doors had been forced. "You hold 'em, Robert. I'll see if I can rouse an officer at this hour. . . . Should be one somewh—"

Saint Sebastien had already unwound his sjambok when he said, "Stand aside, gentlemen." The lash coiled out like something live and predatory, its thin, hard leather cutting deeply into Gervaise's neck above his loosened jabot. Gervaise made a sound like a hiccough as blood welled around the whip, spattering his waistcoat and cloak as he staggered backward. Saint Sebastien slackened the sjambok as if playing a fish on a line, then jerked the whip tight once more. In the silent room there was a sound like a tree branch snapping. Crazily, like a marionette whose strings have suddenly been cut, Gervaise folded to the floor and was still.

For a moment the study was still. Then: *"You monster!"* Even as his yell burst from his lips, Robert aimed his musket, at the same moment that Saint Sebastien flicked the sjambok free of Gervaise's flesh. There was an ear-shattering noise when the musket's charge exploded as the sjambok snatched it from Robert, sending it smashing against a case of antique musical instruments.

"Seize him, Tite," Saint Sebastien said as he gathered in his lethal African whip.

"I will," Tite said, stalking across the study to Robert. On the table, Madelaine saw this and moaned.

Le Marquis de Montalia stepped back from Tite, pulling at his sword which hung in its scabbard at his side under his cloak. There was a scrape, and the weapon was out, and Robert, with a cry, lunged forward, burying the sword halfway to its hilt in Tite's chest.

Tite howled and clawed first at the sword and then grabbed for Robert, his big bloodstained hands crashing into le Marquis' face as he fell forward onto Gervaise's body.

Robert swayed dangerously but did not fall. Tite's blows had been weakened, or Robert would have been stunned. He slipped once on the glass and blood, dropping to one knee before he recovered.

"Vastly entertaining," Saint Sebastien said slowly. "What did you think to prove, Robert?" He came toward le Marquis, negligently toying with the lash of the sjambok. "Surely you did not believe that I would allow you to stop me?"

"I don't know." It had seemed easy when he had rushed out of his sister's house. He had the full force of virtue and love in the face of vice and degeneracy. When he and Gervaise had arrived at hôtel Saint Sebastien, it had been only a matter of holding Saint Sebastien and his Circle at bay while Madelaine was carried to safety. How stupidly simplistic that was, Robert realized now.

"Poor Robert, so righteous." Saint Sebastien motioned to the other men in the room. "But you see, I have her, and now I have you, mon cher Robert." He paused. "I suppose you have told Gervaise's widow where you are? I see I need not have asked. That is inconvenient." He turned to his Circle. "One of you take him to the room in the stable, where Le Grâce is. You, Achille. I am sure you will find a way to amuse our guest until I have made up my mind what to do with him."

Achille's eyes grew bright. "He's a very attractive man, Clotaire. Be sure to allow me sufficient time." He saw Robert shrink as he understood. "He's reluctant." Achille was delighted. "He will not be reluctant when I have done with him."

"Certainly," Saint Sebastien agreed as he pushed Robert toward Achille. "But be sure he is firmly tied. He may have a few surprises left for us."

Achille giggled as he came nearer. "Are you sure you don't want me to minister to him here, where she can watch?"

"Perhaps later. But not now." He went to his chest and removed two lengths of braided leather. "Here. Secure him with these. Do not resist, mon cher Robert, or your daughter will suffer for it." He waited as Achille bound Robert's hands behind him, then said, "I had not planned to leave here until tomorrow, but it may be wise to go to the chapel tonight."

Achille pouted. "How long will I have?"

"Perhaps an hour. No more. There are a few things to finish up here." He slid a sideways glance at Madelaine. "We have not done all we might."

"Very well." Achille shoved Robert ahead of him to the library door. "I

have a knife, Marquis. There are many painful places I might use it."
With a last giggle he thrust Robert from the room, going out behind him.

"Where are we going, Clotaire? I don't mind telling you I don't like interruptions of this sort."

"Neither do I, Beauvrai," Saint Sebastien said slowly. "That is why we are going to the chapel. It is one of the hidden ones La Voison used for la Marquise de Montespan when she practiced the Arts. The police found one, but there are several others, and this is by far the most convenient." He came back to the table and looked down at Madelaine. "You and I will take her in my carriage, I think. The rest of you may follow on horseback."

"But, Saint Sebastien," de la Sept-Nuit objected, "you told me I might have some time with her. . . ."

Saint Sebastien nodded. "So I did. Very well. I have a few notes to write to the others, telling them where we are to meet. You may have a quarter of an hour with her, and then Beauvrai, and then Châteaurose. You may use your hands on her, but you must not beat her yet. You are sufficiently imaginative to invent other torments. But I warn you, her virginity is mine. I will not relinquish that to anyone." He held the door open for the others, smiling at de la Sept-Nuit. "Enjoy yourself."

Madelaine heard the door close, and she held her breath. Out of the corner of her eye she could see the bodies of her aunt's husband and Tite piled together like broken furniture. She could also see de la Sept-Nuit's feet as he moved toward her. She clenched her hands in their bonds. "De la Sept-Nuit," she said as calmly as she could, "why do you do this? It is evil, Chevalier. Think of the penalties."

De la Sept-Nuit ran abusive hands over her. "Think of the power, Madelaine. Clotaire has promised leadership of the Circle when he is done, if I show myself worthy. You are part of the test."

She felt helplessness possess her for the first time. She tried in vain to shut out the painful indignities le Chevalier de la Sept-Nuit worked upon her, to think of other things. But the bodies lying in the spreading pool of blood could not be ignored, nor the pitiful figure of her maid Cassandre, nor the vicious hands that defiled her. More than anything in her life she wanted Saint-Germain to save her, to take her away from hurt and fear and humiliation. But two men had tried to save her already, and one was dead, lying less than ten feet away from her, and the other was a captive in as dangerous a position as she was. So she prayed silently, fervently, wretchedly. She prayed she would go mad.

Excerpt from one of a series of letters written by le Baron Clotaire de Saint Sebastien to the absent members of his Circle; undated:

. . . The chapel may be reached by a secret tunnel that leads from the Seine to the abandoned vaults of the monastery that stood near the river over five hundred years ago. You will find the entrance to the tunnel on the river side of Quai Malaquais between la rue des Saints Péres and la rue de Seine. The tunnel is reinforced with heavy stones, and you should bring a club with you, for there are many rats.

. . . On the other side of the burial vaults is the chapel. It is rumored that practices of our sort were in effect there as long ago as the reign of the Spider King, which is auspicious. Certainly it has seen more recent use, for La Voison mentioned it, and several others like it in and around Paris, to many of that Circle, to which my grandfather belonged.

The chapel itself is almost directly under Hôtel Transylvania. I find myself amused by this contrast. Above us, our splendid equals will be playing at dice, and risking several generations' fortune on the turn of a card, thinking that they have found the answer to power and fame, while we, far under their feet, will perform the rituals that will bring us power as they do not know exists, and the control of France more potent than the throne.

Let me warn you: apparently there is some means of access to the chapel from Hôtel Transylvania, although I have not discovered it, and it is doubtful that the owners of the Hôtel or the staff are aware of it. But you will admit that it would be most unfortunate if any of our number should use it, and even more important if any unlucky member of the Hôtel's staff should happen to discover our presence. For that, and other reasons, I will insist that each of you take turns standing guard. You will not be deprived of the delights of our sacrifice, or the use of our offering, who I find will be excellent. Even the slight taste I have had of her tells me that it will be a splendid thing to destroy her. But we must be secret. Reflection on the scandal that accompanied the last discovery of a Circle should make the need for these precautions obvious to you. One Affair of the Poisons is enough for France. I will not tolerate any of you being so clumsy as was Montespan.

As I write this last message the hour of one has struck. I charge you to be at the chapel by the third hour of the morning, as we have planned. It may be a good thing that we have moved to the chapel ahead of the planned time for it reduces our chance of discovery and allows more leisure to make the offerings acceptable.

If you fail me in this, I will know you for my enemy, and will deal with you accordingly at my first opportunity. If you will not bow before Satan, you may still be of use to him, and to me. Think of the dismal fate of others who have stood against me, and let your decision reflect the benefit of your contemplations.

Until the third hour of the morning, then, and the first ritual, when we will offer on the altar the body of one who has betrayed me, be certain that you are in my thoughts—for advantage and luxury beyond your fondest hopes, or destruction, as you choose. It is my honor to be

Your most devoted
Baron Clotaire de Saint Sebastien

❦ 9 ❦

As the curve of the road brought hôtel Saint Sebastien into view at last, Saint-Germain heard a distant clock strike the hour of one. He pulled in the barb, holding the gray stallion firmly while he studied the rising bulk of the hôtel. The gates would be locked—of that he was certain; and it was reasonable to assume that there would be guards on the grounds. Most of the hôtel was dark, but toward the rear, a few windows gave off a muted golden light. He was not certain which room that was, but even at this distance he could see by the movements of the curtains that one of the french doors was open.

He had made up his mind to try to enter hôtel Saint Sebastien through the open door when the heavy iron gates in the wall that surrounded the hôtel's holdings swung open and two men on horseback appeared. Both spurred their mounts down the road to Paris. Saint-Germain, glad now that he had stopped where he had, pulled his barb to the side of the road into the cover of the flowering shrubs that bordered the small orchard attached to hôtel Saint Sebastien.

The riders plunged by him, and Saint-Germain recognized Châteaurose as one of them. His apprehension, which had deepened steadily since he left Claudia d'Argenlac, now held him with new intensity. He knew enough of these men to realize that they had not abandoned their schemes, and the only other thing that would account for this strange flight was a sudden change of plans.

Even as he watched, he saw another rider emerge from the gate and set off in another direction.

Saint-Germain did not want to risk discovery, and was uncertain how many more horsemen might rush past him in the night. He turned the barb's head into the shrub hedge, forcing the dark-gray stallion through the barrier and into the orchard. When he felt he was far enough from the road, he dismounted and secured his mount's bridle to one of the almond trees.

The lights in the house had gone out, and he could just see the shine of a lantern as two or possibly three shadowy figures moved toward the stables.

He crouched low, running with a swiftness that was not entirely human. He kept his dark eyes set on the figures, and when they disappeared into the stable, he put on a burst of speed that took him up the wide carriage drive and close to the terrace of the hôtel. There he paused, uncertain whether to follow the men in the stable or enter the house through the french doors, which he now saw were broken.

There was an eruption of sound from the stable, and a large traveling coach drawn by four restive light-colored horses bowled into view. Saint-Germain did not need to see the cinc-foil on the door panels to recognize it as one of Saint Sebastien's, for le Baron always drove light-colored horses.

Saint-Germain moved swiftly through the splintered french doors into the darkened room. He slipped, and his hand came away from the floor sticky. He did not need a light to tell him that the substance was blood, for his senses were fired with it. His vision expanded, and he could see the two crumpled figures, Tite, facing him, and Gervaise with vacant eyes on the far corner of the room.

For a moment Saint-Germain stood still, then murmured to the pathetic figures there, "Poor fools. Gervaise, why would you not believe?" He felt it was futile, but he paused to make the sign of the cross on Gervaise's forehead before moving back toward the door.

A moan from the corner stopped him. He turned quickly, prepared to attack who or whatever had made the sound. Then he saw Cassandre huddled against the wall. Moving carefully, he crossed the room once more, and dropped to his knee beside Madelaine's servant.

Cassandre's gaze wandered, and though she undoubtedly tried to move, her body made only a feeble, flopping response to the orders of her will. Finally, with great effort, she said, "They left. Madelaine is . . . with them. . . . I heard them . . ."

Making his voice gentle, insistent, Saint-Germain calmed her, knowing that if Cassandre grew frightened, he would not learn anything from her. "Yes. You are doing well. You need not be frightened. They are gone and I will help you. I want to help you. I want to help Madelaine. If you tell me what you have heard, then I promise you I will find her before she is harmed."

Tears welled in the maidservant's eyes, and she made a vain effort to check them. "Madelaine . . . Madelaine . . . Oh, my dear child . . ." Keening sobs destroyed her words.

"No, no, Madame," Saint-Germain said, his voice soothing her again.

"If you weep, you will not be able to tell me where Madelaine has gone."
He waited then, for what seemed interminable minutes, while Cassandre
put aside her tears and found sufficient strength to speak rationally.

"I am better now," she said in a low voice. "But I am badly frightened.
Oh, very badly. Le Baron has taken Madelaine away . . ." Here she trembled, but held herself in check. "No, I cannot. He, le Baron, has taken
Madelaine and her worthy father with him. He has said he has a place, a
chapel, he called it, but it must be consecrated to evil if that monster can
walk there."

"Be sure you are in the right," Saint-Germain interpolated grimly.

"It is a chapel, where he will kill Madelaine, and le Marquis. Oh, my
sweet Madelaine!"

"But where is this chapel? Did he say?"

Again Cassandre fought down her grief. "It is . . . one that was used
before, by Montespan's set."

"Did they say where?"

"No." Cassandre's face worked, and she did not stop the tears that wet
her wrinkled face.

Saint-Germain felt his hand harden, and he was about to leave, when
another thought struck him. "Is there anyone left here, Madame? There is
still a chance someone might know where Saint Sebastien has gone."

Cassandre shook her head mutely, a thin wail escaping her tightened
lips. Then she said in a shuddery voice, "No . . . wait . . . The stable
. . . Le Marquis was taken to the stable . . . There may be something . . ."

"Bon. You have done well, Madame." Saint-Germain took both Cassandre's hands in his, noting with concern that they were very cold. "Now
I want you to listen to me. I am going to find Madelaine and her father.
You have my word that I will send help to you, but it may not be for some
little time yet. You are not to despair and you are not to be frightened."
He leaned toward her. "You will rest now, Madame, for you have earned
it. You will sleep easily, and your hurts will leave you. Your fear will be
gone when you waken, and your heart will be light. Sleep now." He
passed one of his small hands over her eyes, which closed obediently, and
as he rose, he could hear her breathing become more regular. She would
do well, he was certain.

Before he left Saint Sebastien's study, he pulled down two of the velvet
curtains and flung them over all that was left of Gervaise, le Comte d'Argenlac, and the manservant Tite.

With only moderate precautions, he made his way to the stable, hoping
that there would indeed be some clue to where Saint Sebastien and his

loathsome Circle had gone. He found the stables open to the night, and the horses moving restlessly in their stalls. No person moved there, but the horses sweated with fright. Saint-Germain put his hand down on the flank of a big gelding in a box stall near the door. The horse sidled nervously, his ears lying back against his neck, whites showing in his eyes. All his attempts to quiet the horse were fruitless, and Saint-Germain began to wonder about this. Of all the horses in the stable, this one was the most restless. He was also stalled closest to the tack room.

Determined to investigate that room, Saint-Germain left the box stall, but not a moment too soon, for the gelding lashed out at him with his hind feet. Saint-Germain paused only long enough to fix the brace across the stall door before entering the small door next to the stall that led to the tack room.

Harness and saddlery glowed in the feeble light emitted by one dying lantern. Fine leathers and polished metal, with their distinctive smell, combined with the warm scent of horses. Saint-Germain had always enjoyed that particular odor, and would have taken pleasure in it now if it were not for the man hanging from a singletree. He hurried across the tack room, hoping that this would not be another futile encounter, and that the man was, against all logic, alive.

He came nearer, and saw that the face, though contorted now in fatal agony, was that of Le Grâce.

Le Grâce moved slightly, the singletree swinging with his motion. He saw the dark-clothed figure at the far end of the tack room, and a hideous gurgling filled his throat. Much of Le Grâce's body was burned and torn, and several of the ugly wounds were wet.

Saint-Germain paused about halfway down the tack room, realizing that he must not panic the sorcerer if he was to learn anything from him. "Le Grâce," he said at his most compelling. "Le Grâce, can you hear me?"

Le Grâce whimpered.

"Le Grâce, where have they gone? Where is Saint Sebastien?"

"I won't . . . I can't . . ."

"Le Grâce," Saint-Germain rapped out. "Le Grâce, this is Prinz Ragoczy. You will answer me. Where is Saint Sebastien?"

For a moment Le Grâce's eyes were glazed with terror; then something of the authoritative air of Saint-Germain penetrated his dread-hazed mind. "Saint Sebastien . . . Saint-Germain. Saint-Germain . . ." He ended in a wheeze, and mercifully lapsed into unconsciousness.

Saint-Germain stood still, feeling defeated. It was no use now. Saint Sebastien had outwitted him. He turned from the tack room, moving quickly to hide from himself his sense of failure. But he supposed it was to be expected. Le Grâce was mad with what he had endured. He would do no more than recognize the questions, and abject fear would engulf him.

Saint-Germain stopped still in the door of the stables. Le Grâce did not know he was Saint-Germain. Le Grâce knew him only as Prinz Franz Josef Ragoczy. What Le Grâce had said was in reference to le Fraubourg Saint-Germain, the suburb around l'Eglise de Saint-Germain-des-Près and le Boulevard Saint-Germain—the part of Paris in which Hôtel Transylvania stood.

He paused for only a moment, then began to run toward the orchard and his waiting horse.

Text of a note from le Comte de Saint-Germain to his manservant Roger, written in Latin, delivered by a link-boy at about two in the morning of November 5, 1743:

My faithful Roger:

You will choose two trustworthy servants and dispatch them to hôtel Saint Sebastien. Its master has been busy, and there are several unpleasant matters to be dealt with. You might consider sending Domingo y Roxas with the servants, for he knows something of medicine and drugs that may be used against injury and pain. In the study, which may be discovered by its broken french door, there is Madelaine's maid, Cassandre, who is alive but very much injured, and the bodies of Saint Sebastien's personal servant and le Comte d'Argenlac, the latter two under velvet draperies.

But this is not all. In the stable's tack room Le Grâce has been left hanging on a singletree. By the look of him, Saint Sebastien used the red-hot pincers so much favored by Torquemada's Inquisition. He must receive prompt attention if he is to live. I charge you to be swift in carrying out these orders.

From what I have learned, I very much fear that Saint Sebastien may be going to the vaults under our Hôtel Transylvania. If he is not there, then he may go to the vaults under l'Eglise de Saint-Germain des Près, but that does not seem likely, for that is still holy ground, and I doubt if Saint Sebastien will set foot on it.

When this arrives, I wish you to clear the building of all but the staff, and dismiss those lackeys who do not wish to stay. If you must find an excuse, you may say that there is some contagion suspected in the house, which is partially the truth.

Do not attempt to help me. Prepare our belongings and await me with Hercule, who has been charged to have my traveling coach ready at a moment's notice. You will do me more service if you are there than if you become involved with this battle.

You will also speak to Mr. Sattin and be sure that he and his Guild Brothers get safely away from Hôtel Transylvania. You may give them a cart so that they may carry their equipment and their athanor with them. You may be as frank with them as you think wise, but do not underestimate the danger in which they stand, should they remain.

Should it be that we will not meet again, I trust that you will see my Will executed fully, and that my resting place will be marked in the way I have designated.

Follow my orders as you have before, and know you have my eternal

> Thanks
> Saint-Germain
> (his seal, the eclipse)

❦ 10 ❧

Water darkened the stones of the tunnel, and on the uneven flags that served as flooring, there was a thin film of slime, making it difficult to walk. A pervasive fetid odor filled the close air, making even the torches seem dimmed by the stench.

"Do not drop him!" Saint Sebastien ordered to the men who followed him through the tunnel.

Achille Cressie, who bore the shoulders of Robert de Montalia, complained, "Why did you have to drug him? We should have bound him."

"So that you could be entertained by his dear words, Achille?" Saint Sebastien's tone was poisonously sweet.

This did not have the expected effect on Achille, who chuckled unpleasantly. "You should have heard him in the tack room. How he despised himself when his flesh warmed to me."

De les Radeux, who held de Montalia's legs, gave a deprecating sigh. "It is all very well for you to boast of your prowess, Achille, but you will not let anyone watch, or share." He slid on the watery ooze, cursing.

"Pay attention!" Saint Sebastien barked out the order.

"He is heavy," de les Radeux insisted, sulking.

"All the more reason for you to keep your mind on what you are doing and away from your vain rivalry with Achille. If you cannot do as you are told, you are of no use to me."

De les Radeux muttered an imprecation under his breath, but steadied his grip on the drugged Robert de Montalia, going the rest of the way into the vault in silence.

The air was somewhat better there, not so close, and since the ancient stones were farther away from the river, the vault did not have that clammy cold that had made the tunnel so unbearable. Yet, it was a gloomy place. In the niches around the walls were the partially mummified remains of monks who had died three hundred years before. A closer look showed that most of the bodies had been profaned and that the crucifixes that had lain in their skeletal fingers had been replaced by phalluses, and that where consecrated oil had marked their foreheads as those belonging to God, there were now dried reddish stains in the symbol of Satan.

Saint Sebastien held his torch higher, and went quickly through the vault, arriving at last at a thick door set in the wall. The door was somewhat out of place in the Romanesque setting, for its design was recent, the strong iron hinges and other fittings still showing traces of oil to prevent rust, and the carving on the door indicated to what perverse use the chapel beyond had been put.

The door yawned open on nearly silent fittings, revealing the first area of the chapel beyond. Saint Sebastien sighed as he held the door for Cressie and de les Radeux. It would be an easy matter now. They had escaped detection, and there was no evidence that the chapel had been found and cleansed of the demonic presence.

Saint Sebastien walked farther into the chapel, his torch bringing light to the crude murals that adorned the walls, showing all the excesses of Satanic worship. Saint Sebastien smiled at one particularly horrendous representation, then went to the altar, saying to the panting men behind him, "Here, I think. Strip him and tie him down. I do not want to have to subdue him again."

De les Radeux said at his surliest, "I am honored to do this." He glared at the altar, at Saint Sebastien, at the man he carried. This was not at all what he had anticipated. He had been told that the ceremonies of the Circle were grand occasions. His uncle Beauvrai had dwelt lovingly on the complex gratifications that were offered for every desire as well as the opportunity to advance in power through these practices. But here he was in a cold stone room, under the ground, carrying le Marquis de Montalia and bowing and scraping to Saint Sebastien as if Saint Sebastien were king or archangel and he was the lowest peasant in France. To make matters worse, the damp had quite ruined his satin coat and fine white-silk hose. He wished now that he had had the foresight to keep his riding boots on.

With a last grunt, de les Radeux and Achille Cressie hoisted Robert de Montalia onto the altar, and set about pulling his clothes off, a task that proved to be surprisingly difficult.

It took Saint Sebastien about ten minutes to recite the required incantations as he lit the fifteen torches that lined the walls. The brightness grew, but the flickering of the torches made that brightness unsteady, a leaping, irregular illumination that gave weird life to the grotesque paintings on the walls.

A noise beyond the door brought Saint Sebastien's attention to the task at hand. He called out the password and waited for a response. The proper words came back, and he went to open the door.

Jueneport stood there, Madelaine in his arms. "Where do you want her?"

Saint Sebastien studied the limp figure. "I think we must put her where she can watch what we do to her father. Perhaps there." He motioned to the inverted crucifix that hung over the altar.

"It doesn't look safe to me," Jueneport said slowly. "She's strong enough to pull it out of the wall."

"I see your point." Saint Sebastien considered for a moment longer. "We could tie her there. She would then see what is done to her father, and we would see what is her reaction. An excellent combination." He had pointed to the screen that had once guarded part of the sanctuary, when the chapel had been used by the monks and not the Circles who had come to own it.

"It is strong," Jueneport agreed. "Very well. I imagine there are ropes available?"

"Behind the altar. Take what you need."

Jueneport nodded, then went to where de les Radeux and Achille Cressie worked to secure Robert de Montalia to the altar. Achille worked more slowly, pausing every now and then to run his hands over the nude body, an unpleasant light in his face as he said, "We could bind his organ as well. That way, his pain would be doubled, as would our sport."

De les Radeux shot him a look of tolerant disgust. "Is your lust all that goads you to this, Achille? Have you no other desires?"

The laughter that greeted these questions made Saint Sebastien turn, angered. "None of that, Achille, or I will forbid you to take part in the celebration."

Achille pouted, then shrugged and negligently returned to his task.

Now there was another knock at the door, and the passwords were once again exchanged. De la Sept-Nuit came in, his eyes searching for and finding the pathetic figure of Madelaine. He gestured to the bag he held. "These are the robes, mon Baron. They are all prepared, and need only your curse before we don them."

Saint Sebastien traced the pentagram in the air and said a few syllables of backward Latin. "You may dress whenever you like. Make sure your own garments are out of the way."

"I will." De la Sept-Nuit went away to a side alcove and returned several minutes later in the pleated silk robe of the Circle. It resembled a soutane, but the pleated silk clung to the body in a way no priestly garb did, and the neck opening ran the length of the robe to the hem, so that the material opened to reveal the body as de la Sept-Nuit walked across the chapel.

"I have put your robe aside," de la Sept-Nuit said. "Yours is the red with the embroidery, is that not so?"

"Yes. If you will take this torch and put it in place by the altar, I will invest myself. Are the bracelets there as well?"

"Two of silver, one of black glass. They're with the robe. You will find them. They are still wrapped as you want them to be."

"I am pleased to hear it. That is to your advantage."

De la Sept-Nuit shook his head. "You know what reward I would most enjoy." He waved a languid hand toward Madelaine, whom Jueneport had finished binding to the heavy screen. She was naked, and bruises were beginning to show on her flesh.

"Perhaps. With Tite dead, perhaps." He strolled away to put on his robes.

When he returned, the rest of the Circle had arrived and were concluding the preparations for the first ceremony. Châteaurose was now a little the worse for drink, but he knew the motions well enough that he would complete them without hazard.

"Have the sacrifices wakened yet?" Saint Sebastien asked as he came down the aisle toward the altar. He was gorgeous now in the heavy red silk which hung open showing his lean, hard body that had been only lightly touched by age. Gone was the polish that marked his public dealings, and in its place was a terrible mastery, made even stronger by the signs of office he wore around his neck, the sign of the pentagram and the obscene crucifix.

"Not yet, though the woman is stirring."

"They must be awake in twenty minutes. See to it that they are." He turned away and ignored the efforts of his Circle to force Madelaine and her father to be roused.

Beauvrai strode over to Saint Sebastien. "Well, Clotaire, how is your revenge?" Out of his ridiculous court finery, he was no longer the foppish fool he often appeared to be. In the black-silk robe none of his absurdity remained, and only the malice in him shone at full force, no longer hampered by his outward trappings.

"I have not tasted it yet. But soon. Soon."

"What for Robert? Have you thought of it?"

"Of course." He fingered the two medallions that hung halfway down his chest. "It will please you, mon Baron."

"I hope so." He turned aside, saying under his breath, "That nephew of mine is rather an ass, Clotaire."

"He seemed so to me as well," Saint Sebastien agreed at his most silky. "One would think he was too foolish to live."

"My point precisely." He bowed to Saint Sebastien and walked off to take his place in the first rank of worshipers.

At last Achille Cressie thought to bring two pails of water, and these he threw over Madelaine and Robert de Montalia. He was satisfied as he heard the woman stutter and her father gag. "I think we are ready," he said, very satisfied.

"That is good. We are very near the hour." Saint Sebastien came forward and plucked painfully at Madelaine's breasts and her cheeks. This brought a quick cry in response, and Saint Sebastien was reassured. "Yes, my dear," he said softly, caressingly, "it is I. You have not fled me."

Madelaine half-opened her violet eyes, and felt herself turn an icy cold that had little to do with the water that had drenched her. "Saint-Germain," she whispered in her desperation.

Saint Sebastien achieved a magnificent sneer, "So you long for that hoaxing fop, do you?" He reached out and slapped her face. "It is not that impostor who has you now." He turned away from the fury in her face and walked to the altar.

"He is awake," Achille told Saint Sebastien. "You have only to touch him to see the disgust in his face." He demonstrated this in superb imitation of Saint Sebastien's grand and evil manner.

"You have done well, Achille. I may let you enjoy yourself again before we dispatch Robert." He put one insolent hand on Robert's cold flesh. "How sad, my friend, that I cannot offer you a blanket. But you have my promise that I will see that you are warmed in other ways. You know that I always keep my promises."

Robert, whose jaw had tightened steadily through this new indignity, spat once, most accurately, at Saint Sebastien, then forced himself once again to stoic silence.

"You will make it worse for yourself, Robert." Saint Sebastien stood back, then lifted his arms and called out to the members of the Circle, who waited, robed and silent, before him. "We are met in the name of Satan, that we may grow in his power and his great strength, which is the strength of the great lie. We meet that we may join him in power, be with him in potency and in savagery, and to that end we bring him sacrifices."

"We bring him sacrifices," the Circle chanted.

"Lives, paid in blood, in degradation."

"In blood and degradation."

Madelaine, her arms aching from the bonds that held her to the screen, her body already hurt from the cruelty of the men gathered in the debauched chapel, felt herself sway in her bonds, almost overcome with fear and wretchedness. And she knew that for her the heinous men had not even begun to do what they were capable of doing. She remembered that there would be forty days for her destruction. She told herself in the back of her thoughts that they could not succeed, that she would be missed, and her father, that someone would find her, save her. Again she felt her soul reach out for Saint-Germain, filled with her yearning for him as much as with her panic-stricken desire for escape. But she did not know if she could dare to hope, not with the chanting growing louder.

"This forsworn one, your betrayer, Satan!"

"Your betrayer!"

"Brought back again to make expiation for his duplicity." Saint Sebastien held aloft a curiously curved dagger, letting the blade flash in the quivering torchlight.

"Your betrayer!"

Saint Sebastien put the point of the dagger against Robert de Montalia's chest, and with concentrated precision he cut the pentagram into his skin. "He is marked as yours, Satan!"

"Marked!" This triumph shout covered the groans that Robert could not hold back.

"For your strength is not to be spurned, and your power is not mocked!"

"Power and strength are yours alone!"

Madelaine shook her head, as if the very motion would shut out the sounds that assaulted her. She could not look at her father as he steeled himself against further outrage, and she would not look at Saint Sebastien. The chanting got louder.

"Let him taste of your wrath!"

"Let him taste of your wrath!" came the shout from the Circle as Saint Sebastien brought the blade swiftly down and held up Robert's ear as a gory trophy. A great cry from the Circle combined with Robert de Montalia's scream, and the noise continued rising like a wave as Saint Sebastien put the ear to his mouth and licked it. The Circle surged forward, hysteria pulling them toward the ghastly spectacle. Saint Sebastien motioned for silence, the dagger held high as he waited.

His dramatic effect was quite destroyed when a voice spoke from the rear of the chapel, a voice that was beautifully modulated, and tinged with a slight Piedmontese accent. "I am glad I am in time, gentlemen," said le Comte de Saint-Germain.

Relief, more weakening than her terror had been, filled Madelaine, turning her very bones to water. The tears she had held back welled in her eyes, and a pang sharp as Saint Sebastien's knife lodged itself in her breast.

The members of the Circle turned, each member's face showing that dazed stupidity that often comes with being wakened from a sound sleep. Their movements were jerky, and the momentum of their ferocity faltered.

Saint-Germain came down the aisle toward the terrible altar. All of the elegant frippery of manner had vanished with his splendid clothes. Now his movements suited the tight riding coat of black leather worn over tight woolen breeches that were also black. His high boots were wide-cuffed, and the simple shirt under the coat was adorned with Russian embroidery showing a pattern of steppe wildflowers known as tulips. He carried no sword or other weapon, and was alone.

Saint Sebastien watched him, wrath showing in his narrowed eyes and malicious smile. He nodded, motioning his Circle to keep back. "Ragoczy," he said. "I did not believe. I did not recognize . . ."

Saint-Germain inclined his head. "I have told you before that appearances are deceiving."

"But that was thirty years ago." He moved closer, the dagger held tightly in his hand.

"Was it? I will take your word for it." If he knew that he was in danger, nothing but the hot stare of his eyes suggested it.

"Your father, then?" Saint Sebastien closed in on Saint-Germain, almost near enough to strike.

"I was not aware that I had changed so much in that time." He had taken in the chapel and its uses when he entered it, and now he was prepared to deal with Saint Sebastien on his own ground. He touched the small locketlike receptacle that hung on a chain around his neck.

Saint Sebastien had already raised his dagger, and was about to make a sudden rush, when Saint-Germain's arm shot out, seized Saint Sebastien's shoulder, not to hold him back, but to pull him forward, sending him hurtling past Saint-Germain to crash into the stack of ruined pews at the back of the chapel.

Saint-Germain glanced toward Saint Sebastien, then directed his penetrating eyes to the members of the Circle who stood around the altar. "How absurd you are," he said lightly. "You should see yourselves standing there in your fine robes, with your manhood, if you can call it that, peeking out at the world like so many birds." He waited for the hostile words to stop. "You are foolish. Do you think that you will enhance your place in the world, obtain power and position, by following Saint Sebastien's orders? It is *his* position and power that your profane offices enhance. It is *his* desires that are met. And you, thinking that you get these things for yourselves, give yourself to him without question. If I were the one you worship, I would think poorly of your practices."

Beauvrai was the first to object. "You think we're stupid, you, who came here with nothing to protect you. . . ."

Saint-Germain held up the locket on the chain. "I beg your pardon, Baron. I have this. You are not so far removed from the faith you were born to that you cannot recognize a pyx."

The Circle, which had been growing restless, now became hushed again.

"You are asking yourselves if this is genuine." He held the pyx higher. "You may try to touch it if you like. I understand the burns are instantaneous." He waited, while the silk-robed men held back. "I see."

A sudden noise behind him made him turn, and in that moment he cursed himself for not being sure that Saint Sebastien was unconscious, for now the leader of the Circle was rushing toward Madelaine, and although he no longer carried a dagger, there was a wickedly broken piece of planking in his hands, and this he held ready to strike.

At that moment, the hush, the almost somnambulistic trance that had held the Circle members to their clumsiness and to Saint-Germain's control, ruptured with the explosiveness of a Dutch dyke bursting to let in the sea. With an awful shout, the men in the silken robes flung themselves at Saint-Germain.

Excerpt from a note written by l'Abbé Ponteneuf to his cousin, le Comtesse d'Argenlac, dated November 5, 1743:

. . . From my heart of hearts I pray God that He will comfort you and open your eyes to the glory that awaits all good Christians beyond the grave and the shadow of death. It is my duty to write this letter to you, my poor cousin, but even now my pen falters and I cannot find it in me to tell you what has befallen. I beseech you to marshal your heart to greet this terrible news with true fortitude, for all of us who know and love you cannot but wish that you would never have to endure the ordeal that is now before you.

It was rather less than an hour ago when a coach called for me, to take me to a church on the outskirts of the city. You may imagine my surprise at this unlikely request, for it is not usual to have such a request forthcoming at so late an hour. But I have not been a priest for twenty years without learning to accept what God sends me without complaint. So it was that I went in the coach to the church to which I have already alluded. We arrived in good time, and I was immediately ushered into the sanctuary, where an awesome sight met my eyes. There, laid out before me, were the bodies of three men. One was a mountebank, from the look of him, and I did not know anything of him. Another was one of Saint Sebastien's servants, whom

I recognized by the livery. Saint Sebastien is such an unrepentant sinner of all the Deadly Sins that I did not know the man himself, but his master is not likely to have set his feet on a path toward Our Lord and His Sweet Mother.

It is the third man I must speak of, and it stops my heart to say this. The third man was le Comte d'Argenlac, your own beloved husband, whom you have loved so tenderly, and who has always been your staunch protector. It is further my most unpleasant duty to inform you that he did not die by accident or an act of God. He was, my unfortunate cousin, cold-bloodedly slain by a person or persons unknown.

The curé at this church has given me the use of his study that I might send you news immediately. His understanding is not great, but he is a good man, and I have told him that le Comte is known to me, and that it is only appropriate that you, as my cousin, should hear of this tragedy from one who has the knowledge of your particular circumstances.

Do not let yourself be overwhelmed. Pray to Mary for the saving of your husband's soul. You will find that such religious exercise does much to alleviate your grief, which must surely consume you otherwise. I have often remarked that when God made Woman as helpmeet to Man, He made her prey to whims and weaknesses that her mate does not know. The excellent solace of Scripture will help you to control those emotions which must fill your breast as you read this. . . .

I will take it upon myself to see that le Comte's body is removed to his parish church immediately, and that such notice as must be given of his death be delivered to the proper authorities. If you are not too incapacitated by this terrible event, perhaps you will allow me to visit you and read with you the Great Words that will assuage your sorrow.

In the name of God, Who even now welcomes your beloved husband to the Glories of Paradise, I am always

> Your obedient cousin,
> L'Abbé Ponteneuf, S.J.

~~❦~~ 11 ~~❦~~

Hercule closed the paneled door of Saint-Germain's traveling coach with a grim nod of satisfaction. He had fulfilled all his master's instructions and still had time to help the sorcerers load their equipment on the heavy-bedded cart that stood at the back of the stable. He swung around the coach for one last check of the harnesses, and found them polled up too tightly on the right-wheeler. He made the adjustment and felt new pride as he patted the dappled-gray flank of the right leader. He could hardly wait to take the reins in hand once again, to feel that surge of delight that only driving gave him. His rolling gait was as ungainly as a bear on its hind legs, but with the braces that Saint-Germain had designed for him, he was no longer a cripple. He shouted for a groom, and it was less than a minute before two of them appeared.

"I'm off to the cart loading," he said grandly. "But if there is anything you think needs my attention, then one of you come double time to fetch me. But you make sure there's someone here with these horses. I don't want to hear my master say that these cattle of his aren't properly cared for."

One of the grooms bowed his acceptance, and the other nodded as he quailed under Hercule's formidable stare.

"I'll be back from time to time to see that you're doing it right," he warned them; then, with that curious swaying walk, he swung out of the barn. It was a dark night, he thought, and there would certainly be rain later. He could feel the rain in his scarred knees, and remembered that Saint-Germain had told him that he might feel that discomfort for some while, perhaps his entire life. Most of the time it did not bother Hercule, but tonight, when his driving might mean the difference between death and survival to his master, he did not like to feel unwell. He squared his shoulders and strode toward the cart that was drawn up between the stables and the rear entrance to Hôtel Transylvania.

"Give you good evening," he said to the woman sorcerer who struggled now with two huge baskets filled with boxes of various sizes.

"If you would give me a good evening," she snapped, "you would help me to load these baskets."

Secretly pleased for the opportunity to show the stern sorceress the extent of his capabilities, he pulled himself onto the bed of the wagon, then hauled up the baskets. "Where are the ropes? You will have to tie these down if you are not to have those boxes all over the road between here and the coast."

"Tie them, then."

He did as she told him, securing the ropes with two strong knots. "What else do you have to bring from the cellar?"

Mme. Lairrez put her hands on her hips and directed her intelligent gray eyes on him. "We have several more loads like this one, and of course, the athanor. We will leave the old one behind, but the new one . . ."

Hercule clambered off the wagon. "I cannot leave the stables, but I will help you load whatever you bring up." He felt a warming to the strong-willed Mme. Lairrez. "If I am here, I will be able to hear any call for me. Tell your companions I will do the loading for them."

But Mme. Lairrez was not quite sure she was prepared to deal with this friendship. "We have very special equipment. You may not know what is to be done with it."

He smiled down at her. "I am a coachman, Madame. I may not know about your special equipment, but I know more than any of the rest of you about how to load a wagon."

This argument carried much weight with Mme. Lairrez. She studied the wagon bed, nodding twice to herself. "Very well, friend Hercule. You may do the loading. We would be grateful for your assistance."

"I rely on you to tell me which of your equipment requires special handling."

"There is a great deal of glass," she said slowly, "but it is the athanor which is most dangerous. You see, we have just heated it, and it will soon reach the temperature at which it will produce the jewels. But the heat is terrible. The athanor is made according to the Prinz's order, and has been impregnated with a certain substance, else the athanor itself would melt with the great heat." She stopped speaking suddenly, thinking that she might have said too much.

"You bring me the . . . whatever it is, and I'll see that it is loaded safely." He sounded confident as he said it, but even he did not know what he would do if the thing were as hot as Mme. Lairrez intimated.

"Very well," she said, though her tone was skeptical.

When she had gone, Hercule swung back up onto the bed of the wagon and was standing there when Roger came from the darkened Hôtel, three cases in his arms. "Is the coach ready?"

"It is," Hercule answered. "It could be on the road in a matter of minutes." He felt slightly defensive at being found at the wagon, and added, "The sorcerers need a hand at this."

Roger agreed. "They are unused to being so few. When Cielbleu died, there were too few of them in this Brotherhood to manage all the projects they had developed. I am not particularly surprised that they are working so slowly." He cocked his head toward the brick facade of the Hôtel. "It is strange to see it so, is it not?"

Hercule looked at the dark windows and felt the eerie silence. "It is like a grave," he said, and shuddered.

"I wonder what will happen?" Roger said to the blank face of Hôtel Transylvania.

"Whatever it will be, I have given my word to wait for le Comte, and that I will, though the Devil come and roar at me."

"A noble sentiment," Roger said, looking up at the coachman on the wagon. "I hope your resolve will not have that test." He favored Hercule with an ironic nod and went into the stable, returning somewhat later with empty hands. He stared again at the Hôtel. "It is not natural," he whispered.

Hercule had heard him, and responded, "It is waiting."

"Yes." Roger shook the fatalistic mood off, and was encouraged to see the English sorcerer emerge from the cellar stairs. "You will need some help," he said, relieved.

"Thank you, sir, I will." Beverly Sattin was sweating freely as he lugged two sacks up the stairs. He stopped to catch his breath. "There are twenty-seven stairs between the cellars and here."

"Let me help you with the last six," Roger said, going to take the largest of the sacks.

Sattin thanked him again, then once more bent himself to the task of pulling the remaining sack up the stairs and over to the wagon.

As Hercule was lashing down the second sack, a strange sound caught all three men's attention, and they turned toward the Hôtel, apprehension in their stances. The sounds, like a distant rush of water, died, sounding now like a hive of subterranean bees.

"It comes from the Hôtel," Hercule said softly.

"It comes from the cellars!" Beverly Sattin turned away abruptly and raced for the stairs he had just climbed.

"Do you think . . . ?" Hercule could not finish the question.

"I think that you would do well to get onto your box, coachman. If our master comes through this, he will not want to tarry."

Hercule accepted this without comment, climbing down from the wagon and striding away toward the stables.

Roger stood uncertainly, listening for the sound that seemed to rise from the very ground. It grew neither louder nor softer, but Roger, hearing it, felt fear transfix him. He looked down as if to burrow with his eyes toward the combat he sensed raged beneath him. Then, as if impelled by a vast, invisible force, he raced toward the cellar stairs and plunged down them.

Domingo y Roxas turned in alarm as Roger appeared in the sorcerers' cellar. Mme. Lairrez was occupied with wrapping some earthenware jars in straw and greeted Roger's entrance with the exasperation she had kept controlled for so long.

"Sattin," she said with asperity, "if you want me to finish this task with all our jars unbroken . . ."

But Beverly Sattin, who was holding an armload of very old books bound in heavy leather, was as startled as she. "What is it, Roger?" he demanded as Saint-Germain's servant stared anxiously about the room.

"Don't you hear it?" Roger cried out to them.

"Hear it? Hear what?" Domingo y Roxas put aside the wooden supports that would be used to carry the new athanor to the cart.

"That noise. That sound. It is louder here." Roger glared at the floor. "You must hear it."

The three paused; then Domingo y Roxas said, "It is the athanor." But his tone was dubious, and the others shook their heads.

"I don't know what it is," Sattin said. "It is not the athanor."

"There is a door into the vaults," Roger said as he listened to the sound. "Somewhere, there is a door!"

"His Highness told us earlier," Sattin said, trying to remember now the location. "It is a trapdoor, I think, in the floor. In the north? Perhaps in the north part of the cellar."

"Well, *find it!*" Roger cried, remembering all he had seen when Saint-Germain had set him to watch Saint Sebastien.

Mme. Lairrez stopped her packing once again. "You may look for it if you like, but I have obligations as well. I must have all this on the wagon and ourselves away from here before dawn. I will not allow you to stop me." She took one more straw-wrapped jar and pushed it into the huge basket with the others.

"One of you?" Roger pleaded. "Ragoczy is in danger. He is in terrible danger."

Beverly Sattin put his books aside. "As you wish. I will help you find the door." He refused to meet the reproachful eyes of his two Guild Brothers. To mollify them, he said, "It will not take long, and we owe a great deal to His Highness."

"Go, then." Mme. Lairrez relented. "And may you find him safe."

Roger looked at her. "Amen to that, Madame." Then he set off into the dark behind Beverly Sattin.

Excerpt from a letter from le Duc de la Mer-Herbeux to le Comte de Saint-Germain, dated November 5, 1743:

. . . The plan you have confided to me of your trip to England comes at a most fortuitous time. I trust that your offer was in earnest and that you are still willing to bear one or two messages to the Crown for me. You need not make a formal delivery of these packets, which I have enclosed with this letter. You will do well to hand them to my friend Mr. Walpole, who will know best what to do with them.

. . . I had your note yesterday, but the delicate nature of the communications I am sending with you have delayed my responding until now. I had thought to see you at Hôtel Transylvania earlier this evening, but it was closed, apparently due to some illness in the staff. So I have taken the liberty of sending these by messenger to your manservant, who you have told me has your utter confidence.

While you are in England, I hope you will learn what you can about the matter with the Stuart claim. Charles Stuart is apparently serious about challenging George's right to the crown. Far be it from me or France to question the right of George II to his throne, but you may understand why our Beloved and Most Catholic King Louis XV is concerned in the affairs of Charles Stuart, also a Catholic, and one whose claim to the throne comes from older associations than does His Britannic Majesty George II's. You will be ideally placed to observe the sentiments of the government and any comments you would care to pass along to me would be most heartily appreciated.

I have prepared a note for that scholar of your acquaintance, Mr. Sattin, who you tell me has been studying in France for many years. In this note I commend your friend for his abilities and suggest that he continue in the same manner to the credit of a worthy patron in England. I beg that your friend Sattin will not too much discredit me.

. . . Several weeks ago you made passing reference to a planned visit to Prussia. As you have said you will return to France by summer, I trust we may speak further then of those plans.

. . . It is late and I am eager to retire. I wish you a pleasant journey and calm seas for a swift passage (although my experience has almost always been to the contrary). This and the enclosures by my own hand, are bringing you the humble thanks of

Your most indebted
Pierre René Maxime Ignace Ferrand Vivien
Laurent Montlutin
le Duc de la Mer-Herbeux

~~❦~~ 12 ~~❦~~

Saint Sebastien's headlong rush down the aisle almost reached fruition. Saint-Germain was surrounded by the Satanic worshipers, and though he plucked them away easily, he could not free himself of them.

Madelaine had braced herself for the blow she knew would dash out her brains, and knew a moment of resentment because there had not been time enough, or blood enough, for her to become vampiric and escape the awful finality of the death that faced her.

And then Saint Sebastien fell, the broken plank he carried dropping from his hands in a resounding thud. His rage flared anew, desiring suffering in which to be slaked.

Even that was to be denied him. Robert, Marquis de Montalia, held him back, his hands scraped to the bone where he had pulled them from the ropes that bound him to the altar, his face a bloody mask from the torn ear. His hands which held Saint Sebastien by the ankle sent blood running down le Baron's leg.

Saint Sebastien writhed in this merciless grasp, trying to kick de Montalia's hands away with his free foot. Each blow he gave to those raw hands must have been agony for Robert, but the hold did not break. Robert shouted incoherently, staggering as de Vandonne fell against him, but would not release Saint Sebastien.

De Vandonne lay against the altar, his dissipated young face in a rictus smile. He could not move his arms because Saint-Germain had, in two swift movements, dislocated both his shoulders. He did not think he could stand and did not make the attempt; his feet were pulpy where the heel of Saint-Germain's boot had crushed them. He saw Robert de Montalia, like some monster from the Temptation of Saint Anthony, pull Saint Sebastien toward him, destruction promised in every move he made with his butchered hands.

De la Sept-Nuit had grabbed Saint-Germain by his hair, and tugged, wanting to deliver a series of sharp blows to his throat. He felt a clump of the slightly curling dark brown hair pull out of Saint-Germain's scalp. Then he winced as the beautiful small hands reached back and fixed themselves to his arms at the elbow, tightening, tightening, until there was a giving way, and de la Sept-Nuit screamed and his hands dangled uselessly below badly broken arms. Saint-Germain spun around, turning de la Sept-Nuit so that he could pin the young Chevalier's arms behind him, and in a fast, clean upward snap of his knee, broke the spine of Donatien de la Sept-Nuit.

Though he resisted with frantic strength, Saint Sebastien was being drawn inexorably nearer to Robert de Montalia's deadly hands. He knew beyond question that if de Montalia once fixed those bloodied fingers on his throat, he was a dead man. He fixed his hands on the uneven floor and pulled against the relentless strength of his adversary, but without avail.

"I will kill you," Robert de Montalia said slowly and distinctly, and Saint Sebastien heard the words over the din of groans, shouts, and oaths.

It was Jueneport who took two of the torches off the wall and held them before him like short swords. He motioned his Circle confederates aside and began to move in on Saint-Germain, brandishing the torches in le Comte's face.

This was a moment Saint Sebastien could use. He kicked out desperately, then shouted with all the strength that was left in his body, "In the name of your Blood Oath, help me!"

Châteaurose and de les Radeux heard this, turning toward the cry. They did not hesitate, but threw themselves on Robert de Montalia, bearing him to the floor.

As Madelaine watched this terrible battle, she was almost sure she had been forgotten. Her horror at the wrath of her father, and the brutal attack that even now had defeated him, went beyond tears, or hatred, or madness. She felt nothing, and had to convince herself that this was not happening in a dream, or to someone else far away. Only the sight of Achille Cressie bringing an iron brazier to the men who had brought down her father forced her to sudden action. She made another effort to test the strength of her bonds. On the third attempt she noticed a give in the part of the screen holding her left arm. Grimly she turned her attention there, determined to get free.

Achille Cressie had thrust Châteaurose out of the way with an angry word, then himself stood over Robert de Montalia. He took the brazier by its base and raised it high above his head, shouting to Robert as he did, "No one had you after me!"

An instant later the heavy iron bowl had smashed de Montalia's face beyond recognition as anything human.

Saint Sebastien nodded grimly. "Well done, Achille. That makes up for much." He looked toward Saint-Germain, then leveled his arm at him. "I want him killed. Do it slowly."

Once again the Circle began to converge on Saint-Germain, and he met the threat calmly. He had judiciously avoided the torches Jueneport held, his agility and speed more than once catching Jueneport off guard and forcing him to retreat.

"If you hold him, I will burn him," Jueneport shouted to his fellows.

Those words brought Madelaine's head up, and all her fear, her desolation, rushed back. She remembered that Saint-Germain had told her fire could kill him. After his long, long life, it tore at her vitals to think he would die so stupidly. She renewed her efforts to get free.

Saint-Germain heard these words, but said nothing. Instead, he fell back some little way from Jueneport, as if seeking to escape the torches and the men who fanned out to capture him. But this was deceptive. Quite suddenly, and without warning of any kind, he threw himself to the floor and rolled swiftly toward Jueneport's feet. As he passed under the man's legs, he reached up and delivered sharp blows to the back of his knees.

While Saint-Germain rolled beyond, Jueneport fell forward heavily onto the torches he carried. He made a ghastly scream as the flames licked at the silk robe he wore.

"Madelaine!" Saint-Germain said urgently: "Madelaine!"

She cried out his name and pulled to the limits of her bonds.

"Can you walk?" he asked as he came to her side, keeping a wary eye on the Circle members, who were once again moving to surround him.

"I think so."

"You will have to." He smashed his hand against the screen where it held her, and the wood broke under the blows. Quickly he took the pyx from around his neck and put the chain over her head. "It has the Host. They will not touch it."

"But you . . ." she began.

"The door is at the rear of the chapel, in the little narthex. It will take you into the Hôtel. From there you must find your way out."

"And you?"

Saint-Germain turned to her, and for a moment the hot fury left his dark eyes. "I will follow you, my heart. You have my word on that."

"But Saint-Germain," she said, her whole body shaking as she stood free and unbound for the first time in many hours.

He kissed his fingertips to her. "Go," he said softly. Then he wrenched his eyes away from hers and turned to face the men who were coming closer. He paused only a moment, then rushed to them, his arms upraised.

Startled, the Circle fell back a moment, and that moment was long enough for Saint-Germain to reach for Achille Cressie.

Madelaine did not hesitate. She stumbled down the side aisle, almost falling twice as her feet, both treacherously half-asleep, turned under her. At the end of the chapel she could not find the door, and the dark there made the corners uncertain.

Behind her, Saint-Germain lifted Achille Cressie into the air by shoulder and thigh, then, using Cressie as a battering ram, brought him down full force against Beauvrai, who fell back, bruised. Achille Cressie began a high, quavering wail that grew louder as Saint-Germain hurtled him down at the floor again. The sound stopped abruptly, on a pulpy thud.

"Fall back!" Saint Sebastien shouted, and his Circle obeyed, keeping themselves beyond the range of Saint-Germain's deadly hands and feet.

At the back of the chapel, Madelaine again tried to find the door, and was about to scream with vexation and terror when there was a screech slightly above her, and a sliver of light fell across the wall. In a moment the door was open, and in it stood Roger and Beverly Sattin.

"Oh, God be thanked," Madelaine sighed, and fell into the arms of the English sorcerer.

In the center of the chapel there was stillness save for the spasmodic twitching of Achille Cressie's body.

"Master," Roger said at his most imperturbable, "I think your coach is ready now."

"Thank you, Roger," Saint-Germain said, only slightly out of breath. "I have some little business to finish up here."

Roger bowed, then pointed out, "The unfortunate there in the flames has started a fire, sir."

Until that moment, Saint-Germain had not noticed the flames that were creeping up the piles of stacked pews, feeding hungrily on the dry wood. All the men in the cellar turned toward the fire.

"As you see," Roger said somewhat unnecessarily, "you cannot leave through the vault. There is only this stairway." He stood aside.

Saint-Germain nodded. "I see. Take Madelaine to my coach, then. And keep that door open."

Saint Sebastien motioned to Beauvrai, who staggered to his feet. "The door!" he snapped as soon as Roger, Sattin, and Madelaine were gone.

Beauvrai lumbered toward the door, his silk robe flapping ludicrously about his bandy legs.

"Now," Saint Sebastien said, raising his hands in demonic invocation. He began his chant, and the flames took on a darker color. Saint-Germain moved cautiously toward the door, then stopped as the flames moved higher along the wooden supports of the chapel. He realized that in very little time the ceiling might collapse.

De les Radeux watched his uncle, and then in panicked flight rushed across the room, pushing Beauvrai aside, and ran for the stairs.

If Saint Sebastien noticed this defection, he gave no indication, but continued the sinister chanting, moving his hands toward the fire, then pointing toward Saint-Germain.

The flames roared up between Saint-Germain and the door, narrowly missing Châteaurose, who leaped back with a curse.

"I am loath to leave you, Saint-Germain, or Ragoczy, or whoever you are." Saint Sebastien shouted, to be heard above the eager crackle of the flames. "But I fear our little encounter must end." He smiled at the wall of fire that cut Saint-Germain off from the door. "I am sure you will have some few minutes yet. In that time, you may contemplate the vengeance I will take on your companions." He made an insulting magnificent bow and fled to the door, motioning to Beauvrai and Châteaurose to follow him.

In a few moments Saint-Germain heard the door slam shut and the uncompromising sound of the bolt driven home. He looked at the flames that were eating steadily toward him, devouring the wood and cloth that had been part of that chapel for more than a thousand years. The heat scorched his lungs when he breathed, and he felt his eyebrows singe.

He could delay no longer. Stepping back to the altar, he gathered his strength, then rushed at the flames, leaping into the air and somersaulting over them, his stocky body pulled in on itself, made as small as possible.

On the far side of the flames he came down on his feet, dropped to his knee, and then was up again, coughing as smoke filled his lungs.

There was a warning rumble, and a large part of the ceiling gave way, revealing the empty cellar above and giving new life to the fire as cool air rushed in.

Saint-Germain stood for a moment, debating if he should try to force the door, but the fire was already reaching into the wooden floor of the cellar. He did not have the luxury of time.

One of the ceiling supports that had fallen was not yet burned. This he put against the wall and began to pull himself up its length, hand-over-hand. The heat was becoming oppressive, and his eyes burned with smoke.

As he gained the cellar floor, he heard the sound of running footsteps. He realized that he must have got ahead of Saint Sebastien, and that those dire men were coming behind him. He breathed deeply, then sprinted away for the sorcerers' laboratory, knowing he could intercept them there.

He had barely flung open the door when Saint Sebastien, Beauvrai, and Châteaurose appeared. The sorcerers' room was empty but for the two athanors, and one of them glowed with a heat far in excess of the fire that already was beginning to gnaw at the walls behind them.

"Well met," Saint-Germain said, stepping into the room.

Châteaurose stopped first, and gave a strange cry. His face was that of a man in his worst nightmare afraid to waken.

Beauvrai was too exhausted to speak, but flung up one arm as if to ward off a blow.

But Saint Sebastien smiled. "I think not," he said, and reached for the nearer athanor, which was the newer, larger one.

What he had meant to do with it was never discovered, for as his hands touched the heated bricks, he screamed, and reeling back, he overturned the alchemical oven. There was a muffled crack, and then the brick walls of the overturned athanor bulged, sagged, then burst explosively, revealing gears of white-hot metal, mangled now, and losing the precious molten combination of carbon and azoth which poured onto the floor in a thin, burning stream, flames spreading around it as it ran.

Châteaurose, who was farthest away from this, ran past it, madness distorting his face, and foam on his lips. His robe flirted with the burning elements as he ran, but his flight was too swift for even that hungry flame to take hold.

Where the molten carbon and azoth touched metal or cool wood, there formed little diamonds like the bright bits of salt left on the sand when the tide was retreated. The diamonds winked in the growing heat, shining with the fire that caressed them.

"The secret of the jewels," Saint-Germain said to Saint Sebastien. "Think of that as you die." He was already moving toward the door.

Now the walls were charred and there was heavier smoke in the room. Beauvrai stood at the open door that led back to the chapel, indecision in every aspect of his posture. He coughed once or twice, then said to Saint Sebastien, "You never told me about the jewels, Clotaire. I don't like that." He put his hand to his mouth and retched.

Now Saint-Germain had gained the first riser of the long flight of stairs out of the cellar. He paused to look at the hellish room, saying to the two men on the far side of the fire, "I only regret the loss of my Velázquezes. What a pity they must burn because of you."

Saint Sebastien shouted a terrible curse and rushed over the spreading fire, his hands extended to take Saint-Germain's throat. As he ran, the fire moved around him like impossible wings.

In the moment before Saint Sebastien could touch him, Saint-Germain reached inside his shirt and held up a little golden crucifix so that the light from the fire licked it, making it shine with weird brightness. "It was blessed at Saint-Germain-des-Près not four hours ago," he warned Saint Sebastien.

But Saint Sebastien had already stopped in mid-stride, his hand out to block the sight of the sacred thing.

"I thought so," Saint-Germain said. "I wish you joy of this foretaste of your particular eternity. Adieu, mon Baron. Or perhaps I should say, 'À Satan'?" He backed up the stairs, still holding the little crucifix as a drowning man holds a floating spar. The walls scorched and cracked around him as he moved, but he did not let this distract him for a moment.

The sound of the fire was louder, and all three men knew that it had broken through onto the main floor of Hôtel Transylvania. If Saint-Germain doubted he would ever leave the building alive, he did not show it. At the top of the stairs he slipped out the door, closing it behind him.

Now that the threat of the crucifix was gone, Saint Sebastien launched himself at the stairs, dashing up them, apparently oblivious of the fire and smoke that wreathed him. He pulled at the door handle, and felt his skin peel back from his palm as the metal grew hotter and hotter.

Below him, Beauvrai had retreated to the farthest corner, his hands clapped over his eyes, and his breath coming in gasps as the smoke around him grew denser. Then the breathing stopped.

Saint Sebastien stood before the locked door, rage filling his mouth with bitter invectives that he hurled to the air. His voice was a ragged groan, his eyes almost sightless now as the fire grew, blossoming in bright petals around him. The hem of his robe charred, then sucked up bright fire as if needing adornment. His hair began to smoke, sending out fine wisps as it shriveled. Along his arms the skin began to crack.

With a last cry of hatred, Saint Sebastien turned, and with enormous laughter that might have been only the echo of the flames, threw himself down the stairs, burning, burning, like some terrible falling star plunging into the heart of the sun.

Hercule and Roger stood by the coach watching the first flicker of fire as it showed deep in the heart of Hôtel Transylvania. They had heard the hideous sound when the chapel roof had collapsed, and later, the almost human groan that had erupted as the flames broke through into the upper floor of the Hôtel. They had exchanged looks then, reflecting the worry that possessed them, but said nothing. To speak the words would make them too real, too possible.

Now the flames were tearing at the building, and they dared not hope that their master had survived the holocaust that raged in the depths of the building.

Madelaine stood beside them, wrapped in one of Saint-Germain's long dark cloaks. She stared at the building with a fascination that did not betray the grief and terror she felt as she saw the fire rise.

They had all seen Châteaurose rush from the Hôtel, his fantastic robes flying behind him. He had rushed across Quai Malaquais and thrown himself into the Seine before any of the three could stop him. They waited for another figure, but none appeared.

Now there were little spikes of flame in the smaller gambling salon. Hercule thrust out his lower lip. "I told him I would wait until he comes."

Roger nodded, pulling a long face. He considered the fire. "You had better blindfold the horses, then. They will bolt, otherwise."

Hercule was half done with this task when the fire broke out in earnest in the upper floors. The three looked at one another, and Madelaine put her hands to her eyes, weeping unashamedly.

"Perhaps . . . ?" Roger said delicately.

"No." Hercule climbed to the box.

Two of the huge windows broke, and the fire roared out in hideous victory.

Then, from the floor above, there came a rope, and there was a blackclad figure on that rope, sliding down past the flames, his neat, stocky figure moving with an agility and grace that were surprising in a man his age. He touched the ground, steadied himself, then ran across the narrow space between Hôtel Transylvania and the stables.

"Master!" cried Roger. He wrung Saint-Germain's hand.

"Get mounted, old friend. The Watch will give the alarm shortly, and we must be gone. We have a long journey yet tonight." He glanced up at Hercule on the box. "I see you waited."

The laconic tone Hercule attempted failed miserably. "I followed your orders, sir. I would have driven into the fire, had that been necessary."

He paused. "Saint Sebastien?"

Saint-Germain bowed ironically. "He was detained, I fear."

Hercule's fists clenched. "I wanted to kill him myself. I wanted vengeance."

The smile crept back into Saint-Germain's eyes. "Pray accept my condolences. But why do we wait? Madelaine?"

Madelaine hung back, almost afraid to touch Saint-Germain, to speak to him, for fear he would fade and prove to be nothing more than the embodiment of her wishes. "Saint-Germain?" she whispered.

He turned to her, taking her by the shoulders and looked down into her eyes. "I am safe, my heart. And you are safe."

"Saint Sebastien is dead?"

Saint-Germain glanced back toward Hôtel Transylvania and saw the fire spreading toward the ballroom. "I would assume so." He pushed her gently toward the coach. "Come. It is time that we leave."

She let him hand her into the coach and sat very still while he called out "Hôtel d'Argenlac," to Hercule, and waved to Roger, who would be the out-rider on this journey to England.

"I thought Roger would come with your baggage," she said.

"So did I, originally. But Sattin will do that." He closed the door of the coach and sank down beside her.

For some time they rode in silence—fatigue, hurt and terror leaving little room for anything else. Then, as they moved beyond the close-packed streets of le Faubourg Saint-Germain, Madelaine ventured a few timid words. "Was it very dreadful?"

Saint-Germain turned toward her. "Yes."

"I see." She studied her hands. "And you are going away."

"As I told you, for a time. I will be back in May."

"I see," she said again, and burst into tears.

"Here." He sat up, taking her into his arms, secretly relieved that she could endure his touch. "What is this, Madelaine?"

"You have a disgust of me," she sobbed.

"I? Never." He slid his hands under the cloak she wore, moving cautiously to avoid frightening her. After what she had experienced from Saint Sebastien, he knew she could easily relapse into the abhorrence the Satanists had inspired in her. Slowly, gently, he caressed her. "I have a disgust, a loathing for Saint Sebastien and his Circle. I despise them for what they did to you. But that cannot change my love for you, my heart. Nothing could do that."

She said something incomprehensible and turned her face to his shoulder. He held her that way for some little time, murmuring occasional endearments to her hair, and at last she spoke again. "Your eyebrows are all singed. So is your hair."

"Are they?" He touched her face with one lingering finger.

"Even your lashes." Her grip around his waist tightened. "I almost lost you."

"But you didn't." He kissed her then, and felt his love for her sing in his veins. "My valiant, my cherished Madelaine."

She was breathless as she pulled away from him, and her eyes shone with an inner brightness. She put her hand to his chest as she mustered her resolve. Even the lumbering coach could not soften her determination. "You said you would let me taste of you. Before you left for England. Let me. Let me."

He watched her in the swaying darkness, probing her sincerity with intent eyes. There were bruises on her body, but much of the numbness had left her mind. This was no childish need for solace, but the true seeking of her entire being. In escaping from unspeakable evil she had won the right. He nodded. "Lift your feet."

"What?" The strangeness of his request made her wonder if he was refusing her, and she prepared to insist.

"This is no mockery, Madelaine. Lift your feet." He waited until she had; then he reached to the seat opposite them. A tug of a concealed lever and the seat changed, sliding forward to join its fellow as its back swung down.

Madelaine felt amusement return to her. How like Saint-Germain to have such a contraption in his coach.

"I often sleep while I travel," he explained as he secured the mountings.

Tentatively Madelaine moved onto the bed, and found that the firm cushion made a comfortable mattress. She spread the cloak for a blanket, then reached up to Saint-Germain.

"This cannot be done in haste," he said softly. "Here." He held out his hand, and in it rested the ruby stickpin that usually nestled in the lace at his throat.

She touched the jewel, a certain awe in her voice. "What must I do?"

"Wait." He pulled off his scorched shirt and flung it away. The night touched his smooth skin, and he shivered as he sank down beside her, though not from cold. Carefully he put the ruby into her hand, and then held that hand in his own. Their eyes locked. "You do this." He moved her hand so that the ruby was drawn across his chest.

"I don't want to hurt you," she cried as she saw the dark blood well along the path of the jewel.

"I am not hurt," he assured her at his most compelling. A joyous delirium rose in him. He lay back, his eyes slightly closed, and drew her forward. "This is my life. I give you my life." His voice, deep and low, stirred the strongest yearnings of her heart.

Without a word, she bent to put her lips to the wound he had made, trembling as his body arched at the touch of her mouth. His hands sought out her desires, drawing response on response from her, until the very air shook with the force of her love. Passion blinded her, so that there was only Saint-Germain and the glory of his ravishment. All her soul was contained in his small hands, fused by the white-burning ardor they shared. The fierce sweetness of her heart opened to him as she felt his inexpressible loneliness thaw in the radiance of her fulfillment.

Suddenly she turned away from him, and he reached for her in his turbulent longing. "Madelaine. What is it, my own heart?" He felt apprehension touch him, a terrible fear that even his embrace could not sear away the anguish she had had from Saint Sebastien.

Then he saw that she had the ruby in her hand still, and that she held it poised over her left breast. Before he could stop her she had made a cut in her breast identical to his. There was a kind of frenzy in her eyes as she twisted on the cushions, until she curled around Saint-Germain so that he could share her rapture.

Lightly, gently, he leaned his head against the gorgeous curve of her breast. Their faces were close together and as his lips found the wound she had made for him, he saw the glorious spasm change her features, transforming her.

The horror of the night's ordeal faded before the dizzying triumph that possessed them, and even the rumbling of the coach and the cramped quarters could not recall them from the ecstasy that bound them, exalted them, consumed them with a fervor that fed on its own satisfaction.

At last the coach drew up at the gates of hôtel d'Argenlac. The jingling harness sounded mournful as a dirge to Madelaine as she tore herself away from the elation she found in Saint-Germain's arms.

He sensed her longing and reached to embrace her again. "Be of good cheer, my heart," he told her, his voice filled with music. "When I return we will be together again."

"Pardon, master," Roger said apologetically at the window. "We cannot stay."

"I know," Saint-Germain said sadly. He rolled away from the folds of the cloak so that he would not be tempted by her presence. After a moment he said in a voice that was almost normal, "Go, Madelaine. Go now. I will write to you often, through messengers. In May, my heart. It is not so long."

"In May," she repeated as Roger opened the door for her. She pulled Saint-Germain's cloak more tightly around her, but not for modesty; she was seeking to keep him with her, if only from the familiar warmth of his cloak. She turned her violet eyes to his again, and his hands reached out to her. "I am glad it is you, Saint-Germain," she said. "I am glad you have loved me and I have loved you."

He tightened his grip on her hands. Happiness softened his face, erasing the sardonic twist of his mouth. "I am glad, too, Madelaine. I will always be glad."

She stepped out of the coach. "It is late," she said to the air. The night sky was polished by stars, and a crisp wind ruffled her hair. Once more she said, "In May."

Still he could not leave her. He leaned down from the coach to press one more kiss to her eyes, her mouth. "Now, go, Madelaine, or I will not have the will to send you away."

She nodded and stepped back from the road, one hand holding the cloak closed, the other raised in farewell. She smiled, and her smile was joyous, following the coach until, with Roger riding beside it, and Hercule handling the reins in form, it turned the bend in the road and was lost to sight.

Excerpt from a letter from la Comtesse d'Argenlac to la Marquis de Montalia, dated November 15, 1743:

. . . I grieve with you, my sister, for the loss of my brother Robert, who was your husband. He was a kind man, a good brother, and his fatherly devotion exceeded all his other qualities. I have wept and wept for him as I prayed, but no tears or prayers will restore him to us.

I am told by l'Abbé Ponteneuf, our cousin, that Robert at last made his peace with God, and that his martyrdom suffered on behalf of his child (Madelaine speaks little of this, but we have learned enough of that dreadful night to know that his life bought hers) has given him a place among the Blessed of God. If it is any consolation to you, Saint-Germain has sent money from England to l'Abbé to buy Masses for the repose of Robert's soul. It was he, as you may know, who brought Madelaine away from the fire and restored her to me.

How is it that misfortune always comes in apparently unending multitudes, like drops of rain? It is my sad duty to inform you that Madelaine has not improved in health since that terrible ordeal. I have called priests and physicians, yet nothing they can do seems to help. Her mind has not been too much affected, which is a blessing. She is perfectly lucid. But her soul is possessed of a sadness now. She spends much of her time alone in the night, reading. Her commendable scholarship must be a solace to her, for she is most diligent in her studies, which now include foreign languages and history. Her beauty is not diminished, but rather has become sharper. You would think, to see the keenness of her violet eyes and the slight flush to her cheek that she is perfectly robust. But it is not true. Her physician,

André Schoenbrun, informs me that this travesty of health is but a sign of her disease, and will inexorably claim her.

I have done all I know how to do, and would do more if I could, but I know nothing that will save her now. Nor do her physician and priests.

Pray, Margaret, let me keep her here with me. I do not go out, so she will not be left alone. I still dread the things that people will say, for since my husband's death, the speculation and gossip surrounding his demise have become unbearably painful to me. I realize that Madelaine will not live out a year, but I would like to share those remaining months with her, and find some value for myself in helping her.

For whatever comfort it may bring you, Saint Sebastien and many of his horrible companions were completely destroyed in the fire that gutted Hôtel Transylvania. A group of priests from Saint-Germain-des-Près have searched the wreckage for any remains, but have not found enough bones to make up the whole of one man. They keep vigil at the place, and have performed the rite of exorcism so that any unholy thing left behind by those unspeakable men will be laid to rest.

. . . I beg you will write to me soon, not only so that we may share in our mourning, but so that I may tell Madelaine of your decision.

I do not wish to distress you further, but I know the duty of seeing your daughter die with such Christian resignation, coming so hard upon the death of your husband, is a terrible burden to place on anyone, particularly you, who have a mother's love and wife's affection. I urge you again to let Madelaine stay with me.

In the deepest of sorrow, I have the honor to commend myself to you in our time of mutual distress

> As your most devoted sister,
> Claudia de Montalia
> Comtesse d'Argenlac

Epilogue

Text of a letter written by Madelaine de Montalia to le Comte de Saint-Germain, in inexpert Arabic, delivered in person by the English sorcerer Beverly Sattin, dated April 29, 1744:

My dearest Saint-Germain,

Your gift has arrived quite safely, through the good offices of your Hercule who has returned to Paris as of a week ago. How is it that green chalcedony can be made to glow red when lit from within? I am certain that in time you will teach me even that.

As you see, I have taken your advice of January 10 and am devoting even more of my time to my studies. Arabic is vastly complicated at first, and I am sure that this is clumsy beyond my imagination. But in time, I will master it, as you have.

Schoenbrun has been to see me yet again. He and l'Abbé Ponteneuf put on such good faces when they are with me. I feel quite beside myself, and wish I could tell them that I do not mind dying. For I am dying. It is a gentle thing, no more difficult than taking off my stays at night. By the end of summer I will be in my grave, I think.

How strange it is to say that, and know that there is no terror for me in those words. When you return to Paris next month, you must come to me again, my dearest love. You cannot deny me this. Even as I write these words I glow with desire for you. My physicians say that it is my malady that gives me this vivid color and eyes that burn. But it is not that. It is your blood in me, making me one with you, as inevitable as sunset when the sun stands but at high noon. In May there will be a few days for us to enjoy our sweet rapture, and then I will go down to the good earth, as you did once, and it will give me strength to come to you again.

I will never again need to fear the shortness of hours. I will have time to learn, to study, to know, to see all that there is to see. And if there is loneliness, there is also victory. Across the world and the ages I will always seek your arms, and in time I will achieve that perception that makes you what you are. Because of you, my life is not a wasted thing, nor my death.

In my reading of history there is war and ruin and pillage and lives snuffled out with such profligacy that my breath is stopped by the senselessness of it. One would think that all humanity had nothing better to do than feed on its own carrion. Think of all the destruction you have seen, and the endless foolishness. Whole peoples have perished for a few men's greed, or desire, or sport.

I have thought as I read these books, how many much worse things there are in this world than vampires.

To know your freedom. To live in the blood that is taken with love. Saint-Germain, Saint-Germain, I can hardly wait!

Your Madelaine
Forever

Notes

HÔTEL TRANSYLVANIA

Built in the reign of Louis XIII, Hôtel Transylvania stands today at 9 Quai Malaquais in le Fabourg Saint-Germain. Its name was taken from Prinz Franz Leopold Ragoczy, who stayed there from 1713–1717, due in part to his role in the War of the Spanish Succession.

Much of the Hôtel Transylvania's notoriety developed out of its mention in l'Abbé Prévost's novel *Manon Lescaut*, which was first published in 1728, and has kept up its popularity to this day largely because of the operas of Massenet and Puccini, which are based on Prévost's work (there are in fact, four operas using *Manon Lescaut* as a text, but only two are often performed).

A few of the illustrious people who have lived at or owned Hôtel Transylvania are: la Duchesse de Gramont, who was there in 1724; from 1869 to 1892 la Marquise de Blocqueville lived there, making the place synonymous with all that was splendid in arts and letters; and early in its career, before it gained the name by which it is still known, Hôtel Transylvania was occupied by le Marechal de Tallard.

LE COMTE DE SAINT-GERMAIN

He first appeared in Paris in May, 1743, a gentleman of tremendous wealth, great learning, engaging manners, and much mystery. He was a terrifically conspicuous figure, known to everyone, going everywhere. His passion for diamonds was remarkable even for that gaudy century, and he often claimed to be able to grow his own diamonds. On two or three occasions, he took diamonds from friends and returned them larger stones, saying that they had been made larger by his own process.

He wore black and white almost exclusively, at a time when other men were dressing in colors that would shame a rainbow. His clothes were always of the finest quality, and were particularly neat. Everyone who knew him was impressed with his mode of dress, particularly Grimm and Frederick the Great. To complement his black-and-white clothes, he rode and drove gray horses exclusively, and had carriages of the most modern design.

He is credited with the work *Le Très Sainte Trinosophie*, which he may or may not have had anything to do with, but which bore his seal (the eclipse, with upraised wings) and did contain certain ideas very like ones Saint-Germain expressed. From Casanova and Walpole there is first-hand evidence that Saint-Germain was a practicing alchemist, and apparently quite a good one. In the 1750's, while he lived in The Hague, Saint-Germain purchased an athanor, and added two rooms onto the house he had hired, where he could carry out various alchemical processes.

Music was also a passion of Saint-Germain's, and the encounter with Rameau did indeed take place sometime in the summer of 1743. Saint-Germain wrote quite a few little operas, and the one of *Persephone* mentioned in connection with Madelaine's fête was probably composed before 1750. Saint-Germain played the violin, harpsichord, and guitar and sang in a light, pleasant voice (his range has not been noted). He was an accomplished improviser and would occasionally adlib at the keyboard. His music was collected by the Russian composer, Peter Tschikovsky.

The description of him—a medium-short man with small hands and feet, dark hair, startling dark eyes (everyone who wrote about him mentions his eyes) and the appearance of early middle age—is more or less the same from 1743 until his supposed death in 1786, which is a long time to look forty-five. He claimed to be three-thousand to four-thousand years old, and said that he kept his youth by drinking the Elixir of Life.

Whether he had such a secret or not, it is interesting to note that he was rarely if ever seen to eat or drink in public, and that he did not, under any circumstances, drink wine.

He was an enthusiastic patron of the arts, and was particularly fond of the works of Velázquez. He did some painting himself, and although his work was competent but not remarkable, he did have a secret for blending colors of rare brilliance and luminosity, which more than one painter of his day begged him to reveal.

A gifted linguist, he spoke at least twelve languages, including Russian, Arabic, and Chinese.

Exactly who this man was has been the subject of much speculation from the time he appeared in Parisian society until the present. He may indeed have been the youngest son of Prinz Franz Leopold Ragoczy of Transylvania. If so, he was educated by Gian-Gastone de' Medici and was in fact about thirty when he came to Paris. Walpole, in one of his letters, lists all the stories that were circulating about Saint-Germain at that time, and they include such diverse speculations as: 1) he is a Polish aristocrat exiled from Poland for conspiring against the throne; 2) he is a Portuguese Jew; 3) he is an Italian who married well and murdered his wife; 4) he is the illegitimate son of the Pope; 5) he is a Russian boyar amusing himself at everyone's expense; 6) he is an Austrian diamond merchant spying on France.

Probably Walpole and the French (and possibly Frederick the Great as well) used Saint-Germain as an unofficial diplomatic courier during his long stay in the European courts. He certainly had access to the very highest-ranking men of his time. After 1768 he was lodged in Chambourg so that he would be nearer to the King of France, who spent some time with Saint-Germain almost every day. Frederick the Great liked him as a musician as well as a courtier, and called him "The man who does not die."

His ambidexterity is well-documented, and the business of writing two copies of the same thing at once was a thing he enjoyed doing. What is unusual, even among the very ambidexterous, is that Saint-Germain's signature was the same by either hand. This fact is useful when the question of his death arises, because there are two documents bearing his authenticated signature, dated 1791 and 1793, five and seven years after his supposed death. The original recipients of the letters at the time did not doubt the authenticity of the letters, and there are at least three people who had known him many years who claimed to have seen him and spoken with him in 1793, 1796, and 1802.

Whoever he was, he succeeded in bewildering everyone for quite a long time, and the mystery, even today, is not solved.

VAMPIRES

In deciding which of the general characteristics of vampires would be useful for this novel, I read a great many of the available books on the subject, ranging from scholarly studies to credulous reports. My conclusions are as follows; whatever it is that a vampire finds necessary in blood, nourishment is not the main purpose. Since vampires do not digest or eliminate the way living people do, blood, being drunk, must serve some other function. Apparently this is not circulatory, either, for it would seem that much of the function of the circulatory system is taken over by the lymphatic system, which would in part account for the increased sensitivity to sunlight (although fiction's two Grand Old Vampires, Dracula and

Ruthven, run around in the sunlight without apparent harm). So blood provides food in only a very limited sense, and so long as that blood is mammalian, it provides what little sustenance the vampire requires.

The psychic element of vampirism is another matter. What most vampires seem to seek (at least the fictional variety) is not blood, but life ("For the blood is the life, Mr. Harker," says Dracula). It is the intimacy that makes the blood important, and the physical contact that the vampire truly seeks. In extension of this psychic element, vampires apparently are psychokinetic, for they are credited with the ability to influence human, animal and weather behavior.

There has been a tremendous amount written about the underlying sexuality of vampirism, and of course, most vampiric attacks occur at night, in bed, and leave one exhausted. Now, in most cultures it is agreed that vampires are not capable of genital sexual contact, but that they express their desires through their biting, which will send any Freudian capering with glee. Thus, it is not the blood itself, but the act of taking it that gives the vampire nourishment. Certainly this is consistent with one Chinese vampire that does not take blood from the neck, but spinal fluid.

In European countries there has been a great tendency to attribute heretical and Satanic characteristics to vampires, but this is an inconsistent attitude. If vampires were truly frightened of the Cross, for example, it would be enough to bury them under one and leave it at that. So it is not the religious symbols that control vampires. Nor are they Satanic. There is no element of devil-worship in their behavior. And it is only in Christian countries that it is believed that being a sorcerer in life contributes to vampirism after death.

Whether regarded with horror or curiosity, vampires and the lore that surrounds them have exercised a powerful fascination on humanity for a long, long time, and it is obvious that there is something we find both compelling and repulsive about an undead being who attacks/seduces the living. Much of this stems from a generally ambivalent attitude about immortality, and a certain preoccupation with fears about death.

Varney, Dracula, Lord Ruthven, and their varied children (this Saint-Germain is certainly one of them) have held a very special place in macabre literature. If they did not speak to some hidden part of ourselves, they would not be there.